Mike Carmody operates an expensive weight-reducing salon in New York City. He's got it made—an attractive wife, a sexy secretary, and a group of very rich women who hang on his every word. Then his stepbrother Vance shows up. And suddenly Carmody is being accused of a hit-and-run fatality, and having to answer a lot of pointed questions from Police Captain Gridley Nelson. Then there is a death in the group, an overdose that could be suicide... or murder. It's crazy enough that this police captain thinks he hit someone with his car. Now Nelson is *really* poking his nose into Carmody's business. And who knows what Vance is up to.

## DEADLOCK

Glen Williams is dead, shot through the chest. Lieutenant Gridley Nelson, Acting Captain of Homicide, has more than enough suspects since Williams had a large circle of friends to whom he offered hope and encouragement. To Joss and Morgan Woodruff he promised patronage for Morgan's song-writing talents. To Tom Gaudio, help in promoting his photography. To Sarah Thrace, a has-been actress, he offered the chance of a comeback. And to Fred and Dora Storch, he promised care for their mentally handicapped son. Williams gathered them all around him like a guardian angel. But did he intend to deliver on his promises? Could one of his dear friends have had a reason to kill him?

## RUTH FENISONG BIBLIOGRAPHY (1904-1978)

**Gridley Nelson Mysteries:**

Murder Needs a Name (1942; UK edition, 1950)

Murder Needs a Face (1942)

The Butler Died in Brooklyn (1943; UK edition, 1946)

Murder Runs a Fever (1943)

Grim Rehearsal (1950; UK edition, 1951)

Dead Yesterday (1951)

Deadlock (1952)

The Wench Is Dead (1953)

Miscast for Murder (1954; reprinted in PB, 1956, as Too Lovely to Live)

Bite the Hand (1956; UK edition, 1958, as The Blackmailer)

Death of the Party (1958)

But Not Forgotten (1960; UK edition, 1960, as Sinister Assignment)

Dead Weight (1962; UK edition, 1964)

**Unrelated Mysteries:**

Jenny Kissed Me (1944; reprinted in PB as Death is a Lovely Lady, 1944)

The Lost Caesar (1945; reprinted in PB, 1950, and UK edition, 1946, both as Death is a Gold Coin)

Desperate Cure (1946)

Snare for Sinners (1949; UK edition, 1951)

Ill Wind (1950; UK edition, 1952)

Boy Wanted (1953; juvenile)

Widows' Plight (1955; UK edition, 1957, as Widows Blackmail)

The Schemers (1957; UK edition, 1958, as The Case of the Gloating Landlord)

Villainous Company (1967; UK edition, 1968)

The Drop of a Hat (1970; UK edition, 1971)

# DEAD WEIGHT

# DEADLOCK

## RUTH FENISONG

Introduction by
Curtis Evans

STARK
HOUSE

**Stark House Press • Eureka California**

DEAD WEIGHT / DEADLOCK

Published by Stark House Press
1315 H Street
Eureka, CA 95501, USA
griffinskye3@sbcglobal.net
www.starkhousepress.com

DEAD WEIGHT
Originally published by Doubleday & Company, Inc., Garden City, and
copyright © 1962 by Ruth Fenisong.

DEADLOCK
Originally published by Doubleday and Company, Inc., Garden City, and
copyright © 1952 by Ruth Fenisong. Reprinted in paperback by Dell
Books, New York, 1952.

ISBN-13: 978-1-944520-96-0

Book design by Mark Shepard, shepgraphics.com
Cover art by John McDermott from the original Dell paperback edition
Proofreading by Bill Kelly

First Stark House Press Edition: January 2020

# RUTH FENISONG

By Curtis Evans

Ruth Fenisong, a popular and prolific twentieth-century American mystery novelist hailed in her day as a "virtually faultless pro" by Anthony Boucher, dean of American crime fiction critics, published twenty of her twenty-two crime novels in the very heart of the mid-century, during the two decades falling between 1942 and 1962, beginning with *Murder Needs a Name* and ending with *Dead Weight*, one of the two novels included in this volume. (The other is *Deadlock*, chosen by Anthony Boucher as one of the ten best crime novels of 1952.) Only a poignant children's story, *Boy Wanted* (1964), and a couple of additional crime novels, *Villainous Company* (1967) and *The Drop of a Hat* (1970), appeared from the author's hand in her later years; and, even before Ruth's death in 1978, her name had almost fully faded from the mystery field, with all of her books having gone out of print. Yet in her heyday as a crime writer, from the early Forties to the early Sixties, Ruth Fenisong was a component part of that remarkable corps of women mystery authors who flourished in America, right alongside the more attention-grabbing hard-boiled boys, during World War Two and the early years of the Cold War.

Over these creatively fertile years Ruth Fenisong published non-series mystery novels as well as her Gridley Nelson detective series, the latter detailing the murder cases of an empathetic, prematurely white-haired and Princeton-educated New York City police investigator, Sergeant (later Lieutenant and Captain) Gridley "Grid" Nelson. During the course of the thirteen novel series, which includes both *Deadlock* and *Dead Weight*, Nelson acquires an indomitable housekeeper and cook named Sammy (a black woman who is closely involved in his earliest cases), a lovely wife named Kyrie (first encountered in the fourth novel in the series, *Murder Runs a Fever*) and a lively son named Junie (Sammy's nickname for the boy, derived from Junior); yet as Nelson rises up life's ladder of success he never loses his intelligent sympathy for the unfortunate individuals thrown

willy-nilly into the monstrous maelstrom of murder. Although Ruth
Fenisong somewhat romanticizes Grid Nelson, who as one of fortune's
favorites is even blessed with an independent income in the fashion
of the charming aristocratic gentleman sleuths associated with the
British Crime Queens Dorothy L. Sayers (Lord Peter Wimsey),
Margery Allingham (Albert Campion) and Ngaio Marsh (Roderick Al-
leyn, himself a cop too, however improbably), the world which Nelson
inhabits nevertheless is a grittier one than that of Wimsey and his
gang, more akin to that which one finds in the American mid-century
police procedurals of Ed McBain and Hillary Waugh. Fans of American police procedurals and British manners mysteries alike should
find much to their taste in Ruth Fenisong's appealing crime fiction.

Ruth Fenisong was born on April 29, 1904 in New York City, under
the name Ruth *Feinsong*. Although the author's deliberate transpo-
sition, later in life, of two letters in her surname obscured the telltale
traces of her actual ethnic identity, Ruth in fact was one of two children of immigrant Jews: Maurice Feinsong, a tailor and clothes de-
signer originally from Russian Poland, and his wife Janie (or Jennie),
who had been born in Whitechapel, London to Simon Bobbe, a cloth
cap maker, and his wife Martha, both of whom came originally from
the Netherlands. (Janie would have been nineteen at the time of the
Jack the Ripper murders that terrorized the East End of London.) As
a child Janie had attended a charity school housed in a great three-
story Jacobean Revival structure, the Jews' Hospital and Orphan Asy-
lum (later the Norwood Home for Jewish Children), indicating that
her parents were possessed of no great means. In New York in the
1890s Janie joined her elder brothers Samuel, a tailor, and Louis, an
advertising manager for the department store Koch & Co. and wed
Maurice Feinsong, a successful clothing shop owner, in 1895.

Ruth's sole sibling, her elder sister Martha, married Edmund
Theise, a movie theater projectionist, and with him had one son. Ruth
herself never wed, although for some four decades she resided in
Greenwich Village with her life partner, native Irish schoolteacher
Kathleen Gallagher (1901-1980), the daughter of a lace importer. In
the first years of their relationship, Ruth and Kay, as Kathleen was
known, lodged with Phil Berry (aka Sverre Filberg), a prominent popular women's magazine illustrator originally from Norway, and his
wife, Evelyn, but from the 1940s onward they resided at an apartment
in a five-story, turn-of-the-century row house at 227 Sullivan Street.
"I have many fond memories of my Aunt Ruth and her dear friend
'Aunt Kay'," recalled a great-niece of Ruth's (although unfortunately

she to date has never related any of these memories to me).

How Ruth supported herself in her twenties is unclear. Throughout the 1930s she traveled in Europe, to England (1930), France (1932) and Italy (1937), on the latter trip in company with Kay Gallagher. This suggests she enjoyed either her own independent means or the indulgent support of her father Maurice, or "Pop" as she called him. (Her mother had passed away in 1928.) After the Second World War, Ruth and Kay resumed traveling, though to Bermuda and the Bahamas rather than the war-ravaged nations of Europe. By this time Ruth was enjoying a steady income from the sales of her popular crime novels, many of which were published not only in hardcover but in paperback. Before she began writing crime fiction in the Forties, however, Ruth in the Thirties found herself, as the Depression tightened its dreary grip in the United States, rewardingly (if not necessarily remuneratively) employed with the Federal Theater Project (FTP).

Launched under the Works Progress Administration in 1935, the FTP at its peak provided creative work to over 13,000 jobless actors, artists, writers, directors and stage workers. Despite the success it enjoyed with the public, the FTP was terminated in 1939 after the organization came under blistering attack from the House Un-American Activities Committee (HUAC), an investigative arm of the United States House of Representatives that was tasked with rooting out political "subversion" in the United States. (In practice this came to mean anything, in the eyes of the reactionary gentlemen who led this committee, deemed critical of capitalism and sympathetic to racial integration.) As far as I know, Ruth Fenisong was never singled out for attack by notorious red-baiting HUAC committee chairman Martin Dies, as was future one-shot mystery writer Irving Mendell (who hid under a playful anagrammatic pen name, "Amen Dell"), then head of the FTP's "Living Newspaper" (an innovative theatrical form designed to present factual information on current events to a popular audience). However, during the few short years that she worked with the FTP, Ruth did much interesting work, and her political perspective in that work, when it is discernible, is discernably Left.

As one of the more than three hundred and fifty people in the FTP who worked with marionettes, Ruth wrote and staged Puppet Theater in collaboration with such notable artists as the great Puppeteer Remo Bufano, Director of the FTP's marionette projects. Ruth's marionette plays included *Katcha and the Devil*, *The Mighty Mikko* and *A Valiant Little Tailor*, all adaptations of European folk tales (the last of which her father should have particularly enjoyed); *The Totem*, concocted from Iroquois tribal legend; *Babar the Elephant*, based on the beloved (and then contemporary) children's books by French writer Jean de Brunhoff; and classic English tales by literary giants Charles Dickens (*Oliver Twist*) and Arthur Conan Doyle ("The Speckled Band"), the latter of which of course is one of Sherlock Holmes' most famous and thrilling adventures. More provocative to the likes of Martin Dies, no doubt, were the allegorical *The Children of Salem*, about two children who nearly provoke the killing of a purported witch (the play was billed as "a strong indictment of superstition"), and *The Boiled Eggs*, in which a ruthlessly scheming restaurant owner ("Landlord") and his equally atrocious Wife, attempting to fleece a simple Farmer of $2000 for a meal of a dozen boiled (and very rotten) eggs, have the tables deftly turned on them by a wily Lawyer and a good-hearted Waiter. By the end of the play, the waiter has joined a union and is picketing the Landlord's restaurant, which in a burst of poetic justice is destroyed when the remaining rotten eggs explode. Evident throughout these works is Ruth Fenisong's ardent sympathy for the different and the downtrodden.

With the demise of the FTP in 1939, Ruth, now thirty-five years old, launched out on a second career, one suggested by her composition of the puppet play *The Speckled Band*: writing mystery fiction. In 1942, she published two Gridley Nelson detective novels, *Murder Needs a Name* (dedicated to "Pop") and *Murder Needs a Face*, the latter of which makes estimable use of her background in Puppet Theater. Two more Gridley Nelson novels, the cleverly titled *The Butler Died in Brooklyn* and *Murder Runs a Fever*, appeared the next year, followed by the non-series *Jenny Kissed Me* (1944), *The Lost Caesar* (1945), *Desperate Cure* (1946), *Snare for Sinners* (1949) and *Ill Wind* (1950), rounding off a prolific and highly praised decade for the author. 1950 also marked the welcome return, after a seven years absence, of Gridley Nelson, in the novel *Grim Rehearsal*, which also made excellent use of the author's theatrical background. Eight more Gridley Nelson mysteries followed over the next dozen years, which would prove the perceptive policeman's busiest period: *Dead Yesterday* (1951), *Deadlock* (1952), The *Wench Is Dead* (1953), *Miscast for Murder* (1954), *Bite the Hand* (1956), *Death of the Party* (1958), *But Not Forgotten* (1960) and *Dead Weight* (1962). Interspersed among these winning works was a fetching pair of non-series crime novels, *Widows' Plight* (1955) and *The Schemers* (1957).

In addition to clever mystery plots, Ruth Fenisong's impressive crime corpus offers readers sensitively rendered portraits of people from a variety of social and ethnic/racial backgrounds—or, as an admiring Anthony Boucher in his 1952 review of *Deadlock*, the seventh Gridley Nelson mystery, memorably put it, "beautifully realized [characters], on every level of Manhattan from café glitter to basement sordidness." No mere "puppets" they! *Deadlock*, one of the most ingeniously constructed of Ruth's novels, concerns the shooting slaying of charming dilettante Glen Williams (discovered dead on his couch on the book's first page), a Lord Bountiful wannabe whose actions, it turns out, had banefully affected the people he had greedily gathered around him (including a couple trying to care at home, in the unsupportive 1950s, for their Down Syndrome child). This naturally makes these people leading suspects for Grid Nelson in his murder investigation. Although there are a myriad of meaty material clues for Nelson to sink his teeth into, the problem presented is as well a deeply psychological one, requiring penetration into the mercurial mind of the deceased, concerning whom Anthony Boucher lauded the author for bringing off "an extraordinary task of fully characterizing [someone] who never appears alive." Readers who share Gridley Nelson's keen sympathetic insight into the lives of others will have an advantage in cracking this tough case.

*Dead Weight*, the final Gridley Nelson novel, takes readers back to a milieu which has more in common with the murderous comedies of manners of the British Crime Queens, though there is seriousness at its heart. Here the main theater of criminous events, including theft and suspicious death, is a pricey New York weight loss salon with a tony clientele of wealthy city matrons (derisively dubbed "the beasts" by cynical salon owner Mike Carmody). In his review of *Dead Weight*, Anthony Boucher justly praised the author's "fine use" of this setting, while noting more cryptically that the novel "is an all but unprecedented detective story in a surprising way which a review cannot particularize." This introduction cannot particularize in this respect either, although let it be said that the puzzle in *Dead Weight*, like that in *Deadlock*, is simultaneously neatly clued and boldly unorthodox.

The last pages of *Dead Weight*, which take place in the Nelsons' cozy living room as Grid and Kyrie discuss the recent case, have the feeling of a coda, as indeed they were, *Dead Weight* turning out to have been Grid's last recorded case. "Capt. Gridley Nelson is as quietly perceptive a detective as ever," noted Anthony Boucher in his review of the final Nelson novel, neatly bookending his 1943 observation, in his review of *Murder Runs a Fever*, that then Sgt. Gridley Nelson was "one of this department's favorite gentlemen coppers." Over his twenty-year recorded career Grid Nelson remained one of the most likeable and appealing of fictional American detectives, a testament to the admirable creative vision of his idealistic and kindhearted creator. "Will you please stop trying to remake the world?" a lovingly exasperated Kyrie asks Grid, in the novel's closing lines. "Sometimes you seem to have a sneaking idea that you can change it singlehanded." There doubtlessly was a limit to what Grid Nelson–or Ruth Fenisong for that matter–could accomplish in society singlehanded, but in their mysteries, at any rate, Grid and Ruth made pieces of it better for a time, giving Ruth's readers a reassuring feeling that there could yet be some measure of justice meted in an unjust world, to both the guilty and the innocent.

—Germantown, TN
August 2019

Curtis Evans received a PhD in American history in 1998. He is the author of *Masters of the "Humdrum" Mystery: Cecil John Charles Street, Freeman Wills Crofts, Alfred Walter Stewart and British Detective Fiction, 1920-1961* (2012) and most recently the editor of the Edgar nominated *Murder in the Closet: Essays on Queer Clues in Crime Fiction Before Stonewall* (2017) and, with Douglas G. Greene, the Richard Webb and Hugh Wheeler short crime fiction collection, *The Cases of Lieutenant Timothy Trant* (2019). He blogs on vintage crime fiction at The Passing Tramp.

# DEAD WEIGHT

## RUTH FENISONG

## CHAPTER 1

He was the only one in the elevator who rode all the way to the roof. He stepped from the cage to the elegant outer reaches of "Carmody's," and with exactly the right air of indolent assurance made his way across a calm sea of broadloom to the receptionist's island.

The girl at the desk observed his progress through the mascara-stiffened fringes of her eyelids. To her he suggested a type encountered in the fashionable places of the world. She had never visited those places, but in illustrated magazines she had met his counterpart wearing swimming trunks and sunglasses, or slacks and cashmere jackets.

When he came to a halt and removed his hat he looked somewhat older than her magazine heroes. She noted that the horn-rims on his aristocratic nose were not even tinted, yet found compensation for this in the distinguished splashes of white at his temples, and in his deeply tanned face. A moment before his arrival she had been dreaming unchaste dreams of her employer. To absolve herself of fickleness, she used the businesslike voice that she reserved for salesmen.

"Can I help you?"

The horn-rims lent him a studious look. There was no doubt that he was studying her. She smoothed her golden hair with fingers tipped by iridescent polish.

The "What are you doing tonight?" implicit in his scrutiny was not uttered. "I should like very much to see Mr. Carmody," he said.

Unconsciously she mimicked his beautiful diction. "I'm afraid that's impossible at this hour of the morning. Mr. Carmody has given strict orders not to be disturbed while he's conducting a class."

His lips sketched a smile. She wondered what she could have said to amuse him, and why a man like him should seek out Carmody. A husband to one of the "beasts"? She did not think so. The few who occasionally called for their wives wore sheepishness like a badge. "Why don't you leave your card," she said, "or call between one and three for an appointment?"

He shook his head.

She said uncertainly, "If it's important I could send a message to him."

"That's just what I don't want you to do." He removed the horn-rims and let them dangle from a narrow hand. His eyes did not seem defective. The light gray irises, sharply outlined in black, had a candid all-seeing stare. "It would rather spoil the surprise," he said.

The impact of those naked eyes unsettled her. She relapsed into her native brand of English. "That's a new one on me."

"I beg your pardon?"

"Your line. I see why you don't need to carry it in a briefcase. I hate to disappoint you but Mr. Carmody doesn't go in for surprises."

"Not even a long-lost brother descending out of the blue?"

"You! Now I've heard everything."

"I quite understand what you mean," he said solemnly. "Poor Michael never did take advantage of his opportunities."

"I don't understand what *you* mean." She averted her eyes from that curly smiling mouth and grasped her slippery loyalty by its tail. "Mr. Carmody's a very successful man—one of the top names in the reducing field. You've only to see the furs and jewelry on the ladies who walk in here and eat right out of his hand."

"I'm delighted for him. Perhaps I've been away on my travels so long that I've lost touch."

She was appeased. The panorama of his travels unfolded before her; the yacht bobbing on blue seas, the convertible speeding along winding foreign roads, the smart restaurants, the villas ...

"... and above all," he was saying, "my brother is to be congratulated for having such a faithful little sentry at his gates. I shall tell him so, Miss—?"

"Spofford—Edna Spofford."

"I expect we'll be meeting frequently, Miss Spofford. I do hope we'll be friends." He offered her his hand.

Self-consciously, she took it. Its clasp was unexpectedly fervent, as though he were sealing a bargain, the nature of which was as yet unknown to her.

The ten large women were ready to drop in their tracks as they left the conditioning room. But there was no rest for them at Carmody's. Next came the ordeal of the swimming pool. Submitting to its cool embrace they thrashed about like a school of dispirited porpoises.

Vigilant at the pool's tiled edge, Carmody raised his voice. "You won't take it off that way, Mrs. Grimes."

Annie Grimes had been floating in a dream of happier days. Reluctantly she turned over, a memory of grace implicit in the movement of her body. Crashing into the dream the words used by Carmody had almost made her raise a hand to undo the strap of her circumspect

bathing suit. Amusement at the sensation she might have caused re-
vivified her. She gamboled with the rest of the porpoises until Carmody's assistant blew the whistle.

In the dressing room after a shower, she endeavored by means of
custom-made garments to achieve an acceptable semblance of human
form. A few of her classmates were already seated at the long shelf
that served as a vanity table. She took her place and gazed hopefully
into the glass above it. She saw no welcome change. Her features had
the look of delicate furniture lost in an overlarge salon. She twisted
them into a grimace and carried her distaste further by producing a
derisive raspberry.

Mrs. Atmore, seated next to her, jumped at the vulgar explosion. "Really!"

"Excuse please—just a little exercise I thought up by myself."

Mrs. Atmore said repressively, "One could wish for more privacy."

"One should get it," Annie Grimes said, "what with the fees Carmody
charges."

Mrs. Atmore jumped to the defense of Carmody. "I'm sure he was far
too busy to concern himself with the arrangements. Undoubtedly he
left them to his wife." She ducked to avoid the spray of her neighbor's
atomizer.

Annie Grimes, friendly soul that she was, sighed. Lack of privacy
had never troubled her. She felt quite at home in the dressing room.
Barring its cleanliness and costly scents, it might have been backstage
at one of the better houses she had played. She glanced at the lineup
on either side of her and barred it too, because it would never have
passed muster on any self-respecting runway.

She put the finishing touches to her face, batting a puff against skin
that was still clear and fine in spite of its years behind grease paint.
The chair creaked insultingly as she stood up. She went to claim hat,
gloves, jewelry, and mink from her locker, the last in a row of lockers
stuffed with similar treasures. She slung the coat across her arm. It
was Friday, and the session would not be over until Carmody had
given his weekly talk.

The reducing establishment shared the roof of New York's Hotel
Easton with a few exclusive apartments and a nightclub, each divi-
sion supplied with a bank of elevators. Carmody's territory was the
largest. The solarium where he exhorted his pupils had a magnificent
view, yet the women seldom gave it more than a passing glance. Carmody, not very tall but with every inch of him male and muscular, was
view enough for them.

He spoke from a lofty dais that recalled to Annie Grimes the pulpit of a Cape Cod church she had visited during a summer tour. Wherever she went she had always been one for taking in the sights, but then as now her mood was far from reverent. The exercises had induced a ravenous hunger and Carmody's voice glanced off her well-groomed head. She was thinking guiltily of forbidden foods.

Carmody's wife, more cultivated than he, wrote his "talks." Her choice of words was somewhat at variance with his street-flavored accents. Fortunately there were no critics present.

"... you have been attending this special class for two weeks," he said, "and on the whole I am gratified by the progress shown on your charts." There was an involuntary bowing of heads as a portion of his audience attempted to scale the barrier of bosom in hasty self-examination. He went on, "Of course there are those among you who have raised the average of pounds shed—and those who have lowered it. You will know into which category you fall and it is not my purpose to create embarrassment by naming names." He waited for the ripple of laughter to ebb. "I think I may say in all modesty that I am fulfilling my part of the bargain." His raised hand stopped the applause. "But unless you fulfill yours, the time you spend here is wasted. I cannot stress too often that exercise is not enough. You must—I repeat must—follow the diet that has been prescribed. You are an intelligent group. Therefore I need not pull my punches by minimizing the discipline I require of you. Ladies of your standing in life are undoubtedly subject to more temptation than those who cannot afford the luxuries of the table. Yet—if you are really sincere—if will and not whim has brought you to me—we can—by working together—achieve the desired result." At the second flurry of applause he allowed a smile to stretch his mouth. The effect was brief but flashy. "How long the process takes depends solely upon you." He paused to let that sink in, and noted that one of his audience was not with him. He began to ad-lib, trying to follow the style of his wife's script. "I can't dog you every place you go to see that you win your fight against the cocktails, the lobster thermidor, the spicy casseroles, the butter-soaked hot biscuits, the rich desserts, or the between-meal snacks of fudge sundaes and sugared beverages and ..."

He had succeeded in winning the attention of Annie Grimes. The full flavor with which he laced each separate taboo played havoc with her salivary glands. She took out a handkerchief and dabbed at the corners of her mouth, relieved to find the precaution unnecessary. She observed without comfort the restiveness of those around her who too were being seduced by guilty yearnings. So strong was the illusion of the feast conjured up that delicious odors seemed to be rising from the hotel's kitchens to plague her flared nostrils.

She was the first to leave the solarium, struggling into her coat as she went, and ruefully conscious that its overlap had not increased. When she reached the receptionist's desk near the elevators she slowed down, half of a mind to put paid to the whole experience.

"Miss Spofford—if you've got a minute to spare—"

The receptionist said, "Always at your disposal, Mrs. Grimes. Do you know what I was remarking to myself as you came through the archway? I had to take a look at my desk calendar to make sure it was still February because I was remarking I could hardly believe you'd only been with us for two weeks. You look so—"

Annie Grimes shook her head. "My clothes tell a different story. They don't seem a bit looser."

Edna Spofford said hurriedly, "You mean to say you can't see what the regime's done for your skin and your eyes? Take my word for it the rest will come later. According to Mr. Carmody's theory, weight reduction has to be slow in the beginning—even in the accelerated class. You won't catch him stooping to quack methods that—"

"But my skin and eyes were always—"

"Speaking of clothes, Mrs. Grimes—you have wonderful taste—especially that coat. In my position I naturally see loads of furs—but nothing to compare—if you'll excuse me for being personal."

Annie Grimes excused her. The girl knew her job. She had probably been schooled to spot malcontents a mile off.

"Let's both get personal, Miss Spofford. How's for giving me a rough idea of when I can expect to breeze out of here with your kind of shape?"

The girl seemed to consider the question gravely. "In my case it took—"

"Wait a minute." Annie Grimes glanced at a strategically placed display board exhibiting photographs of impossibly obese and dowdy women transformed into impossibly slim and modish sylphs. "Are you going to sit there and tell me you're a 'before and after'?"

The girl fingered her gleaming yellow hair, the only part of her that belonged in the "before and after" category. "Well—I wasn't a real client like you—but while Mr. Carmody was satisfied with my ability to do the work when I applied, he didn't think it in his best interests to employ anybody whose figure wouldn't be a credit to the establishment—so he was generous enough to put me through a free course."

"Next you'll be convincing me that Mrs. Carmody once weighed in at a couple of hundred pounds."

The girl said distantly, "So far as I know she doesn't have to count calories."

Carmody appeared, surrounded by his disciples. To Annie Grimes he suggested a raisin in a field of dough. Seeing her, he extricated himself and walked toward the desk.

She felt that she had swallowed quite enough of him on an empty stomach. The vanguard of the next class was debouching from an elevator. Picking up her heels she broke into an oddly light-footed sprint, and safe in the descending cage resolved that if she did resign it would be by mail. That way she could avoid the strain of trying to resist persuasive counterarguments.

Onyx-eyed, Carmody had followed her retreat. Recalled to his duties he greeted the one-o'clock arrivals who proceeded to the dressing room to peel off their girdles. They were a postgraduate group supervised by his assistant in order to give him a lunch break.

When the last of both classes had disappeared, the receptionist tried to detain him, but he said, "Not now," and stalked away.

His private quarters consisted of an office whose rear door led to a three-room apartment. He rubbed himself down, put on a clean jersey, and made for the kitchen where a savory beef stew was holding its heat upon the electric range. Home cooking was one of his wife's economies, and he had to admit that she was good at it. He filled a plate, sat at the kitchen table to eat, arose for a second helping, and again for coffee and dessert. The meal consumed, he loosened the belt of his slacks and lit a cigarette. A few minutes later he was at his desk in the office.

Outside he could hear the "beasts" thudding along the corridor. They were being herded to a small mechanically equipped gymnasium which, in a jocular mood, he had christened the department of "losing horses."

A scowl worked alteration upon his features, making him look like the tough little man he was. He knew all about losing horses. Those he had been betting on lately could have done no worse had they been of the variety clamped to the gymnasium floor. In fact he might as well have placed his money on the rowing machines or the electrical massage tables or the "thigh cycles" that kept them company. He had not yet hit upon a foolproof means of keeping his most recent run of ill luck from his wife. But he was working on it, and if all went well he would not have to worry about a thing.

There were some manila folders on the desk. They contained the vital statistics of the earlier class, and should have been returned to the files by the receptionist. She doubled in brass as secretary, or in any role that was required of her. She was a very obliging girl, he thought, having reason to know.

As he was about to summon her on the intercom his eye was caught by the topmost folder. Someone had been writing on it. With lowering brow he read the penciled message.

"I meant to surprise you but decided it would be kinder to cushion the shock. I reached town this morning. Quite an interesting setup! See you later. Vance."

A rising rebellion took place in the region of Carmody's stomach. He tried to settle it by breathing deeply four or five times. Ten years, he thought. Ten years—and he has to turn up and—but he's not going to spoil it for me.

He did not need to ask why, with a stack of clean paper on the desk, his stepbrother had seen fit to spoil the folder. He was convinced that Vance, who had reason for everything he did, wanted to convey that the contents had been studied.

Carmody raised the manila cover and riffled through the enclosed pages. The marginal notes he had added were not incriminating, he told himself. Just simple facts about a client's background such as might be gathered by any businessman who prided himself upon using a personal approach.

He picked up the telephone receiver and stabbed a button on the intercom. "Get in here, Edna."

The receptionist achieved a quick and hopeful entrance, hips waving all the way. She had decided that the visitor of the morning was definitely a bush bird. She smiled sweetly upon the bird in hand.

"First of all," he said, "you don't want to leave these folders out. I keep adding notes to the forms filled in by the accelerated class. It's to help me in my work because they're the cream and pay for special treatment—but they could get insulted if they happened to—"

"I was wanted at my desk before you got through with them this morning. Besides—the clients hardly ever come in here."

"That's another thing," Carmody said. "Nobody should come in here without an invite—so what's the idea of showing a strange man—?"

"You didn't give me a chance to tell you. He wasn't a strange man. He was your brother."

Carmody did a successful job of swallowing his bile. "You shouldn't believe everything you hear."

"Well—wasn't he?"

"My stepbrother—which don't happen to be the point. How long did he hang around?"

"Not long." She looked ready to cry. "I don't see why you're jumping on me."

"Okay—okay—the damage is done."

"Damage? He acted like a perfect gentleman—and brothers don't always resemble each other. How was I to know—?"

"You know now," Carmody said.

Life had not encouraged him to expect a bed of roses up to the time his old man got hitched to a widow with an eight-year-old son of her own. He had been a runty half-starved six, thrown in as part of the bargain. But from the moment he entered the new mama's house damned if she hadn't treated him like he was the surprise package delivered from the best store in town. So of course there had to be a snag—the pretty boy with the mouthful of butter who pushed him around and lorded it over him and ...

"Did he say when he was coming back?"

"No—just that he'd changed his mind about waiting and had left a note."

"Yeah." Carmody dropped the subject, grimly aware that it would not stay dropped. "What did you do to the Grimes that made her shoot out of here?"

"Me?"

"You were talking to her—weren't you?"

"You ought to be glad I was instead of barking at me. She was like a state getting set to secede until I started oiling her up. I even hinted you'd cut me down to my size." She arched her body, outlining it with her hands.

The sensuous maneuver was wasted. He said absently, "We don't want to lose the Grimes. She should be good for the course and then some."

"Well—I'm doing my bit. Not that I get any thanks for it." She walked around the desk.

"Huh? Oh—sure." He grabbed her.

She gave a happy squeal. "Mike—stop—your wife might walk in and—"

"You're right." He released her, pretending not to notice her disappointment. "You better blow before I lose my head." He drew the back of his hand across his mouth.

Hurt, she said, "My lipstick doesn't come off that easy. Talk about losing your head. What do you think I lost last night?"

He said flatly, "Nothing if I'm any judge. And I am."

"Listen—don't get the idea I'm a pushover." She thought of the morning's unexpected yield and convinced herself that she had renounced a sun-tanned playboy for her true love's sake. "If I'd wanted to I could've—"

"Are you going to give me trouble, Edna?" He liked her. She was provocative both fore and aft, with the type of cheaply pretty face that attracted him. Still, it had been a mistake to start anything. Counting repairs to the car last night could cost him plenty.

He stood up, tightening his belt to its premeal notch.

Diverted, Edna said, "You've got such a narrow waist, Mike."

"Move."

"What's your hurry? The next group isn't due yet—not that it would hurt them to sweat it off by waiting." Spite bubbled from her wounded ego. "They're nothing but a bunch of rotten-spoiled women."

"They pay your salary."

"I earn it. There are lots of jobs open for a girl like me. I don't have to—"

"Write your own reference and count on me to sign it any time. I'd be the last to keep you from getting ahead."

She recanted. "I didn't mean it that way. You know I love my work here—all of it. You know that, Mike."

"So get back to it."

She glanced at the folders on the desk. "I'll file those—"

"Okay. Make out a new cover for this one. It got dirty." He extracted the contents, tore the manila to scraps, and dropped them into the wastebasket.

She lingered over the small chore, and when it was done seized upon any excuse to linger. "There was something I wanted to tell you. I was listening on the intercom to that Number Four talk you gave this morning—and if you promise not to get mad again it seems to me you piled it on too thick. Mentioning all those groceries like that only reminds them how hungry they are—and it's human nature they'll stuff themselves first chance they get. I bet none of them made it past the dining room in the lobby."

He said, "You think so?" His grin puzzled her.

"Of course. It's bad psychology—that's what it is. You'll undo all your work."

He kept grinning. "Never mind. You attend to your knitting—I'll attend to mine."

"All the same, Mike—"

Good-humoredly he picked her up, dropped her at the door, and gave her a parting slap. "Beat it—and none of that 'Mike' stuff in business hours. There's a time and place."

Greatly encouraged she made a face at him and bounded down the corridor.

She was the least of his worries, he thought, removing a silky yellow hair from his black jersey. It would not take much to keep her happy. Behind that boldly touting front she was just a dumb chick with a torch. It had not even occurred to her that the comparatively low rental of the premises was due to a tacit contract with the management. He had argued that since none but the rich could afford his fees there were side benefits to be reaped before the beginners settled down in earnest to the prescribed regime. And I'm keeping my end up, he thought, or that bus boy I tip for reports is lying. What with second breakfasts, lunches, and teas, not to mention the bar bills of types like the Morrison dame, they're nicking the "beasts" for plenty. It lengthens the course too. Who can blame me if my orders are disobeyed?

He looked at his watch. He had a class at three, but the postgraduates never felt they were getting their money's worth unless he put in an appearance before they left. The doorknob turned as he reached for it. He thought his wife had come to call him to the colors and he assumed the noncommittal mask he had taken to wearing in her presence.

He kept the mask on as his stepbrother entered the office, closely followed by Edna Spofford.

"I couldn't help it, Mr. Carmody." She looked less indignant than she sounded. "He wouldn't listen to me."

His stepbrother greeted him as though there had never been anything but love between them, crushing him in an embrace before he could duck. "Cro—I've been looking forward to this across miles of country. What could have given your lovely young dragon the impression that you wouldn't be glad to see me?"

Carmody said, in a voice like a hard push, "You're excused, Spofford. Send word to have the class in the gym dismissed."

But when she had slammed the door he was all apologetic charm. "Got to keep them on their toes or the joint would fall apart. Well—well—this sure is a surprise."

"There are more to come," Vance said.

## CHAPTER 2

A few members of the accelerated class made virtuous tracks for home to eat low-caloried lunches washed down by strong hopes of recapturing straying husbands. The widowed Annie Grimes had no such problem, nor had it existed during her married life. She was among those who did not get past the main-floor restaurant. So was Mrs. Atmore, who entered five minutes after her.

Annie Grimes called across the large room, "Yoohoo—Mrs. Atmore—" happily unaware that she was violating the subdued atmosphere and that her self-conscious prey accepted the invitation to prevent it from being reissued.

Seated across the table, Mrs. Atmore nibbled at a salad without dressing. Perhaps this was why the meal ordered by Annie Grimes had tasted much better in fancy than it did in fact.

Looking with astonishment at the food that remained on her plate, she said, "Maybe that yogurt I've been swilling has shrunk my stomach and if so the rest of me is bound to follow. Or else you're shaming me by setting a good example."

"I consider it foolish to consult an expert unless I'm prepared to take his advice," Mrs. Atmore said.

"You're right—but I've done bumps and grinds and tried to diet till I'm blue in the face. It just doesn't work for me. You see—when Arthur took sick he was restless if I left him alone with the nurses, and that was how the weight crept up on me. I hung around the house so much that eating was the only fun I had—and when he passed away, the habit stuck."

Mrs. Atmore murmured something that sounded like an embarrassed expression of condolence.

Annie Grimes said quickly, "That's all right. As it was, poor Arthur had more than his share of suffering. He lingered on for months after the doctor said there was no hope. Still—prepared for it or not you kind of get used to somebody." Almost at every turn she was confronted by the gap that Arthur had left. Its size seemed disproportionate because although she had grown increasingly fond of him during their years together she had never been in love with him.

Mrs. Atmore chewed away, stoic and silent. Direct probing in the dressing room had revealed that she too was a widow. Annie Grimes swore at herself for reviving painful memories. She endeavored to atone. "I have to admit I was kind of surprised when you walked in here. You didn't seem the type to put on the feed bag right under Carmody's nose, so to speak."

Mrs. Atmore smiled faintly.

Encouraged, Annie Grimes said, "I'll bet you haven't fallen from grace once—and you're really getting results." It was not flattery. "Even without losing another pound you're what my old dad called a fine figure of a woman. Let me in on your secret—or is it just a case of that will power Carmody's always raving about?"

"I—we all owe it to ourselves to look as well as we can." A wash of red was creeping up Mrs. Atmore's neck.

Annie Grimes lowered her cornflower eyes and busily flicked a crumb from the tablecloth. Looks like I went and put my foot in it again, she thought. Could be something to that gossip about how bad she wants a man.

She said, "You'll think I'm crazy at my age—February nineteenth I'll be forty-four—but I have a specially important reason for slimming down. I want to get back in show business."

Mrs. Atmore's blush had given way to cold disapproval. "You can't mean—?"

Annie Grimes laughed. In the dressing room she had made no secret of her former occupation. "No—that's over and done with. I've seen too many flabby has-beens trying to do what don't come natural after thirty-five. But I played a bit part in a turkey Arthur backed before I married him because everybody said it was better for a man of his class not to marry a wife right out of burlesque. Well—anyway—flopperoo or not—I got rave notices—and there might be some legit producer willing to take a chance on me for a character role if I can ever do more than waddle across the stage."

Mrs. Atmore made a polite attempt to show interest. "I've known people who invested in the theater. Wouldn't that be more suitable than taking an active part?"

"No—all an angel does is part with his moola and cross his fingers. I need to be in there pitching. I get so sick and tired of sitting around I could bust. You think maybe I haven't given Carmody a fair chance?"

"You'll have to decide that for yourself. Although I have great confidence in him I make it a rule not to give advice."

But the effect of her uncompromising presence was more potent than advice. If she can do it so can I, thought Annie Grimes. I'll string along with Carmody for a while longer.

"Cancel my dessert," she said to the waiter. "Just black coffee."

Vance, seated without invitation, looked like a man relaxing at his favorite club. He had taken on more than a tan since Carmody's last sight of him. His long-limbed boyish frame had filled out just enough to enhance an aura of success, and horn-rimmed glasses bridging his fine straight nose added to the whole effect a seeming of knowledgeable maturity.

"Put your eyes back in your head," he said. "I can't be as fascinating as all that."

"For all I know you suddenly got fascinating to the cops," Carmody said. "Or are those trick cheaters for real?"

Vance removed the horn-rims. Something dangerous flickered for a moment in his eyes. "Was your somewhat stilted greeting due to your failure to recognize me at first glance?"

"I'm laughing." He had no urge to laugh. The old diminishing forces were at work, transforming the office into a scrubby boardinghouse kitchen, and himself into a stringy brat who had fought to preserve his entity under an elder boy's rule. He could almost feel the air leaking out of him, and the muscles dissolving in the arms that were weighted to his sides by his tightly balled hands. He thrust the hands into the pockets of his slacks: involuntary admission that fists were useless weapons against this enemy. He thought of a scene that had taken place in that kitchen, and shouted as though the heat of his voice might destroy a rising crop of goose pimples, "Shave your head—grow a pot—lose your teeth—I'd know you!"

"It's gratifying to be so deeply etched in your memory," Vance said.

The deceptively gentle tone warned Carmody that he must hold tight rein upon himself. Losing his head in anger would not help him to find out what, if anything, he had to fear. He said pacifically, "You could always juggle the language, Vance. Why wouldn't you be etched—or whatever you want to call it? Maybe we didn't always see eye to eye but we were kids together—weren't we?"

"Ah yes. One must never underestimate the bonds of the past."

Carmody said a little too abruptly, "What brings you to town?"

"Business—some old—some new."

"It's been so long I don't even know what racket you're in."

Vance reproved him mildly. "Running a legitimate business yourself I should think you'd have forgotten words like 'racket.'"

"You said a mouthful. Everything here is strictly on the up and up—no gimmicks—no angles. The customers got something to get rid of and they pay me to take it away." He almost added, "Put that in your pipe and smoke it." Instead he ended the statement with a boastful "Not bad—huh?"

"Not on the face of it." Vance's eyes disowned the smile upon his lips.

Carmody glanced around the room for reassurance. It was no crummy kitchen. It was his office, a suitable orderly setting for a solid businessman. He withdrew his hands from the dampened linings of his pockets. He inflated his chest.

Observing this, Vance said, "Local boy makes good."

"I got no complaints."

"Congratulations. But I shudder to think of how hard you must have worked to amass enough money to finance the enterprise."

Carmody could not look at him. "It wasn't easy. I had to start small and leave it to satisfied graduates to spread the word around—and by the time this hotel went up, things were going good enough for me to chance the move. What about you? You still haven't told me—"

"There will be ample opportunity for that." Vance pulled his chair closer to the desk, lifted the lid of an empty cigarette box, and let it fall quickly, as though he were attempting to ignore a glaring social lapse.

Carmody mislaid his resolution to keep calm. His voice was corrosive. "I'm also clean out of champagne and fish eggs—so by now you should be asking yourself, 'Is this trip necessary?'"

"Times may have changed but you're the same old Cro."

"Don't call me that—"

"I'll admit the name you're using is more distinguished than—"

"It's legitimate. I—"

"Of course. You adopted it for business reasons. Quite usual."

"How did you find me?"

"Don't be modest. Those spot announcements on television have spread your fame."

Carmody damned his wife. She had insisted upon the advertising campaign, and the one logical argument he could advance against it was the one he dared not use. So he had submitted to the cameras and the lights, squaring his shoulders, thrusting his chest out, stiffening his features like a man with his head in a vise. And later he convinced himself that the end result, no more than a flash and gone, had the anonymity of an old tintype.

"Relax," Vance said. "None but your nearest and dearest would hitch that winsome lad on the screen to a shady past. I might not have recognized him either—if I hadn't been sentimental enough to keep track over the years."

"What do you want? You—you don't look like you're short of pocket—but I guess anybody could use extra cash—and for old time's sake I could maybe raise—"

"Your generosity overwhelms me," Vance said. "I—" Then the door opened and he was on his feet. He did not so much as nod his head, but Carmody had the odd impression that he had bowed from the waist in gallant appreciation of the woman who entered.

Her velvety brown eyes made brief acknowledgment of his presence before they settled upon her husband. "I came to remind you of the time," she said. "I didn't know you were busy."

"I'm not. I'll be out in a minute." He mumbled to Vance, "Nice of you to drop in."

"And altogether rewarding," Vance said, "at least from my point of view."

His point of view was clear. His point of view was Ceil.

Her black hair shone. She wore it combed straight back from a smooth broad brow. The simplicity of her dress was almost arrogant, as though she had decided that her figure needed no gilding. She did not appear aware of the rapt attention she was receiving. She gave her husband a questioning glance, patently expecting an introduction.

Vance might have been portraying a connoisseur of rare wine, busily rolling the first sip on his sensitive tongue. Distraught, Carmody borrowed at random from a salesman who had called several days ago. "This is Mr. McLean."

She looked bewildered. He wished she'd stop holding her goddam beautiful neck as stiff as if she expected a noose to drop over it. He wished she'd go away before ... He saw Vance emerge from his phony trance, and heard his phony chuckle.

Ceil said, "Mr. McLean—? Oh yes—you're representing the Vitrate Company. I hope there isn't going to be a delay with the order. We plan to start using it next week."

Vance shook his head. "If I were representing any company that served you there would never be any delay. In fact I stand ready to apply for a job with Vitrate so that I can push your order through. What is it by the way? It sounds lethal."

Carmody had almost forgotten the lift of her lips when she smiled. "It's a food concentrate—a sort of meal-in-one that's been tested with very good results on groups of people who need to lose weight. Of course there are a number of them on the market but we thought that a formula made especially for us would—"

Carmody said rudely, "We can't stand here talking. You better run ahead, Ceil, and get Graham to—"

"Give me at least a moment," Vance said, "to clear up the misunderstanding that's been created."

"Some other time." He suffered the frustration of knowing that Ceil was no Edna Spofford to be bounced from the room.

Vance had turned back to her. "I'm Vance Manning. Introducing me as 'McLean' was meant to be a joke, I suppose, although its point escapes me—but withholding your name comes under the heading of sheer selfishness. How many beautiful ladies does he want all to himself?"

Her lips had straightened. "I'm Mrs. Carmody."

Carmody's satisfaction at the effect of the cold pronouncement did not last. Vance looked thunderstruck, but made such swift recovery that his shock could have been as phony as the rest of him. He took Ceil's hand and touched it with his lips.

He said, "If I were greedy I'd claim my right to kiss the bride properly."

Carmody shouted, "'Bride' nothing—we been married eight years."

Vance dealt him a painful clap on the back. "I do congratulate you." His sincerity flooded the room. "There must be more to our Cro than meets his brother's critical eye."

Ceil said aloofly, "I'm afraid, Mr. Manning, that I've missed the point of *your* joke."

"Why wouldn't you?" Carmody tried to keep his voice down. "You must've heard me mention him—but being he's a stepbrother it probably didn't cut as much ice with you as—"

Vance said over him, "Cro and I were much too close to split hairs about whether or not there is a blood tie. We've shared everything since we were youngsters—including our deepest secrets."

It sounded friendly. It carried the same force as the clap on the back. Carmody, on the brink of open war, was pulled back by Ceil.

It was impossible to judge from her face or voice how much of his tension had been communicated. "How long will you be in New York, Mr. Manning?"

"'Vance,' please. I'll be here for quite a while. A combination business and pleasure trip."

"If you'd let us know in advance we could have prepared a better welcome."

"Meeting you is welcome enough for a king. Will you and Cro be my guests for dinner tonight?"

She hesitated. Carmody jumped in. "We're dated up."

Vance said sadly, "I got off on the wrong foot with him. I've never been able to resist teasing him, and it seems that the years between haven't cured me of it. I confess that I kept pulling his leg until he came to the conclusion that I either wanted to borrow money or be taken into the business. Poor Cro. He should have known better than anyone that this sort of thing isn't my line of country."

Ceil was too polite to ask what his line of country was. She said, "Why do you call him 'Crow'?"

"Just one of those boyhood nicknames. I've forgotten how it started. Let's see—it couldn't have been short for 'Cro-Magnon.' I don't think we were that well informed. Besides—scientists say they were a race of tall erect men—"

Carmody said hoarsely, "Now we're running a history school."

Vance smiled. "He never did have a musical voice—so perhaps it stemmed from 'Croaky.' You will celebrate with me tonight, won't you?"

Carmody did not give her a chance to answer. "Celebrate what?"

"Why, our reunion. Speaking of history, February seventeenth should go down as a memorable date."

## CHAPTER 3

March second was an ugly threatening day. On its eve, Gridley Nelson of Homicide West phoned his wife from a Brooklyn hospital and told her not to hold dinner. If he cared to check, she said, he would discover that even the most fashionable dinner hour had come and gone, so he must forgive her for not being bowled over by his announcement. Then she laughed, and assured him that her "acid wit" had been inspired not by him but by the absence of their son, Junie, who along with some of his classmates was on an educational tour of the nation's capital. Nelson said that Junie, a man of eleven, had his own life to live, and that they had better get used to it. Whereupon she accused him of never having been a mother, but added a pious "thanks be." She did not ask him when he would be home, but mentioned that a neighbor had invited her to drop in and review a wardrobe designed for a trip to Europe. Nelson said that by all means she must give the neighbor the benefit of her superior taste, which was tantamount to saying that he would not be returning within the next few hours. At her demand to know if he had eaten he made vague allusion to a late lunch. She was not fooled. She said that he was to sit down to a decent meal before he tried to tackle whatever else was on his calendar.

As always the sound of Kyrie's voice gave her to him, complete with deceptive fragility, ash-blonde hair, and violet eyes. He smiled as though she could see him too, but as soon as he hung up his expressive mouth sobered.

He stepped back into the antiseptic corridor and did not break stride until he reached the frosty air. The object of his visit, casualty of a hit-and-run driver, had left earlier, quitting the hospital and the world.

Nelson eased his car out of the driveway and headed for Manhattan. Ordinarily he drove with minimal conscious effort. Now the power beneath his hands seemed inimical; part of a growing conspiracy of moving vehicles to depopulate a land that loved mechanization too well.

The girl had lain comatose for over two weeks. There had been no hope for her beyond the hope that she would return to brief awareness and utter a clue to aid the police in their search for the missing killer. She had not uttered. But she had seemed to recognize Nelson when he appeared, and her fingers had clung to his in a last convulsive attempt to cling to life.

Nelson's reason for being in at the death was not entirely professional. Young Alice Thwaite had been employed as a nursemaid in his neighborhood.

At times his activities ended when hers were well begun, and walking the last lap from garage to house he would stop to greet the vigorous little figure wheeling the large perambulator. He welcomed these encounters. The girl and her plump pink charge had come to herald a return to normality after some mean journey along the byways of his vocation.

Word of the accident had not been received through his office. It was Sammy, friend, cook, and housekeeper extraordinary, who brought it to his attention. He had come downstairs to a very early breakfast, careful not to disturb his sleeping wife. Sammy, as usual, beat him to the kitchen. She allowed him to finish his bacon and eggs in peace, but when his plate was clean she said, "You acquainted with Alice Thwaite?"

He said, "Yes," preoccupied with nothing more important than whether a third cup of the good coffee would be superfluous.

Sammy persisted. "I talking about the girl I recommend to the Mortons—and they so pleased because she care for that baby like he the most important business there is."

Sammy rarely made small talk, and he had never known her to gossip. He said tentatively, "She does seem dedicated to her work."

"She dying in a hospital," Sammy said.

He should have been shockproofed. None the less he was shocked. He said, "Accident?"

Sammy nodded. "Her sister live in Brooklyn and that where Alice spend her day off. Only this trip she stay late because the sister bedridden and the husband delay himself till midnight in a bar. She walking to the subway alone when a car knock her down. It happen where they building a project which nobody lives in yet—so ain't a soul to say how long she lay before she found."

He had not yet finished with the morning paper. He reached for it.

"Page nine," Sammy said. "They don't waste no big letters on it. You got to look real hard."

Aside from including the exact location of the accident and the name of the hospital, the commonplace item added nothing to what Sammy had told him.

"You think they let me visit with her?" Sammy said.

"I'll inquire."

He called the hospital and, by pulling rank, was connected with a staff doctor. Among the details of a black prognosis were severe concussion and internal bleeding.

"She hasn't regained consciousness," he said to Sammy. "Her employers left orders that she's to have every possible attention—but no visitors are allowed. I've asked to be notified if there's any change."

Sammy's handsome face brooded. "You fixing to get to work and catch that runaway?"

"So far it's a case for the local precinct."

Her deep rich voice was scornful. "So far what they done?"

"It's not an easy job, Sammy. No witnesses have come forward with the license number or a description of the car. Even the sex of the driver is unknown."

"That wouldn't make no difference to you—once you set your mind to it. And she just happen to be in Brooklyn so what a Brooklyn precinct to do with it? She live with her old pa on the West Side before she come to the Mortons—and that where she vote did she last long enough. It truly a case for your Homicide West."

He kept in touch with the hospital and followed the fruitless course of the police search. Even if he had been less interested he could not have done less under the pressure of Sammy's deep concern. But pressured as he was by the demands of his own office he could not do more.

The final moment in the hospital room had provided grim sanction for further effort in that the Homicide Squads of Brooklyn, Queens,

Manhattan, and the Bronx would be alerted to the hunt for a featureless criminal in a featureless car. And with luck they might stumble upon him. Extraordinary luck, Nelson thought. Lacking it, there was always room in the file of unsolved cases for yet another failure.

Slowed by the heavy traffic he looked with jaundiced eye upon the crawling line ahead. For all he knew, one of its units contained a driver who either by carelessness or misfortune had maimed or slain, thereafter to carry the act concealed in the reaches of an accommodating conscience.

Before he pulled up at the drab building that housed his office, snow had begun to fall. It brightened the dirty streets but not his mood.

He had been away for three hours, leaving behind him a reasonably cleared desk. Without surprise he saw that it was piled high again with data that had accumulated during his absence. There was also an accumulation of stale air because someone had closed the narrow window. Nelson raised it, meeting the familiar resistance of warped wood and rotting sash cord.

Slowed down by interruptions he worked his way through the mass of typed or penned material. In the main it consisted of reports on current investigations. Most of them were dull and repetitious, contributing little to the sum of painstakingly gathered information. Some of the detective-authors were on the late shift and sat in the ready room awaiting further assignments. Occasionally he summoned one of them to discuss a point obscured by illegible writing or cumbersome sentence structure.

He had neared the bottom of the pile when the Brooklyn call came in.

"Captain Nelson? Lieutenant Werner speaking. I've got a little something on the Alice Thwaite business—an anonymous letter delivered in the morning mail. From what you told me at the hospital I thought you might be interested."

"I am." He had talked to the lieutenant in the hospital corridor, careful to explain the unofficial nature of his presence because precinct men were often allergic to the aid and comfort given by "Special Squads."

"Here goes for what it's worth," Werner said. "No salutation." He began to read in a slow uninflected voice:

"'I saw the Thwaite accident from start to finish. I had my reasons for not sticking my neck out. Let's put it I can't afford to have cops asking me questions that have nothing to do with the case. But it was

him. I swear it was and I ought to know. We swabbed the same decks
day in day out for months. Thinking it over I don't owe him a thing.
He had no excuse except he was in a hurry. He always was. He
speeded out of nowhere while she was crossing the street. She was
flung high and hit the asphalt like a bomb. It shook me right off the
sidewalk. First I was squatting beside her expecting him to get out
and next thing I knew he went into reverse and I started running after him. The street was lit pretty good so don't worry. I made him plain
as day but I'll bet he didn't make me. His mind was strictly on the get-
away. He backed around the corner and shot forward down the avenue
quicker than it's ever been done before. I chased him a block before I
came to with egg on my face. I didn't return to the scene. The rate bad
news travels I was sure somebody else had found her and anyway she
looked too dead to care. But when I read in the papers how she lay
in the cold alive and maybe suffering I stopped sleeping. Like I say I
don't owe him a thing so why let him get away with murder? Could
be it's not the first time or the last. It was a green sports car. I could-
n't tell the make or get the license. Too crazy mad to know what I was
doing I guess. But I got better than that and never mind how. I hear
he's come up in the world since he went to sea. You can collar him at
the Easton Hotel in Manhattan. The name he goes under is Carmody.
Take it from there.'"

Lieutenant Werner dropped the flat delivery and said in his normal
robust tones, "It's signed 'A First-time Squealer.' If I hadn't been out
all day the lab report would be ready. Not that these things pay off
more than one in a thousand."

A simple sum had been posed by the penultimate line of the letter.
Nelson set it aside. He said that anonymous communications were a
mixed blessing, and thanked the lieutenant for the call. He was dou-
bly grateful, he said, piling it on a little, since he realized that a man
in charge of a busy precinct had little time to devote to friendly ges-
tures.

"My pleasure, Captain. Knew you before we met—by reputation,
that is. In fact I'd begun to feel I was the only member of the force who
hadn't made your acquaintance. If you don't mind me saying so
you're kind of a legend. Not many of us would be sticking to the job
if we'd inherited money enough to retire in style." He seemed in no
hurry to end the conversation.

Neither was Nelson, who wanted more of the letter than had been
provided by its content. He said, "Your 'First-time Squealer' indicates
that he's absorbed a certain amount of education. He expresses him-

self quite clearly."

Werner gave further proof that he was not a man who jealously guarded his preserves against interdepartmental poaching. "He's not a top-notch speller or much on punctuation. I threw in a few periods and commas as I went along." He paused. Nelson guessed that he was staring at the letter. His findings seemed to depress him. "I wouldn't make book the mistakes aren't phony. That goes for the hint about having cause to shun the police—and the deck-swabbing bit too. If we do catch up with him he could turn out to be a college professor or a cute little kid with a big imagination." He paused again. "Only the writing's too much like a kid's to be true—and risking any kind of fist instead of piecing it together from newsprint shows too much self-confidence to suit me—or else he's never heard of handwriting experts."

Nelson said, "You've told me a great deal without benefit of lab equipment. Let's hope he's never heard of fingerprints."

"Remains to be seen." The precinct man tossed the compliment off, but his voice was brighter for it. "They might be able to trace the stationery. Cheap stuff—no watermark—eight and a half by eleven—but green—same as the car's supposed to be. The envelope's ten-cent-store white with a Brooklyn postmark—which doesn't mean he's a resident of Brooklyn. More likely the opposite."

Nelson agreed.

Werner said, "The Easton's one of the newer hotels, isn't it?"

"Yes—and one of the more expensive." Nelson added as though it had just occurred to him, "A place of its size could very well have several Carmodys registered—but there's a reducing school of that name on the roof."

"You don't say!" Werner chewed on it for a moment. "Come to think of it I've seen the ads somewhere."

"Are you a bachelor, Lieutenant?"

"That's right." He sounded puzzled.

"That might explain why your home hasn't been invaded by telephone calls soliciting clients. Carmody's is a 'ladies only' enterprise so perhaps it has a system of checking its prospects."

"Or maybe Brooklyn's not considered tony enough to bother about." Werner chuckled. "Say—you had me worried you'd spotted a button missing from my shirt. Well—I won't wait for the lab to get busy. I'll send a team to the Easton right away—or on second thought I'll roll, myself. It might need more finesse than ..." His voice tapered off.

Nelson turned his head toward the rattling window. Fat white flakes were blowing in to cushion the sill and glisten in a melting patch upon the worn linoleum beneath. He hoped that the weather was even worse in Brooklyn, and that there was a window near the precinct man's desk.

He did not hope in vain. Werner assented glumly to a comment that driving would be no picnic on a night like this.

"I'm nearer to the Easton than you are," Nelson said. "It would hardly be out of my way to stop in for a preliminary look-see."

Werner hesitated for as long as it took to hunt for the catch. Then he said slowly and earnestly, "I've always been a great believer in co-operation, myself—and everyone knows you're no hog for credits. Confidentially, I'm up to my ears in work here and I'd be sore as a boil if this turned out to be another false lead—especially when I could have been spending the time catching up on the garage reports. You'd be surprised how many car washes and minor repairs took place right after the night of February sixteenth."

Nelson made a sympathetic sound. He said that since he had started his career as a rookie it would be like old times to work for a lieutenant.

The edges of Werner's voice crisped. "You'll be sure to call me so I can follow through if necessary?"

Nelson promised.

Before he set out he called the hotel garage and asked a few brief questions. The garrulous man in charge answered at length. Nelson said that he was in the neighborhood and would continue the conversation in person.

Once a week Carmody closed early. By so doing he made way for a men's club whose membership was wealthy enough to pay through the nose for the privilege of using the swimming pool and other available facilities.

On this particular day he got into his street clothes as soon as the early afternoon class had been dismissed. "I need a change of scene," he said, taking careless aim at the air around his wife. "Don't count on me for dinner."

She too needed a change of scene but she waited until the rest of the staff, with the exception of Carmody's assistant, had departed. The assistant would remain to keep an eye on the men's club and to supervise the small brigade of charwomen who mopped up after it.

She went for a long walk, stopping when she tired to dine at a counter. Snow had begun to fall in earnest before she returned to the hotel, but she did not, after the fashion of wives, worry because her husband had worn neither overshoes nor waterproof. She knew him well enough to be certain that he was basking comfortable as a cat in some warm shelter.

The Easton lobby was crowded. She walked alone through its companionable noise until Vance Manning reached her side. Her eyes had been turned inward. She blinked her damply clustered lashes at him.

"What must a man do to attract your attention?" he said. "Where have you been?"

"I went for a walk."

"So I see." He reached down to brush snow from her coat. "But I meant where were you now—not to hear me calling across the lobby?"

"Thinking about dry clothes, I suppose."

"And what's our Michael thinking of—to allow you out in this weather?"

"He—he doesn't know. He's out in it himself."

"Well—take Dr. Manning's advice and swallow a hot drink before you do anything else."

"I will." She did not ask him to come up, and he did not seem to be seeking an invitation. In the weeks following his initial appearance he had chosen to regard himself as a member of the family, welcome to drop in at any hour that suited his fancy. Often he came bearing flowers or other small gifts for her, courting her shamelessly in the presence of her husband, but never staying longer than a few minutes if he found her alone. So she assumed that his interest lay not in her but in baiting Mike.

"*Bonne nuit*, dear Ceil," he said. "Rest well."

Yet he was an added element to her unrest.

An elevator whisked her to the roof. She said, "Good night, Denis," to the operator, glanced at Edna Spofford's desk, vacant in the surrounding emptiness, and wondered in passing if the girl's plans for the evening had corresponded with Mike's. She did not worry about that. The acute pain caused by the first of a series of Ednas had lessened with each successive infidelity until it was no more than dull discomfort.

She let herself into the apartment by way of the office, leaving the door between open. She changed wet clothes for dry, and with a book to keep her company sat down in the living room.

Mike's outings had become more frequent lately, and more prolonged. She should have been resigned to her peculiar solitude in the midst of the life that was lived on other parts of the roof. But tonight, as on other nights since the advent of Mike's stepbrother, the silence of the apartment condensed around her, seeming as heavily explosive as a chemical compound awaiting the spark that would bring destruction.

On the surface there was nothing alarming about Vance. The precarious nature of her existence had manifested itself long before his coming. And he had given her no valid reason to suppose that he was the lighted match. Possibly, she thought, his constant baiting of Mike was good-humored, and not the hostile thing it seemed to her. Possibly too she was exaggerating its effect upon her husband. An only child, she had no means of judging sibling relationships, or of knowing whether unrelated children brought up under the same roof were subject to the emotional stresses of siblings. What she did know was that even in the early days when Mike had pretended to confide in her, he had never so much as made casual allusion to Vance. He had said that like herself he was an orphan without kith or kin and that she was all the family he ...

The knock at the door hurled her to her feet.

## CHAPTER 4

Approximately three quarters of a mile from the Hotel Easton, Doris Atmore sat alone in her living room. For once self-pity was no part of her mood. She felt relaxed and drowsy still, even though she had awakened only a short while ago. And she smiled lovingly and indulgently at herself for having fallen asleep at such an unconventional hour.

Acting on an impulse to spread some of the joy that had come to her in the late afternoon, she reread and answered a letter from her daughter. The girl was away at college, and had filled up a great deal of space with the details of an Easter house party which was being planned by her roommate. Easter was a long way off, but quite obviously she was giving her mother ample time to adjust to an empty holiday.

Doris Atmore's pen rode happily over the paper leaving none of the usual reproaches in its wake. "Dear Joan—accept the invitation by all means," she wrote. "You're sure to enjoy it, and I am glad you are choosing the right kind of friends. The Beales are a fine family. Your dear father always spoke highly of ..."

The shadow cast by her dead husband caused the pen to balk. But he would not want me to grieve forever, she thought. His dearest wish was for my happiness.

Presently she was able to continue. "When you do come home you will hardly recognize me. I believe I mentioned that two weeks ago I was one of several in my reducing class to be put on Vitrate. It's one of those formulas that contains all of the protein, fats, carbohydrates, and minerals necessary for perfect health. Along with the exercise I've been taking it has done wonders for me, and the best part of it is that my hunger is completely satisfied."

In every way, she thought. All of my hungers.

"So you see," she wrote, "that the reducing course has proven a wise investment. Forgive me, dear, for sounding like a testimonial, but I want you to know how well and cheerful I've become. My outlook has changed so completely that there's not the slightest need for you to worry about your mother who knows what a trial she's been to you at times."

Here she decided to inject a humorous note. "Of course every rose has its thorn, and it would be untruthful to say that the reducing class is an exception. There's a perfectly dreadful woman who sits next to me in the dressing room and she uses proximity as an excuse to shower me with her boisterous attentions. If you can imagine me being forced into the position of lunching with a former queen of burlesque it will give you some idea of my predicament. To be fair, however, I must concede that she is a disarming sort of creature. She too was chosen for the control group and now that she has begun to take off weight she gives me the credit for it instead of Vitrate, because she appears to think I encouraged her to stay the course when she was on the verge of resigning. I did so unwittingly, I assure you...."

She added a few maternal injunctions to the letter, and closed with love. She was filled with love. She could hardly contain its almost unbearable sweetness. It brimmed out of her eyes and was reflected in her bedroom vanity as she prepared to rejuvenate face and neck with a hormone cream that was said to accomplish miracles. Yawning luxuriously, she was tempted to skip the routine for once, but now of all times she could not afford to do so.

About to dip into the jar she paused to stare at her bare hand. Some time ago her wedding band had become imbedded in surplus flesh, and she had suffered the indignity of having a surgeon remove it. The operation had misshaped it, and although she had bought a replacement it was now too large and kept slipping off her finger. Probably in the bathroom, she thought indifferently, because it had never had the significance of the original. Then she was really concerned. My emerald. I could not have been careless with that—not under any circumstances.

She went to the adjoining bathroom. The wedding band was there on the edge of the washbasin. She frowned at it. Surely I had the other on when ... Her face cleared. In my jewel box, of course. I must have taken it off automatically and ...

The jewel box was locked. Could she have been so deliberate as to open it, deposit the ring, and lock it again with the onlooker standing close? She fumbled in a drawer for the little key, fitted it, turned it, and raised the lid of the box. The small collection of jewelry that she did not keep in a bank vault winked up at her. But the emerald had its own special compartment, and the compartment was empty.

She had trouble with her breathing. Feverishly she searched the apartment. Her head began to throb in the moments before she lost it. Her rush to the telephone was purely reflex action.

But before the police detectives arrived she had faced her error in summoning them. She forced herself to make the tumbled bed. She tried to force coherent thought. The jewel box! Hide it—make it appear as though thieves had—later I'll find a way to waive the insurance ...

She was weeping shameful bitter tears as she dragged herself to the door.

Not many city blocks away, Annie Grimes had passed the evening by taking stock of her wardrobe. Quite recently there had been reason to congratulate herself for emulating Mrs. Atmore. Her girdle was beginning to fasten without struggle, and the dresses she tried on showed a regional looseness where all had been snug before.

She wished there were someone to rejoice with her. The occasion called for a girl friend ready and eager to discuss the pros and cons of having her clothes altered or of waiting a bit longer and discarding them for new. It was too bad, she thought, that none of her late husband's friends could supply her need for a confidant. They were all fine people but their ways were not her ways. The only bond had been Arthur Hamilton Grimes himself.

The excitement of being wooed by one of the richest bachelors ever to cross her path, the stimulating envy of the other girls in the show, had catapulted her into the marriage. "Grab him while the grabbing is good," they said. "So what if he's older? Don't be a dope, Annie Dale. There's the future to think about—and what will you have when your face and figure go?"

So she had grabbed Arthur, and given such good value in return that he never once regretted his choice of a wife. As for her—well—she had enjoyed her new estate for as long as her gay and often rowdy companions took advantage of ungrudging invitations to free-load. But eventually they went on tour, or scattered to follow their separate stars. And after they dropped away she had only infrequent postcards mailed from distant places to remind her of their existence. Finally even the postcards stopped coming.

She sighed. Arthur had given her a good life, but it was simply not the life she was meant to lead. The novelty of a whole house to call her own, servants, jewels, excellent food at regular intervals, came to be taken for granted, and to be viewed as pale compensations for the tinseled world she had lost.

The telephone call inviting her to avail herself of Carmody's "Special Offer" had come soon after Arthur's funeral when she was at lowest ebb. She had hoped to reap the side benefit of a boon companion, but obviously the women there were not inclined to enlarge their circles with the addition of a quondam stripper. Mrs. Atmore was somewhat more polite than the others, now and then lending an ear under duress. Not by any stretch of the imagination, however, was she the stuff of which boon companions are fashioned. There was nothing personal in her being so stiff, thought Annie Grimes. Just that she seemed to have no use for women in general. She probably felt that any man was preferable because she even quivered when Carmody drew near.

Annie Grimes helped her unresponsive maid to replace the modeled garments in the closet. Then she played some noisy records to bolster her flagging spirits.

At night no visitors were permitted to use the private elevators without announcement over the house telephone. Mike had insisted upon that, and in the beginning Ceil had believed he was being considerate of her.

The knock came again. Angry with her pounding heart, she took deliberately measured steps to answer.

"Who's there?"

"It's Denis, Mrs. Carmody. I hope I've not disturbed you." The familiar reedy tenor reassured her. She pulled the door wide.

The elevator operator said, "The night manager vouched for this gentleman and asked me to show him the way."

She composed her startled face. She said coldly, "Is the house phone out of order?" But Denis had turned his uniformed back and was racing along the corridor to his abandoned cage.

She said to the man left standing there, "I suppose you want my husband. He's not at home."

"Then perhaps you can help me." The voice was deep and pleasant. "My name's Nelson—and before you fault the hotel service will you have a look at my credentials?"

She looked. She thought in confusion that here was the lighted match. A numbness armored her against the expected explosion. "Come in," she said, meaning, "I'm ready." But she had to sit down in the nearest chair before the closed door shut her in with him.

He carried his coat over his arm. It looked wetter than hers had been. He wore no hat. His white hair gave him a spurious claim to an age negated by the vitality of face and body. He stood tall beside the desk until she made the reluctant gesture. Then, as though the place of authority was his by right, he sat behind it, pulled out the wastebasket, and slung his coat across it.

"What time do you expect your husband, Mrs. Carmody?"

"I don't know. Probably quite late."

"I see."

She thought that perhaps he saw too much; that her tone had revealed too much. She sat straight-backed, rigid with pride. "He can rarely go out during the day," she said. "We—he works very hard."

"I'm sure this is a demanding business." There was a stack of blank paper on the desk. Absently he realigned its edges.

It was such a proprietary gesture that it made her feel it was she who had invaded his domain. Glancing down at her housecoat she experienced the dismay of a figure in a dream who has rushed inadequately clad to an illogical tryst.

"Has your husband ever been a seagoing man?"

To her the question seemed as much a non sequitur as wearing her housecoat to a formal interview, and quite as irrelevant to her conscious fears. She said, "No," and although in her waking hours she seldom gave confidences, could have gone on to say, If he had been it wasn't one of the things he boasted of when we met. A girl I knew introduced us. I'd given up teaching to care for my invalid mother until she died. Mike looked like all of life to me—and so did I to him because—you see—my mother had invested her money wisely.

The police captain's groomed hands were folding and refolding a sheet of the blank paper. His deep-set eyes were fixed upon her. They were friendly eyes, but he was not a friend. She had to remind herself of that. She averted her head. When next she looked he had disposed of the paper.

He said, "Does he do much driving at night?"

"I don't think so. Only around the city." To his bookie and back, she thought. Or to the nearest of his current fancies, or ...? Then the question took on meaning for her. She shivered, and her hands met and twined together for warmth. "Has he been in an accident? Is that what you've come to tell—?"

The pleasant voice was firm and reassuring. "I had no reason to expect that he wouldn't be at home and well."

She could not label the emotion that had come to her with the sudden vision of Mike dead or dying. "Then why *are* you here? Surely I have a right to know."

His face neither granted nor denied her right. He produced another apparent non sequitur. "Does your husband have friends or connections in Brooklyn?"

"None that I know of—except—" She stopped because the exception could not be pertinent to whatever information this man wanted.

"Yes?"

"Nothing. I started to say that one of our employees—the receptionist—lives in Brooklyn. If you want me to answer you intelligently you'd better give me at least a faint idea of what this is about."

"Very well. I'll try not to drag it out. The police receive a great deal of mail purporting to assist the course of justice. A large percentage of this mail is written by cranks—but we've learned to neglect none of it. Today a letter arrived accusing a man named Carmody of hit-and-run driving. It stated that he could be found at the Easton Hotel."

She could not take it in. It was so far removed from anything she expected. She said stupidly, "But that's impossible."

"It happens all the time." There was a noticeable drop in the climate around him, "And there hasn't been another Carmody registered here for the past month."

"I didn't mean that hit and runs were impossible. I meant that my husband wouldn't—it isn't the sort of thing he'd—" But she could not finish the sentence, and fixed by those gravely attentive eyes she realized that she should not have started it.

"The hit-and-run referred to," Nelson said, "took place a few weeks ago—at night on a Brooklyn street."

"Was—was anybody hurt?"

"A girl was injured. She died today."

"Oh—that's too bad." She took refuge in the flimsy words, afraid of what she might say if she said more.

It seemed that no more would be required of her. The man was on his feet. "I'll see your husband tomorrow," he said. "What time does he start to work?"

Her answer was mechanical. "At ten—but he has things to do before that. About one o'clock would be more convenient—during his lunch break." The protest came in spite of her. "But I don't see—you said yourself that the letter could have been written by a crank. Who sent it? There must have been something beside a name and address to bring you here on a night like this."

"Policemen aren't expected to notice weather conditions. The writer claimed to have witnessed the accident—and as proof he gave a description of your husband's car. So you can understand why it was necessary to disturb you. Good night, Mrs. Carmody." He was gone before she could rise from her chair.

Mike Carmody did not come home late. He missed Nelson by about three quarters of an hour. He had swallowed a moderate amount of liquor, but his mellow mood was dispelled, when he entered the lobby, by what he thought was a glimpse of his stepbrother making an exit with a crowd of barflies. He tried to persuade himself that he had been mistaken but his nerves were jumping as he got into the elevator.

He said to the boy, "Any visitors while I was out, Denis?"

"Maybe I did take somebody up," Denis said. "But yours isn't the only floor I stop on—and one night gets to be like another in this job."

Carmody said, "You got a grouch? Here—massage it with this."

The tip brought him a mumbled thanks, making him wish he had pasted the slob for insolence, which was what he deserved.

Lights had been left burning in the office and living room. He switched them off in passing, shed his coat, loosened his tie and collar, and yawning loudly strode to the bedroom. His wife had removed the spreads from the twin beds and was undressing. He glimpsed known beauty before she covered it with a robe.

"Don't worry," he said nastily.

He came out of the bathroom to find her reading in bed. "I know you weren't waiting up for me," he said. "So how's it going with Vance?"

She looked as though she had never heard the name.

"Okay," he said. "I just saw him in the lobby—but have it your way."

I'm too tired to play the heavy husband." He forced another yawn and went to his side of the room.

Stretched flat beneath his blankets, he reviewed the day. On the whole he thought that it had gone well, and that if his luck held it would not be too long before he was exactly where he wanted to be. But would his luck hold? Vance elbowed into his mind, pushing optimism out.

He had expected, if Vance ever caught up with him, anything from threats to bullets. But he was not prepared for a "man-who-came-to-dinner" haunt who exuded the innocent pleasure of one assured of welcome even while he needled his suffering host. What was his game—what did he know or guess? Why was he sucking up to Ceil?

Carmody could not figure him. If money, the obvious answer, was what Vance had decided to settle for, he was wasting his time on Ceil. She grudged every nickel that was not plowed back into the business, and paid all bills except bookie bills with the speed of light, instead of holding back and living a little.

But Vance had been hanging around her long enough to get the picture. It did not have to be spelled out for him. He was not a fool. And judging by the dough he flung around what he could pick up here would be small change. He sure looked as though the world had been treating him well. No "Sam the Tailor, one flight up" dealt in the suiting that clothed him. No chain store had produced his shirts and shoes and ties, and no flat wallet had paid for that dinner on the night of his arrival.

Carmody shrugged off the second obvious answer. Ceil had class; the same type of class that had rubbed off on Vance from who knew where. And she was an eyeful. But even in the early days before Carmody had decided that marrying her would be to his advantage, his usual approach had got him nowhere.

Was Vance having better luck? Carmody's insides responded with a dog-in-the-manger yelp. He turned over and dug his face into the pillow. Nuts! That's what he wants me to think. And if it's true why the hell should I care? Pretty soon I'll be on velvet and ... But it isn't true. The flowers he brings and the syrup he spouts are a cover-up for ... For what—?

He had to break the circle of his thoughts. He broke it by shouting, "Turn off that damn light," and rolled over on his back again to let the air from the window dry his face.

She put the book on the table between them and pulled the lamp cord. A while later she said, "Mike?"

"I'm asleep." He had faked a sleep-sodden voice to prove it. Things were in a fine state if a man started breathing fast because his name was called in the darkness.

"I'm glad you can sleep," she said.

"What would there be to stop me?" He gave the blankets a vicious tug that left his feet exposed. "Who the hell made my bed?"

"You did," she said.

He was slow to absorb it. Then he said, "Maybe your lover-boy appreciates the fancy cracks. If you got nothing else to sell sign off."

"A detective came here to see you tonight."

He shot up. "What for?"

"I'd like you to tell me."

"Sure you would. A murder confession and a ticket to the execution thrown in would suit you fine. Too bad I can't oblige." His hand was on the lamp cord. He pulled it. She lowered the arm she had raised as a shield against the sudden light. Her brown velvety eyes focused upon him. "Well?"

She was staring at and, for all he knew, through him. All the scars on his conscience began to itch. He pushed back the silence. "So you woke me up and I'm listening," he said.

"It was something about a hit-and-run accident."

He let out the breath he was holding. "Where do I come in? I haven't used the car since—not for weeks."

She said slowly, "Did you lend it to anyone?"

"A brand-new car? Am I punchy?"

"There was a bill for repairs in this morning's mail."

He swung himself out of bed. He turned his back and got busy anchoring the loosened blankets. I'll fix that moron at the garage, he thought. I told him not to send the bill—that I'd be in to settle ...

He said aloud, "All right—if that's what's bothering you. The time Spofford stayed late to work on the books I drove her home. She didn't ask for overtime so it was the least I could do. On the way I rammed a truck that couldn't decide whether it should stop or go. The big lug drove off before I could make something of it—so with no witnesses or anything it wasn't worth the headache of bracing the insurance company."

"You drove her home to Brooklyn?"

"She don't live in the Bronx." At any other time he would have congratulated himself for disposing of the Spofford business so easily. "Maybe this dick was after one of the clients," he said. "A lot of those rich dames think they can get away with anything."

"It was you he asked for. When I told him you'd be out late he said he'd come back tomorrow."

"Where are my cigarettes?" He padded out to the living room and padded back empty-handed. Climbing into bed he said, "Well—if this dick really thought I was his boy he would have stuck around until I showed. Was the victim hurt bad?"

"Killed," she said.

He picked up the carafe on the night table and poured water into his glass. He drank and set the glass down. "Tough," he said, "but in a town full of jokers who shouldn't be driving in the first place—why pick on us? There couldn't be enough cops to count every car that's been up for repairs lately."

She said as though she were reciting a rather dull lesson, "Someone who witnessed the accident wrote to the police. He gave your name and address and described your car."

Carmody looked wildly around the room. He could almost hear the click of the sliding gate and see the bars on the windows. He stuttered, "S-search me!" And then he said to his fellow prisoner, "Ceil—what are you shivering about—you know I wouldn't pull a caper like that."

## CHAPTER 5

Some of the money left by Nelson's father had been used to buy the house in the East Sixties. Nelson entered the hall, dropped his coat, and headed for the large colorful living room. Only one lamp was lit and no logs burned in the fireplace, but a great deal of light and warmth came from Kyrie. She switched off the television set and went the length of the room to meet him.

"You shouldn't have waited up for me," he said.

"What sort of woman could lie snug with her man out braving the elements?"

"You're lifting your share of the dialogue from the 'Late Late Show.'"

"The little I've seen of it isn't that good. Until about ten minutes ago I was next door looking at Mrs. Whitman's late late fashions. Grid—your hands would ice a drink. Shall I get you one?"

Nelson released her. "I think I'd like food. It's a hungry sort of night."

She said accusingly, "You didn't have dinner."

"My memory's frozen too."

"If your customers are as slippery as you no wonder you have to work so hard. Come with me."

He followed her to the kitchen, and together they looked into the tidy refrigerator.

"I vote for the roast beef," Nelson said.

"Shouldn't you have something hot?"

"Coffee. I'll put it on. You do the sandwiches."

Kyrie made several of heroic proportions and joined him at the kitchen table to eat them. "Your coffee's almost as good as Sammy's," she said. "It will keep us wide awake."

"Is that bad?"

They smiled at each other. He thought of Mrs. Carmody and wondered what sort of homecoming she would give her husband.

"Our son remembered to call from Washington," Kyrie said.

"How did he sound?"

"Like a seasoned politician. I hope he won't choose to be one."

"If he does we'll try to live it down. Any symptoms of homesickness?"

Kyrie shook her head. "I don't know whether I'm glad or sorry."

"Be glad—because it means he's secure enough to feel that he needn't stick around to keep an eye on us. He's certain we'll both be here when he gets back. Did he talk with Sammy?"

"He asked to—but she'd gone out."

"Is she upstairs now?"

"No. The Mortons sent her an SOS. They had to keep an important engagement, and the baby's taken a violent dislike to the new nurse," Kyrie added soberly, "The hospital notified them that Alice Thwaite died today."

"I know. I was there."

"At the hospital? But I thought—didn't you tell Sammy that the case wasn't in your territory?"

"I've been cooperating with the Brooklyn precinct."

"Is that what delayed you tonight?"

"Partly. Anything to keep from being blackmailed in my own home. Sammy's taken to calling me 'Captain' with discernible irony."

"Yes—I've noticed. Her sense of justice isn't bounded by boroughs. To her you're the be-all and end-all of the whole force. You will go on with the case—won't you, Grid?"

"I'll make a tactful try at getting official permission."

"I know your tactful tries. You'll get it. I know something else—and don't stop eating while I'm talking to you. Not even Sammy could make you do what you didn't want to do."

"I want to all right—but until tonight it seemed like a needle-in-ahaystack business."

She leaned across the table. "You found something! They've been working on the case for weeks and in one night you've—"

"Not so fast. I undertook to do a routine job for Lieutenant Werner of the Brooklyn precinct—no more than following a lead that he furnished."

"A top-secret lead?"

Nelson said, "No—he was all ready to release it to the press when I checked back—but I hinted that it might be wise to withhold names pending further developments." He told her about it, sparing her the pathos of that final moment in the hospital. His account of Lieutenant Werner's call, and of the interview on the Easton roof, was more detailed.

When he stopped talking Kyrie said, "You seem to think that Mrs. Carmody wasn't as surprised as she might have been by your visit."

"It's only a feeling. There are no valid conclusions to be drawn from it. On comparable occasions I've seen even the most blameless citizens react like hardened sinners."

"But you've made her sound so tense and—"

"Her tension might have been part of the syndrome of universal guilt—or it might have stemmed from a realistic problem that has nothing to do with the case." His wallet was in his hand. He removed a folded piece of paper and opened it on the table.

"What's that, Grid?"

"I took it from a stack on Carmody's desk."

"But it's blank. Does it mean anything—or has green become your favorite color?"

"So far it's the operative color. Our 'First-time Squealer' wrote his letter on green—and described Carmody's car as green—which turns out to be a fact."

Kyrie said, "I suppose it could be common garden coincidence. I suppose it's occurred to you that it might be someone working there who has access to the paper and doesn't like the boss."

"Yes—it's occurred to me."

"It wouldn't necessarily have to be a male either," Kyrie said. "It might even be Mrs. Carmody working out her real or fancied problem."

"Maybe—but we haven't got around to comparing this with the 'First-time Squealer's' letter." He refolded the paper and put it back in his wallet.

"You don't like the idea of Mrs. Carmody stooping to such measures—do you?"

Nelson said absently, "Not very much."

"Have you had enough to eat?"

"More than." He got up and did a little jig step to flex his long legs. He went through the motions of helping to put Sammy's kitchen in order.

Kyrie took the dish towel from his hand. "I'll do that. Your mind isn't on it."

Something in her husky voice alerted him. "Neither is yours."

"I was thinking that Mrs. Carmody sounds glamorous as well as unhappy. If your description was half as lyrical when you checked back with the lieutenant, you haven't a hope of going on with the case."

He turned to her and nodded thoughtfully. "Green is the operative color all right."

"If you're under the impression that I'm jealous after all these years—" She began to laugh. "It's remarkable—but I really am."

Annie Grimes slept like a healthy child that night, and breakfasted the next morning on a beaker of Vitrate. She could not honestly say that it hit the spot, but it was doing the trick, and that was what mattered. Besides, she could look forward to a light lunch that would at least keep her from forgetting the taste of honest-to-goodness food. This was a concession gained from Carmody by her insistence that just the mention of a liquid diet three times a day gave her gas.

She had been surprised to be included in the control group, since the others selected were model pupils and she was not. She had also been surprised when Carmody came off his perch to explain that she was essential to the experiment because if Vitrate helped her it would help anybody. He was not such a bad stick after all, she thought, smiling to herself over his unexpected flash of honesty.

Later, as she went through her paces on the Easton roof, she worried a little about Mrs. Atmore, who was absent from class. She wanted to ask if anyone knew why, but repeated slights had succeeded in dampening her natural spontaneity. Moreover, Mrs. Atmore's aloofness had been equally distributed, making it unlikely that the cause of her defection was known.

But the noonday session in the dressing room threw light upon it. At first the talk had centered on Carmody, the consensus being that he was definitely off his usual form.

A Mrs. Morrison said, "He might not enjoy the idea of his wife having a boyfriend."

There was a chorus of "No—do tell!"

"Well—I was in the neighborhood last night with a friend —and we stopped at the Easton for a drink. And there was this chap in the lobby brushing the snow off her coat as though he owned her."

A Mrs. Ogden said, "What was he like?"

"Like I couldn't imagine what he saw in her—handsome—well dressed—the most."

"If he is her boyfriend," Mrs. Ogden said, "I don't think it would break Carmody's heart."

A Mrs. Pierce took it from there. "You're so right. He's got plenty of candidates ready to fill her shoes. But speaking of being off form— Doris Atmore can't be feeling too well today either." Her voice sounded challenging rather than sympathetic. "And she didn't even make the headlines."

"That sort of thing doesn't rate much coverage—it happens all the time." It came from Mrs. Morrison, who smelled as though she had been on a whisky diet. "But this time it certainly has a peculiar twist. She must have been full of sleeping pills."

Mrs. Ogden shook her head. "She told the police she'd never taken a sleeping pill in her life."

"I believe it," Mrs. Morrison said scornfully. "She won't even take a sociable drink so she's got to have some kind of—"

Annie Grimes horned in, too interested to care whether or not they thought her pushy. "What's happened to Mrs. Atmore?"

Mrs. Pierce stopped painting her eyebrows. "I hadn't realized you were a particular friend of hers."

"I guess that puts us in the same boat." She appealed to Mrs. Ogden. "Would you mind telling me—?"

"Mrs. Atmore's apartment was robbed yesterday afternoon in broad daylight while she was taking a nap. You must have missed it in the morning papers."

"I generally catch the news on television. She wasn't—they didn't hurt her?"

A Mrs. Milrose spoke from the far end of the room. "It's painful enough to have valuable jewelry stolen."

"Oh—that's too bad." Annie Grimes was relieved that it was not worse. "I missed her in class and got to wondering. I didn't think she was sick because she's been looking so fine lately—blooming, you might say."

Mrs. Pierce laughed. "If such a winter plant could be said to bloom."

Annie Grimes ignored her. "On the whole it's a good thing she slept through it. She might've been murdered if she tried to stop them. Do the police have any clues to—?"

Mrs. Milrose said, "They seldom do."

"You can't altogether blame them," Mrs. Ogden said. "There seem to be more robberies than policemen."

Mrs. Morrison disagreed. "The streets are full of policemen—but they're too busy giving out tickets and closing nightclubs to have time for anything else."

"Too true." Mrs. Pierce lowered her voice. "You get the *Tribune*, of course." She included everyone but Annie Grimes. "Were any of you under the impression that our Doris held something back when they questioned her? The *Tribune* didn't exactly say so but—"

"Lorna Pierce—you don't mean she's trumped it up to collect insurance—not one of the high and mighty Atmores!" The whiskyish Mrs. Morrison quivered with mirth.

"She's only an Atmore by marriage. I understand that she came of quite common—"

Several voices were raised at once, none in defense of the absentee. Annie Grimes strode to her locker. Grabbing her possessions, pulling her coat about her, she made comment with a penetrating "Mi-aow," and swept out of the room, slamming the door behind her.

In the corridor she collided head-on with a tall dark girl.

"Excuse me, Mrs. Carmody—I hope I didn't knock the wind out of you."

Mrs. Carmody assured her breathlessly that no harm had been done. "Are you the first?" she asked. "Or have the others gone on to the solarium?"

"The solarium? Oh no—I'm the first." That catty bunch had made her forget what day it was.

"I'm sorry to give such short notice," Mrs. Carmody said, "but my husband asked me to announce that the talk will have to be postponed. He—"

"Think nothing of it," Annie Grimes said warmly. "I could see for myself he wasn't feeling right. I hope it's nothing serious."

"Thank you. Have a pleasant day, Mrs. Grimes." She entered the dressing room without allowing time for the politesse to be acknowledged.

A nice well-spoken person, Annie Grimes thought. They're jealous of her is why they want to spread that mean gossip. Very attractive she is even with hardly any makeup and her hair sleeked back off her face. It isn't everyone can get by with so little fuss or feathers. I wish

I'd kept her long enough to get a straight account of the robbery.

She decided to see if Miss Spofford knew anything, but the receptionist was not at her desk. The whole place had a forsaken air and no one got off the elevator to enliven it.

The postponement of Carmody's talk had lengthened the day a little. Annie Grimes did not regard the extra time as a bonus. The weather interfered with her chief recreation of strolling from shop to shop and buying things that she did not need. Of course she could go to a movie, but she looked upon that form of diversion in the afternoon as a public confession of loneliness.

Downstairs in the restaurant she lingered as long as she could over a clear consommé, melba toast, a dab of grilled beef, and some watercress. She kept a defiant watch upon the door but saw no familiar face. The nonappearance of her classmates brought her to the wistful conclusion that she was the only one among them with a blank engagement book. She wished she had not quit the dressing room in such a hurry. It might have been amusing to stay and see how the cats reacted to her scorn. But she had always been too much of a trouper to spoil a good exit.

Nelson's morning was crowded with work. Beyond a few routine measures and a non-routine call to the Commissioner's office, the case of Alice Thwaite was shelved until he looked up at half past eleven to see Clevis in the doorway.

"Judging by the way you're swaddled," Nelson said, "it's very cold in Brooklyn."

"Yeah. Bad enough I live there without having to work there. It got even colder in the precinct when I asked the lieut to surrender the material—but telling him you'd do the work and he'd get the marks was as good as a coal stove." Clevis removed his scarf and stripped off his heavy coat before he shambled up to the desk. "I would've been back sooner but I stuck around for the lab's two cents' worth." He handed a large envelope to Nelson. "This is it—plus your contribution and the original letter."

Nelson silenced a shrilling telephone, replaced the receiver, and extracted the contents of the envelope. Clevis, detective first grade, did not interrupt the process of study and comparison. He slouched indolently against the desk, his baggy suit concealing trained muscles, his slack-mouthed, button-eyed face fronting a serviceable brain. He could move faster than most in the field. Shamble and slouch were his means of husbanding energy.

Nelson said, "You've had a look at all this?"

"A quick one." Clevis shrugged. "Aside from the fact your stationery matches—it don't carry much of a punch."

"The fingerprints are more of a punch than I expected—and if the graphologist is right no attempt has been made to disguise the writing." Nelson glanced at the wall clock. "Since you're all but sitting you might as well go the whole hog for a few minutes."

Clevis grinned as he took the extra chair. He and his superior officer were friends of long standing. "Those prints would be more than anyone expected," he said. "If the photos are for real they're the paws of a nine- or ten-year-old."

"The writing points to a child too. The graphologist confirms that."

"Which gives us a pint-sized punk who'll grow up to be a juvenile delinquent if he plays his cards right—or else we got a mixed-up midget."

"Lieutenant Werner offered a similar theory last night."

"Good for him. Most precinct boys act like there's a law against using their heads. What beats me—I hadn't noticed things were so slack around here we had to ask for handouts. Ain't this business kind of far afield?"

"On the contrary—it's very close to home." He explained Sammy's involvement in the case, knowing that his own would be incomprehensible to a cynic like Clevis.

"That's different," Clevis said. It was often necessary for him to come to the house in the East Sixties, and he had been known to invent an excuse for the chance to feast upon Sammy's cooking. His air of boredom vanished. "You found out yet if Carmody has a past?"

The change of attitude amused Nelson. "They're working on it at 'Records.'" He nodded involuntarily at the old red brick building across the street. Row upon row of files weighted its creaking floors, and every file contained prints, mugshots, descriptions, and the *modus operandi* of prisoners past and present.

"I don't envy them," Clevis said. "With tracks to cover he'd be using a brand new alias providing he's halfway smart—which he must be with a front like that. When are you seeing him?"

"In a little while. His wife asked me to make it during his lunch break."

"You saw his wife?"

"Last night."

Clevis looked skeptical. "Then she's given him time to prepare a good story—or do a vanishing act if there's fire behind the smoke." He reached for the Brooklyn reports and thumbed through them.

"What are you looking for?"

"The bit in the handwriting analysis where it says something about uniform spacing—and how the lines don't slant up or down."

"You *have* decided to take the matter seriously."

"Well—it didn't seem like our headache till you brought Sammy into it." He found the place and mumbled the words aloud, his diction clearing as he came to the end of the paragraph. "... no discernible break for thought."

"Well?"

"I still don't get any big fat message—except it was copied out of a mag or something." He shuffled the papers until the letter was on top, eyed it, and said, "Nah."

Nelson, who had formed an opinion, said, "Why 'nah'?" It was not the first time that Clevis had served as a sounding board, and often he produced more than an echo.

"Because the punctuation would've been copied too—and even the crummiest mags do better than that. My guess is that all the stopping and thinking went into a rough draft and what we have here is the final edition. As for not slanting up or down—the stationery's thin enough to see through—so what about the dodge of placing a ruled sheet under it to guide him or her?" He decked the papers and shoved them back to Nelson. "Nuts to graphology. It can't even tell the sexes apart."

"Leaving sex out of it, there's a possibility you haven't mentioned. The letter could have been dictated without benefit of punctuation."

Clevis said in disgust, "So we start by finding a kid sent to do a skunk's work. This Carmody got any?"

"No. According to the night manager none of the residents have children." Nelson got up and went to the wooden clothes rack.

Clevis said hopefully, "I could go along."

"Your afternoon is set."

"Judd can take care of the Sunderland business single-handed." Judd was his partner in the field. "It's in the bag anyway." He wound the woolen scarf around his neck, flung his coat on, and jammed his hat down over his ears.

## CHAPTER 6

Carmody, barricaded by his desk, left no doubt as to who was the intruder. Nelson in a facing leather chair said patiently, "Read the letter again. Take your time."

Carmody gave him a long-suffering look from darkly pouched eyes. "It don't mean a thing to me," he said. "There's not a word of truth in it. If I ever swabbed decks in the Navy it's news to me." He added, "Or Merchant Marine either—so that settles that."

Nelson looked pointedly at the stack of green paper. "So what? Anyone could walk in here and help himself—or buy it wherever they peddle office supplies."

"Why should anyone want to?" Nelson said.

"Who knows? It takes all kinds." He scratched at a razor nick on his chin.

Nelson said, "You do own a green sports car."

"Me and who else? Stand on the street and watch them roll by."

"The problem," Nelson said, "is to discover how many of them were up for repairs on the night in question."

"That's for you to kick around, Captain. I explained how my car came to be dented. If you don't want to take my word for it ask the receptionist."

"Where did you say your accident took place?"

Carmody muttered the name of a street.

"Is that on route to your receptionist's house?"

"Maybe not—but it's the route I took. I don't know Brooklyn. I got lost. Ask—"

"Before I do that I'd like to see Mrs. Carmody. It's possible, of course, that she didn't think your minor accident important enough to mention to me last night—although it happened at approximately the same time as the hit-and-run."

"Watch it, Captain." Carmody's grin was feeble. "You're giving me an alibi."

"Yes—if it can be substantiated."

"But I told you—"

"On the other hand," Nelson said, "I don't believe I fixed the time of the hit-and-run when I spoke to Mrs. Carmody. Since she knew you were somewhere in Brooklyn that night, her reticence might have been caused by a natural desire to protect you."

Carmody's exclamation was short and ugly.

Nelson made what he could of it, and tried to make more. "Wives do have an instinct to protect their husbands."

"Sure they do." Carmody wore the look of a poker player who had inadvertently revealed his hand. "What I meant—why would I need to be protected?" He fumbled in a pocket and brought his hand up empty. "I got to keep in training," he said. "I'd be smoking every minute if I had them on me. You don't happen to—?"

Nelson's lie was full of polite regret.

Carmody took substitute satisfaction by chewing his lip.

Nelson watched with interest.

Carmody said, "It's this way, Captain. If you have a wife I'll make book you don't tell her everything. Mine couldn't mention the accident for the simple reason she didn't hear about it. Let a woman know a truck backs into you and she starts worrying that worse is waiting to happen every time you get ready to take the car out."

Nelson nodded amicably. His ear caught a sound in the corridor. It made him think of Clevis, who, by agreement, had made a separate entrance. He wondered if Clevis had come upon a pool worth fishing, and carefully rebaited his own hook. "Too bad you didn't get the truck's license."

"Not as bad as it could have been. I'm lucky the damages weren't too steep." It did not seem to occur to Carmody that his luck might lie in producing a witness who was not on his payroll.

Nelson was sympathetic. "But if you're like most people, even a scratch on a new car is cause for mourning."

"You said it." His negligent tone suggested that with the business of the interview concluded, both of them could afford to relax. "Bet you if I'd settled for a secondhand heap the truck wouldn't have touched me."

Nelson topped the cliché. "That's the way it goes." He added, "A less expensive car would have served you just as well. According to Mrs. Carmody your driving is limited to the city."

"Right. No time for long trips. You got to be a galley slave to break even these days. Not that I'd make for the open road in this kind of weather."

"We can't complain. Yesterday's snowfall was the first we've had since January—and there's been very little rain."

Carmody grunted. He looked at his wristwatch as though he had a train to catch.

Nelson said unhurriedly, "We haven't quite exhausted the topic of the weather. With hardly any precipitation—and not enough mileage to detract from your car's new look—I can't help wondering why you had it washed."

"You don't miss a thing." Carmody's facial expression did not match the implied flattery.

"Visiting your garage was normal procedure—a means of determining how much weight the letter carried. I might have forgone this meeting with you if your car had turned out to be an antique purple sedan."

"It happens I'm not queer for purple—or antiques either—but with city soot and buildings coming down and going up all over the place I run into plenty of flying dirt."

"Including flying gold-colored hairpins that land on the back seat?"

Carmody said sourly, "If I plan to go in for liquidating pedestrians I better find a garage where the help don't run off at the mouth." He caught the suggestion of a leer on Nelson's face and seemed encouraged by it. He became excessively man-to-man. "Okay—I can see you get the picture —but don't make my wife a present of it. She's the kind won't even let you look. Like I said I drove the receptionist home because she'd worked late. There'd been a turnover of clock-watchers before her and I did it to show I appreciated she was different. I had nothing else on my mind until she started waving all the flags in my face. I had to pull up because she was all over me and I don't believe in one-arm driving. I figured if I gave her a fast brush she might quit the job and I'd be stuck with another of those chicks who do you a favor by sitting around and breathing from nine to five. That's how come the hairpins in the back seat. Not that I let it get out of control—just some wrestling to keep her happy—and a spiel about it was a shame for such a sweet kid to waste herself on a married man." He laughed sharply. "Sounds like I'm trying to clear myself with the Vice Squad—but Spofford's over twenty-one and she was a lost cause before I laid—" he braked his skidding tongue, "eyes on her. It's one of those things any man can tell at a gander—you'll see for yourself when ..."

Nelson allowed him to complete his claim to innocence, relevant only as a gratuitous presentation of character.

Outside in the corridor there were further sounds, this time small and stealthy. They receded as Carmody emerged from his circumlocutions. "Anyway," he said, "I told your gabby pal at the garage to give the back seat a going-over while he was at it. Dames are always shedding hair and losing lipsticks and stuff and it turns out I wasn't being too careful. The wife doesn't use the car much—but with my luck she just might—and—"

"Then she didn't know you were driving the receptionist home?"

"Sure she knew—why would I keep it dark when there was nothing in it? All the same she wouldn't expect Spofford to ride alone in the back seat like the queen of the May."

"The man who washed the car said there was more than building dust and soot on it."

"I wouldn't be surprised. We parked near a vacant lot—and don't ask me where it was because it was dark and I was lost—but some punks sneaked up behind and started chucking rotten fruit. Good thing it wasn't garbage from a butcher store or you'd have had me. Look, Captain, you've got as much help as I can give—and while I enjoy chewing the fat with you I wouldn't mind chewing a bite of lunch before the next class catches up with me."

"I have a few more questions. I can ask them while you have your lunch if you like—unless it would interfere with your digestion."

"Why should it—except I like a little peace and quiet when I feed—so let's get done with it here and now."

"How many people are employed here?"

"Not many. My wife insists on keeping the operation small." Carmody's tone expressed contempt for her limited vision. "There's Graham, my assistant, who's also a lifeguard—Ma Hagen, a practical nurse who pitches in as needed—and Cora. She tidies up after the ladies and helps out in the steam room. Aside from my wife that's it—except a square-head named Halversen comes every Tuesday to massage those who want it—but he's not on the payroll. I gave him the concession."

Nelson thought "gave" was the wrong word.

"A clean-up crew is supplied by the hotel and tacked to the bill," Carmody said. His mouth twisted sarcastically. "I also hire four or five girls from an agency to drum up trade by telephone whenever the registration drops. They work off the premises and I've never seen hide nor hair of them or vice versa—but I wouldn't want you to think I was holding out on you."

Nelson said, "For the moment we'll proceed on the assumption that only those who know you would want to injure you. Has either the nurse or the steam-room attendant any children?"

"Knock it off, Captain. Ma Hagen's an old maid. I tag her 'Ma' the way you tag a tall guy 'Shorty'—and if Cora has brats—which I wouldn't know—chances are they take after her and can't copy 'c-a-t' from a blackboard. Besides—the help likes me. I don't walk around cracking the whip. You ask them."

"I will. It might expedite the inquiry if you supply full names and addresses—including Halversen's. A list of your clients and other business and social acquaintances might help too."

"Lay off the clients."

"Isn't it possible that you've offended one of them?"

"Do I look like the type who offends his bread and butter? Not to blow my own horn I'm popular around here. I got to be or they'd go somewhere else—which they will if you don't lay off. It stands to reason high-class dames don't want to be bugged by the police even if there's nothing behind it." He brought a fist down upon the letter. "You don't think one of them is responsible for this!"

Nelson said dispassionately, "Mental disturbance isn't limited to low-class dames."

"That's right." Carmody made visible effort to veil his antagonism. "Screwballs crop up where least expected—but I never had one here was screwy enough to dream up a stunt like framing me. Take my word for it, Captain, you're barking up the wrong tree."

"I've been hoping you'd point toward the right tree."

"All I can do is give you odds some psycho wrote this—or had it written—and thought I'd do for a fall guy. Maybe my name stuck in his head from an ad—or maybe he picked it out of a telephone book. He could have been triggered by reading about the hit-and-run."

"The telephone book doesn't list a description of your car."

"A psycho wouldn't let a little thing like that stop him. He could have got my address where he got my name—and braced a hotel flunky for the rest of it. He could also have sneaked up here while I was in the gym and grabbed himself a couple of sheets of paper to pass it off as an inside job. Spofford isn't always at her desk to watch who comes and goes."

"It seems rather a lot of trouble to go to if you were picked at random."

"Who knows how a mind like that works? Maybe he don't like skinny women and is on a crusade to wipe out the reducing business." Carmody's lips stretched to a grin to illustrate that humor was intended.

Nelson said, "I can see you've been giving the matter a great deal of thought."

"Sure I have. Knowing I didn't put a foot wrong don't stop me from thinking. If you want the truth—since last night when my wife told me—I been chewing away at it, trying to figure why me. But of course if I'd seen you last night I'd have rested easier. You got what it takes—and I'm no slouch at sizing people up. In your place I'd have been here myself to take a look—but I bet nothing will sidetrack you for long."

"I wouldn't be justifying your confidence if I left without the receptionist's account of the night you took her home."

"Sure." Carmody made haste to use the intercom. He issued a considerate invitation. "You busy, Edna? A gentleman wants a word with you."

Nelson stood up. "I can see her on the way out. Enjoy your lunch."

Carmody came from behind the desk. "That's all right—I won't be satisfied until I know you are." He assumed a cocky stance, legs spread, hands pocketed. His head did not clear Nelson's broad shoulders. "Besides—here she comes."

There was nothing stealthy about the approaching steps. Edna Spofford managed to thrust the door open without breaking rhythm. She waved neither hips nor bosom as she entered the office, but the flags of war rippled in her eyes.

Seeing her, Nelson came to a conclusion about the identity of the eavesdropper who had overheard Carmody's more or less true confession.

The unsuspecting Carmody took command. "You didn't have to run, Edna. Nothing to be hot and bothered about. All you have to do is tell the Captain here what happened the night I drove you home."

"Happened?" She drew a steadying breath and jerked her voice from its precarious height. "What should happen?"

Nelson's guess took firmer root. Carmody winked. "You know—the truck that backed into us." He turned on his flashiest grin. "Being a lady you can skip the swearing I did when I got a load of my bumper— or what I promised that bruiser if I ever caught up with him."

She might have been a Method actress. Her bewilderment seemed to rise from the core of her being. "I'm afraid I haven't the faintest idea what you're talking about, Mr. Carmody."

"Truck—t-r-u-c-k," He ironed out his scowl before it set. "Come on, Edna—it's not like you to be so slow on the uptake."

"I'm sorry." She pumped real tragedy into it. "But it must have been on your way back to Manhattan. Otherwise I'd be sure to remember."

"Are you kidding—!"

"Of course not, Mr. Carmody. After all—you only drove me home that once—which was kind of you, I'm sure." Her diction was very precise. "But it certainly would not have slipped my mind if there had been anything out of the ordinary during the drive." She added decisively, "So you see you've merely forgotten whether you were going or coming."

"The hell I have!" His skin had mottled. "This is no time for jokes—"

"I wouldn't joke in business hours, Mr. Carmody. If there's nothing else you wanted I'll go back to my desk."

"There's plenty else I want—now you look here—"

But she had turned on her spiky heel and was away.

Nelson did not try to detain her. He saw to it, by planting himself in the doorway, that she was safe from pursuit. To Carmody, who seemed on the verge of a seizure, he said, "It might not be a bad idea to advertise for that truck driver."

Downstairs in the Easton, Clevis had nosed around for a while, coming to rest upon a padded bench that faced the elevators. There, for the count of three or four return trips, he exercised his wits by sizing up the passengers who trickled out of the elevator Nelson had taken. He paid special attention to those who disembarked whenever the last light on the indicator had flashed. Most of Carmody's pupils, he observed, bore a stamp in common. It had nothing to do with bulk because several of the fur-bearing specimens were not what he would have called fat. He did not use such terms as boredom or discontent or lack of inner resources, but they vapored formlessly through his head and came out capsulated as "rotten spoiled." Peering over his newspaper he thought, Blubber's the least of it. They've got too much of everything and don't know how to put salt on it.

He made an exception of the overblown female who had been the first to come down. "Nice" was his snap judgment of her plump, hopeful face. Looks like she could laugh hearty and mean it. Looks like—?

He dived into his mental records and remained submerged until he found the answer. Training prevented him from an overt show of satisfaction. He folded his newspaper, got up quietly, and appeared to be watching the revolving street door as he marked Annie Dale's progress through the lobby. He had not filed her under her married name although he recalled that at least one marriage had taken place. When she turned in at the entrance to the restaurant he sat down again, glancing at his watch to create the impression of one whose expected companion is inexplicably late. His mind was divorced from this routine performance. She ought to have a pretty shrewd slant on Carmody, he thought. He would have liked to approach her at once but he decided against it. Obviously she had risen in the world, and it followed that she might be snooty if he tried to strike up a conversation without revealing his official status. She would be easy to find if the proceedings upstairs warranted a contribution from her. Clevis had no doubt that she was Annie Dale. She had not changed all that much. There was even a hint of the come-on walk beneath the drape of her coat. He had been titillated by it in the old days when he visited burlesque houses, either as a policeman or just because he felt like it.

He spent what remained of his wait by studying her classmates. It was not, on the face of it, a fruitful occupation. But he had learned during enforced periods of idleness to occupy himself with some sort of "busy work," much as a woman resorts to embroidery or knitting.

The elevator operator squinted at him as he sauntered into the cage. Clevis said, "I'll bet you see all kinds."

The operator's eyes said, Not your kind. His voice said, "Floor?"

"Roof."

The operator leaned out of the cage, looking for additional passengers to make the trip worthwhile.

"I got all day," Clevis said.

The operator was unmoved. "That why you took so long to get your nerve up—making out you were sitting there waiting for somebody?"

"You keep your eyes open all right," Clevis said.

"My ears too." He glanced at the prop briefcase that Clevis carried. "Chances are you don't sell Mr. Carmody a thing. He's sick."

"Where did you get that hot tip?"

"Straight from a couple of his customers. They talk—I listen. You still want to go up?"

Clevis said dolefully, "Might as well—long as I got this far." His clownish features drooped.

"You don't look like a salesman. New at it?"

Happily aware that he did not look like a detective, Clevis nodded.

The operator closed the sliding gate and the elevator shot upward. "Try to get past Miss Heatwave to see Mrs. Carmody," he said. "At least she'll stand still for the pitch."

"Thanks. Who's Miss Heatwave?"

"The hot-shot's receptionist or what have you. Some of him must have rubbed off on her."

"I take it you don't warm to him?"

The operator said flatly, "I'm crazy for all the guests. Courteous and friendly service like it says in the Easton ads."

"You been a friend to me," Clevis said, and let it go at that. No sense in shucking a clam until it was time to eat it. Besides, he doubted that this one would have much meat to offer.

The operator said as he stopped the car, "You peddling a new reducing gimmick—or what?"

"I'm a policeman sent to raid the joint."

The operator guffawed. "You look it. Well—if you need a hand ring my bell. I'd like to pinch Miss Heatwave myself."

Clevis heard the click of the elevator gate behind him as he breasted the sea of broadloom. When he had advanced far enough to realize that the receptionist's desk was deserted, he took bearings and shifted his course.

He went under the arch without interference. The other side was crossed by a corridor. He chose the left turn, which seemed to be a mistake. All it led to was the swimming pool. The centered double doors were closed, but he sniffed chlorine even before his eyes explained its source. Swimming pools anywhere were dead ends so far as he was concerned. But he could not resist the invitation of the eye-level glass panels.

The pool itself, set in a large tiled enclosure, was not in use. He had expected that at this hour. The two who stood near its edge were unexpected.

There was no reason for him to duck. They faced each other, not him, and their profiled jaws moved in turn. He wished he could hear what they said because it struck him that this was an odd place for a fully-dressed couple to select for ordinary conversation. Not so much as a mumble reached his ears. It was like viewing a silent film without subtitles and he dared not open the doors a crack for fear of raising an echo.

The man placed his hands upon the girl's shoulders as Clevis watched, and now he seemed to be delivering an uninterrupted speech. Clevis wondered who he was and eliminated Carmody on two counts. Carmody was probably in camera with Nelson, and this citizen had more the appearance of a Who's Who entry than of a muscle merchant. Neither did Clevis think that the girl could be Mrs. Carmody even though she was "standing still for the pitch." Miss Heatwave more likely, considering the vacant desk, and a neckline low enough to show part of her radiation equipment.

The man's jaw ceased wagging at last, but his hands remained on her shoulders. He did not remove them until she nodded slowly. That broke it up. As soon as he freed her she cut a straight course for the exit.

Clevis shot toward the opposite end of the corridor. Since he had skipped the entrance formalities he could hardly expect a cordial reception, especially in his role of Peeping Tom.

The walls to the right of the arch were broken by several doors. He spotted one that was ajar, and after cautious survey stepped inside.

He had taken cover in the dressing room. He left the door open but moved to a point where he could not be seen by passers-by. Leaning against a row of lockers, ears cocked, nose filled with the rich leftover scent of women, he did not stir until he was satisfied that there was no immediate danger of being discovered. For want of other busy work during this short interlude, and not because he vested it with importance, he reviewed the scene at the swimming pool. If the leading lady *was* "Miss Heatwave," she had evidently sneaked off to further some interest of her own while the boss was sewed up. Full faces instead of profiles might have provided a clue to the interest. The way it had been, with no wiring for sound, there was skimpy basis for conjecture. Except, he thought, the peepshow had none of the earmarks of a lovers' tryst. No contact but that hand-on-the-shoulder bit, as if the guy were conning her into something she did not want to do. And not even a parting smack to sweeten her nod of consent.

Clevis edged to the door, peered out, and immediately withdrew his head. One-half of the swimming pool team, clearly recognizable by her dress, was crouched three or four keyholes away.

He wondered if this was a follow-up to the recent *tête-à-tête*. He let a few minutes go by before he peered out again. She was still there but she had straightened up to a listening instead of a looking posture. In the light of his own frustration he grudged her the opportunity to use her ears, and hoped that what she heard was dull enough to send her about her business so that he could go about his.

His present surroundings had been left in a rather untidy state. The lockers hung open, which he took as a sign that they would not repay inspection. The plastic surface of the room-length vanity was splotched with powder, and some of it had arisen to film the mirrors. The wastebaskets beneath contained wadded tissues stained with lipstick. Disgruntled, he thought that fingerprint experts and serologists would have a field day here, collecting a glut of souvenirs that unfortunately had nothing to do with the case. If there were a case.

He took another look at the corridor. Miss Heatwave had disappeared, but he did not have time to give thanks for a clear coast. The door next to the dressing room was pulled inward and a voice assaulted his rear.

"Hey, Mister—"

He stepped back over the threshold as though he had bought and paid for the premises. The aproned woman, lugging a pailful of cleaning paraphernalia, followed him. She was large and had a large pink face.

She said calmly, "The ladies' room is where I came out of—they're always complaining that a door should be cut through from here but Mr. Carmody didn't get around to it yet."

Clevis said, "You don't tell me."

"It's the fourth sink as you go in." She looked no more alarming than a cow, and showed no further symptoms of insanity. She thumped the pail down, bent over it to extract a cloth, and set to work with no great energy.

"What's your name?" Clevis said to her back.

"Cora Jenkins." She was dusting one of the mirrors. Her face, reflected in it, looked surprised that he was still there. She twisted her head around to make sure. The briefcase under his arm caught and held her eye. "I guess you didn't come to fix the plumbing. A plumber don't carry that kind of bag."

"One bag is like another in my business," Clevis said. "You been a maid here long?"

"Who says I'm a maid? I take care of the ladies in the steam room—but I have to empty the baskets and dust in here to get it ready for the next batch."

Clevis made a clicking sound with his tongue. "That's slave labor. I'll sic the union on to Mr. Carmody."

"I don't do it for him. I do it for her and she pays me good and sends the kids presents at Christmas. So if you're from some union don't make trouble. I got a real nice job. The hotel does the heavy cleaning at the end of the day."

"Don't worry," Clevis said. "As long as I know he ain't taking advantage of you and your kids. I'll bet your ten-year-old is a smart boy."

"Stanley won't be ten till—say—how do you know I got kids?"

"I can see it in your face—also that you're a widow."

"I'm not a widow either—my husband's a merchant seaman and don't come home much even when he docks." Then she said, "Go on—you don't see nothing in my face. You seen Stanley times when he hangs around waiting for me after school. Some people got nothing better to do than keep other people from working." She began to put vigor into her dusting, but the spurt did not last. She stopped to scrabble in the sandy ridges of her hair as though she were digging for buried thought. The smoothing of her puckered forehead indicated success. She dropped the cloth, went to the row of lockers, and thrust a pink arm into the first one.

Clevis ambled over to watch. "Treasure hunting?" he said.

She withdrew the arm. "I got orders to do this all the time in case they leave something behind—and hand it in if they do so's nobody makes off with it. Yesterday it was a glove—but Mrs. Pierce came back for it." She had forgotten her annoyance with him. "You'd be surprised how rich ladies hate to lose stuff—like the time Mrs. Morrison made such a fuss—and she hadn't even worn them in the first place."

"I can see you have a position of great trust," Clevis said.

"I have," she said proudly. "I been bonded by the bank same as everybody who works here." She had reached the next to the last locker. She gave a triumphant exclamation and pulled out a narrow cardboard box. "Chocolate peppermints," she said. "Don't that picture on the cover look good enough to eat?" She rattled the box experimentally, and seemed to be struggling with her conscience.

"Go ahead," Clevis said. "Help yourself." To him the rattle had not sounded like peppermints.

She looked shocked. "It's not that. It's whether turning it in would be snitching. Somebody wants to break the rules by eating candy it's not up to me to—" She removed the cover. "Well, what do you know about that!"

"What do *you* know?" Clevis said.

"It's Mrs. Atmore's ring. I seen it on her plenty of times. It must have been here since yesterday."

"Wasn't she around this morning?"

"She should've been—she's in the special class—but I guess being robbed yesterday she didn't feel up to it."

"Was she robbed here?"

"No—where she lives." She fished a clipping from her apron pocket. "It said so in the paper. I cut it out."

He took the clipping from her and read it.

"Give it back when you finish," she said. "I want to show my girl friend." She took it from him and stowed it away, juggling the peppermint box in her other hand. "Still and all it's got a silver lining to it—because if the ring was with the rest of her things they would have taken that too."

"Didn't you go through the lockers yesterday?"

The significance of the question escaped her. "I always do—first

thing. I would've done it first thing today too—but with you making
out to be a plumber I forgot." She had taken the ring out of the box
and was trying to push it over the knuckle of her forefinger. It balked.
"It's one of them real emeralds," she said, "but it's so big you'd swear
it came from the five-and-ten." She wafted her large pink hand before
her eyes to study the effect. "Funny it don't go on me. It began to slide
off her as soon as she started losing."

"You'd better turn it in before something happens to it."

"You're right. I better. He'll be in his office—he's always there until
nearly three o'clock—but it ain't three yet. I hope the gentleman's gone
because Mr. Carmody don't like anybody to go in his office even
when he's not busy." She walked out of the room, the ring still gird-
ing her finger above the knuckle.

Clevis retrieved the box she had left behind, and tailed her. He did
not doubt her honesty, but he wanted to meet Carmody, and he
wanted to compare notes with the gentleman in his office.

## CHAPTER 7

Carmody and Nelson were both standing. Nelson seemed to be on
the verge of departure, but kept resisting hints that should have sped
him. Carmody's stomach rumbled loudly. His voice competed. "If
there's anything to that saying about a man being innocent until he's
proven guilty it strikes me that it's up to you to dig up that truck
driver. Suppose I do advertise—would he stick his neck out when he
knows the collision was his own damn fault?"

He was in no state to distinguish one set of footfalls from another.
Until the office door opened he thought that Spofford, with an eye to
keeping her job, had decided to corroborate his story.

His bubble of relief burst at the sight of Cora. "What the hell do you
want?"

She was unmoved by her reception. "I'm handing something in like
I'm supposed to."

"Don't bother me now—I'm busy."

"That's what I told him."

"Who?"

"Him." She pointed over her shoulder.

He saw the flash of green as she gestured, and had no time for Clevis, who had come in behind her. He snatched at her hand.

She backed away. "You don't have to pull my finger off. I'm giving it to you."

He held the ring at stiff arm's length as though it were exuding poisonous fumes.

"I found it in the locker Mrs. Atmore always uses—in a candy box like it was a peppermint," Cora said. "He told me 'Open it,' so I opened it and he—"

Consciousness of an audience returned to Carmody. As a sop to it he muttered, "You did right, Cora." But the effort fell flat because the tall Captain's eyes and ears had been pre-empted by Cora's "he."

Clevis's muted barrage of words did not spread beyond its target. Carmody coughed experimentally. No one but Cora paid the slightest attention. "Do you want a drink of—?"

His facial contortions closed her mouth. He edged to the desk and leaned over to ease out a drawer. The silence hit him as he straightened up. So did all the eyes in the room.

The sloppy newcomer had separated himself from the Captain. Carmody took the offensive by barking at him, "You got business with me you don't barge in—you go through channels."

Clevis performed a mock salute. "Police officer—special duty."

Nelson said, "He brought a message for me that wouldn't keep."

"Don't tell me—let me guess. They nabbed the hit-and-run driver."

"It has nothing to do with the hit-and-run. May I use your phone?"

"I'm surprised you ask. Press button three for an outside line." He was almost gracious because no reference had been made to his latest worry. Most likely they stuck to the work in their own department, he thought.

He told himself that the call had nothing to do with him. Nevertheless he tried to listen to Nelson's end of the conversation. But he was distracted by Clevis, who had drawn Cora to the other side of the office. He wondered uneasily what she could be blabbing about that would hold the interest of a plain-clothes dick. To put a stop to it, he forsook the telephone area although the call was not yet underway.

He prodded Cora with his thumb. "You taking a holiday?"

"My chief wants her to wait," Clevis said.

"Your chief don't pay her wages."

Clevis said, "Do you?"

Cora was pleased to be the center of attention. "I make out real good. Mr. Carmody lets me keep the tips and his Missus gave me a five-dollar raise at Christmas—so even take away the Social Security I can't complain."

"There aren't many of us who can say the same," Clevis said.

"Well—it's not all roses," Cora said. "Those ladies keep me hopping in the steam room—wanting this and that and sending back to the dressing-room lockers to—"

"I'm sending you," Carmody said. "Hop."

"He says the gentleman wants me to wait." She turned to Clevis for support, but he had gone back to the desk.

Carmody saw that the call had been completed, and more than suspected that he had been lured from the listening post by foul means. Nelson held one of the desk pencils in his hand and was studying something he had written on a sheet of the green paper. He passed it to Clevis, who scanned it quickly and nodded.

Carmody strode up to them, dogged by Cora. "Anything else you want," he said, "don't mind me. Go right on making free."

"I want the ring you put in the desk," Nelson said.

"Huh?" He blustered into the pause that followed. "You running a private Lost and Found? A client leaves something behind it stays right here till she claims it in person."

"You'll have to break that rule for this particular client."

Cora droned to herself, "Mrs. Atmore sure is particular—yes sir—particular as they come."

Clevis encouraged her. "She is?"

"That's right. She's who you're talking about, isn't she—being it's her ring?"

"You're certain it's her ring?"

"Yes sir! If I seen it once I seen it a million times."

Carmody snorted.

Nelson said to him, "You have too—of course."

He shrugged. He took it from the desk drawer and stared at it vaguely before he placed it in Nelson's outstretched hand. "Could be. I'm kept too busy to notice who wears what. They don't sport jewelry in class. Only time I see them dressed up is when they come in and go out."

"But I told you," Cora said. "As soon as I handed it in I—"

Carmody winked at Nelson. "She might have told me at that—but I'm in the habit of turning off the ear trumpet when she's around."

Nelson did not respond. He was consulting the notes he had jotted on the green paper. Cora did not hear. "... and like I was saying in the dressing room if she hadn't left it behind it would've been taken off her by them robbers. All the same—"

Carmody decided to look as though the dawn were breaking. He thumped his head. "Well—how about that? If it is Mrs. Atmore's ring she sure won't scold herself for being careless." He condescended to explain. "This client of mine was in the morning papers, Captain. Her apartment was broken into and they got away with all her jewelry."

"It's been brought to my attention," Nelson said. "In fact I used your phone to get a full report."

Carmody wrote his act as he went along. "Are they getting someplace? I wouldn't want her to recoup her losses by signing off with me."

"She must have had a lot on her mind not to miss it before she got home," Cora said. "A particular lady like her."

"You've got something there," Clevis said.

"Well—I would've if it was mine—and I'd a turned right around and come back for it before the next batch used the lockers—because you never know—like when we were first married—that sterling-silver ring with the blue stones my husband bought in Mexico—"

Carmody gave Nelson an anguished look and would have followed it up, but Nelson's face stopped him.

Cora continued to jog placidly along the single track of her mind. "I took it off to wash my hands in the movies and left it on the sink—and wearing it so much I could feel something missing as soon as we were stepping on the bus—but there wasn't a sign of it when I went back and nobody turned it in."

"I'll bet that's why you're so careful to go through the lockers every day," Clevis said.

"Yes sir! After every class. I got orders. Yesterday it was a glove. I was on the way up the hall with it and there was Mrs. Pierce who'd missed it and—"

Carmody said, "You've got your dates mixed," his tone so sharp that it penetrated.

She showed her wound. "No such thing."

"You didn't find a glove yesterday. Yesterday you slipped up on the job."

"I never. Ask Mrs. Carmody. Mrs. Pierce was into her pocketbook to give me something for my trouble only she saw Mrs. Carmody in the hall and forgot. She said to Mrs. Carmody how losing one glove was worse than losing two and I thought of it later when it started to snow and my Margie couldn't find her other fleece-lined mitten."

Nelson said, "Is Mrs. Pierce in the same group as Mrs. Atmore?"

"Yes, she is—they pay extra for that group—but Mrs. Pierce ain't friendly with Mrs. Atmore. Mrs. Atmore don't mix—not even with Mrs. Grimes, who's as friendly as they come. You won't believe it but she used to be a strip lady on the stage—"

Carmody yelped, "For God's sake—"

Nelson smiled at Cora. "Thank you very much."

She said mechanically, "That's all right," mulled it over, and looked surprised.

Clevis took her arm. "Yes, ma'am—any time we need more help we'll know who to ask." He guided her to the door and closed it upon her.

Carmody said to him, "You could teach me a trick or two about getting rid of pests—starting with present company."

"Is that nice? When we're spending valuable time helping you to clear yourself?"

"Clear myself of what!" He addressed Nelson. "First I'm accused of knocking down some cluck who could have been too stupid to tell a red light from green—and when you can't make it stick the subject is switched all of a sudden to something that's not even your department. Talk about valuable time. Holding me up while you put that cow through a crazy rigmarole—"

Nelson said, "The information I received a few minutes ago may help you to grasp the sense behind that 'crazy rigmarole.' This ring was one of the few pieces of jewelry Mrs. Atmore described as missing before an attack of hysteria prevented her from completing the list. I've written the description down. Would you like to read it?"

Carmody waved the paper away. "I'll take your word for it but what's so exciting? She left it here and never gave it a thought till she discovered the robbery. Then she sees it's gone too and naturally she lumps it with the other stuff."

"You seem determined to believe that she did leave it here."

"How else would it get in her locker?" He did not wait for an answer. "Listen—they don't come any dumber than Cora. If you take any notice of what she says you're—"

"You took notice, Mr. Carmody. You were quick to tell her that she had her dates mixed. Yet her detailed account of finding a glove yesterday was quite convincing. I mean to ask your wife about it, of course. If she was there when Cora—"

Carmody was turning purple. "I've had it up to here. What are you trying to prove—that I go in for second-story jobs on the side and hide the pick of the loot in a candy box? Search the place for the rest of it, why don't you—and when you get through you better be ready to crawl because you're heading straight for the wrong end of a police shake-up. That goes for your 'messenger' too. Don't think I'm overlooking the way he was snooping around the premises while you had me boxed in here. I wouldn't know what's in it for you but I'll find out.

You can bet what's left of your future on that—"

When the waiter asked for the third time if Madam would like dessert, Annie Grimes paid her check and went back to the lobby. There she lingered indecisively, pretending purpose by casting a buyer's eye at the hotel gift shop's window. It displayed chinaware, depressing ornaments, useless gadgets, and greeting cards that ranged from saccharine, of which she approved, to sadistic, of which she did not. She moved on and was tempted by a line of telephone booths. Why don't I give Mrs. Atmore a friendly call? she thought. It might take her mind off her troubles. I could say something like the class didn't seem natural without her this morning.

The booths were occupied, and several impatient people with prior claims waited for vacancies. She walked to a directory rack and looked up the number. The fact that the exchange was the same as her own caused her to note the address. For goodness' sake, she thought, I didn't realize she lived so near me. Real convenient if we should get to be on visiting terms.

More people had gathered to wait for an empty booth. Annie Grimes's shrug was a philosophical tribute to fate. I can call her at home later, if I still want to, she thought. Turning away she saw a familiar figure click-clacking toward the street exit.

"Miss Spofford—?"

The girl did not stop until Annie Grimes caught up with her near the doors. There she halted, tapping her heel, her attitude marked by a complete absence of deskside manner. "What is it?"

"I just wanted to ask after Mr. Carmody's health. His wife said he wasn't feeling—"

"He's sick all right."

"There—I had an idea he was the minute I saw you. I know you wouldn't be taking the afternoon off unless—"

"I'm in a hurry." The girl dashed through a door.

"Well—I must say!" But Annie Grimes had to say it to herself. That little snip is giving her manners a holiday too.

She replayed the theme with variations as she billowed out to the cold pavement. Seems everyone acts as if it costs money to be polite these days. I never got a chance to ask what was wrong with Mr. Carmody—or if she'd heard anything else about the robbery....

The crossings were hazardous with tight-packed drifts of yesterday's snow. There were no cabs in sight. Standing under the Easton canopy she forgot Miss Spofford and wished, not for the first time, that she had learned to master a car instead of being such a dunce when it came to anything mechanical. Soon after her husband's death she had dismissed the chauffeur because it seemed absurdly pompous to employ him for herself alone, in a city where all manner of public transportation was available.

The doorman stood where canopy met curb. She caught his eye and he nodded. He blew his whistle in vain as a taxi rounded the corner. It stopped about forty feet short of the hotel, and that "snip," who must have been hugging the building walls, came tripping forward to grab it.

But Annie Grimes softened toward Miss Spofford when she saw a passenger get out, assist her to enter, and climb in beside her. A heavy date, she thought. That accounts for the big hurry.

She tried to get a glimpse of his face as the cab rolled by. He had looked quite handsome from a distance, with a build that was nothing to sneeze at, and somehow that helped to excuse the girl's rudeness. She might have been late and started walking, thinking she'd been stood up. Or else she did not want to wait in front of the hotel for fear that somebody she knew would horn in on her private life. Some busybody like me, thought Annie Grimes.

Several pre-empted cabs passed. Several people came out of the hotel, and summing up the situation allowed themselves to be blown westward by the penetrating river winds that whirled along the street.

In spite of her swaddling, Annie Grimes began to feel the cold. She joined the doorman at the curb.

"They're kind of few and far between, aren't they? I had trouble getting one this morning."

"Yes, Madam. It's partly because the weather discourages walking—even for those in the habit of it." His quick assessment excluded her from that dreadful category.

"Well—maybe I'll have better luck if I try the avenue." She had tucked her pocketbook under her arm, and made a muff of her mink sleeves. She freed her hands to rummage for a tip.

He thanked her by shouting as she started away, "There's an empty one coming now."

It was a small cab. One more thing in favor of reducing, she thought as her hips met the seat. A relief to be out of the wind, though. She said as much to the driver for the purpose of launching a conversation, but he was not the talkative kind. She studied his picture and put him down as a family man with worries. Take that boil on his neck—and a wife and kids to support. Arthur had wanted kids. She didn't honestly know what her own feelings were at the time. She'd been too busy comforting him when the doctor reported that he wasn't up to scratch in the "begat department." But it would have been nice now if ... Never mind—a lot of things would be nice. She'd settle for a heavy date like Miss Spofford's. She'd settle for less—like just having somewhere to go instead of home.

She looked out of the window. The sight of a bleak-faced woman breasting the wind for the sake of two overdressed poodles moved her to make silent comment that people often liked dogs better than people. She might get that way herself, she supposed, if she owned a pet. But as things were, it seemed too much like a last resort.

It sure is slow going, she thought, and although she peered up at a street sign she was not referring to the progress of the cab. She identified the location as about halfway between her house and Mrs. Atmore's, and tried to recall the exact address of her classmate. She succeeded, and what she had really been toying with sat up and hit her.

Why not? If I was to call her on the phone it's likely she'd ask me to drop in. She almost sold herself on that "likelihood." So as long as I'm out anyway I might as well. I don't have to stay if she's got company— and if she hasn't I should think she'd be glad to have some. I know I'd be nervous sitting alone if such a thing had happened to me.

Annie Grimes allowed the "errand of mercy" aspect to settle it for her. She took another look at the driver's framed card and said, "I've changed my mind about going home, Mr. Lucca. Take me to—" She gave Mrs. Atmore's address.

Usually they seemed pleased to be called by their names. This one showed no pleasure. He accepted the new destination with ferocious patience. "You sure?"

She was by no means sure, but she did not say so.

## CHAPTER 8

In the lobby Clevis said, "Something I left out—one of his customers is Annie Dale. Married, I guess—and Cora's friendly strip lady."

Nelson smiled. "I've more than heard of her."

Clevis looked cheated. "They lectured on her at Princeton, no doubt."

"No—she came into my life after I was graduated."

"How come? You weren't much over twenty when she kissed her

public good-bye. Now that I think of it neither was I—the difference being you never had to get your kicks that way at any age."

"Remind me to tell you the story of my life another year."

Clevis paced him to the exit. "Meaning I should take a fast walk to the lab. There won't be a thing on the peppermint box the way Cora smudged it up but I got her prints for comparison on the off-chance."

"Did you get Carmody's?"

"Yeah—I dropped the prop briefcase and he picked it up and handed it to me like 'what's your hurry here's your hat.' I'm carrying it right side out so don't shove me. What I was getting at—I saw Annie Dale go into that restaurant—and reducing or not—her upholstery says she's still a serious feeder—so if she's there yet, maybe she can add to the general picture. It couldn't hurt to get her slant."

"At the moment I'm more interested in Mrs. Atmore's slant when I show her the ring."

"I hope it's worth the trip." He turned his collar up as they pushed through the door. "Wow what a winter! Beats me how you can go without a hat."

"Run back to nice warm headquarters. See you later."

"You skipping lunch today?"

"Haven't you eaten?"

"A cup of coffee would go good. There's a lunchroom near where you parked."

"All right—but no lingering over the port and cigars."

Clevis made for a booth when they reached the lunchroom, and set the briefcase down with care. Attacking the sandwich Nelson had ordered for him, he said, "I kept what's maybe the best for the last. Cora has a kid around ten—name of Stanley. He turns up once in a while to wait for her. The pop's a merchant seaman."

"You've been earning your bread. Put Miller onto it after you take that briefcase to the lab. Tell them to send the findings over to 'Records' as soon as they can."

"Sure—is that all you're going to eat? Why so hell-bent on the Atmore dame? I wouldn't believe Carmody if he swore it was cold outside. All the same he don't strike me as thick enough to leave stolen property where the help has to find it—and I got to agree with him about where's the connection between robbery and vehicular homicide."

Nelson was inclined to agree too, but something other than logic demanded a look at the unfriendly Mrs. Atmore. "Call it plain curiosity," he said.

He dropped Clevis at a crosstown bus stop and drove on to Mrs. Atmore's house. Carmody had surrendered unwillingly the names of
staff and clients, after a futile attempt to locate Edna Spofford, who
was not, it developed, on the premises. Mrs. Carmody, who was, had
not seen her leave, and could give no explanation for her absence. She
answered a few questions with remarkable detachment. Yes, she remembered the episode of Mrs. Pierce's glove, and made no attempt to
weasel out when she was told about the ring. She merely said quietly
that Cora might have skipped one or two of the lockers.

Nelson thought about this as he drove, and about the swimming-
pool conference described by Clevis, and about Graham, the assistant,
an ex-prizefighter who impressed him as thankful to have landed
where he was and of no disposition to spoil it for himself, and about
Ma Hagen, from whom he had gleaned nothing but fulsome praise of
her employer. He was thinking about Cora's husband and Cora's Stanley when he found and utilized parking space across the street from
Mrs. Atmore's residence.

Annie Grimes braved the ultramodern entrance to the apartment
house, her nervousness mating pleasantly with a sense of anticipa-
tion. I'll bet the rents are real steep, she thought, surveying the
lobby's area of crimson rug and glass and stainless steel and trailing
potted plants. The building can't have been up long. She must have
moved after her husband died. Maybe that's what I should have done.
But selling or storing the things that belonged to Arthur's family did-
n't seem exactly ...

A man in uniform came from the rear of the lobby, touched his cap,
and went to take up his post outside before she had a chance to ask
him for Mrs. Atmore's apartment number. I don't blame him for
ducking in once in a while to get comfortable, she thought, and kept
going. There were two elevators to the right of the entrance and two
to the left. She said, "Eenie minie mo," and chose the left. She hoped
they were not self-service, pushed the button, and was relieved when
a cage descended complete with operator.

"Mrs. Atmore's apartment, please."

He accepted her right to be there at a glance, and said agreeably,
"Yes ma'am—4-A."

As the cage went up she wanted to mention the robbery, but decided
that he might be reluctant to discuss it with an outsider. She wondered if the thieves had gained entrance during one of the doorman's
breaks. They had probably known where the stairs were and made

a beeline for them. It must have been kind of risky in that open and aboveboard lobby with anyone liable to spot them. But she supposed they had their ways of doing what they set out to do. They could have used the roof....

"First door on the right, ma'am."

"I beg your—? Oh—thank you."

She stepped out of the cage and advanced upon 4-A, adjusting the set of her hat, patting a few blown ends of hair into place before she rang the bell. Nothing ventured, nothing gained, she thought, and prepared to be as haughty as the stiffly correct maid she had invented for Mrs. Atmore.

She listened for sounds of life inside, let a few minutes pass, and rang again. Turning away at last in disappointment, she poked fun at herself. The joke's on me—all strung up for nothing. But it could have been worse. I could have had, "My madam is seeing no one," and the door slammed in my face. Only it looks as if she doesn't have a maid—or not a full-time one.

She waited for the elevator, as anxious to be away as she had been eager to come. I shouldn't have, she thought. It was nothing but nerve—and it would serve me right if that nice young fellow brought her up right now and she gave me the cold shoulder in front of him.

When the operator came up alone, Annie Grimes found it necessary to account for her quick reappearance. "Mrs. Atmore isn't home. It doesn't matter though—I just happened to be in the neighborhood."

He said doubtfully, "If she isn't home she would have had to leave before I came on at half past eight—and she never does. It's ten on the dot every morning."

"I know but—"

"Sure she's home. As long as I've been here she's never walked down. The bell must be out of order."

"It works—I could hear it—"

But he was the kind who had to hear for himself. He left the car and a few strides brought him to Mrs. Atmore's door. He rang, shuffled his feet, and rang again. After the third and longest try he came back scratching his head.

"Couldn't she have used the other elevator?" Annie Grimes said.

"No—Paul's home with the flu—so mine's the only one running on this side of the house." He followed her into the car and jerked his head at the indicator. "You mind an extra ride? They're buzzing like crazy up there."

"I don't mind a bit. I guess you have double the work with the other man sick."

"It don't matter about that—only they act like it's my fault the manager couldn't get a replacement for him." He returned to the subject of Mrs. Atmore. "Funny. I kept a special eye out for her this morning because—" He closed the door upon the rest of it.

"I was anxious to see how she was too. No picnic being broken into and—"

He made a discouraging sound. Annie Grimes moved to the rear as he took on a soured-looking middle-aged couple and then two pretty young girls in short coats and long stretches of leotards. The girls started to joke with him, calling him Roddy, and promising not to squeal if he shared the jewels with them. The soured woman, who had been blocking her husband's view, "tsk-tsked." The girls tossed their artichoke hairdos and silence followed. They made a dash for the street as soon as they were freed. Annie Grimes lingered behind to speak to Roddy, but the soured couple had him cornered, so she went her way.

Outside, the doorman was talking to a tall hatless man. She heard the tag end of a sentence and could not resist being helpful.

"Excuse me for butting in—but I came to see Mrs. Atmore myself. She's out."

The tall man turned to her. He had an alert, prepossessing face and she thought with a pang of envy that Mrs. Atmore was lucky to have a caller like him. Real distinguished with those shoulders and that hair ...

The doorman said, "You must be mistaken, Madam. I'm sure she hasn't gone out."

She remembered his "break" but did not give him away. "Roddy wouldn't believe it either till he rang himself. Coming down in the elevator it struck me she might be asleep—or not feeling well enough to answer—but the way Roddy rang I should think she'd have to. Her sleeping through the robbery was different. I mean a thief would take care to be extra quiet." She looked expectantly from one to the other, "I was just about getting nervous enough to ask Roddy if there was a passkey—"

The soured couple came out of the house. The female half broke up the little group by beckoning to the doorman and drawing him aside.

Mrs. Atmore's caller said to Annie Grimes, "I think that passkey is a good idea." He was holding the door for her. Bemused but game she re-entered the house merely because he seemed certain that she would. But inside the now familiar lobby she hung back.

"Do you—I mean—should we? I didn't want to scare you about her not feeling good. I guess you know her pretty well but I—" She could not quite admit to her own effrontery in being there at all. She lowered her voice. "Between you and me and the lamppost she could be out regardless of what they say. I wouldn't be surprised she lost her patience with only one elevator running—and walked down. Four flights isn't so much—and if the doorman was talking or getting somebody a cab he wouldn't notice. Why—there's Roddy. It just goes to show they can't always be on the spot."

Roddy was walking from the rear of the lobby accompanied by a shorter stockier figure who took two steps to his one. Mrs. Atmore's caller said, "Excuse me," and went forward to meet them.

He seemed to be in command of the huddle that resulted. Annie Grimes, standing about ten feet away, saw something passed from hand to hand, but could not hear the words that were passed. Her curiosity became much stronger than her urge to retreat in good order, and when the three men headed for Roddy's elevator she hurried to crowd in with them. Roddy gave her a look which she translated as, Are you back again! The stocky man was vocal and more polite. "Would you mind waiting down here for a few—?" But Mrs. Atmore's caller intervened. "Since we're following your suggestion," he said to her, "it's no more than fair that you join us."

She was pleased that the others accepted her on his say-so. In her opinion too few men had genuine authority these days. Going up she studied him covertly, convinced that he must be a very important person and that she had seen his face somewhere, either on television or in the papers. Trying to place him she nearly forgot where they were bound and why. But as soon as the car stopped, her qualms started again. In or out, now or later, Mrs. Atmore could hardly be expected to take kindly to her entrance on a passkey.

She said, "I know! With both the elevators working on the other side don't tenants sometimes—?"

The stocky man said, "It's a rather narrow passage across. Even tenants visiting friends in the house prefer to ride down to the lobby and go up from there." He was evidently the manager. He told Roddy to stay with his job, and led the way to the apartment. He rang and knocked by turns before he used the key. The door gave on to an oblong foyer that smelled strongly of the sweetheart roses shedding their petals upon a carved pedestal. The stocky man eyed them with an odd expression, shrugged, and raised his voice. "It's me, Mrs. Atmore—Ed Welsh—"

The ensuing quiet was a stay of execution to Annie Grimes. She turned to her newfound friend. "You see—she *is* out."

He did not answer. He was crossing the foyer to the large room beyond. The stocky man went after him.

Hesitantly she progressed as far as the threshold of the room, halting there because it did not seem right to go farther. What she saw looked more like Mrs. Atmore than did the sweetheart roses, or would have if its order had not been relieved by an opened newspaper trailing off a sofa, and by a tall unwashed tumbler that had sweated or spilled whitish blobs upon the polished surface of a table.

She narrowed her eyes, trying to catch a glimpse of the men through the door at the far end. They were not in sight, but she could hear movement and voices. She did her best to inhibit the onset of apprehension, wanting to think that they were carrying things unnecessarily far; telling herself that Mrs. Atmore, who was even fussy about leaving a sprinkling of powder on the dressing shelf, had not only gone out, but gone out in something of a hurry.

Her legs began to move, independent of reason or scruple. They carried her the length of the room and past it.

Her steps were silenced by the pile of the rug, spread wall to wall throughout the apartment except where tiles or thick linoleum lay. The men did not know she was there until she cried out. Then the manager jerked around as though she had pulled his strings, and turning slowly, the tall white-haired man walked to where she stood.

She could not tear her eyes from the inert mass on the double bed. Her heart was beating fast, as though it must compensate for the heart that she knew had stopped. She said breathily, "I knew it—I felt it in my bones."

At Nelson's request the distraught manager took Annie Grimes to his own apartment and gave her over to the ministrations of his wife. Left alone, Nelson used the telephone in Mrs. Atmore's bedroom.

When he had reported his findings he returned his attention to the double bed. There on its edge was the impress where the woman had sat to remove the shoes that toed each other on the rug. Perhaps she had intended to remove her dress as well and put on the robe that was draped over the footboard. But some agency stronger than will had overpowered her, and she had surrendered dressed as she was, hair scarcely disarranged, and only the dropped jaw mocking a habit of neatness.

Most of this he had seen at first glance. He had also noted a faint suffusion of throat and cheek suggesting oddly the affronted blush of one who is the victim of highly improper advances.

According to Cora's treasured clipping from the *Daily News*, the victim had denied that sleeping pills in the afternoon accounted for her failure to hear the intruder. She was reported to have said that she considered such aids a weakness, and that there were none in the apartment.

The bottle on the night table was stamped with a December date. It did not negate her alleged denial. The label advised "one every four hours for pain," which at least ruled out, as did the size of the remaining tablets, the Phenobarbital so widely and so often unwisely prescribed to combat insomnia.

Without touching it, Nelson made further study of the bottle. The name of her physician was typed in below the name of the pharmacy. He drew the telephone toward him again and dialed.

He allowed it to be assumed by the nurse who came to the phone that he was a friend calling on Mrs. Atmore's behalf. The doctor was out but the nurse said that he could be reached if it was urgent. Nelson, feeling that there was no profit in spreading the word until necessary, said that it was not urgent. He waited a moment, and asked what the doctor had prescribed in December. The nurse took it for granted that he was relaying a question from the patient. She told him to hold on while she consulted Mrs. Atmore's card. An intranasal solution, she said, to relieve congestion, and codeine to relieve the pain. Was Mrs. Atmore having another attack of sinusitis? The doctor had read about the robbery and mentioned it when he came in that morning. So perhaps it was not her sinuses but migraine. Mrs. Atmore was a—um—sensitive woman. Nelson was sure she had started to say "neurotic." No, she had always refused to take sleeping pills or tranquilizers either, although the doctor had suggested a mild form last year when she was suffering from those asthmatic symptoms which had no—um—er—clinical basis. Too bad. She'd been so well since she began to reduce. The doctor was expected back at ... Nelson thanked her and broke the connection.

He had toured the bedroom several times. He did so once more. Neither the dressing table with its fastidious complement of creams, astringents, and cosmetics, nor the bureau, nor any other surface offered what he sought. He gave the body a final bleak glance and went to explore the rest of the apartment.

There were two bathrooms. The contents of the medicine cabinets were quickly assessed; toothpastes, packaged soaps, bath salts, aspirin, antiseptics, and a few cathartics, all of which would receive closer scrutiny should the findings of the medical examiner so indicate.

The appointments in the second bedroom were of a youthful taste, and the closet door, half open, revealed garments suitable to a slim girl. There had been nothing said about another occupant. He added "daughter?" to his unwritten list of queries.

He did not expect to discover a farewell note in the kitchen. He entered it on the premise that potential suicides could rarely be classified as rational. Somewhat sheepishly he investigated cabinets, an unnecessarily large refrigerator, and even the innards of a wall oven. Then he paused before two large cans upon a shelf. They were identical, each flaunting a tall "V" for Vitrate. He lifted the lid of the one that had been opened and held the can under his nose. On the way out he pressed the foot lever of the garbage pail. There was not a crumb or scrap within to evidence the consumption of an honest meal. He quit the cheerless place.

The tiny dining room was equally unyielding. He had left the living room until the last. It was the most obvious location, but although he had walked through it quickly, he felt that a propped-up note on the mantel or desk or console or coffee table would have given him pause. Logically, if a note was not prominently displayed to ensure discovery, the probability that it had been written was slight. Yet his observations had drawn a portrait of Mrs. Atmore, and such an untidy loose end was at variance with it.

He sniffed at the unwashed glass. He scanned the page to which the trailing newspaper had been turned. He pulled down the top of a Sheraton desk and surveyed its cubbyholes. Most of them were empty, but a few held decks of letters preserved in their envelopes and bound, according to their character, by ribbons or rubber bands. Beyond sampling a few postmarks on the personal variety, he did not disturb them. They were not of recent vintage, and not, for the moment, pertinent.

The leather wastebasket beside the desk earned more of his time. He had finished matching and reading the jagged bits of paper it contained before an assistant medical examiner arrived. And by the time the crew of a mobile laboratory unit stamped in, there remained little doubt that their presence on the scene was justified.

## CHAPTER 9

Annie Grimes, insisting that she had no intention of fainting, allowed herself to be led away by the manager. He seemed relieved that
there were no other passengers in the elevator, and broke the news
to Roddy by announcing that Mrs. Atmore had died suddenly of
causes unknown. Annie Grimes was too busy exerting mastery over
legs that had gone rubbery to open her mouth, and Roddy, quelled by
a signal that she missed, did not ask for elaboration.

The manager deposited her in his ground-floor rear apartment, had
a few private words with his wife, and ducked out. Annie Grimes sank
into a chair, accepted a cup of hot sweet tea, cried hard, and felt the
better for it.

The eyes of the manager's wife teared in sympathy. She dabbed at
them and said, "Poor soul. I didn't know her well but all the same—"

"It's sad to see anyone go," said Annie Grimes. "It is. Still—we all
come to it sooner or later."

The two women had taken to each other on sight. Annie Grimes
thought it a pity that such a black cloud hung over their meeting. She
said, "In my opinion Mrs. Atmore should have come to it a whole lot
later. If there'd been a thing ailing her she couldn't have stood the pace
at Carmody's for a minute." She explained about the accelerated class.

"It's a good thing I'm skinny," the manager's wife said. "I'd never be
able to afford anything like that."

"Money isn't all it's cracked up to be. You're lucky to have kept your
nice little figure."

"Thank you—but I've always envied the big girl. I wouldn't lose
much more if I were you."

"I wouldn't have lost a pound if Mrs. Atmore hadn't been a real inspiration to me. I just don't believe she died a natural death. Yesterday
morning she was as chipper as a bird and I can't help thinking—"

She was not encouraged to say what she could not help thinking.
The manager's wife offered more tea and murmured something
about Mrs. Atmore's orphaned daughter.

Annie Grimes, who knew nothing about the existence of a daughter, could have wept afresh. She admitted her ignorance and pressed
for details.

"She's pretty in a quiet sort of way. I don't run into her often because
she isn't home from college more than a week or so out of the year.

Children do drift away. I haven't any of my own—but whether you have them or not it seems to amount to the same thing in the end."

Annie Grimes said that she did not have any of her own either. It established another stretch of common ground.

"Still—blood is thicker than water," the manager's wife said, "so she's bound to take it hard."

Annie Grimes nodded. "I'm wondering if the gentleman who went up with me is a relative or just a close friend?" Her description of the gentleman did not help the manager's wife to place him. Disappointed, she said, "Well—for the girl's sake I hope he's a relative—because I'm sure he could be depended upon to get her over the hurdles. He was so kind to me when I barged into the room. I saw him looking down at the bed like he might have been saying a last good-bye—and somehow it hit me in a flash she wasn't just sleeping. Oh dear—"

"Now don't you start crying again," the manager's wife said.

"I won't—but it's terrible—dying alone like that—not even a maid around."

"The maid only comes mornings since a few weeks ago. The rest of the day she works for another tenant on the same floor. I guess from what you told me about drinking food instead of cooking and eating it and washing the pots and pans, there wasn't enough for her to do."

"Mornings!" Annie Grimes generated excitement. "Then Mrs. Atmore must have been alive when she left today or she'd have set up a holler. Do you think I could have a talk with her before I go? She'd be the one to say whether—well—whether Mrs. Atmore complained of a pain or—"

The manager's wife said sharply, "I wouldn't do that if I were you. Nothing she says can bring the poor soul back. I was only trying to take your mind off—"

"I know—but I can't get rid of the notion there's something—"

"There's nothing that the doctor who has to sign the death certificate can't tell without needing help from you or anyone else. Bad news spreads through the house soon enough and my husband wouldn't care for it a bit if you gave that maid an excuse to start gossiping. You just let it alone."

Annie Grimes was hurt by her tone. She showed it. "You've been very hospitable but I'm sure you have things to do and I don't want to go on being a nuisance. If you'll tell me where you put my coat—"

"Oh no—please don't take it that way. You aren't a nuisance at all—but my husband's job is no cinch even when things run smooth—and sometimes it gets the best of me. The tenants seem to hold him responsible for whatever happens—the elevator boy coming down with the flu—and thieves breaking in—and now this." She put a handsome cap on the apology. "But it's an ill wind—isn't it—because it blew you in—and making your acquaintance is a real pleasure."

Annie Grimes said, "Likewise." She did not mention the maid again, and soon the air was filtered of constraint. They exchanged bits of personal history, and had progressed to "Annie" and "Irene" terms when Irene got up to answer the door. She came back with the white-haired man, announcing his name in a stilted voice that was drowned by Annie Grimes's full-throated "Am I glad to see you!"

Nelson said, "If you're ready to leave I'll drive you home."

She jumped at the offer, seeing it as a reward for her deference to Irene's sensitivity. "I appreciate your consideration," she said, "especially at a time like this."

She told him where she lived as he held her coat, and hoped it would not take him too much out of his way. He assured her that it would not, and she sent Irene a look which said, There—what did I tell you about him? Her good-bye was hurried because she did not want to keep him waiting, but she managed to crowd in the promise of a future meeting at her house.

His car was parked on the opposite side of the street. Crossing with his hand at her elbow she was bursting with questions, but before they could be asked, her rules of etiquette demanded a toll of small talk. Stepping carefully, she said, "March came in like a lion all right—a dirty one dropping snow all over the place."

"It was spring when we met the first time," he said.

The words were so strongly reminiscent of episodes in her past that they startled her for a moment. Impatiently she reminded herself that in those days she had been an entirely different kind of eyeful, and that furthermore this was no ordinary pickup. Even if it were, she thought, the white-haired man would not stoop to such a rusty line.

She looked upward to confirm her opinion of him. "It did cross my mind that I'd seen you someplace but I couldn't pin it down."

He did not reply until she was seated beside him and the car underway, a transition accomplished so smoothly that it was scarcely an interruption.

"You're Annie Dale—aren't you?"

Pure pleasure curved her lips. It was so long since she had been Annie Dale to anyone. "In the flesh," she said, "and far too much of it. But I must be doing better than I thought or you wouldn't have recognized me. Would you mind saying who you are again? When Mrs. Welsh introduced us I'm afraid I was woolgathering and didn't quite—"

"Nelson—Gridley Nelson."

It seemed discourteous to let him see that the name meant nothing to her. She said, "It's been a long time—hasn't it? I'm Mrs. Arthur Hamilton Grimes now—or—well—the truth is I hardly know who I am since Arthur passed away—and so much water has gone under the mill that I can't exactly put my finger on where it was I met you."

He had an attractive smile. "Perhaps it wasn't tactful to mention it."

"Now don't tease." A few minutes ago she would not have believed that anything could take precedence over Mrs. Atmore. It's been an unexpected day, she thought, happily forgetting what kind of a day it was. "Why shouldn't you tell me? Even the best of men have what they call misspent youths—and I never made any bones about mine. Did you come backstage?"

"Yes—but unfortunately not for romantic reasons."

She said delightedly, "Then you're in show business yourself. I thought you might be."

"There are times when I wish I were."

A good old gossip couched in the language she had so sorely missed would have added exactly the right color to the encounter. She hid her disappointment. "Let's see if I can guess your profession. How does that button thing go?" She started to chant, "'Rich man—poor man—beggar man—thief—doctor—lawyer—'"

"Warm," he said. "I could be called a middleman for lawyers."

"Whatever that means."

He stopped for a red light and handed her his opened wallet.

She read the cellophaned identification, dropped it, and retrieved it from her lap. "You could knock me down with a feather! A police captain!" Her voice accused him of deliberate intention to mislead. "Then you're not—you weren't a friend of Mrs. Atmore?"

He took the wallet from her and stowed it away. "Policemen do make friends," he said, "but our paths hadn't crossed."

She remembered how he had leaned over the bed. Not grieving as she thought. Not saying a last good-bye. Just taking a cop's impersonal look at a defenseless corpse. She said, "How did you happen to be on hand? You couldn't have known what—?"

"I'd come for information about the robbery."

"Well! If I'm not the biggest fool that ever was. I didn't think to connect— But you're from Homicide. Why would they send someone from Homicide to—?"

She saw him turn the ignition key. With so much stopping and starting, arrival took her by surprise. She wailed, "We can't be here so soon."

He got out and assisted her to the sidewalk. She stood there, so loathe to lose him that she said resentfully, "You put me off—wasting the best part of the ride with that business of meeting me before— and now I suppose you're in too great a hurry to come in and talk it over."

"I'd like that very much."

"You would!" She exhaled gustily. "Then what are we standing in the cold for?"

The maid opened the door to them and took their coats with less than her customary hauteur. Annie Grimes, behaving as though handsome visitors were an everyday affair, led the way to her own special nook on the ground floor.

The assistant medical examiner had pronounced Doris Cunningham Atmore "D. O. A.," and the technicians had finished their work and packed up, taking various oddments and treasures with them. The treasures had been cached in a jewel box under the bed. One of the oddments was an opened can of Vitrate spiced pungently with nutmeg.

Death, according to the assistant medical examiner, had occurred between the hours of twelve and two, caused by paralysis of the respiratory centers. In the grudging manner of his kind, he said that this was no more than an educated guess, and refused to commit himself further, pending the performance of an autopsy.

After the body had been speeded on the first lap of the last journey, Nelson had done what more could be done on the spot: squeezing Roddy dry, and tracking the harassed manager to the basement where he had gone to escape tenants who had witnessed the transference of corpse to ambulance.

Roddy had been eager but apologetic. He could keep pretty fair track of the tenants' exits and entrances, he said, but neither he nor the doorman could keep track of strangers unless they looked suspicious or asked directions. Too many came and went. No, there was no special service elevator. When heavy stuff came in they padded Paul's car to keep it from getting scratched. Regular delivery boys went up the same way as everyone else. Yes, he seemed to remember seeing someone with a florist's box yesterday, but not to describe. It might not even have been yesterday, or the car could have been too crowded, with Paul out, for him to notice who got off where. He would not have connected flowers with Mrs. Atmore anyway. He had never known her to receive them as a gift or buy them for herself. He would give Nelson a buzz if more about the man with the box came back to him. Sure, if people were up to no good they could ride up on the opposite side and use the passage across. If Nelson wanted to question the two other boys, okay, but he doubted that he'd have any better luck. And he was right.

Under duress the manager produced the part-time maid, and she in turn produced the fact that when she left for her second job at noon, Mrs. Atmore was alive, and kicking a little more than usual. Maybe because she was coming down with something. Her eyes looked headachy and she breathed kind of heavy, like she used to when she had her old asthma. "I guess she wanted to get rid of me and be alone," the maid said, "because when I offered to—" She was inhibited by an impatient glance from the manager. She decided not to finish the sentence, but grumbled instead that she had to get back to work. But she did confirm the existence of a college-girl daughter, and threw in a brother-in-law who lived on Eighty-Sixth Street.

The brother-in-law was listed in the telephone book as a stockbroker. Nelson called his office. He had an old voice that quavered at the news. He was less appalled for the dead, it developed, than for the living. He asked with avuncular concern if his niece had been informed, and promised to get in touch with her at once. He seemed to know nothing of Mrs. Atmore's private life. Nelson put a mental "reserved" sign upon him, and terminated the conversation before return questions could be phrased.

Then, because Annie Grimes was on the premises, which indicated more intimacy with Carmody's late pupil than had been supposed, he made his casual offer to give her a lift.

Even after her little sidewalk speech she did not rush to make up for lost time. Being a hostess came first.

She plumped herself down on a tufted settee and invited Nelson to "take a pew." "This is the coziest place in the house," she said. "I always have a fire going in the grate whether I'm home or not. It's good company—something to come back to. Arthur called it my 'Green Room' when I'd finished adding the bits and pieces."

She had decorated the walnut-paneled walls with glossy prints of former cronies. Costumed and semi-costumed they overflowed to the carved mantelpiece, and to the top of a small piano. Other surfaces, including the flat-topped cabinet of a combination television, radio, and hi-fi, were weighted with copies of *Variety*, old programs, sheet music, and records. A large gilt cage dangled from a stand between the crimson window hangings. She pointed to it.

"The kids in the show chipped in for that—only it's never been lived in. I don't go much for birds except outside where they belong—but of course they meant it as a joke. They got the idea from the old song." She hummed a few bars.

The chairs were man-sized and comfortable. Facing her, Nelson declined an offer to name his "poison," but did "light up."

"I never smoked, myself," she said, "though maybe I should. They say it cuts the appetite. Arthur was partial to cigars—the brand that comes in separate aluminum cases. Every so often he'd stick some into the packages I sent to a couple of comedians at the retired actors' home. Somehow I couldn't get over them ending up there. They weren't young when I met them on tour but they seemed like they'd go on forever. Laughs! One night while they were doing a blackout a sandbag broke loose from the flies. It landed plop between them—and without turning a hair, Tubby—the short fellow—said, 'Drat those pigeons,' and went right on with the act. I was standing in the wings and I nearly ...'"

Wasted time was an occupational disease for which Nelson had found no cure. He realized the futility of trying to rush Annie Grimes.

The room and her freewheeling reminiscences were a savory compound. Midsentence she stopped to introduce the alien ingredient.

"There I go—off to the races as if I had no feelings at all. You see—after Irene—that's Mrs. Welsh—let fall there was a maid worked mornings, I could tell she didn't want to talk about it anymore—and she took the attitude it wasn't my place to ask the maid questions—but somebody should because—" She made a fresh start. "You might feel it's none of my business either but—" Her eyes begged for encouragement.

Nelson gave it. "I spoke to the maid. When she quit the apartment at noon, Mrs. Atmore was alive—"

"And in her usual health too, I'll be bound."

He did not contradict her.

She said, "That does it—I was right," and bounced with the joy of self-vindication. "No two ways about it—there's been foul play."

"It's a possibility."

"Of course it is—coming right on top of the robbery. That thief—or thieves—" She paused to interpolate kindly, "Sometimes there's an extra one along to act as a lookout—but be that as it may they didn't get all they came for so they played a return engagement expecting to find her out like she was every morning—only she wasn't and they had to kill her. After all—on television the crooks keep tabs on their prospects—so why wouldn't they in real life?"

Nelson heard himself saying, "Life does imitate television sometimes. Will you tell me exactly when you suspected foul play?"

"I don't know—right away. At least—" She mulled it over.

"Was it after you learned that the maid had been there?"

"No. It was before—even before I saw for myself."

"You weren't in the room very long—and there were no bloodstains—or other indications of violence."

It jolted her, as it had been meant to do. She looked for a moment as though he had fed her something too unpalatable to retain. Then she said weakly, "I guess I had what you'd call a—" She shook her head. "No—it was more than a premonition. All I can tell you is what I told Irene. Mrs. Atmore didn't suffer from heart trouble—and if there's anything else that takes people suddenly she couldn't have had that either because Carmody wouldn't let us join the accelerated class without a doctor's okay."

"I see your point—but didn't it occur to you that she might have committed suicide?"

"Mrs. Atmore!" The exclamation was scornful. "Easy to see you never met her. Besides—would anyone with suicide in mind bother to take last licks at her diet? You must have noticed that goblet in the living room." She barely waited for his nod. "Well—I've forced enough Vitrate down to recognize the remains of it—and furthermore it doesn't taste that delicious you'd choose it for a last meal."

Nelson said, "Perhaps the glass was used last night or early this morning—and the maid overlooked it."

"Mrs. Atmore wouldn't have a careless maid. She was as neat as a pin, herself, and expected everybody else to be. I've heard her scold Cora—the attendant at Carmody's—if there was a smear on the dressing shelf when she sat down. No—that glass and the newspaper on the sofa came later." Annie Grimes added positively, "Too late—or she wouldn't have left them there."

Nelson said, "You've thought it through very carefully."

She looked pleased. "Oh, it just came to me—I've never been much of a thinker." Something else came to her, bidden by his approval. "What would prevent a thief from walking up the stairs—hearing voices inside—and hanging around till the maid came out? Then he rings the bell like anybody would and pushes in when Mrs. Atmore answers the door. She's been taking her Vitrate lunch—so unbeknownst he slips poison into the glass. I wouldn't know how he gets her to drink it but that's neither here nor there. She might be so scared she looks as if she'd faint and he holds it to her lips pretending to help her. And when the poison works he carries her into the bedroom, steals the rest of the jewels, and walks out as bold as you please."

Nelson's nod was a salute to the television screen. Annie Grimes translated it as acceptance of her reconstruction. She was undaunted when he said, "Would the thief leave the glass unwashed—and if he expected Mrs. Atmore to be out why did he arm himself with poison?"

She tossed that off with ease. "He'd have learned to prepare for emergencies—and using a gun or a knife his clothes could get spattered with—" She gulped. She said huskily, "I hope you didn't wash that glass. It's evidence sure as you're born." Then she struck the side of her head with her palm. "Don't mind me for trying to teach you your job."

"I need all the help I can get. And as a friend of Mrs. Atmore you're in a key position to—"

"One thing—every time I take a drink of Vitrate I'm going to think of her." She sighed.

"If you stop taking it for a few days the unhappy association may disappear." Nelson was not dispensing idle advice. He thought it unlikely that the entire supply of Vitrate had been doctored, but steps were being taken to halt its consumption until further notice.

Annie Grimes said, "I think I will give it a miss at that. I can make up for it by being extra chinchy with real food." She seemed to cheer up at the prospect. "Fact is, the company puts it out stood Carmody up on the reorder and most of the ladies have used theirs up. I wouldn't have any left either if I'd been as religious about it as they are."

The Seth Thomas clock on the mantelpiece cleared its throat and chimed the hours. Nelson said on the count of five, "How well did you know Mrs. Atmore?"

She looked a little shamefaced. "Not as well as you might think."

"You were on visiting terms."

"Not really. Between you and me I just decided to drop in on the spur of the moment. She's not anyone you'd know well—or maybe I'm not anyone she'd know well but we sit—" she corrected herself, "sat next to each other in the dressing room and talked of this and that."

Nelson threw nothing into the reflective pause. His silence worked like a suction pump.

"She didn't go out of her way to be chummy with the rest of them either," Annie Grimes said, "so I don't think her being standoffish with me was personal. It could be she just had no use for women."

Nelson thought of the letter he had pieced together from the waste-basket.

"For instance—she wasn't a bit standoffish with Carmody, who's even hard for me to take sometimes. Like once in the beginning when she was trying to touch her toes and he gave her a whack on the fanny. I think I would have slapped him down myself—and I could hear all those high and mighty tabbies stop breathing to wait for the fire-works—but she didn't do more than get a little red in the face. It was-n't an angry red—more as if—"

Somewhere in the house a telephone shrilled. It dragged her out of the bog of Mrs. Atmore's inconsistencies. "Probably a wrong number," she said, but sat forward with touching expectancy until a few mo-ments after the shrilling stopped. "Where was I?"

Nelson said, "You were criticizing Carmody's lack of finesse."

She seemed surprised. "Now how did I get into that? I thought we were talking about Mrs. Atmore. It's true I don't go for his nibs in a big way. His type's not as new to me as it would be to her—but I've got to admit he's good at his work."

"I should think that making himself popular would be an important part of his work."

"I suppose so—and from the way they all carry on I guess I'm the only holdout. It's nothing I can put my finger on except he reminds me of a reformed gangster I ran across once who wasn't reformed enough. *He* had a wife too—though he never advertised it. Not that Carmody can make a secret of his—her being right there on the spot."

"Isn't it a happy marriage?"

"They seem to pull together all right—but I wouldn't be surprised she has her troubles. I know if I were her I'd soon send Edna Spofford packing—not that there's as much danger as might be on that score what with her having other fish to fry."

"Mrs. Carmody?"

"Oh no—she's a lovely person and the dressing-room gossip about her having a boyfriend is just plain spite started by Mrs. Morrison, who happened to see her talking to a man in the lobby. But I was re-ferring to the receptionist—Edna Spofford. Seems *she* really has a boyfriend. He came along in a cab as I was leaving today and she al-most knocked me over getting to him. Still—I didn't mind—because she's young and won't do herself good by sniffing around Carmody. This other fellow's a better bet from what I saw. Tall—with a real pol-ish to him the way he got out and helped her in. I tried to get a closer

look when the cab passed but aside from horn-rimmed glasses—" She
thought that Nelson's attention had strayed, and stopped to shake a
finger at him. "You're too polite—sitting there letting me rattle away
as if you're drinking in every syllable. What's that you've got?"

He had an envelope in his hand. He removed the ring and placed
it on the coffee table between them. "Have you seen this before?"

Her eyes began to fill. "Of course. It's Mrs. Atmore's. You went to tell
her you'd found the stolen jewelry—and now—now she'll never know."
She gave an inhibiting sniffle. "Did you get all of it?"

"I think so."

She misinterpreted his slight hesitation, and said consolingly,
"Never mind—you will. Rome wasn't built in a day—and she wore this
ring such a lot that it must have meant more to her than the rest of
her things put together. One time I remarked on the setting and she
let drop her husband had it specially designed. It makes me real
mad—Mrs. Pierce and Mrs. Morrison hinting in the dressing room the
whole business was staged to collect insurance. Could insurance
take the place of something she prized so highly? And besides—if
what they say is true—she had a fortune—more than Arthur left
me—which is going some." She was cradling the ring on the fleshy
palm of her hand. "Here—you better put it away again. You don't want
to lose it. Her daughter will—did you know of the daughter?"

"Yes—she's been notified—by an uncle."

"That's good. I'm glad the poor girl has someone to turn to. Not finding the thieves yet how did you happen on the ring?"

"In an obvious place. It was listed as missing but—"

She spared him the necessity of inventing a substitute for Carmody's. "I understand. It wasn't really missing—only mislaid in the
apartment. Well—that bears out what I said about them coming back
to get something else. They'd heard about the ring and—" Her eyes
widened. "Oh dear—maybe they were still there when I rang the bell.
Maybe that's why they scooted off without it." She was crestfallen. "I've
been a big help—scaring them away when you might have nabbed
them."

Nelson smiled. "You can't be convicted of that until your guilt is established." He had been trying throughout to spot a few flowers in the
weedy mass of her words. To make sure that he had missed none, he
went over the terrain again. "As you said earlier, cases of breaking and
entering have been facilitated by a knowledge of the victim's habits.
The list of those who might have acquired such knowledge is endless—delivery boys, repair men, apartment-house staff, neighbors,

members of the intimate circle—"

She could not await her turn. "We can rule out the apartment-house staff," she said. "That Roddy seems a nice fellow—and the manager's too conscientious to hire people without looking into their references. That goes for the tenants he'd let in too. Also he can't be a crook himself or Irene wouldn't have married him. As for delivery boys—I shouldn't think there'd be any from the local markets lately on account of her sticking to her diet—and department stores generally use a parcel service which is too rushed to do more than dump the merchandise and run."

She had whittled it down to the point for him. He said without stressing it, "Then we'll have to look elsewhere. You've kept your eyes and ears open to such a remarkable degree that perhaps if you think back you might remember hearing Mrs. Atmore mention—directly or indirectly—someone who in retrospect seems to have shown undue curiosity—a casual acquaintance, for example—or a newly acquired friend."

Obediently, Annie Grimes prepared for a voyage of concentration, pleating her brow and narrowing her eyes to slits. She did not leave port.

"It would have to be a male," Nelson said, "since you believe she wasn't eager to form friendships with women."

"I'm sorry—I can't say I heard of anyone like that. Outside of Carmody's—who she met and what she did was a closed book. It was only how she acted with Carmody that gave me the notion she'd be willing if Mr. Right came along." Her face smoothed out. "Wouldn't the detectives have thought to worm that sort of thing out of her when they turned up last night?"

"They tried—but as I understand it she was too distressed to provide a coherent answer."

"Who wouldn't be distressed? I know I would. The idea of anyone I'd given the time of day to sneaking in behind my back and pinching my belongings is somehow much worse than being robbed by a perfect stranger." Her voice swelled with indignation. "I'm beginning to see where Mrs. Pierce got the crazy thought she was holding out on the police. I ask you!"

Nelson contemplated the nosegay he had gathered and hoped it was worth keeping. He stood up.

"You're not going so soon?" Reluctantly she too arose. "Well, I suppose you've plenty to do and I shouldn't try to hold you." But she had a question in reserve, and no intention of allowing it to go unanswered. "I still can't get myself to believe you're really a police officer—especially if it's true we met before." She giggled. "Because time was when we wouldn't have been so pally."

"Time was," Nelson said solemnly, "when a rookie helped the Vice Squad to close a show on Fourteenth Street."

"Fourteenth—? Well I'll be—!" The giggle swelled to a full-bodied laugh. "Wait—it's all coming back—the first and last time I was ever mixed up in a raid—and that's the gospel truth." She regarded him with fresh interest. "You wouldn't be—? Yes you would—I can see you like it was yesterday—a fine young strapper in uniform—and the ladies in the cast dreaming up stories you'd gone white from being crossed in love—and every last one of them ready to mend your heart—but know what? There's something about you now says somebody did—somewhere along the line."

"I'm happily married—but the stories had no basis. Premature white hair runs in the family."

"It still looks premature—and that Fourteenth Street shindig happened longer ago than I want to admit. But you *did* recognize me—which is more than I had a right to expect. I'll bet your wife doesn't have to diet."

"Sometimes she thinks she does." He lied with a purpose. "I've caught her studying the liquid-food ads."

"I imagine the advertised brands would be more appetizing than Vitrate. I wouldn't put it past Carmody to order the flavor left out just to make us think we're getting our money's worth. Didn't they used to say something like 'the nastier the medicine, the quicker the cure'?"

"Something like that."

Annie Grimes grasped at any means to prolong his stay. "I take it your wife suits you the way she is."

"Yes—she does."

"Tell you what—I'll give you a can of Vitrate to take home. If that doesn't discourage her she really needs to lose weight."

"That's generous of you."

She thought she saw a "but" coming and said earnestly, "Go on—take it—unless you're afraid you'll be accused of graft when one of those police investigations comes along. You couldn't be—not with me doing all the insisting. I'll have it wrapped for you."

She kept him another few minutes, pressed the wrapped can of Vitrate upon him, and begged to be informed of Kyrie's reaction to it. In the same breath she begged for news of his progress with the Atmore case. He left, feeling that on the whole the time had been well spent.

## CHAPTER 10

The afternoon of the truant Edna Spofford had an auspicious start. "I didn't think you'd wait," she said, as Vance Manning assisted her into the taxi.

"I've been cruising around on the wings of optimism."

Edna never knew when he was fooling and when he was not, but she liked the way he talked. At the sight of him her eavesdropping rage had dissolved.

He fed her at a very expensive restaurant whose name was often mentioned in the columns. She tried to identify celebrities at the other tables, gave up, and behaved like a bored habitueé until she had swallowed a second martini. Then she was more herself. "I hardly ever drink in the daytime," she said. "He'll be wild if I go back smelling of liquor."

"Why go back at all?"

"I can't walk out just like that—with nothing else lined up." She added plaintively, "I've got my living to earn."

She left room and to spare for the insertion of a "Don't worry, little girl, I'll take care of you." But the long menu engrossed Vance Manning, and he missed the opportunity.

She said "Yes" to the items he suggested, checking the prices surreptitiously to make sure that she was not being short-changed. She would have preferred overdone steak and French-fried potatoes to the underdone guinea hen and wild rice that was placed before her. And she thought that the dry white wine, a Pouilly-Fuissée, would be vastly improved by a scoop of sugar. But all in all the meal had its advantages. Untempted, she ate little, which should prove, she felt, that her mind was on higher things than food. If Vance had expressed solicitude about her lack of appetite she would have said she was too upset to eat. But he did not, which was just as well because she could not resist the dessert he ordered.

It was difficult to look mortally wounded after she had licked her lips of whipped-cream traces. She applied a new coat of lipstick, and did her best. "Mr. Carmody was still in the office with the police captain and another man when I sneaked away," she said. "I still don't know whether I did right or wrong. I hate to believe the worst of people—and even after what you told me at the swimming pool I was ready to back him up. But I couldn't let him lie about me—could I? Not when I happened to overhear with my own ears how he was tearing my reputation to shreds."

Vance made "tsk-tsk" sounds.

"Then he had the nerve to send for me to get him off the hook." She had given Vance most of the details in the taxi. She went through the scene again, embellishing it with cutting phrases that she had not used, and attributing statements to Nelson and Carmody that would have astonished both of them.

Vance said, "I'm glad for your sake that you've taken the true measure of the man."

The "for your sake" was too objective to suit her. It was for his sake that she had practically burned her bridges, and she began to be doubtful about the outcome. Yet it stood to reason that his purpose in turning her against her employer was to clear the field for himself. Else why would he invite her to an expensive lunch afterward? A man did not spend money on a girl unless he had an ax to grind. And what other ax could there be?

"I can't imagine why you're so nice to me," she said.

"All men have a duty to protect innocent damsels." The horn-rims dangled from his hand. His eyes had a faraway look.

She made an all-out effort to pose as an innocent damsel. "That first day you walked in," she said, "I didn't dream we'd be having lunch together. And here we are."

"Yes—here we are." He hardly seemed to be there at all.

The waiter refilled her coffee cup. She did not want more coffee. She drank it to keep the lunch from petering out before anything was settled.

"You still haven't explained why I shouldn't be friendly with Mi— Mr. Carmody. At the swimming pool you only hinted he'd done something terrible and I took your word for it. But maybe I was too hasty. I've worked for him nearly six months and he's been a very good boss—while you and I are—well—only just getting to know each other."

He passed over that opportunity too, when the least he could have said was, "Here's to a long friendship." He had summoned the waiter while she talked. The check was placed on a salver before him, to be buried under a large bill.

Like money was dirt, she thought covetously.

When the waiter had whisked it away, she said, "You should have added it up. It doesn't pay to be too trusting." She leaned forward, drawing attention to the resultant exposure by making modest adjustment. There was no time left for subtlety. "What you need," she said, "is someone to take care of you."

"That's a chore I wouldn't inflict on anyone."

A soulful stare conveyed her readiness to perform the chore. But except for a passing gleam in his eye when she tugged at her slipping neckline, he remained aloof. Brief as it was, the gleam did away with a starting suspicion that he might be queer. Married? She supposed she could take that for granted, because it seemed improbable that such a prize had not been hooked at least once. Evidently, though, a famous place like this would have been out of the question if the current wife kept tabs on him. So what held him back?

The waiter had returned, bearing the depleted salver. He accepted the tip with a smile, and so he should, since by her calculations it was a lot more than the required percentage. She sat like a stone when the hireling would have pulled back her chair. "Those martinis really relaxed me," she said to Vance. "I could sit here for hours chatting with you."

"I've enjoyed it too," Vance said.

She fought to keep it in the present tense. "I wish you'd come right out and say what you've got against Mr. Carmody. You didn't have a thing against him that first day. In fact—"

"Let me put it this way," he said. "Perhaps I'm pro-society."

She thought crossly that he sounded like those politicians on television who were always putting it this way and that way—and never putting it any way at all. She wished she knew what he was running for, and kept on wishing it after she had been maneuvered to the street. It was almost as though treating her to lunch were some sort of obligation that he had felt honor bound to discharge. She made a final pitch as they waited for a cab.

"Please drop me at the Easton."

She was encouraged by another of those quick glances. "You're a brave girl."

Her substantial lower lip quivered. "A girl in my position has to be brave. But it may not be so bad—not if I promise to put it right with the police—and explain that I only let him down because I was cut to the quick." She thought, That ought to get him going.

But he only said quietly, "In your place I'd sleep on it. The climate might improve later."

She shook her head. "I guess you don't know your stepbrother as well as you think. The longer I postpone it the worse he'll be—especially with me taking two hours for lunch when I've got him used to having me snatch a bite in any room that's vacant while she relieves me at the desk."

"'She'?"

"His wife. No—there's nothing to do but face the music and get it over with."

"If you insist I won't attempt to dissuade you."

She wanted him to dissuade her, and she had an uneasy feeling that he knew it. "I don't see any choice. I can't impose by letting you take me home."

"I'll be glad to."

"No—it's much too far. Anyway I simply couldn't bear it right now—not the way I feel. You see—I share an apartment with a girl who's kind of common—and her riffraff friends keep dropping in because of her being unemployed right now. Is that a cab coming?" She thrust back her drooping shoulders. "If it isn't I'd better start walking."

It was a cab, and Vance Manning commandeered it.

Until the afternoon ended, Ceil Carmody occupied Edna Spofford's chair. When the last word had been said to the last lingering client, she got up and followed her husband to the apartment. "Are you having dinner here?"

"What dinner? You been cooking it on the desk?" Carmody looked tired, and his normally clean sweat exuded an unfamiliar odor.

She wondered if it could be the smell of fear, and felt a twinge of pity for him. "What would you like to eat? I'll send down for it."

"The appetite I got you don't have to spend much. Tomorrow when that tomato shows I'll brain her."

Ceil said, "She may not come back."

"She don't and I'll have her blackballed at every agency in town. She knows that. She'll come back all right—on her hands and knees—and be lucky if she goes out that way."

Ceil called room service while he was in the shower. When he came out, the waiter was transferring the contents of his wagon to a folding table.

Carmody manipulated the television dials before he sat down. This was recognized procedure at meals shared with his wife, a substitute for the failure of personal communication.

Through the tail end of the "Early Show," and all but through the seven o'clock news, he chewed and swallowed, eyes trained upon the screen. Then Ceil swallowed the wrong way.

"For God's sake!" Carmody shoved a glass of water at her, his attention still riveted to the commentator. And above the sound of her own gasping she heard the first broadcast of Mrs. Atmore's death. A simple statement untrimmed by details, of a socialite found dead in her midtown apartment, cause as yet undisclosed.

The commentator slid on to other matters. But Carmody had no ears for other matters.

"Where the hell is the evening paper?" His voice was unrecognizable.

"We haven't one. Mike—?"

His chair scraped and overturned. By the time she had righted it he was on his way down to the lobby.

He did not reach the newsstand. As soon as he left the elevator he was stopped by that dick with the baggy pants.

"I was just coming up to get you," Clevis said.

"Get me?"

"Figure of speech. They want you to drop in at headquarters to help them clear up a thing or two."

Carmody looked around to see if he could spot any other dicks in the lobby. "I'm in the middle of dinner—"

"Do you always eat it on the run?"

"What would I run from? You can see I haven't even got my overcoat on." He tried to dispense with the hand upon his shoulder, but its grip was strong. "Let go of me. I've got a good name in this hotel. Do you want to spoil it by starting something?"

"No. Do you?"

"All right—I don't mind helping the police—but I just shot down for a paper and a pack of—"

"We'll tell you all the news downtown."

"I've got to let my wife know I'm going out or she'll—"

"Send a bellhop up for your coat and hat. That will tell her you're going out—and if you're too bashful to trust him with the rest of the message we'll give her a call from headquarters."

Ceil received the call within the hour. The officer at the other end of the wire made light of her panic with lavish use of the word "routine." Everyone who had known Mrs. Atmore was subject to interrogation, he said, and sure she could get a lawyer if she had cause to believe it was necessary. She asked to speak to her husband, and was told that he was free to use the phone but had not availed himself of the privilege.

She sent down for the late editions. They were on the waiter's wagon when he came to remove the dishes. She waited until he had gone, to scan them, imagining that he knew whatever there was to know. Yet Mrs. Atmore's death had not been treated as front-page material, and only one reporter had mentioned the name of Carmody. The deceased, it was stated, had been taking Carmody's accelerated reducing course, and a chance visit from one of her classmates had led to the discovery of the body.

She went through the next paper and the next. A by-liner in the fourth and least conservative of the lot offered his readership a multiple-choice quiz. "Accident—Murder—or Suicide?" he asked, and supplied a scattering of helpful hints. No suicide note had been found, he said, but there were factors pointing to an overdose of an unspecified drug. He hoped that the detectives, who were attempting to establish a link between the untimely death and the jewel theft of the previous day, would not neglect the "wealthy widow" aspect. "*Cherchez l'homme*," he advised, since all too often lonely women of means were driven into the arms of calculating suitors. His last few lines wept for a beautiful young daughter gaily pursuing her studies at college while tragedy struck her remaining parent down.

Ceil refolded the newspapers slowly, because when that was done what else was there to do? If her husband did not come back within a reasonable length of time she would try to reach one of the partners in the law firm that handled the salon's business. She would ask that a lawyer be recommended who specialized in ... In what? She whitened. It seemed to her that her thoughts were shouting a condemnation of Mike, to be heard and acted upon by those who were questioning him.

I must be mad, she thought. Of course he will come home. Why should they hold him? He is no—? Our existence will continue as before, with even its assets negative. Her mind scrawled a heading for those assets. It was "Absence of Open Disgrace."

How long should she wait before calling a lawyer? Would Mike thank her for calling one at all? He had refused the privilege of speaking to her on the telephone, which meant that he wanted nothing of her. It had not entered his head that she might want something of him; that she could have accepted with mendicant humility the smallest coin of reassurance.

Had she tipped the waiter? She spent a few moments trying to remember, unconscious that her absurd preoccupation was a talisman to ward off the real anxiety. A little later she was in the kitchen filling a kettle with water. Mike called her a biddy for drinking tea but

... Had he finished his coffee at dinner? She could not, herself, recall its taste or temperature, but it was seldom hot enough when they sent it up. Did he feel as cold inside as she felt? Did any of his feelings ever match her own?

She left the kettle in the sink. The house phone rang and she went to answer it.

Last night the police captain had walked in unannounced. Perhaps it was he again, using a formal approach to suit the occasion. He would not fob her off as had that officer who telephoned to tell her where Mike was. He would say, "Your husband has been charged with—"

She put the receiver to her ear. She said, "Hello?" and heard Vance Manning's voice.

"Mike isn't here," she said, and thought he answered, "I know," but was not sure.

"May I come up, Ceil?"

"I don't—" She threw that start away and said, "Yes." He was some-one to turn to in a world that held no one to turn to. He did not like his stepbrother. She had known that at once, as would anyone with an ounce of perception. But he had been at pains to seek him out, which meant to her that the roots of a common childhood had en-twined to produce a species of loyalty, however wizened it might be.

She switched on the office lights as she passed through. She opened the door to the corridor and stood there, waiting.

It had never occurred to her to ask Vance Manning what sort of work he did. She had judged from his appearance that he either lived on income or was engaged in something unexacting that left him free to spend most of his time as he chose. But now as he stepped into the full light of the office he looked like a man whose day had been given over to hard and unrewarding labor. She murmured a greeting and he followed her to the living room, dropping his hat and coat on the way.

He remained on his feet after she had seated herself on the edge of a chair. His aura of control over any given situation had vanished. He said abruptly, "Why didn't you leave him long ago?"

She could not answer. He was no one to turn to, and she wished him gone.

"Pride," he said. "Your face is stiff with it. Pride—or conditioning by self-righteous little forebears who put divorce on a par with original sin."

The truth of it burned her cheeks. "You have no right—"

"That's so. I have no right."

His voice was different too. She said involuntarily, "Something's happened to you, Vance. Can I—would you like a drink?"

He smiled then. It so transformed him that she felt as though his dejected entrance had been imagined; merely a projection of her own stress.

"Ceil—you'd probably emerge from the anesthetic after a dangerous operation and inquire about the surgeon's health."

"I'm glad you can smile," she said. "You didn't seem very cheerful when you came in. I was afraid you might be going through some personal crisis."

"You were afraid—for me?"

He was standing too close. She sat well back in her chair and said coldly, "To be truthful—no. I was afraid for myself. I really have no room for troubles that aren't my own—and the way you looked made me think you might have decided to burden me with yours."

His smile had left no traces. He picked up the topmost of the newspapers, rolled it, and brandished it like a weapon. "I can guess the source of your troubles, Ceil. Our boy seems to have done it again."

"What do you mean? Why are you so ready to assume he's done anything?"

"Now there's a question that should have been asked and answered before you married him. I only regret I wasn't on the spot to open your poor blind eyes."

"I wouldn't have been interested in your boyhood grudges. I'm not now." His proximity was sending forth a tide that threatened her. She forced anger, using it as a bulwark. "It was you who sought *him* out. Up to the time I found you in the office he hadn't once referred to your existence—so you couldn't have been there by invitation—and it couldn't have been family feeling that—"

"Family feeling stretches more ways than you know."

"I'm sure it does. I'm sure your peculiar brand of devotion led you to suppose you'd find him in the gutter. You came prepared to gloat—didn't you? What a disappointment it must have been to see how he had prospered."

"One of the contributors to his prosperity has found her way into the news tonight." The paper was still clubbed in his hand. He gestured with it toward the stack on the table. "But you seem to have gone into that pretty thoroughly."

She had to steady her voice. "Does it seem strange to you that I show interest—when a woman I've seen almost every day for weeks is suddenly—suddenly—please—will you stop waving that at me?"

He dropped the paper club. He said defenselessly, "I left you out of my reckoning, Ceil. How could I have known about you?"

That revived her. She treated it with the scorn she thought it deserved. "Don't bother to put on a performance. I haven't enough vanity to expect a pass when Mike isn't around to be annoyed by it."

"I wasn't—never mind. You think he'll be home tonight?"

"Of course he'll be home. If you must know, he's gone to the police of his own free will to see if he can help—"

"It didn't look like free will to me. I happened to witness his exit as I entered the hotel."

"You couldn't have. It was nearly two hours ago—"

"Yes—I've spent all that time deciding just how to tell you—"

"It doesn't matter what you tell me. I won't listen—I don't trust you."

"Trust yourself. He's a sinking rat—"

"Aren't you reversing the proverb?"

"Yes—to suit the case."

"Then if I'm to be the deserting ship what role have you reserved for yourself?"

He did not answer. But when she arose to dismiss him he would not be shown the door.

## CHAPTER 11

Carmody said to Nelson, "All I know is what I heard on television."

"Which was enough to make you rush out of the hotel without your overcoat."

"I wasn't rushing out of the hotel. Your stooge rushed me. Just the same it shook me—a good customer dying like that."

"Dying like what?"

"You've got me. The television announcement was a teaser. The evening papers hadn't been delivered so I went to get one in the lobby to see if she'd slipped and cracked her head or something."

"First the robbery—then death," Nelson said.

"Yeah. Hard lines. Who says bad luck has to come in threes?"

"Perhaps the bad luck started when she enrolled with you."

"You feel like insulting me—enjoy yourself. I still got no explanation for that ring except she left it in the locker. It don't tie in with a thing."

Nelson's office had been small enough at first glance. As the questions went on there were times when it narrowed to cell-size for Carmody. It was much the same sensation he had experienced in his bedroom on the night Ceil told him the police were nosing around.

Clevis had handed him over, said a few words, and disappeared. He was alone with Nelson or almost alone. He did not know at what point a stenographer entered and seated himself near the door. Sensing the unobtrusive presence and twisting around to check, he tried to make a joke of it. "Taking down what I can contribute won't give him writer's cramp. Besides—with your memory you don't need a steno."

Nelson did not smile. Instead he pulled a fast one. "Your comment after reading the anonymous letter was that if you'd been in the Navy it was news to you. You added, 'Or Merchant Marine either.'"

Carmody remembered. He thought it had been a smart play at the time. But at the time he had thought he was smarter than Nelson. He said, "We ran that subject ragged this afternoon."

"There have been developments since this afternoon."

"I hope so for your sake. You were getting no place fast."

Nelson was patient with him. "The letter didn't specify the Navy—or any other branch of our government services."

Carmody kept his mouth shut. Nelson followed suit, utilizing the pause to consult a folder on his desk. Carmody twisted his head again and caught the stenographer scratching himself as though the opportunity were heaven-sent. Carmody received the impression that both men would cheerfully go on doing what they were doing all night.

He broke the deadlock. "Considering the letter didn't mean a thing to me it figures I wouldn't bother to read it word for word."

Nelson lifted his eyes from the folder. "It figures it shouldn't have suggested the Navy to you—considering recent findings."

Carmody said, "I'd have to know what you're talking about to give you an argument."

"I'm not inviting argument. Obviously you felt quite safe in mentioning the government services or you wouldn't have called my attention to them. That left private shipping companies as a more likely source for checking the letter out, and somehow the pains you took with your earnest disclaimer spurred me to the task."

It looked like a second deadlock until Carmody said, "That deck-swabbing pitch suckered you into buying an empty package."

"I neither bought the package nor turned it down," Nelson said, "but my sales resistance has been weakened by information dealing with your past."

"Excuse the horse laugh—mine and the ones you got from all those private shipping lines. You think they keep files on every hand ever

signs on? And with what you were after, it would have to be pretty
long ago because my business is nearly eight years old. Also—I'm not
saying my name runs neck in neck with Smith or Jones but I would-
n't mind having a fin for every seagoing harp who's tagged with it."

"You've hit upon more successful devices for increasing your wealth."

Carmody did not like the sound of that, but he made no complaint.

"The name isn't as common as you might suppose," Nelson said. "As
an alias, however, it does provide a degree of anonymity—and it
does have a truer ring than 'Smith' or 'Jones.' No doubt that's why you
chose it."

Carmody looked like a man with a hearing loss politely trying to follow the conversation.

Nelson seemed to commiserate. "Unfortunately for you we didn't
have to tap the files of all commercial shipping. Your fingerprints on
a property briefcase pointed to a shorter cut."

Carmody heaved mightily to push back the converging walls. "Next
you'll tell me I also obliged by leaving prints at the scene of whatever
you're trying to pin on me."

"I'll tell you first—or remind you—that you were persuaded to
leave them with the police nine years ago—shortly after a tearless
parting with the captain and crew of the *Fiona Driscoll*. Not incidentally, your papers were made out to Michael Crokey. At the start
of the voyage your shipmates called you 'Mick.' Later they dropped
that for coarser designations."

Carmody's voice fought free of his tightened throat. "So I spent a
lousy six months with that outfit. Who wouldn't want to forget it?"

"Who—in fact—would want to remember the suspicion aroused by
a winning streak at cards—still less its immediate result—the crip-
pling of a man in foul fight?"

"Lies—a bunch of sore losers—anybody's smart enough to take
them it has to be foul."

"And suffering from the injustice of it you proceeded to relieve a
woman of cash and sundries a few weeks after you had been put
ashore."

"Talk about a stacked deck!" Carmody swallowed. His own bitter
saliva seemed to act as a sedative. "The old bitch gave me presents
and walking-around money—and reneged when I couldn't take more
of what went with it. Even a bum rap was a nice change." He spoke
with gathering confidence, as though the worst had come and he could
deal with it. "But frame or not it's past history—and short of sprout-
ing wings I've lived it down. As for changing my name—where's the

law that says I couldn't pick something classier for business reasons? So what else have you got up your sleeve?"

"The old saw about history repeating itself," Nelson said, "and its possible application to Mrs. Atmore's death—the recovery of a valuable ring—and a case of vehicular homicide."

"You think you're entitled to grab the pot on that? It's not even three of a kind."

"This isn't a poker game."

"I wouldn't know what to call it—but the mug should be sitting in isn't me. If Spofford hadn't made me out a liar in the first place you wouldn't be giving the 'oh yeah' treatment to every word I say."

"You haven't said much of anything."

"Not anything but the truth. I've been telling it from the beginning."

"Then let's go back to the beginning. Now that you've had time to mull it over are you still sure that none of your acquaintances is bent upon doing you injury?"

Carmody groaned and shook his head. "That tune really bugs you. If I didn't know different I'd think you were trying to get me off the hook."

"That seaman you crippled—"

"Drop it—will you? If you dug that scuttlebutt out of my 'make' read me the place where it says anybody pressed charges."

"The captain of the freighter may have hesitated to press charges. You were signed on at the last minute to replace a defecting crew member—and consequently some of the formalities were overlooked."

"That had nothing to do with it. The bastard was coming at me with a knife—and the other bastards ganging up for the show as if fights on that rotten hulk were something special. I didn't have time to pat him on the head and coax him to be a good boy. I rammed him with the first thing handy and all of a sudden he was Joe Popular instead of a type whose own family would congratulate me for putting him out of commission."

"Would there be rejoicing in your family if you came to grief?"

Carmody was busy brooding aloud over his wrongs. "I should never have told that old bitch I'd sailed on the *Fiona*—" Nelson's question penetrated, taking him by surprise. "You think my wife would start dancing if—?"

"I was referring to your mother—father—sisters—brothers—"

"You're mixing me up with two other guys. When I paid my so-called debt to society, I testified I was a lonely orphan. It still stands."

"Does it? You wouldn't have been the first prisoner who tried to keep his loved ones out of it. But now—by your own account—they'd have reason to be proud of you."

Carmody said piously, "Right—and I sure hope there's a grapevine where Mom and Dad are so they know how their boy made out."

Nelson matched the intended bathos. "No doubt it was grief at losing your parents that drove you to take ship so suddenly."

"To be frank it wasn't. They'd both been gone a couple of years and even the house I was born in was torn down to make room for a development—like the police found out when they tried to get a line on me. But I was still in my hotheaded twenties when I got the bug to sample life at sea. I guess by 'sudden' you mean I had to cut a few corners—but in those days it was now or never with me—no stopping to think things through."

"But in these days you compensate by thinking things through with the utmost care."

"Running a business like mine I have to."

"Yes—I should think so. Are you on visiting terms with any of your clients?"

Carmody's eyes blinked. He covered with a show of rubbing them and yawning loudly. "Like you see I'm out on my feet from getting too much of them in working hours." He stared at his watch, shook his wrist, and held it to his ear. "Must have stopped. It couldn't be that early."

"It's ten after ten," Nelson said. "We've ample time to get down to facts."

"Don't you ever knock off?"

"When my chores are done. According to your dossier you were born in Brooklyn."

"Something else you're holding against me? Have a heart—"

"Yet you stated that you had lost your way in Brooklyn on the night of the hit-and-run."

"I'm stating it again. People who live there all their lives lose their way—I hadn't been back for years and I wouldn't even have recognized my old neighborhood with all the new buildings—"

"And none of the old neighbors around to recognize you—and with the school you attended torn down as well—not one of your teachers left to vouch for your character. How very sad."

Carmody could not keep the hint of smugness out of his, "Sure—that's right."

The phone rang. Nelson spoke into it, and listened, his responses monosyllabic. After a terminal "Thanks" he pushed cigarettes and matches across the desk.

"Things must be looking up. Your stooge wouldn't let me stop to buy a pack." Carmody helped himself and made a fumble of striking and applying a match. He took in smoke as though it were food and drink.

"Things aren't looking up for you," Nelson said. "There are those around me who accuse me of having too much heart—but I thought you might need something to cushion the shock."

Carmody went on smoking. When he removed the cigarette, the lengthening ash broke, powdering his clothing. He dusted himself off. "What bush are you beating around?"

"I've just had the first installment of a laboratory report. Your prints have made another appearance."

"I'll bite. Where?"

"In a bathroom. Mrs. Atmore's, to be exact."

"I'm disappointed in you. That trick's got a full head of moss."

Nelson pushed an ashtray toward him. "You'd better put that out. It's burning your fingers."

It had burned them. Carmody swore, and dropped the cigarette butt. He spread his hand, wet the smarting spot with his tongue, and narrowed his eyes to inspect the incipient blister.

Nelson said, "Take all the time you need. I want a convincing explanation as much as you do—but don't labor to produce a flea."

"Look—you asked me was I on visiting terms with my customers. Right?"

"Right. And you avoided the lie direct."

"Avoided nothing—except to stop you from taking off in the wrong direction. I wasn't at Mrs. Atmore's on a social call. The firm that makes the low-calorie diet for me goofed on the reorder. Their excuse was they had to do some experimenting—me telling them the ladies were complaining that the regular stuff on the market was much tastier. But what I'm getting at—they promised to send it Thursday morning and it didn't come until after the accelerated class went home. Even then it was only a few cans which they said would have to tide me over and the rest would come on Monday. Anyway—Mrs. Atmore was clean out on account of she stuck closer to the rules about drinking it than the others. And being such a stickler she started to make a noise. I had to swear she'd have a family-size can by suppertime and I told Cora to deliver it on her way home from work. But I didn't get a chance to remind her before she left and the way she is I figured she could forget. Well—to keep Mrs. Atmore from raising a stink next morning—I decided to drop it off myself." His grin was too

feeble to live for more than a moment. "What happened to me should-
n't happen to a dog. I walked over—and it could have been due to my
lunch not agreeing with me and on top of that the cold hitting my
stomach—but I got the hell of a cramp going up in the elevator—and
the minute she opened her door I had to bust out with 'Where's the
john?' I don't embarrass easy but you should've got a load of her face.
You'd have to know her to—"

Nelson said, "Unhappily, she was dead when I met her."

"Yeah—I can't get used to that—it don't want to sink in."

"It will. Meanwhile—try not to lose the thread of your composition."

"Brother! You sure are out to get me over a barrel."

"You *are* over a barrel." The stenographer caught Nelson's signal. He
studied his notes and read aloud, "'... you should've got a load of her
face. You'd have to know her to—'"

"I don't need help," Carmody said. "She cleared her wires to give me
directions and I shoved the can of Vitrate at her and took off. I had
to run through her bedroom to get to the john and on the return trip
I hung back to take a few drags. What I really wanted was a drink before I showed—with her acting like plumbing was for the common
people. About those fingerprints—scouting around for an ashtray I
guess I could have touched a bureau or something."

"Did you find an ashtray?"

"Sure—I mean—come to think of it—" He came to think of it. "No.
Fact is the room was so prissy I went back and flushed the butt down
the toilet."

"The episode stands out as one of those rare occasions when you carried your own cigarettes."

"I always carry them outside of working hours. I'd have bought some
in the lobby tonight if your stooge—" He shrugged. He met Nelson's
eyes, his own radiating frankness and honesty. "Well—that's the
story."

"We'll edit it for discrepancies. There are two bathrooms in Mrs. Atmore's apartment—the one she doesn't use is quite close to the living
room. Consensus has it that she's a fastidious woman who might not
permit anyone but a close friend to enter her private domain."

"If that ain't what the agencies call nit-picking!"

"My job often hinges on a capacity for nit-picking."

"Then you're a natural for it. I'll take your word on the layout of the
apartment—and you can take mine she wasn't giving it a thought—
not with me about to—"

"You disposed of your cigarette—and?"

"I came out to find she'd recovered enough to let bygones be bygones. She invited me to sit down—which I did—hoping it would raise my stock. I asked her if Cora had brought the Vitrate and she said it had been left a good half hour ago. Seemed she'd already had a glass on account of missing lunch."

"Did she mention that the flavor had improved?"

Carmody looked at Nelson as though he were debating his sanity. "A little thing like running out of sensible questions don't stop you. Okay—she mentioned the flavor—but not to say it had improved. They got to beef about something—so she claimed she liked the old taste better. But after she got that off her chest she thanked me for being too conscientious to trust Cora—and threw in a bunch of compliments about how the course was helping her. And I said I better leave while my hat fit."

"Did you speak to the elevator boy on your way up or down?"

"No. The car was full—and I didn't have to ask him the apartment number. She'd given it when I promised the extra service."

"I'd call it extraordinary service."

"It never hurts to keep them happy, and I knock off at three every Thursday anyway. I don't lose by it. A men's club rents the use of the swimming pool and gyms with my assistant standing guard to see the wear and tear don't swallow the profits. Also I wasn't going out of my way. I had to be in the neighborhood."

"Why?"

"Why did I have to be in the neighborhood? There's a place near her carries the type shoes I work in and the last couple of pairs were too tight. They said my foot must've spread and wanted me to stop in to be fitted again. Name of the store is Buckman." He added, "Only what with one thing and another I didn't get there."

"I'm interested in the one thing and another."

"I hate to disappoint you but it ain't interesting."

"What time did you reach Mrs. Atmore's apartment?"

"About twenty to four. All told I didn't stay more than a half hour. If she was robbed that afternoon it had to be after I left."

"We don't know at what time of day the theft occurred," Nelson said, "but her call to the police that night was undoubtedly prompted by her discovery that her favorite ring was missing. That was what she described first." He did not say that the ring was all she had described.

"And it turns out the ring was the only thing not stolen."

Nelson looked unimpressed by the observation. He said, "Mrs. Atmore kept her jewel box on the bureau. Did you notice it when you were in the bedroom?"

"I was hunting an ashtray and I didn't notice a thing except I couldn't find one. And if I was trying to help myself out by lying I'd say, 'Sure I noticed it,' which would have to mean that it was lifted later. Only I wouldn't put it past you to insist I picked it up and sat talking to her with it bulging under my coat."

"There wouldn't have been a bulge. The box was found under the bed."

"It was?" Carmody seemed to assume that the box had been empty. "Well—I didn't put it there."

"When Mrs. Atmore came to the door did her appearance suggest that she had arisen from—or was preparing for a nap?"

"The shape I was in I wouldn't know. But the second time around I saw she was wearing a robe zipped to the chin and had maybe run to your other bathroom to put on a fresh face—so at that I must have noticed she wasn't fixed up to start with. Also—now that you remind me—she did yawn a couple of times before I left." He added, "It could have been a hint for me to get going though."

"Where *did* you 'get going'?"

"With the weather so rotten I didn't feel like mushing to the shoe store. It wouldn't make sense trying them on over wet socks—so I went into the bar of the hotel on the corner. It was the right day for breaking training. I sat there relaxing—watching the crowds drift in."

"Of course it was too crowded for the bartender or anyone else to note your presence?"

Carmody said innocently, "That's right—plus the lighting was too gloomy for me to swap vital statistics with anyone. Mostly I thought about how to kill the evening. As a rule—closing early on Thursdays— me and my wife live it up a little—dinner—and sometimes a show or a nightclub afterwards. But this once she wasn't in the mood and wanted me to go alone and enjoy myself." He paused, as though for disconsolate tally of a wasted opportunity. "When I stepped outside again it was coming down hard and the rush hour had crept up and all the cabs were full. I wished I had my car but it seemed screwy to go get it with nothing particular in mind. So in the end I went back to the bar—had another drink—ate a bite in the coffee shop—and did some phoning. Finally I got on to a pal who said why didn't I stop in for a beer and a friendly game. I said I would if I was lucky enough to catch a cab—which I was. We played till eleven or so and called it a night. Satisfied?"

"At least your pal can vouch for the end of your saga. His name and address please."

"No soap. I'm not setting him up for you. The laws in this burg being what they are how do I know the police won't decide it wasn't a friendly game?"

"You seem to be making a habit of destroying your alibis as fast as you give them."

"Why should I need an alibi for—?"

"Provided you did—and provided you could cause this 'pal' to materialize—I gather that his value as a character witness would be nil. Did you lose as usual in the friendly game?"

"What's with 'as usual'? I don't—I broke even."

"I'm toying with the possibility that habitual gambling has depleted your assets to an alarming extent."

"Sure you're toying—and you want it both ways—but the joker who made off with that jewelry wouldn't be worrying win or lose—not when he could recoup by a run to the nearest fence."

"Jewels like the emerald ring will not be easy to dispose of for a while. The description has been broadcast and even if the stone were removed from the setting and cut, no fence would pay a high price in view of the depreciation and risk involved."

"I wouldn't know." Carmody tried not to look knowing.

"It also occurs to me," Nelson said, "that the thief might have been accumulating other pressing I. O. U.'s—not necessarily those racked up at cards. There are other forms of gambling—"

"Look—I been going along with you a hell of a lot further than I have to. I gave you a run-down on my afternoon—which by all accounts is when the dirty work happened—and if her dying so sudden was more dirty work there's cast-iron proof of where I was today. So what's the time between got to do with you?"

"Let's say I'm attempting to establish your credibility."

"Goddamit—you wouldn't have to if that Spofford—"

Nelson cut the tirade short. "I've sent a man out to see her—on the chance that she's had a second thought."

"Thanks for nothing. If you sent a man you sent him to see she sticks to what she said the first time—but you could have saved yourself the trouble. I know how to handle the conniving little—"

"That's all for now," Nelson said.

"No, it's not all—not by a—"

"If you can't tear yourself away I'll be glad to supply free bed and board."

Carmody gave him no time to change his mind.

## CHAPTER 12

He had torn himself away, not feeling the wrench at all. He reached the chill sanctuary of the street without stopping to button his overcoat. It flapped about him as he put distance between himself and the inquisitor of Homicide West. At first his relief at being free was insulation against the winds of March. Then he was heated by a fire of rage which he fed with makeshift fuel. His bookmaker was cast upon the flames. Next it was the dead woman's turn, to be followed by Spofford, Nelson, and everyone else who had crossed him. But beneath these logs the kindling that had started the blaze would not be reduced to ashes. It burned on, perverse and indestructible. He knew its name. He had known it for the greater part of his life.

Temporarily he had mislaid the fact that there was such a thing as transportation. Striking out in the general direction of the Easton, he inhaled the beery smell of a corner saloon. He entered, ordered a shot of rye that his inner climate did not need, and tossed it down. He pictured Ceil, tense and waiting, and to prolong her anxiety he signaled for a refill. She would not be thinking of his welfare, but of what would happen to a business hit by scandal. Let her suffer. Her penny-pinching had forced him into his present situation. He gained a measure of comfort by persuading himself that this was true.

The whisky tasted like rotgut. He decided that he could not afford to punish his stomach further for the pleasure of punishing Ceil. An absent-minded drink later he threw a five-dollar bill on the bar and it was replaced by a single and a few coins. He accused the bartender of short-changing him, and left with the sound of yet another defeat in his ears, accepting it as part of the plot to undo him.

There was a cab parked in front of the saloon. The driver was talking to a man in a windbreaker. Carmody asked without charm if the cab was free or not, and got in without waiting for reply. He expected an argument, and in his bellicose mood would have welcomed one. But it developed that the other fellow was not a prospective passenger. He and the driver must have been cronies because he hopped into the front seat and went along for the ride.

Carmody's threatening statement concerning the illegality of extra freight was not contested. He appeased himself by scowling at the extra freight's neckline. Its spruce look was enough to fan his rage although he had not even glimpsed the face that went with it.

To compensate for his rout in the saloon he did not tip the driver. He dashed into the hotel before protest could be launched, regretting that it would be folly to start a slugging match on home ground. He had to wait for the elevator but exchanged no words with Denis when it came. He was saving the words for Ceil, and maybe more than words if she so much as uttered a wrong peep.

He let himself into the office and slammed the door. He heard voices and charged the rest of the way.

The cool appraising stare of his stepbrother brought him to a standstill. All but pawing the living-room rug he bellowed, "What do you think you're doing—!"

Vance stepped in front of Ceil as though it were his duty and his right to shield her from unpleasant sights. "I came because I was sure you had taken up permanent residence elsewhere."

"I believe you!"

Vance turned his back and spoke to Ceil. It was her answering murmur, soft and intimate sounding, that did it. Carmody did not see her move away from Vance. Through the red glaze of his eyes he saw only that arrogant back. The table lamp felt weightless in his hand. He hefted it easily, swung it high, and brought it down with all his strength.

Carmody had not been permitted to go forth unaccompanied. He was tailed by a detective named Bonino whose patrician features and general bearing would have carried him far as a confidence man. When the suspect entered the saloon Bonino had time to plant a cab outside and arrange a temporary swap of his elegant topcoat for the driver's windbreaker. The plan to pose as the driver's buddy and hitch a ride to the next destination was not orthodox, but if Carmody wanted a cab it seemed wise to have it ready. At eleven thirty in that part of town, a second one might not have appeared soon enough to be helpful to Bonino.

Bonino kept his face averted, took his place up front, and the ride ended at the Easton. He was familiar with the layout there. He reclaimed his coat and followed Carmody into the lobby in time to see him board an elevator. He was rather disappointed that the chase had ended so tamely. On the chance that Carmody would reappear he decided to wait a while before he called headquarters for further instructions. The lobby was fairly well populated with homing guests and patrons of the Easton's supper club. He selected a chair near the desk, so situated that those entering and exiting had to pass it, and wedged himself into a stock-market discussion with two affluent gentlemen from Oklahoma. He managed to seem as affluent and knowledgeable as they, but was not carried away to the extent that he missed what went on around him.

He contributed to the discussion for five or six minutes, in the course of which a man with a doctor's bag came in from the street and went to the desk for his key. He had started to walk away when a man who had been busy at the other end of the desk called, "Just a minute, Doctor," and hurried out to intercept him.

The two stood talking in front of Bonino, blocking his view. He was about to resign from his seat on the Exchange and rise, when he heard Carmody's name. He listened, trying to shut out the lesser talk. Not all of the words reached him, but among those he heard were "emergency" and "roof," and the doctor added to their significance by nodding and heading in the right direction.

Bonino was abreast of him before he reached the elevator. He opened the conversation by simulating great relief.

"I'm glad you got back, Doctor. They just told me at the desk that you were on the way up."

The doctor grumbled, "Every time I make an outside call I'm wanted here. It never fails." He assumed quite readily that Bonino was a friend or relation of the couple on the roof. "What's the trouble? The assistant manager doesn't know but he appears to think it's serious."

"I don't know either," Bonino said. "The message I received was garbled—but it sounded urgent enough to bring me here in a hurry."

"Well—we'll soon see."

They were stepping into the elevator when he said it, and it served as Bonino's passport. The operator knew the doctor, at least by sight, and found it unnecessary to challenge anyone who was on speaking terms with him.

He said, "Where to this time, Doc? You haven't ridden with me since Mrs. Tupperman sprained her back."

The doctor said tartly, "That's right, Denis—and it's unlikely I'd be riding with you now if Carmody had been able to raise his own physician."

"Carmody? I took him up a few minutes ago. I wouldn't say he was sick—exactly."

No one asked him what he meant by "exactly," and he did not explain. But prompted by either curiosity or courtesy he got out of the car with his passengers and led them to the Carmody apartment.

A woman opened the door. Denis said, "I've brought Dr. Oates, Mrs.

Carmody. Is there anything else I can—?"

She said, "Thank you," but did not really see him or Bonino, who stood behind the doctor. Her eyes were on the arm holding the black bag. "Please—in here."

The doctor followed her. Denis would have tagged along, but Bonino said, "We'll manage, Jack," and shut the door upon him. Then he moved quietly across the office.

He could have tramped flat-footed into the other room without arousing protest. No attention was paid to him.

A longer length of man than Carmody lay stretched out on the couch. He had bled upon the upholstery under his head, and there was a patch of blood on the rug several feet from where he lay. The front of the woman's dress was stained too.

She looked down at the couch. "Vance—?" She turned to the doctor. "I'm afraid he's unconscious again—he got up and—it's the back of his head—I tried to bandage—"

The doctor addressed the patient. "Can you hear me?"

There was no answer.

He reached for a limp wrist and held it for the count. Poker-faced, he said, "I'll wash my hands before I have a look."

"I'll show you—in the kitchen—I think my husband's using the bathroom."

If the doctor had believed the man on the couch to be her husband, he did not say so. When he came back he looked Bonino's way. "Can you help me to shift him on his side?"

Bonino came forward. He expected to strain against an inert weight. The "unconscious" body seemed to lend assistance.

Just below the crown of the head the fairish hair was caked. The doctor cut some of it away. He asked for a razor and a small one, obviously the woman's, was brought to him. He passed the new blade through a flame before he used it. The cut disclosed looked nasty, and there was a swelling to boot. Bonino saw the patient's broad shoulders tense, but there was no other manifestation of pain beyond a grimace on the profiled face and a show of pallor beneath its even tan.

The woman's face was a starker white, as though she too had bled. She evidenced no surprise at Bonino's presence. Her actions and reactions, he thought, were like those of a sleepwalker. He helped her to fetch and carry, disposing of wads of crimsoned gauze, bringing hot water from the kitchen, and measuring—at the doctor's orders—a purplish disinfectant into a basin.

As he moved about, his foot crunched something into the rug. He looked down and saw fragments of pottery lying where they might have eluded a hurried sweeper's eye. He had noted before a perfect circle of dust on one of the small tables, such dust as accumulates under a static object.

The doctor beckoned again. The patient now wore a neatly wound turban. Bonino helped to support him while a spoonful of liquid was forced between his lips. His swallowing reflex functioned. No drop of the liquid was spilled.

The doctor straightened up. He did not let the question break on the woman's lips. He said, "How did it happen, Mrs. Carmody?"

She transferred her asking gaze to the man on the couch. It seemed to have the effect of actual contact. He opened his eyes and spoke. "An accident."

"Vance—I thought you were—"

He raised his head. "Playing possum. I didn't want the doctor sidetracked before he'd done his work—besides—it took all my energy to refrain from making unmanly noises."

The doctor said dryly, "I advise you to go on saving your energy. You've lost quite a bit of blood."

"No more than I've donated at a throw to the Red Cross." His voice was fairly strong. He was sitting up, his head resting against the back of the couch. He smiled at the woman. "I'll be able to leave in a few minutes."

The doctor said, "I must insist that you spend a night or two in a hospital. I can't rule out the possibility of concussion. You sound clear enough but it's often delayed—"

"No hospital, Doctor. A night's sleep in my own bed will set me right."

The doctor hesitated. His eyes went to the stain on the rug. He was torn, the interested Bonino supposed, between professional integrity and the temptation to spare the hotel embarrassment, since it was probably his chief source of income. Bonino had not heard the absent member of the ménage come out of the bathroom. He wondered what he was up to. The sum total of his observations made him feel that he had ample justification and nothing to lose by identifying himself. But he waited for the doctor's next move.

"You say it was an accident?"

"To my extreme mortification, yes. I was showing off by doing parlor tricks. I lost my footing and grabbed a lamp for support. It came down and whacked me as I fell and smashed to bits against my thick skull."

"Hmmm—well—I can't send you to a hospital without your consent." The doctor had voted to spare the hotel. He began to repack his bag. "Where do you live?"

"Downstairs."

"In the hotel?"

"Yes. Would you like me to settle your bill now, Doctor?"

Bonino saw the woman's startled face. She took a step toward the couch but the patient did not look at her.

The doctor said, "That will be quite all right, Mr.—?"

"Manning."

"I'm Dr. Oates, Mr. Manning. If you should need me during the night don't hesitate to call my room."

Bonino stopped being a spectator. "Mr. Manning—was Mr. Carmody assisting you with the parlor tricks?"

The light eyes found him and focused upon him. "Are you a member of the hotel staff? I'm sorry but there are so many managers and assistant managers that I—"

"By strange coincidence," Bonino said, "I'm a member of the police force." He had his credentials in his hand.

No one asked to see them. The doctor had gone an uneasy red. He said, "But I thought—you led me to believe you were a friend of—" He looked at Mrs. Carmody, who looked numb.

"Perhaps you're too trusting, Doctor," Bonino said.

"See here—I don't know what business you have with these people but I suggest that Mr. Manning is in no condition to be harassed."

"You haven't insisted that he go to a hospital. That satisfies me as to his condition."

"The question you asked won't set me back," Manning said. "Mr. Carmody didn't arrive in time to assist me with the parlor tricks. He entered just as I'd wound them up so clumsily."

"And locked himself in the bathroom because he gets sick at the sight of blood," Bonino said. "I'm afraid I can't afford to be as credulous as the doctor. Mrs. Carmody—I want your husband's version of what happened. Will you please call him?"

Manning said, "I heard him leave the bathroom. He's asleep in his bed by this time."

Carmody gave him the lie. His hangdog entrance contrasted strongly with the aggressiveness he had shown when last seen. The starch has been taken out of him, Bonino thought. But he was wrong.

Carmody almost knocked him down in a sudden dash for the office. Bonino righted himself too late. The connecting door had slammed. The key had turned in the lock, and a moment later the outer door slammed too.

Nelson intended to go home as soon as he had rid the office of Carmody. But one of his men came in with a problem concerning another case, and by the time that had been disposed of, the stenographer brought him the transcribed notes. He looked them over, remembered that Clevis was still on the premises, and summoned him.

"Go home," he said wearily. "You've been putting in time and a half."

"That dinner I had at your house was like the start of a new day." Clevis had entered at an unusually fast clip. He stared at the empty "guest chair" and adjusted his sagging jaw. "I give up—where is he?"

"I doubt he knows, himself."

"You didn't hold him?"

"He won't leave town. Bonino's tailing him."

"Well—that's a help." His disappointed face did not bear out the words. "Or would be if he was part of a gang and you expected him to finger the top man."

The transcription did not appease him. He read it carefully and put it back on the desk. "So now I'm up to date. You think a jury would be snowed by the part where it says he delivered a can of Vitrate and was afflicted by colic en route?"

"It depends on the jurors. With Cora's shortcomings as a witness they'll want more than the ring as proof of guilt. They might not be impressed by Carmody's moral tone—but neither will he strike them as being inherently stupid. And with a boxful of trinkets to choose from, the selection of the most incriminating item surely implies a very low I. Q.—unless they're prepared to accept the theory that criminals have a subconscious desire to be caught."

"You can give that one back to Freud. You want a real theory—I got it. The ring didn't have to be in the box. Maybe it was laying around loose and he couldn't resist. That much was stupid. But come right down to it there was nothing stupid about the locker as a hidey-hole. He'd have figured to retrieve the ring himself before Cora found it— or else he'd have figured the dressing room for empty when she made her rounds—and counted on it being out of sight out of mind with her once she'd turned it in. He didn't count on us—but any old way the locker provided that ready-made bit about dames forever leaving stuff behind."

"And your theory on the jewel box hidden under the bed?"

Clevis said halfheartedly, "Simple. That's where she always kept it. They been known to get screwy kinks at her age. Or maybe she shoved it there afterwards—like locking the barn door."

"Why did she tell the police it was missing?"

"That's only the way we heard it. But if she was still hysterical when the detectives came she'd have made even less sense when she phoned for them. So the precinct could have got the message wrong and just thought she said the whole works. One thing I know for sure—she'll never give us the straight of it—but you got Carmody dead to rights with those fingerprints."

"Invention on my part—inspired by a telephone call that had nothing to do with the case. According to the maid the apartment was thoroughly dusted—which means there's slim hope of fingerprints anywhere."

"Not on the box either?"

"Just hers."

"So what? Your invention wasn't a patch on his—but it paid off some. You made him admit he'd been there."

"But not on the day of her death."

"No—but if the lab reports and the P. M. were in it's ten to one they'd show he gave her a slow-acting poison."

"The P. M. won't be completed until tomorrow—but I stopped at the lab after dinner and got a partial lab report—including the Vitrate analysis. Mrs. Grimes's supply had not been doctored. One half of Mrs. Atmore's had."

"One half had been—? You knew that when you set him loose?"

"Stop looking at me as though I've lost my grip. Do you want the gist of the lab report?"

"What harm could it do me?"

Nelson said, "The formula donated by Annie Dale Grimes consisted of ten ounces of powdered skim milk, less than an ounce of corn oil, and a pinch of saccharine—which is more or less what the brands on the open market—"

Clevis shuddered. "People eat that?"

"They add water and drink it. Some of the commercial products come ready-mixed and contain low-caloried flavoring agents to make them more palatable. But Carmody doesn't believe in pampering his clients. He yielded only when they complained of the taste. That part of his statement has been confirmed by our Annie."

"Okay—so he yields by adding a little poison."

"I haven't used the word. What had been added to one of the two cans in Mrs. Atmore's kitchen was a nonlethal dose of crushed barbiturate pills and a generous sprinkling of nutmeg."

Clevis looked as though the mixture had been forced down his own throat. "A nonlethal—?" He gagged on it.

"The exact amount couldn't be determined because more than a third of the Vitrate had been consumed and the additions hadn't been evenly distributed. The P. M. will be more accurate—but even with three times the lab's estimated dosage the barbiturate alone could not have caused death."

Clevis mumbled, "I had all my eggs in that Vitrate. Now every time my wife puts nutmeg in the custard I'll be eating crow."

Nelson said gravely, "So far not too much is known about the pharmacology of barbiturates combined with nutmeg but—"

"Go ahead—needle me. The transcription reads he delivered the Vitrate personally. I should've realized he wouldn't own up to anything that could backfire."

Nelson said, "Cora is supposed to have delivered the opened can. The one he said he delivered was innocent of barbiturates—but the nutmeg was present in smaller—"

"I'll drop it if you will—but all the same—ain't you mislaying a green car driven by a man who'd been to sea—and the fact he did time for rooking a middle-aged dame who was high and dry in every place but the cash department? Just show me the difference between the M. O. then and now."

"He didn't murder the other middle-aged dame."

"He might've if she hadn't got her innings first. Mrs. Atmore wasn't so lucky. It's my latest guess she caught on to him and threatened to make it hot—and he went to her house on Thursday to coax her to shut up—like over a poisoned cup of weak tea—or whatever she drinks when she ain't drinking Vitrate."

"And they had this tea party in the bedroom?"

"Sure—it being the same M. O."

"If they were on such friendly terms at that point why would it be necessary for him to kill her? He could only hope to profit if she were alive. Her lawyers tell us the wealth was her husband's and will revert to her daughter."

Clevis said, "See what I mean about letting him go? Me, I would've kept at him and at him until he coughed up his guts— You want me to take that phone?"

Nelson took it. When he hung up, Clevis said, "Bonino?"

"Yes—with a full plate of crow for me."

"How's that?"

Nelson told him. Before he came to the punch line, Clevis stopped being a critic. "Now we've really got him," he said enthusiastically. "Assault and battery with intent to kill—and with that on the ticker it won't be long till we get the whole sad story from his own eggy lips. Bonino should be bringing him in pretty quick. Can I—?"

"You haven't heard Bonino's whole sad story," Nelson said. "He can't bring in a man who isn't there."

## CHAPTER 13

A pale sun came into the bedroom. Nelson raised his eyelids and saw Kyrie standing over him. She was wearing a dress he liked.

"Early bird," he said, smiling up at her.

"It's after nine."

"Kyrie—why didn't you wake me?" The concerns that sleep had held in abeyance flung him out of bed.

"Don't take it to heart, Grid. Most people oversleep every Saturday of their lives. You do once in a blue moon and nothing dire comes of it."

"I'm going to get me a room and an alarm clock." He put on his robe.

"No right-thinking alarm clock would have had the heart to wake you. I didn't even hear you come to bed."

"Yes, you did. You wound yourself around me and sighed, 'High time.'"

"Force of habit—but probably true. Whenever you're home to dinner and have to go out again you think it gives you license to work all night."

He kissed the top of her head and disappeared into the bathroom. He did not sing in the shower. Nor did he think blithe thoughts while he shaved and dressed.

The phone calls he made before he went down to breakfast did not lift his spirits, and neither did Sammy's benign smile or her observation that it appeared to be a good morning. She left the kitchen as soon as she had seen to it that he and Kyrie were well served. If he was thankful for anything, it was that she had made no reference to the case of Alice Thwaite.

"You're letting your eggs get cold," Kyrie said. "There's nothing worse."

"Except an error of judgment."

She gave him a quick look but did not ask why he had chosen that particular exception. "Sammy's off to do some extra-special shopping.

Want to know why?"

He tried to show interest. "It seems quite a while since she's been so cheerful."

"You can thank Junie's classmate's toothache."

"Would you mind backing up a little?"

"You're still oversleeping, Grid, or you'd have caught the scent of new-baked chocolate layer cake. The Washington tour was cut short because young master Richard refused to sit still for a strange dentist. He screamed for Dr. Joel whose chairs are equipped with television screens. So Junie will be home this afternoon."

Nelson felt somewhat cheered. "Here's to young master Richard. What time?"

"Two o'clock. Sammy and I will drive to the airport to meet him."

"I wish I could make it. But I'll try to join the welcoming committee here as soon as I can."

"Of course you will."

He thought he detected the sound of martyrdom. "Why don't you say it, Kyrie?"

"Say what?"

"That if I hadn't resisted promotion I'd have more regular hours and could spend more time with you and Junie." He knew that he was being uncommonly touchy. She had made no attempt to influence him when he declined to fill a vacancy left by one of the seven deputy commissioners.

Kyrie said, "I never believed for a moment you'd accept that latest offer. For one thing, deputy commissioners are civilians, which meant you'd have to resign from the Force."

He said defensively, "If I wanted to be an executive I wouldn't have joined the Force."

"I know that. You even fought making captain because you thought it would curtail your activities in the field—and you still grudge every bit of legwork you have to assign from behind a desk—because you want to do it yourself and know you could do it better."

"My wife understands me."

"As well as anybody can understand anybody. It took practice and I still have far to go—but I've managed to gather that being a policeman pure and simple comes closer than anything else to your need for direct contact with every type of human being extant—and it's lucky for you the extra money and the status that go with promotion aren't what you want or need."

"But not so lucky for you."

"True—only I'm such a fool for punishment that if there were more of you around I'd turn bigamist."

"Pure and simple policeman notwithstanding?"

It was unlike him to ask for reassurance. Kyrie said lightly, "On second thought not very pure—and even less simple." Then she said, "If you did make an error of judgment it will probably turn out not to be. Is it in connection with the reducing business?"

Last night at dinner, Nelson had told her of his visit to the Easton and of his subsequent encounters with the lively ex-stripper and her unlively classmate. "I had another go at Carmody," he said, and gave her a condensed account of it. He paused to light a cigarette before he went on to Bonino's call from the hotel.

Kyrie filled the pause. She seemed inclined to agree with Clevis. "I should think you had enough to hold him on suspicion of murder. Why didn't you?"

"Chiefly because I was influenced by his refusal to admit that he might have been framed or to name anyone who might have framed him. Yet he'd been grasping at far weaker straws." He looked at her. "Am I making sense?"

She said candidly, "Not much. He doesn't sound like a man who'd risk a lot to protect anyone who'd framed him—or anyone else for that matter."

"I don't think he would—unless by protecting someone he was protecting himself."

"His wife?"

Nelson shook his head. "It would have to be someone whose vengeance he feared more than he feared due process of law—and it's my impression that no matter what his wife knew or suspected she'd exercise her right not to testify against him. Or it was my impression. I had him spotted for Bonino, who followed him when he left the office. A bit later I sent for Clevis and was soundly criticized for allowing him to remain at large."

Kyrie did an indignant right-about-face. "There's nothing new about criticism from that quarter—and what you've done isn't irrevocable—not with Bonino on the job."

He smiled faintly. "Hold the phone. Clevis was still going strong when Bonino called back to say that he'd lost the 'suspect.'"

She had met most of the men on the squad. She said, "Oh no! Bonino's one of your best—"

"It wasn't his fault." Nelson went on to tell her the means by which Bonino had landed in the Carmody apartment, and of what he had found there. "Bonino's convinced," he said, "that Carmody, returning after a hard night's work in my office, conked his wife's gentleman caller on the head. He'd had a few drinks to begin with, and gave evidence in the cab that he was spoiling for a fight. Bonino holds that if Manning's story were true there'd have been no reason to bolt—or no more reason than there was when he left headquarters—and he could have attempted it then if he wanted to because he seemed completely unaware of a tail."

"But Bonino's so resourceful," Kyrie said. "I should think he'd have got that locked door open in time to pick up the scent."

"He found the telephone first—with the intention of having Carmody stopped at the desk. But the operator was slow to answer so he ran to the door and did the key-recovery trick, poking it until it dropped onto a sheet of paper which he drew back inside. That took time—and when he unlocked the door and rushed out, the elevator had come and gone. There was no point in trying the fire stairs. It would have taken at least fifteen minutes even if he broke all records. On the next ascent the elevator boy said sure he'd taken Carmody down. He'd asked him if Mr. Manning was the one who'd needed the doctor, remembering that he'd taken him up earlier, and Carmody said to mind his own business. No one noticed him in the lobby, and none of the cab companies have had time to come up with anything. Points of exit ditto."

"You'll find him," Kyrie said, "and now at least you know he has something to run from."

"You and Clevis must have gone to the same school."

"Grid—does the elevator boy recognizing Mrs. Carmody's caller mean that he's a regular—or that he's seen him around the hotel?"

"Bonino asked him that. He said he'd taken Manning up several times. His room is in a different section of the hotel. He'd take another elevator to get to it. There's something odd about that too. When the doctor asked him where he lived he said, 'Downstairs,' and Bonino saw Mrs. Carmody jump as though she had heard startling news."

"Maybe he doesn't live there. Maybe he just said that to keep the doctor from sending him to a hospital."

"No—he's registered. I'll have a talk with him this morning. With Mrs. Carmody too."

"I can see why your first impression of her has altered," Kyrie said. "But there isn't necessarily anything wrong with entertaining a male guest."

"I don't know whether that's an example of 'we girls must stick together' or whether you're trying to comfort me for my shattered illusions. But I'll weather her defection if I must. Annie Dale mentioned that there had been dressing-room gossip of a handsome man courting Mrs. C. in the lobby."

"Does that fit Manning?"

"In spades—according to Bonino."

"He couldn't be as handsome as you are—especially when you smile."

"I wish I didn't have to wrench my handsome self away from here."

He got his coat and she went with him to the door. "What was all that about nutmeg, Grid?"

"Take a look at a book called *Science in Crime Detection*. It's on the shelf near the door in the living room."

He was barely out of the house when she called him back. "Grid—Mrs. Grimes is on the phone—do you want to talk to her?"

"Not now. I'm sure she just wants to know how you like Vitrate."

Nelson went directly to the Hotel Easton and rode up to the fifth floor. A chambermaid answered his knock, her arms full of towels and crumpled bed linen. She started to stuff the load into a hamper on wheels, and dropped a few towels and a pillowcase. Nelson swooped to pick them up for her. One of the towels had been used to remove makeup. He asked thoughtfully if Mr. Manning was at home. She said he had just gone into the bathroom to shave and should she tell him he had a visitor. Nelson said it was dangerous to interrupt a shaving man, and he would just go in and wait. She left him to it.

The bed had been made. The very modern room was tidy and impersonal. Nelson itched to explore it but sensibly refrained. Vance Manning stuck his bandaged head out of the adjoining bathroom and called, "You forgot to leave clean towels, Lily."

She had left them on a chair. Nelson tossed one to him. He caught it, dried his face, and stepped into the bedroom. "And what can I do for *you?*" he said.

Nelson identified himself.

"Are you here to make a mountain out of last night's molehill? I assure you that my attempt to assassinate myself wasn't voluntary." He was wearing faded pajamas and a rather shabby robe. He sat on the bed and yawned as though he would have preferred to get into it. His eyes were quite clear but his fading tan had a grayish cast. "Turn that chair around and sit down. It hurts me to crane."

Nelson obeyed. "At that you've made a quick recovery," he said.

"I can remember feeling better. I never could stand the sight of my own blood. In fact if you've come to ask me a lot of tiresome questions I must warn you that my mind isn't working too well."

"In that case it would have been wiser to take the doctor's advice and go to a hospital. I can arrange it now if—"

"No thanks. I'm on vacation. I don't mean to waste it in hospital."

"Vacation from what, Mr. Manning?"

"That comes under the heading of tiresome questions." He studied Nelson and said tentatively, "I suppose I could take a turn for the worse and have you removed as a health hazard."

"That would really be a turn for the worse. Perhaps I should state my position before we go any further. I'm investigating a murder in which Carmody figures as a suspect—and you are on visiting terms with him—although obviously you're not a cherished visitor. If you want me to spell that out, I've had a report which suggests that your explanation of last night's molehill is the only parlor trick you performed."

"I have a vague recollection of a dressy individual appearing out of the blue. Is he your informant?"

"He seemed to think that you were a dressy individual."

"Did he now?" Vance Manning lowered his eyes for a significant glance at his shabby attire. "You see? I wouldn't place too much reliance upon him if I were you. After all he did permit your suspect to steal a march on him." He threw the next line in. To an untrained ear it would have passed as idle conversation. "Or has he redeemed himself by tracking him down again?"

"If you want an answer," Nelson said, "I might give it in fair exchange. You've registered here as Vance Manning, Los Angeles, California. You can either tell me whether that much is true and proceed from there—or I can take steps to verify or disprove it."

Vance Manning said, "I'd hate to put you to unnecessary trouble. It is true—although I'm beginning to wish I'd registered under a false name—but a spotless citizen whose reputation hasn't been smirched by so much as a traffic ticket doesn't expect to be sought out as a suspect's suspect acquaintance."

"Are you employed?"

"I hold a modest but respectable position."

"In what capacity?"

"Next question."

"Is your salary modest?"

"In other words, can I afford to stay at this hotel? I can't. I've been scrimping and saving for years to give myself a taste of luxury—not a laudable ambition but then—"

"Has it been worth it?"

"Is anything ever? I've been wondering if I shouldn't have tried the Summit. I understand that they atone for the sore-thumb appearance of the architecture by piping champagne into the rooms."

"Probably an exaggeration," Nelson said. "Moreover they don't have Mrs. Carmody at the Summit."

"My choice had nothing to do with Mrs. Carmody. I hadn't the good fortune to meet her until I came East. Does that take care of that?"

"Partly. Had you met Mr. Carmody before you came East?"

"No."

Nelson said, "He may be new to you under his present name so I'll rephrase the question. Did you know Mr. Carmody when he was Mike Crokey?"

"Aliases too? He does begin to sound shifty."

"I'll accept your shifty answer. Now all you have to do is tell me where and when you met him and what came after."

"I'm sure you're not trying to be subtle but I simply have no grasp." He leaned sideways and reached for a bottle of aspirin on the night table. He swallowed two and chased them down with water from a half-filled glass. He replaced the glass and said, "Dizzy but ready. Carry on if you must."

"When did you come East?"

"Mid-February."

"That isn't the date on your registration card."

"You asked me when I came—not when I arrived. I drove—sharing the car of a friend of a friend of a friend. We took our time and saw the sights."

"Is this twice-removed friend in New York?"

"No—he went on to somewhere in the wilds of Canada."

"Predictable. You're not a native Californian, Mr. Manning?"

"Aren't they predictable—or do you ask that because I lack the West Coast speech coloration? I rather pride myself on using the brand of English adopted by cultivated Americans the country over. I include you in that category, of course."

Nelson had to remind himself that he was not there to be amused by the man. He said, "Where were you born?"

"Not too far from here."

"Where?"

"That aspirin isn't helping a bit."

"Connecticut—New Jersey—New York—the Bronx—Brooklyn?" He gave "Brooklyn" extra emphasis.

"You could start a new trend in station announcers," Vance Manning said. "Fine voice—clear enunciation—"

"I won't insist that you pin it down," Nelson said. "Something tells me I'd only discover that your old homestead had been razed, and its environs altered beyond recognition so that none remain who remember you or yours."

"That might have happened," Vance Manning said. "I can't say for certain because I haven't embarked on a sentimental journey to find out. Shall I let you know if I do? It could well be that you've just given a remarkable demonstration of precognition."

"Are you related to Mike Crokey?"

"I'm crushed that you should entertain the thought—and frankly curious to know why."

"Your evasions are on a higher plane than his—but you might have learned them at the same knee."

Manning winced and pressed his hands to his bandaged head. Nelson could not be sure that he was shamming. Neither could he afford to sympathize. He said, "The detective saw the base of that lamp and some of the broken pieces in the kitchen while he was on an errand for the doctor. He says that one of the pieces could have caused the cut, but that the lamp itself wasn't heavy enough to cause a swelling or a severe headache. To gather the necessary momentum it would have had to be brought down from a higher point than that very low table where it stood. Yet your story is that you slipped to the floor and brought it down after you."

"Yes—that's my story—and I have got a devil of a headache—so your man must be wrong again."

"Carmody's sudden exit would seem to prove him right."

"I don't see how. If the detective's nose was more than a fixture he'd have told you that Cro—Carmody had been drinking. I attributed his melodramatic escape to one of those strange impulses that seizes drunken men. But then—if as you say—he had reason to dodge the police—finding a detective in his own living room invests his dash for freedom with a certain amount of logic."

"If your own logic had been working immediately after you were struck you might have treated your audience to a more plausible tale. I won't go so far as to say you'd have told the truth."

"Ah what is truth?"

It was murmured in a vague dreamy tone, but Nelson treated it as a literal question. "Truth is that Carmody had been drinking. He came home—found you there—and interpreted or misinterpreted the situation. You outweigh him. He waited until your back was turned to attack. Perhaps the sight of your blood didn't mix too well with cheap alcohol so he shut himself in to recuperate. At first he might have had some befuddled notion that if he hid long enough the whole thing would blow over—but it couldn't have been long before he realized that you were not to be counted on to suffer in silence, and that in his position he could not afford another strike against him. When he came out he intended to keep going. The sight of the extra people in the room merely strengthened his resolution."

Manning said, "I've heard that men with impaired vision hear better than others—but it doesn't seem to work with me. I wonder if my specs broke when I fell or if they're upstairs intact."

"I'll ask Mrs. Carmody. I'll be seeing her in a few minutes." He saw dismay in the gray eyes. "It surprises me that she hasn't been down to see you."

"Does it?"

"Surely she would be concerned about the extent of your injury. But perhaps she spoke to you on the phone—or you called her to give her reassurance."

"I imagine Mrs. Carmody has other things on her mind—especially if her husband hasn't returned."

"One way or the other I imagine she has. Still, in the circumstances she'd have room for more than a passing thought of you."

"What circumstances?"

Nelson said, "I mean, of course, that she would want to know if you were clinging to your initial reluctance to prefer charges. It would naturally influence what she tells me."

"I have no influence at all upon Mrs. Carmody."

"It occurs to me that if you wished you could exert quite a bit of influence where women are concerned."

"Shall we compare notes?"

Nelson thought of the towel he had retrieved for the chambermaid. In swift succession he thought of a number of things: Edna Spofford, who wore eye shadow and light pink lipstick; Clevis's eyewitness account of the swimming-pool conference; Annie Dale's mention of the girl rushing to meet a date who wore horn-rimmed glasses. He said, "Do you know Edna Spofford?"

Manning nodded indifferently. "She's Carmody's receptionist."

"Do you visit there during business hours?"

"It's a fascinating place. I've been shown over it between classes."

"By the fascinating Miss Spofford?"

"Is she?"

"I should think you'd know. You were seen taking her for a taxi ride."

Manning laughed. "I did pick her up in a cab. No gentleman would have done less. I was on my way to a late lunch and it was cold and she was walking. It ended by my feeding her at a restaurant I'd been meaning to try."

Nelson said patiently, "Did she tell you that she had quit her job?"

"No. In fact she was worried about staying away so long. She moaned about it until I hailed another cab and took her back."

"She hasn't been seen since. From last reports she didn't go home last night."

"I assume she has loving friends who would be delighted to put her up. But why are you so interested in her private life?"

"Any associate of Carmody's interests me. When you brought her back to the hotel did she come up to this room?"

"How you talk."

"The chambermaid dropped a towel stained with pink lipstick."

"She may have been collecting laundry from other guests."

"I'll ask her." He had an impulse to shake his head in order to rid it of a very nasty thought.

"You can make even a dirty towel sound important. To go a step further you almost succeed in making a harmless lad like me feel guilty. What am I supposed to have done with the girl—and don't answer. I did not."

He looked boyish and defenseless with his bandaged head and his faded robe. The maid, Nelson thought, had been in the bathroom to remove the towels, and there was no other hiding place. The sliding door of the shallow closet exposed a few good suits, a few pairs of treed shoes, and a suitcase on a shelf against the back wall. Spofford was a sizable wench. Barring a dismembering operation she could not have been smuggled out. Nelson exorcized the preposterous thought.

"You can't seriously believe she spent the night here," Manning said. "Even if I'd entertained such a base idea—and she willing—it would in the course of events have been knocked right out of my poor head."

"But you did escort her back to the hotel."

"I dropped her off, kept the cab, and rode on to the Metropolitan Museum to see if their most touted Rembrandt was worth the money they'd spent for it. I got back in time for dinner which I ate by courtesy of room service. Then I began to get bored with my own company and went up to the roof. Mrs. Carmody and I spent the evening in conversation until the accident occurred."

"Conversation?"

"So be it. No parlor tricks—but yours is an empty win. Who—aside from a confirmed teetotaler—would prosecute a man in his cups?"

"An innocent and righteously outraged citizen might—if he were set upon by a husband who had jumped to the wrong conclusion."

The gray eyes looked frostbitten. "It would take a great deal more than that to make this citizen either outraged or vengeful."

The almost brooding note that had been struck marred an otherwise skilled performance. Nelson said, "What *would* it take to make you vengeful?"

Manning strove to regain his light touch. "You must have kept your poor papa on his toes when you were a little boy."

"He never tried to fob off my questions. What would Mike Crokey have to do to make you want to punish—?"

"Crokey? Oh yes—of course—Carmody. Excuse the interruption. I so seldom meet a man with an alias."

"His real name isn't unfamiliar to you. In one of your few unguarded moments you started to use it." Nelson glanced at the door.

The knob turned and the doctor came into the room.

## CHAPTER 14

On Saturdays the reducing salon profited by holding classes for "career girls" who could not take time off during the week. Ceil Carmody had left the reception desk and gone with Nelson to the office. She did not seem surprised by his reappearance. Nor did she show hostility.

"No—I don't know where Mike is." She looked as though her composure was hard won.

"Would you tell me if you did know?"

"Yes—I would—not because I want to betray him but because I'm sure he has nothing to fear. I suppose you've heard about last night but his—Vance Manning isn't going to prefer charges. You can't make an arrest if he doesn't—can you?"

"I thought that you and Mr. Manning had agreed to stick to the parlor-trick story."

"He wanted to but I'm not very good at—at that sort of thing."

"Have you spoken to him this morning?"

"He called me as soon as he woke up to say he felt fine." She looked anxious. "Doesn't he? Have you seen him?"

"Yes. The doctor came while I was there. He couldn't find much to worry about—but to be on the safe side he persuaded him to have an X-ray taken. They left in the doctor's car." Manning had needed no persuasion. He had started to dress at once.

"Was he really well enough to go?"

"He seemed a bit washed out but of course I don't know how he looks ordinarily. His mind is perfectly clear." Too clear, he thought. From his point of view the doctor's entrance could not have been more ill-timed.

"I'm glad you saw him," she said. "I wanted to but I was afraid to leave in case there was word from Mike. He must be terrified thinking of the serious trouble he'll be in if Vance was badly hurt."

"He is in serious trouble. I've been criticized for not holding him on suspicion of murder."

The depths of her eyes were haunted. They were beautiful eyes. He hoped they were honest as well. "Mrs. Atmore—?"

He nodded.

"But we heard it announced on television and it—it shocked him. He wasn't acting. I can tell if he's acting. He ran down to get a newspaper. Then he sent for his coat—and later a police officer called and said they were questioning everybody who knew Mrs. Atmore—and he kept repeating that it was only routine."

"It starts off as routine. The way it develops depends upon the way the questions are answered."

She was shaking her head. "It's impossible. I don't know what you asked him or what he answered—but he can't have had anything to do with her death."

"Most wives take that attitude. Most mothers too. 'My husband wouldn't kill—he's a good man.' 'My son's not a bad boy.' But crimes are committed—and husbands and sons and wives and mothers and daughters have been found guilty of them."

"That isn't what I'm saying." She went on painfully, "He isn't a good man. There are things I've discovered about him that I don't even whisper to myself—but I'm married to him and I've got to help him. I've got to make you understand that he isn't capable of deliberate murder. He's quick-tempered—violent at times if he thinks he's being threatened—or if something he owns is being threatened. He's vain and weak and dishonest and he divides people into categories— those who can further his own ends and those who can't—or won't. That's about the level of his sins. He discards or runs from those who are useless to him—but his instinct for self-protection is strong. It would never let him commit an act that would mean his destruction if he was caught. Surely in work like yours you've learned how to judge men. You've talked to him—made him talk to you—just as you're making me talk—" She tried to read his face. "You talked to him here on the day Mrs. Atmore died. He was *here*. You saw him."

Her estimate of Carmody was similar to Nelson's. He asked himself if the unexpected frankness of a very reserved woman could have other purpose than the purpose expressed. He said, "He was with Mrs. Atmore on the penultimate day. We think the drug used had a delayed reaction." He reminded himself that he did not yet know the results of the post-mortem, nor had he heard from the man sent to talk with Cora's Stanley, nor received further word on Spofford, nor finished with Vance Manning.

He did not show that he was pressed for time. "We'll find your husband and give him all benefit of any doubt. But meanwhile it must be hard for you to manage alone."

"The assistant—Mr. Graham—is bearing the brunt of today's classes."

"I remember meeting him on my first visit. He impressed me as a conscientious worker—but with Miss Spofford absent you have her work to do as well as—"

She interrupted him. "That wasn't your first visit. You'd come the night before—yet I've heard no more about the hit-and-run. If you were misled about that couldn't you be mis—?" Then she said, "I'm sorry—it's quite a different thing—isn't it? I didn't get much sleep and I'm not thinking straight." She tried to smile. "I wish all my troubles were as minor as Miss Spofford's absence."

"Have you heard from her?"

"Yes—she called an hour ago to say she was sorry she'd walked out yesterday. Her excuse was that she'd been starting a cold and felt so miserable she didn't know what she was doing. She promised to be in on Monday."

Nelson said mildly, "It isn't much of an excuse—not when a simple explanation before she left would have served." He could not make himself believe that Mrs. Carmody was lying about the call. "Did she sound as though she had a cold?" He meant, Are you sure it was her voice?

"She sounded the same as usual—but it doesn't matter. I'll take her back. It's not worth making a change when everything seems so—so temporary—and she's good at her job." She looked at the clock. "Do you think Vance could be back from the X-ray place?"

"No—not even if he was taken at once—but I'm sure the verdict will be satisfactory. Was your husband's temper tantrum based on anything stronger than the drinks he'd had?"

She answered the ringing telephone eagerly, and engaged less eagerly in conversation. "No—Miss Spofford isn't here today. This is Ceil Carmody.... Yes, Mrs. Morrison, it's very sad.... I don't know.... The newspapers didn't ... Yes—naturally ... He isn't feeling too well. Mr. Graham is taking over his classes.... Thank you, I will.... Flowers for ...! I didn't mean to sound that way. It's kind of you to think of taking up a collection. I expect the funeral will be announced ..."

When she hung up she said, "I thought it might be Mike. It was a client who'd heard the news."

"You handled it tactfully," Nelson said. He noted that although she had avoided the direct lie she too could be evasive on demand.

"I wish Mike would call."

"If he and Vance were on good terms before last night I expect that remorse has been added to his troubles."

She spoke absently. "I don't think they ever got on too well. It was hard to understand why Vance looked him up after so many years."

"There must be more of a bond than you suspect."

"There must be or he wouldn't have behaved so generously."

"Could he have provoked the attack deliberately and then had a change of heart?"

She came to attention. "There was no provoca—" Her conflict seemed to lie in not knowing which of the pair to defend.

"What was the nature of his former association with your husband?"

She looked puzzled. "Didn't he tell you?"

"He seems to enjoy being a man of mystery. He didn't even tell you he'd been staying at this hotel."

"I never thought to ask him where he was staying." Her voice put distance between them.

"Had they been partners in some business enterprise that he asked you not to mention?"

"No, but—"

"Yes?"

"He'd have told you if he wanted you to know."

"He didn't tell me. I hope you will—even if you believe you have reason not to."

"He's Mike's stepbrother. I don't see how information like that could mean anything to you—or any reason that I could have to keep it secret."

"Can you think of a reason for him to keep it secret?"

"No—unless he's ashamed of his connection with a man who might receive publicity as a murder suspect." A little color had come into her face. Her voice was colored with pride. "I know next to nothing about him. I'd never met or heard of him until he turned up a few weeks ago."

"Didn't it seem strange to you that you had never heard of your husband's stepbrother?"

"It's strange that you make so much of it."

"I think there's a possibility that Manning is involved in more than last night's incident."

"I don't understand."

You don't want to understand, he thought.

"You believe my husband is—that he had something to do with Mrs. Atmore's death—and now you drag someone into it who's not even aware that she existed."

"Are you sure of that?"

"Of course. Do you think I wouldn't jump at any chance to clear my husband?"

Nelson did not think she would jump at a chance to implicate Manning. But he did believe that she wanted to help the husband whom she no longer loved, if she had ever loved him. Either her integrity would not permit her to discard the "for better or for worse" clause in her marriage vows, or, as she had suggested of Manning, she was moved solely by a determination to avoid the public shame of being linked to an accused murderer.

He felt that she had exhausted her supply of pertinent "Vanciana." As he arose he said, "Does Cora work on Saturday?"

"Yes—until one o'clock."

"May I see her for a few minutes?"

She was too dispirited to ask why. "I'll send her to you. I'd better stay out at the desk."

Left alone he went through the open door of the apartment. Detectives were covering the front and service exits of the hotel, but Carmody had departed unobserved, and it seemed wise—with apologies to Mrs. Carmody—to make sure that he had not managed to sneak back.

Cora entered at full steam to find Nelson waiting for her. She spoke in a loud whisper which kept breaking to let her normal voice escape. "Oh—you're the other one. Mrs. Carmody says you want me. Funny not to have him up and around." Evidently she assumed that Carmody lay ill in his bed. "He didn't look none too extra yesterday. Ain't it terrible about Mrs. Atmore—?"

"You needn't whisper," Nelson said. "He can't hear you. You were almost the last person to see Mrs. Atmore before she died—weren't you? I'm told you delivered a can of Vitrate to her on Thursday afternoon."

The large pink face was regretful. "No, I didn't. I got off early on purpose but I couldn't go into such a classy house without putting on my good clothes first. It's different here—where I work—and anyway we don't live very far—near the U. N. Ours is about the only house they didn't tear down yet but we got notice and what with the high rents I don't know where they'll find us an apartment we can pay for. It's convenient too—saving carfare and all. When Mr. Carmody gave me the Vitrate right after lunch I put it with my coat not to forget it and when I went home Stanley was there. He knew I was mad at him because instead of going back to school that afternoon he'd come here saying he'd lost his lunch money and was hungry which didn't fool me—there being plenty home in the icebox. Well, I caught him near the solarium talking to that gentleman so I—"

"What gentleman was that?"

"I seen him around once before—some friend of theirs—lucky the ladies were in the gym and the steam room but the boss don't want Stanley around anyway so I told him to go home I'd attend to him later. He wanted to make up with me so when I told him I had to go out again he said he'd do it for me—and my feet hurt so I gave him the bag with the can in it and told him to go into the kitchen first for a cup of hot chocolate—he likes to mix it himself—that instant stuff and I didn't want him out in the cold without something hot in him. Margie, my youngest, wasn't home yet so I went to soak my feet and think about what to have for supper and before you know it Stanley was back. I asked did she give him a quarter and he said no she just called out for him to leave it at the door. I don't think I'll tell him she died. He don't like people he knows to die—it makes him mopey—"

Nelson mined for ore until the vein petered out. She looked at him doubtfully when he thanked her, and instead of returning to her duties accompanied him as far as the reception desk. He did not want to leave Mrs. Carmody unhappier than he had found her but could not think of a cheerful parting word. As he went toward the elevators he heard Cora say, "He must have forgot, himself, what he wanted me for."

Vance Manning's key was in its cubbyhole, but the clerk called his room to check and hung up shaking his head. Nelson left the hotel and drove to headquarters. It was after one. The morning had been consumed.

Judd, the man he had sent to Brooklyn to talk to Miss Edna Spofford, was waiting in his office.

"I didn't want to take a chance on missing you, Captain."

Few of Nelson's men came close to resembling the stereotype of the hard-bitten police detective. Good-natured Judd, plodding and unimaginative, might have been cast from birth for the modest role of "the clean-cut American" who works at some essential but pedestrian job, marries the girl next door, settles down in suburbia, entertains and is entertained by neighbors, and further enriches his lot with assorted household appliances, children, civic affairs, church suppers, and back-yard barbecues. But Judd had wandered out of context into the Homicide Squad, where his assets were physical courage, tenacity, conscientiousness, and an open face that inspired confidence. Nelson saw now that this face was chapped and weary. It looked as though it had been left out in the cold too long.

"I didn't expect you to wait all night if she wasn't home, Judd. It wasn't that urgent. Sit down, and have a cigarette."

Judd sat down and said apologetically, "I thought I could tell you quicker than write a report. I haven't seen the girl. She didn't come home and her roommate was kind of sore because they'd planned to go somewhere together and she hadn't phoned to say she'd changed her mind. The roommate asked me to wait and how about a drink but I said maybe I'd be back a little later. I didn't want to use her phone to check back here. As it stood she thought I was just a friend, so I left and went to a booth. I couldn't get you—but Lippert was on the desk and he thought I should stick with it. I had coffee and doughnuts and went back to see if she'd come home in the meanwhile. She hadn't and her roommate said there was no telling when she would if she'd got herself a heavy date but she'd be home sometime because she hadn't slept out since working at Carmody's." Judd quickened his tempo, unconsciously switching to present tense. "The long and short of it, the roommate disappears and comes out in a robe and a nightgown as if she's ready for bed, so I say good night. They live one flight up. I stand in the vestibule watching the street through the glass door. There isn't much doing. The few people coming in or out don't give me more than a quick look. After a while it gets quieter than that till it looks like I'm the only one left awake. I've fixed on half past one as reasonable for a city girl with a date and I tack on another thirty minutes for luck. I'm ready to quit when this cab stops and a drunk nearly

falls out of it. He gets up the fare and the cab takes off. He's squint-
ing at the house and trying to stow his wallet away at the same time
and he misses. He doesn't notice he's dropped it. He comes in, hunts
for the right name in the bell, finally gets the buzzer and heads for
the stairs. He doesn't give me a tumble. I fix the door and run to pick
up the wallet. There's no money in it. I guess the driver got the last
buck or so but I find Carmody's name and address on a couple of cards.
I'm back in time to hear the roommate yelling stuff like 'Tell it to the
Marines you're a pal of Edna's—you're a bum and you better get going or I'll call the police—she's not home anyway—' Doors are opening and shutting and somebody yells 'Beat it!' He beats it and I follow him to a subway station on the next block because before I left H.
Q. Clevis told me he was going to pick him up for questioning and it
smells kind of funny that he's where he is at two A. M. He's really
stoned. He almost falls down the stairs, fumbles for the price of a token and it's a miracle how he manages to fit it into the slot and push
through the turnstile and not roll off the platform before the train
comes. I'm right with him. We get out at Grand Central and he stag-
gers uptown. We cover better than half a mile and I begin to think he's
trying to sober up with air and exercise and hope it won't take him
as far as the Bronx. But he seems to have something in mind. Every
so often he stops to puzzle out a street sign. At last he finds one that
suits him and turns west. The hike ends at a small private house. The
number's on the door with a light over it and he shoves his face up
close to read it. Then he rings the bell and doesn't give up until a
woman looks out of the second-floor window. I'm across the street under a canopy by this time. I can't hear what he says to her because
he seems to have sense enough not to shout louder than he has to. The
upshot is she comes down and lets him in. He doesn't come out. At four
o'clock I nail a passing patrol car and tell the boys my troubles but I
don't say who he is because I don't want them horning in. They get
in touch with the desk and Hen Sleifer comes on the double to relieve
me." Judd's closing was matter-of-fact. "I hear from Sleifer that Carmody's 'wanted,' so at least I wasn't wasting shoe leather. But what
should I do about Edna Spofford—?"

"Never mind Edna Spofford. What's the address?" By tracing the
course of the hike he had made an easy guess. Judd's confirmation was
less of a surprise than an additional worry. He picked up the phone
and issued some terse instructions.

Judd was disconcerted. "I thought of making a collar on 'drunk and
disorderly,' but then I thought he might lead us somewhere impor-

tant—and afterwards I couldn't go in without a warrant and when
Hen got there he said we'd hold it until you gave the word."

"Why wasn't I told when I called in this morning?"

"Well—I expected you here as usual and so I didn't talk it over with
anybody. The woman couldn't have been afraid of him or she would-
n't have been so ready to let him in—so I figured she wasn't in any
danger."

Nelson smiled at him. "Go down to the basement and get a car to
drive you home to Flushing in state. When you get there do nothing
but eat and sleep away the effects of that cold vigil. I can't afford to
risk the health of one of my best men."

"Thanks, Captain." For a weary man he made a very brisk exit.

The Atmore P. M. had come in. It topped the papers on the desk. Nelson gave it priority. Boiled down, it bore out the "educated guess" of
the assistant medical examiner who had arrived before the crew of
the mobile unit. His opinion had been that a drug had paralyzed the
respiratory centers. He had said "drug." The post-mortem made it plu-
ral. A derivative of rauwolfia had been present in the stomach, along
with a quantity of the highly flavored diet.

Nelson studied the conclusions reached by the medical examiner,
and put the report aside for further reference. But his mind did not
relinquish it. Next on the heap was a memo that said a Mrs. Grimes
had called three times and refused to state her business to anyone
else. She had left her number. The telephone rang as he picked it up.
He tried not to show frustration at the sound of the male voice. Lieutenant Werner of the Brooklyn precinct took his time. He seemed relaxed and smug.

"I've been trying to get you, Captain. You're a hard man to reach....
Yes—I hear you've got a plateful but I have a hunch you've been on
the wrong track about that hit-and-run...."

It was not what Nelson would have termed a hunch. There had been
a strong lead from one of the Brooklyn garages alerted by Werner's
men. A new customer had driven in on the night in question. He said
he had just moved to the neighborhood and was shopping for available garage space. He had been accommodated, paying a month in advance, and when he mentioned that he would probably be too busy
to use the car for several weeks, space was assigned him between two
vehicles whose owners were off on cruises. The night man was called
away several times while attending to him. He had taken his name
and address but it had not occurred to him to check the license for
proof of ownership. He could offer no better description than that the

man was well dressed and of average height and build. He remembered seeing him remove something from the car but he had been too busy to pay much attention. He had not seen him leave. The car, a "Tourer," was the latest model. It had occupied the same space until yesterday when some shifting around became necessary. The employee who did the shifting noticed the cracked windshield. He was afraid he might be blamed for it, started to look for other damage, and discovered that the license plates had been removed and that there were dried brown stains on the fender and head lamps. On a new car it seemed improbable that the stains could be rust, especially when said car had been stripped of any means of identification. The information had been passed on to Werner. Scrapings of the dried stains were tested, and proved to be human blood of the same general grouping as the blood of Alice Thwaite. Not conclusive evidence, Werner admitted modestly, but what with a false name and address plus the rest of the steps the owner had used to remain anonymous it took on weight. If he *was* the owner, Werner expected no difficulty. He could not remain anonymous if he had bought the car at a reputable agency and taken out license plates in his own name. Perhaps he had been too desperate to think straight.

"I'll let you know what comes of it, Captain," Werner said. "Something warned me at the start that our 'First-time Squealer' was from hunger. But I understand that unbeknownst he did you a favor by letting you in on the ground floor of something more in your line."

Nelson said that depended upon the way you looked at it, and wished Werner good luck and good-bye as quickly as he could.

The telephones went on ringing for a while. He was tempted to steal a little mulling-over time by asking the desk to withhold all calls until further notice. But in hurrying out of the house that morning he had neglected to answer a call that would have saved him anxiety, and perhaps time as well. Simultaneously he lifted receivers, made responses, and took quick readings of the papers in front of him. There was a report from the detective who had been sent to investigate the firm and lab that were responsible for the Vitrate. Nothing questionable had been uncovered there. As soon as he had a clear wire he called the ready room but the man assigned to interview young Stanley had not returned. A message from the D. A.'s office asked him to call them soonest. He filed that with other non-immediate items and was about to call Annie Grimes when Kyrie's voice came through. It was rare for her to interrupt his work. He said her name on a sharp urgent note.

"Have I disturbed you at a particularly awkward moment, Grid? I'll hang up—"

The unfounded fear ebbed out of him. "A lady doesn't hang up on her lord and master. Speak."

"Annie Grimes wasn't calling to ask if I'd enjoyed the Vitrate. Did she manage to get in touch with you?"

"Not yet."

"Well—she called me back about a half hour ago and said she'd been trying all morning on and off. She wouldn't tell me why but I thought it might be something important."

"It's all right. Everything's under control." A somewhat premature statement, he thought.

Kyrie said, "Good." She did not quite change the subject. "Sammy and I are leaving for the airport right away."

"Watch your driving going and coming."

"I will." She added with dogged optimism, "See you soon." He called Annie Dale at last, but her maid said impatiently that she had stepped out. She sounded as though his call had delayed her own exit. He wondered if, with her employer gone, she was stealing off to regale kith and kin with a juicy account of shenanigans that had gone on under her nose.

## CHAPTER 15

Nelson himself stepped out, but not for pleasure. Within two hours he was back at his desk where he settled down to various matters that did not concern the Carmody case. But at intervals he took time out to call the Easton Hotel.

Vance Manning did not answer his telephone. And if he was on the roof, a detective, who had been instructed to let Nelson know as soon as he reappeared, was falling down on the job. On one of the tries Nelson spoke to the doctor, who said that the X-ray had confirmed his own opinion that Manning had suffered no serious injury. After it was taken, he said, Manning had felt well enough to go for a walk. He had no idea of where he might be.

That was how matters stood when five o'clock came. Nelson, who had skipped lunch, decided that there was no law against a man going home to celebrate the return of his only son from parts unknown. The telephone rang as he took his coat from the rack.

"Captain Nelson? ... Ed Welsh speaking—the manager of the apartment house where Mrs. Atmore ... Yes—I wasn't sure you'd recall my name. I tried to get you earlier. I don't think it can be important but my wife insisted ... The maid who worked for Mrs. Atmore has been worried. I'm afraid I was terse with her when she tried to answer your questions but ..." He worked his way through the long preamble, but when it was out of the way he stated the rest with laudable brevity.

Nelson thanked him, complimented him, and reread the P. M. as soon as he bade him good-bye. Then he left word that he was to be notified if even doubtful need arose, and went home without further let or hindrance.

Junie must have been watching from a window, or else his ear was attuned to the voice of his father's car. He reached the door before it was opened, a slim strong boy with coloring like Kyrie's. His ten-year-old's dignity would not have permitted a demonstrative greeting in public, but with no one there to see he flung himself at Nelson.

Nelson hugged him hard, held him off, and growled, "You must be an impostor. My son's in Washington on an important mission. Besides—you're at least three feet taller than he."

Junie said solemnly, "It's a disguise—I couldn't have got here otherwise. I'm being watched."

They went on with the game until he had to laugh.

As they entered the living room Kyrie gave Nelson a look of warm approval. The fireplace glowed. She and Junie had been feasting before it. Sammy appeared with a tray of reinforcements and Nelson joined the party.

"Eat a lot," Junie said kindly, and took his own advice. "We're having a late dinner and I can stay up late because tomorrow's Sunday."

He had started to tell his parents how their government worked when Sammy announced that Detective Gregor was in the study. She added mysteriously that he had brought a friend. Nelson felt his relaxed muscles tighten. He arose and said he would see what that was all about. Kyrie diverted Junie, who would have followed him.

The "study" was at the right of the living room. Originally it had been designed for Nelson, but he preferred to use an upstairs room when he worked at home. Junie, at the age of five, had pre-empted it as a finger-painting studio. Since then his interests had widened. It testified to most of them.

Gregor was blocking the door. Red-faced, he made way for Nelson. "Sorry, Captain, but Stanley here had me chasing him all over town and I'm taking no more chances. He's a regular eel."

He was a well-fed eel with hair the shade of a "color added" orange.

He had his hands in the pockets of his buttoned-up reefer. His blue-jeaned legs were firmly planted. His eyes were on a baseball bat in a corner. He brought them around to Nelson.

"Hello, Stanley. Take off your coat—it's warm in here."

"This isn't a police station. I think I better go home. I think I'm kidnaped."

Gregor said, "I showed him my badge but he didn't believe it was real. I had to crowd him into a booth with me while I called in for advice. They told me you'd gone home so I took a liberty and brought him here. I couldn't get a thing out of him myself—with my kids grown I guess I've lost the touch."

"I'm glad to see Stanley," Nelson said. "Will you tell my son I want him for a few minutes on official business? Give him a partial briefing first. Then find Sammy and hint that you could do with some coffee."

"Right."

Stanley would not sit down. He occupied the wait by busily taking inventory of the room.

Junie came in and stood at attention. His official bearing suffered a little when Stanley said distrustfully, "You're not his son."

"I am so."

"I bet he kidnaped you too."

Junie recovered. "This is my house and I live here and this is my dad. He doesn't kidnap. He's a police captain and he arrests people who do bad things."

"I didn't do anything bad."

Junie was only slightly at a loss. "Then maybe he'll let you help him find somebody who did—if you know anything."

"I know a lot. What's your name?"

"The same as my dad's. But Sammy started to call me 'Junie'—short for 'Junior' so she wouldn't get me mixed up with him."

"Junie's a sissy name. You're a sissy."

"That's not fair. I can't hit you because you're in my house." He added hopefully, "Unless you hit me first."

Nelson touched his shoulder. "I'll see that you get a promotion out of this. Company dismissed."

Junie went reluctantly.

Stanley said, "I could fight him."

Nelson looked at him doubtfully. "I don't know. He's a pretty fair boxer."

"I can box better. Is that his bat?"

"Yes."

"The football too—and the mask?"

"Same boy."

"How about the clay and the paints and the books and that crazy kid-typewriter?"

"All his."

"Then he's a sissy."

"You keep that up and you may *have* to fight."

Stanley said nonchalantly, "I don't have time. My mom left a note in the door that she and Margie had gone to Aunt Violet's and I got to be home by seven or she'll get mad."

"That will just about give us time to have a talk and see if there's any more chocolate cake in the kitchen."

Stanley perched on the edge of a chair. "My father's a real captain—on a ship. He's been in a place called Near East for two months."

"Does he send you letters?"

"Postcards sometimes with 'How are you and Margie and Mom?'—and where he'll be when the ship stops next—and whenever Mom has to tell him something she says I should write it for her."

"Do you?"

"Sure—I write good—I wrote a letter for—" He began to cough like a ham actor.

"That's a bad cold you've got," Nelson said. "Did your friend at Carmody's pay you to write the letter for him?"

The little boy's eyes were blue disks. "Who told you—?"

Nelson thought ruefully of the game he played with Junie. "My spies."

"How did they find out? He said it was a funny joke and we'd spoil it by telling. I didn't even tell the man who brought me here."

"If it was only a funny joke why did you run away when he asked you about it?"

"I didn't run away for that. He said he was a policeman and I didn't think so—and once when my father was home he told me not to talk to strange men."

"You talked to Mr. Manning."

"He isn't a strange man. He knows the lady at the desk where Mom works because I heard her say, 'Hello, Mr. Manning'—and he owns a room downstairs but it's a secret from everybody but me. That's where I wrote the letter. My fingers got stiff but he gave me three quarters. I saved one of them."

"Did he say the Vitrate was another joke?"

Stanley shook his head vehemently. "But the green ring was. I had
to go to the bathroom and Mom said I could sneak into the 'ladies' and
the ring was on a sink. I wanted to give it to Mom but she was in the
steam room and everybody was busy—so I stuck it in my pocket and
went down to show it to Mr. Manning. He was going out but he let me
come in for a minute anyway. He had a box of peppermints for me. I
like them—I like chocolate cake too."

"You haven't finished telling me the joke."

"I forgot. Well—I showed him the ring and he said I should take it
right up and put it in the desk in the boss's office because the lady
wouldn't want to lose it—but Mom told me never to go near there so
I'd ate all the peppermints and I put it in the box—and they weren't
in the dressing room so I put it in back of a locker to surprise her. That
was the joke." He looked at Nelson expectantly.

Nelson laughed. He was a better ham actor than Stanley.

Stanley grinned at him. "I knew you'd laugh. It was because I knew
Mom went through the lockers every day. She told me and Margie lots
of times how we'd be surprised the things they'd leave behind and she
always said the lady who used the next to the last locker in the morning never forgot anything so I thought I'd fool her."

"When she found it did she tell you?"

"She told Aunt Violet—but she don't like me or Margie to butt in
when she's talking to Aunt Violet so I made out I wasn't listening.
Aunt Violet always thinks I'm laughing at her when I laugh."

Nelson said, "You can fool people so well that I think you're fooling
me too. I think the Vitrate was another joke. You took some of it to the
lady who lost the ring—didn't you?"

Stanley said earnestly, "No—that wasn't a joke—that's what the fat
ladies eat. Mom told me it didn't taste too good but they had to eat it
anyway to—"

Junie said from the doorway, "Wanted on the phone—important."

There was no extension in the room. Nelson said, "Remember he's
a guest," and sprinted for the telephone in the entrance hall.

The call was from the Easton. "He came in and went up to the roof,
Captain."

When he hung up he called Ceil Carmody's number. She said shak-
ily, "Have you—is Mike—?"

"He's in a safe place. You may see him as soon as—hello—are you
all right—?"

The next voice he heard said angrily, "What did you say to her?"

"Manning?"

"Yes—Manning. What—?"

"I want to talk with you—but not on the telephone. A detective will be at the door in a few minutes. I think you'll prefer to make it easy for him. A small friend of yours named Stanley has been telling me some very funny jokes. I expect you to join us within the next half hour."

He hung up. Stanley was not in the study. He found him in the kitchen.

Gregor said, "You through with him, Captain? I want to get him home before—"

Stanley spoke through a mouthful of cake. "That's all right. Mom is always later than she says. I have to go upstairs to see Junie's boxing gloves when I finish eating."

"You care for more milk?" Sammy said.

"Yes, Ma'am. 'Sammy's' not a lady's name."

The doorbell rang. Nelson said, "I'll get it." As he left the kitchen he heard Junie say, "What's so great about the name 'Stanley'?" He was glad that the name "Gridley" had not been up for discussion.

Kyrie had answered the door and was taking Annie Grimes into the living room. They were talking as though they had known each other forever. He followed them unnoticed, and stood in the doorway.

Annie Grimes stopped in the middle of a sentence to say, "Oh—there you are. They said at your office you were home and you'd like to have me drop in if I had time. As if I wouldn't make time. I've been calling all day—first to tell you about it—and then to ask how it turned out. Your wife is a lovely girl. She didn't need that Vitrate any more than I need mashed potatoes."

"I hear you've been leading an eventful life," Nelson said. He was in debt to her because she had prevented the fugitive from wandering far afield, but he knew more or less what her contribution would be and he wanted her to get on with it before Manning arrived.

"What beats me," she said, "is how you knew where Carmody was. You could have knocked me down with a feather when your men turned up. My maid will never be the same again but that's no loss. I was the one who had to let him in—she was too scared to open the door at that hour. Did you throw him in the drunk tank?"

"We gave him a bit more privacy than that."

"Poor twerp. I couldn't help feeling sorry for him the way he stumbled into the house and started crying how I had to let him hide out because everybody was against him and especially Mrs. Atmore who dropped dead when he was ready to divorce his wife and get hitched

to her and now they were trying to pin her death on him. Maybe I
haven't got that exactly right but it was about the size of it. Can you
imagine Mrs. Atmore marrying him! I didn't know whether to laugh,
cry, or call the police."

"The last course would have been the safest," Nelson said.

"Well—I've handled drunks in my time so it wasn't as if I was afraid
of him—and if he was just raving it would only have shamed his wife
to have him arrested—so I thought I'd find out more about it first. But
he passed out on the 'Green Room' sofa so I threw a blanket over him
and went upstairs with his shoes to finish out my sleep. I forgot there
was a little bar in the Green Room. Anyway—he must have come
awake with a thirst. He'd gone two-thirds down a bottle of bourbon
by the time I was up and dressed. On and off he just about knew who
he was and who I was—and darned if he didn't try to make a pass—
bawling that if I hadn't played hard to get he never would have bothered with Mrs. Atmore. Right about there I couldn't hold back. I had
to roar with laughter or slap his face—and he wasn't in any condition
to have his face slapped. But he wouldn't take 'no' for an answer and
he didn't smell like a rose—so it was kind of a good thing he'd taken
some of the flab off me or I might not have been able to defend myself. You should have seen the dirty look he gave me before he passed
out again. That was when I started phoning you for advice. Does his
wife have to get wind of it? She's such a nice ..."

Nelson managed to convey a message to Kyrie before the bell rang
again. She suggested tactfully that Mrs. Grimes might like to see the
upstairs part of the house.

When he opened the door, Vance Manning strode in followed by the
detective. He wore a new and smaller bandage, and to Nelson the
anger on his face was new.

"Where's Stanley?"

"He's being third-degreed in the kitchen." Nelson turned to the detective. "Go give them a hand, Scott." He led Manning to the living
room.

Manning said furiously, "It must be fun to bully a child."

"More fun than making him an accomplice. Did you smuggle a drug
into the Vitrate he delivered to Mrs. Atmore?"

"You must be absolutely mad if you think I'd use a little boy as an
instrument of murder. What I did was bad enough—" He shrugged
and sat down as Nelson gestured toward a chair. "Where's Cro? I
promised Ceil I'd—"

"He's taking an enforced rest."

Manning said bitterly, "If he's in prison it's too late—much too late. His crime dates back to years and years ago. That was when he killed—not the day before yesterday. I don't believe he had any more to do with the death of Mrs. Atmore than with what I accused him of in that letter."

"Suppose you tell me more about that letter."

"Why not—if you've got the stomach for it. I saw an item about the hit-and-run in the newspaper on the day I arrived in town. For some reason it stuck in my mind—perhaps because it had happened near the place where I was born. But that's another story. As you've un-doubtedly surmised I've been at some pains to cultivate the lush Miss Spofford—not for the purpose that she may have imagined—but be-cause I felt that she was in a position to supply me with bits of data that might aid and abet my campaign to harass her employer. To his disgust I had taken to dropping in frequently—for nuisance value if nothing else—and on one of these visits I struck what seemed to be pay dirt. The Spofford looked disgruntled—and with a little judicious coaxing she revealed that she was unhappy about Cro. He'd changed toward her. Of course he was married—but still—Mrs. Carmody was such a cold woman—so she didn't think it was wrong to—well—be so-ciable since it was plain he needed sympathy and understanding. She had done her best to give it to him—especially on the night he'd been considerate enough to drive her home to Brooklyn in his beautiful new green car—the very night before I arrived on scene. They'd become real friends that night—or so she'd believed—only after that he be-gan to act as though he hardly knew her—and she just didn't know what she'd done to make him sore. It couldn't have been the accident with the truck that had turned him against her because that wasn't her fault. She hadn't told him to drive with one arm—had she? Not, she said, looking at me soulfully, that it had gone any farther than that. Well—I listened—as the saying goes—with all my ears. And when I came across a second item that the poor hit-and-run girl was not expected to recover and that the driver was still at large, I was pro-vided with the opening salvo for my war of nerves."

Nelson was grimly silent.

"Anything else you'd like to know before you lower the boom?"

"I'm sure you'll be equally informative on the matter of Mrs. At-more."

"I suppose you mean in regard to the plans he had for her. I saw them outlined in a folder I found on his desk. There were annotations in the folder of a Mrs. Grimes too, but obviously Mrs. Atmore had been first choice. It wasn't difficult to figure out. I'd caught him at the game of extracting money from women when he was still in his teens. This time I gathered that he was so awed by the amount of the jackpot that he was prepared to go a step further and make an honest woman of his target."

"He has a wife."

Vance Manning nodded, his face somber. "A wife with rigid notions about divorce. But if it suited him he'd have found a means to break down her resistance. And for her sake I could have wished him success."

"Nothing you've told me so far is justification for sending a letter to the police which might have resulted in calling off the search for the real criminal. And in your own words, the letter was merely the opening salvo."

"I'm not trying to justify myself. I admit to having been obsessional where Cro's concerned."

"Having been? What cured you?"

"This morning you asked me if I had any influence upon Ceil. You didn't ask if she had influenced me. She's suffered enough. Last night I discovered that I couldn't add to her suffering—not even to purge myself of my own sickness. And as soon as I came to that decision my sanity returned."

"Too bad it didn't return before you sent the letter—or drugged the Vitrate."

Manning said, "I'll take your word for it that Mrs. Atmore did not die a natural death—but I don't believe that the Vitrate could have been responsible—nor do I see your point in insisting that it was. That sort of thing would not occur to Cro even if he had anything to gain by it—and his gain was in keeping her alive. Surely you've had the stuff analyzed—?"

"The analysis proves that it had been tampered with."

"Of course it had—but you can't accuse Stanley of anything but the best intentions."

"Tell me what you think his intentions were."

"I don't think. I know. That child hasn't learned to lie. If you've come to any other conclusion you're in the wrong job."

"My job is to check and double check."

Manning said impatiently, "Very well—his mother had brought it home and he offered to deliver it for her. He took it to the kitchen where she had sent him to drink some hot chocolate and he couldn't resist prying off the lid of the can to see what it tasted like. He wasn't impressed—and according to him his mother had said that the fat ladies weren't either. There was nutmeg in it, he told me, but not enough, and he thought he'd surprise Mrs. Atmore by adding more and making it 'real tasty' so that she wouldn't mind taking it anymore. His mother had nutmeg on the shelf so he dumped some into it. He didn't have time to sample it again because his mother called out for him to hurry up—but he was sure he had made a considerable improvement."

"When did he tell you this?"

"He stopped in for a moment on his way home. He was so pleased with himself that he had to tell someone. His father's away most of the time and I don't imagine his mother is a very good listener."

Nelson went out of the room. When he returned, Manning looked at him curiously. "I take it that Stanley's still here."

"Just leaving."

"Did he mention the ring he'd found?"

"Yes."

"That's an indication of the channels my spleen took—small petty channels. It should help to convince you if nothing else does that I had no compulsion to take the woman's life. I told Stanley to put the ring in a drawer in Cro's desk. I intended to see to it that Mrs. Atmore learned where it was before Cro did. And when she asked him for it his denial would have gone a long way to disillusion her. It rather pleased me to feel that a little good should stem from my activities—that I might be rescuing her from the hell Cro brings to everyone he touches."

"Did good come of turning Miss Spofford against him?"

Vance very nearly smiled. "She didn't lose by it. I made her see him in a somewhat clearer light—at least to the extent that she refused to alibi him for the hit-and-run. And I took her to lunch as a reward. Incidentally, I didn't go to the museum that day. When I brought her back to the hotel I absent-mindedly asked for my key. After that it seemed the better part of valor to allow her to accompany me to my room where she washed her face, redid it, and showed a disposition to linger. In the end she settled quite cheerfully for a lone but I'm sure not lonely weekend at the Summit, with a few additions to her wardrobe thrown in. If you care to verify that you might call the Summit and ask if she's registered."

"When and how did your Crokey-Carmody obsession start?"

"Isn't it enough that I've admitted to it? In what I thought was my right mind I went about working what mischief I could—and I'm ready to pay whatever penalty there is for deliberately misleading the police. The rest can't matter to you."

"It may matter to you."

Vance Manning told the story tonelessly, as though he had told it to himself over and over and over; as though repetition had staled it. He told of the boardinghouse his mother had started after his father died. He told of the man and the child who had come to live there. The man was gentle, beaten, and very grateful for the home he had found at last. Jobless for the most part, he made himself useful to the widow by shouldering chores too heavy for her to perform.

"He couldn't do enough for her," Manning said, "but I think she married him because of Cro. She felt that the skinny neglected boy needed care and love, and she gave him both. I don't believe I was jealous. She had so much to give. I tried to like him and help him but he was a congenital biter of the hands that fed him. And is. My mother was too good to recognize the meanness in him. And of course he realized that it was advantageous to behave like an ill-used lamb when he was with her. Elsewhere he was something else. Many children who lie and steal outgrow it. Not Cro. I can't count the times I shielded him and tried to set him straight for my mother's sake. She wanted him to have an education but he barely scraped through grade school. He left home when he was eighteen. He said he had found a job in New Jersey—too far away to commute. But he did come back to see her whenever he wanted money.

"I had started at Columbia on a scholarship. My mother was very happy when I told her I was going to be a teacher." He paused. He said flatly, "I am one—but I won't be when they hear of my recent activities. It was a woman instructor at Norton University who told me about Carmody's. She'd gone there to lose weight when she was on vacation in New York. I knew that Carmody was Cro. I'd kept periodic track of him, but for some reason her mention of him made me decide that the time was now. I was due for a sabbatical too." Vance was sweating. "I seem to have skipped the most important part."

Nelson nodded.

"I was a senior at Columbia when it happened. Cro's father had been dead a year, and shortly before that my mother's heart had begun to give her trouble. But she was still a fairly young woman and the doctor said that with reasonable care there was nothing to be alarmed about. She'd prospered enough to hire additional help and was doing far less work." He went on in the same flat tone, "Then one night I came home and found her lying near the door. She'd had a stroke. Her speech had been affected, but she tried desperately to tell me what had happened. I wouldn't let her until a few days later when the doctor insisted that it might ease her mind.

"Cro had been there to ask for money. As nearly as I could gather she thought he looked ill and she tried to persuade him to come home to live. He might have thought it was the overdue brush-off—or else he had urgent reasons for laying his hands on some cash. The boarders had paid for their keep that evening and the money was in her pocketbook ready to be deposited the next morning. He snatched the pocketbook and ran, thrusting her out of his way. Her heart couldn't take it. When she told me she said, 'Why did he? I would have given him whatever he needed.' It wasn't the loss of the money that grieved her. She lived on for a week after the stroke—still asking herself how she had failed him and why he had turned against her. And by the time I'd started to hunt for him he had taken ship. The pocketbook was found on a rubbish heap near the waterfront."

He brought his dulled eyes into focus and stared at Nelson. He said, "Would you consider that I had cause to wish him well?"

Junie had gone up to bed after the late dinner. His parents sat on in the living room. Nelson put some records on the turntable of the hi-fi, and when he got up to replace them, Kyrie shook her head.

"Don't bother, Grid. You haven't really been listening to the music."

"Who says?"

"I do. You're wearing that postcase depression face that says, 'Oh lord—I've just sent a human being on his way to the chair.' Only this time there doesn't seem to be any basis for it."

He said, "That's why I'm depressed."

"I know you'd just as soon drop the subject but—?"

"It's all right. My mind won't drop it anyway."

"I still don't understand how Mrs. Atmore died."

"Did you get a chance to look at Morland's book?"

"No—things were a bit rushed and I wasn't even sure you were serious."

He took the place beside her on the couch. "Clevis didn't believe I was serious either—but powdered nutmeg was first used as a drug in Egypt. It's contended to be more harmful than hashish—and in combination with present-day tranquilizers it's pretty well guaranteed not to be good for what ails you."

Kyrie looked horrified. "I can't bear it. Not that little boy!"

Nelson said, "The nutmeg couldn't have done the job unaided—and

Stanley was innocent of wrongful intent. He was spurred by a child's normal curiosity and a purely altruistic impulse." He went on morosely, "The maid was also out to perform a good deed. She had high blood pressure and her doctor had prescribed a tranquilizer. She told the manager of the house that the pills 'calmed her down something wonderful,' and that Mrs. Atmore's edginess and headache and the way she got red in the face had looked like high blood pressure to her. She didn't dare offer the pills knowing they'd be refused but she felt so sympathetic that she slipped a couple into the Vitrate, thinking they'd do the trick when Mrs. Atmore drank her lunch. Little round things, she said. The only way she could keep them from rolling off the kitchen counter while she crushed them was to put them in a napkin and pound away with a knife handle. Then, of course, she had to mix them in a little in case they were noticed. But she didn't mind going to the trouble. Mrs. Atmore had been nice to her in spite of the people next door saying she was a snob—and she'd put in a word with the manager too when some of the other tenants wanted a maid for part-time. 'And please—the pills couldn't have hurt a flea—could they?' And she'd have told me about it that day if the manager hadn't made her nervous."

"I don't see—?"

"Take a woman with inflamed sinuses and a tendency to asthma when upset. Take codeine and the additive effect of nutmeg and a tranquilizer—and you have the respiratory centers slowing down until complete paralysis sets in. Result—death."

Kyrie shivered. "Did you ever have anything like that before?"

"Plenty of deaths by misadventure—but I can't remember anything quite so misadventurish. I was almost sure Vance Manning was responsible for the nutmeg. Education-wise he seemed the only one who might be aware of its possibilities. But Stanley insists proudly that it was his idea and his alone."

"I hope he never finds out that it wasn't a good idea."

"He won't if I can help it—but an admonition to keep hands off other people's property might be in order."

"Will the maid be admonished too?"

He nodded. "But when doctors write out prescriptions for drugs it should be mandatory for them to lecture their patients on the subject of one man's meat being another man's poison. That might curb some of the indiscriminate sharing that goes on. Too many laymen take it upon themselves to diagnose and treat the aches and pains of their friends. Cigarette?"

Kyrie said, "No thanks—and you don't want one either. It doesn't make sense lighting them and stubbing them out after a single puff."

He glanced at the full ashtray. "Nothing makes much sense to me at the moment."

"Not even Annie Grimes? She's accepted an invitation to dinner next week."

"Stop trying to cheer me up."

"All right—wallow in it. Does the handsome stepbrother get off with just an admonition?"

Nelson said, "Lieutenant Werner seems to have lost interest in the letter. Also he made it clear that he no longer requires my assistance." Grudgingly he returned her smile. "When I told Sammy that the precinct all but had the Alice Thwaite case made, she consoled me by saying I'd have beaten them to it if they hadn't had such a big head start."

"Did you tell her she'd given you a big head start in the Carmody case?"

His face darkened again. "A head start in a race that has no finish line."

"Grid—why does it have more than an average bad effect on you?"

He said savagely, "Because Carmody's guilty and there's nothing I can do about it. If he hadn't launched his project the woman would still be alive. She would never have left that valuable ring in the washroom if she hadn't been preoccupied with thoughts of the coming tryst—and if she hadn't left it she wouldn't have jumped to the conclusion that he'd stolen it—or worked up a headache and taken codeine—or aroused the sympathies of the maid and prompted her donation of tranquilizers."

Kyrie murmured, "This is the house that Jack built."

"It's the house that Mike tore down."

"How do you know she jumped to the conclusion that he stole the ring?"

"Why else would she have tried to fob off the police? Her subconscious had probably warned her of the type of man she was taking on as a lover—and she may have realized that if cornered he'd have no qualms about making the affair public. She'd lived a conventional life. The thought of her daughter—her own violated pride would have forced her to do anything to avoid the attendant scandal."

"But you can't even be sure she did have an affair unless—?"

"Yes—the P. M.—and before that it was indicated by the letter she'd written to her daughter. In addition there was Vance Manning's story—and Carmody's whining saga when I saw him today."

"How long can you hold him?"

"He's arranged to hold himself for a while—in a hospital bed."

"You didn't tell me that."

"Getting out of the police car he swatted an officer and tried to break away—but he slipped on an icy patch of sidewalk and broke his leg instead."

"Well—that should keep him out of the reducing business for some time to come—and then there's the charge for resisting arrest."

"Small comfort in the face of his other crimes."

"What about his wife? Will she try to carry on alone at the Easton? I hope she doesn't. I hope she divorces him and marries Vance. Being a teacher's wife would be a lovely change—"

"Vance is working on it—and it's not impossible that the grounds for divorce will be desertion. Carmody has overdrawn on the joint accounts and I gather that from his angle the salon hasn't lived up to its promise. Then too he stands in mortal fear of his bookie, who seems to be taking a jaundiced view of his indebtedness. So it's likely that when we run out of charges he may decide to seek safer climes."

"There—you see? He doesn't get off scot-free."

"He shouldn't be free at all—there are too many of him running around loose. In my book he's a murderer. If his plans had succeeded he'd have killed Mrs. Atmore by inches."

"Will you please stop trying to remake the world? Sometimes you seem to have a sneaking idea that you can change it singlehanded."

He put an arm around her and said pacifically, "Even in my most deluded phases I don't dream of changing you."

THE END

# DEADLOCK

## RUTH FENISONG

# CHAPTER 1

A chair was overturned. A silver box had been swept from a low coffee table. Its content of cigarettes made angular patterns on the thick gray pile of the rug. Water from a broken vase trickled along the polished acre of the desk, overflowed a shallow indentation that had been cut in the thick surface, and dripped down into the half-opened drawers. The peonies that the vase had held died lingeringly upon the floor beneath.

But these indications of violence were isolated in the large room. The windows were open, but June was short of breath that year and could not even lift the raw-silk drapes. The gray walls, hung with vivid splashes of color, seemed remote from whatever it was that had taken place. So, at first glance, did the young man on the long, deep sofa. He was smiling broadly. He did not move when the outer door of the apartment opened.

The girl closed the door and padded across the square entrance foyer. She moved like an animal habitually on the alert. She was a small, meager girl. Too little food and too much experience had been her portion. But somewhere along her unpaved road she had acquired vanity. She slowed her steps to smooth the new silk dress which bagged pathetically because it had been designed for somewhat more of a figure, and raised her gloved hand to pat the brittle elegance of a recent permanent.

On the threshold of the room she came to a full stop. Like an animal scenting danger she sniffed, and her bright knowing eyes, slanted in their bony sockets, went in turn to the upset chair, the fallen cigarette box, the vase, the dying flowers, the man.

She made neither sound nor gesture of surprise. She was so still that she might have been gathering for a spring. But after a moment the tension went out of her and she walked toward the couch.

"Hey," she said. Her voice had been hoarse since babyhood. The people of her slum had always to strain their vocal cords in order to be heard. "Hey—mister—"

His fair hair was rumpled, his blue eyes wide. He wore slacks and a fine white shirt opened at the throat, and there were soft leather slippers upon his narrow feet. She noted all this before her mind registered the peculiar glassiness of his stare, the rigid smile, the hole in the shirt outlined by a dark petallike design.

One of his hands dangled over the edge of the couch, and she was impelled to reach out and touch it. Then she recoiled, shaking her own hand, much as a cat shakes its paw after contact with something new and strange. Yet death was not strange to her. She knew death when she met it.

"Just my luck," she muttered. "Just my luck." And feeling, perhaps, that some expression of sympathy was required, she raised her voice a little. "I'm sorry it had to happen to you, mister, but I guess you were playing out of your league." If it was my fellow, she thought, my dream boy, I'd turn on the floodworks. She shook her head, attempting to clear it for more practical matters. This was no place to get mushy about her dream boy. The sooner she was out of it, the better. She was an hour late as it was, thanks to the old woman.

She stroked the red pocketbook under her arm. Her eyes narrowed. He expected me, so he should have left the cash ready. Last time it was on the desk in an envelope. She went over to the desk. "Holy smoke!" she muttered. "What a mess." Then she saw the envelope propped against a bonbon dish. She pounced. Like a bonus, she thought, because I don't have to part with nothing in exchange. Yep, it's all here. Her eyes returned to the bonbon dish. Only a few left, she thought. Wonder if they're the same kind he gave me last time and laughed because I ate so many. Poor guy. Almost sentimentally she unwrapped one of the silver-foiled confections and popped it into her mouth. A noise startled her and she swallowed the candy whole. She giggled nervously because it had been only her own pocketbook knocking against the desk. Act your age, she admonished herself. Might as well see what else is kicking around. There won't be another chance, and it don't look like the cops have been wised yet.

She pulled the half-open drawers out further and rooted through them. I seen him take dough out of the desk once when the cleaner's boy came, so you never can tell. But the drawers were so untidy that her hopes fled quickly. Jeez, she thought, that killer sure was looking for something. Funny he didn't spot my envelope. Her mind continued with its commentary. Will you look at all them pencils and paper—a regular store. And them letters! He must have saved every one he ever got—most of them from dames, too, I'll bet. Rich dames. He wouldn't be bothered with any other kind.

In one of the drawers she found a flat cigarette case that looked like real gold. She was tempted to help herself to it, but she did not yield to the temptation. Sooner or later the cops would arrive and they might have some way of knowing what was missing. The cops were tricky bastards, and she was not looking for trouble. One racket was enough to handle at a time. But even the cops wouldn't stoop so low as to count candies. She emptied the dish into her bag.

Leaving the apartment was a wrench. Its luxury had captured her starved little soul. She regretted that now it would be closed to her forever. The low good-by she uttered was the good-by of a lover resigned to the end of love. She addressed it to the beauty of the room and not to the deep sleeper.

He climbed four flights of musty stairs. He unlocked the door of the railroad flat and threw his hat on the hall table. He drew a few deep breaths and shouted, "Joss—are you home? Joss!"

"I'm here." Joss Woodruff came hurriedly from the kitchen. She laughed and struggled. "Unhand me. What would you do if we'd been separated for weeks instead of a few hours?"

"Dunno. Eat you, I guess." He kissed the fine smooth skin of her neck.

"Quit—you'll get flour all over you."

Morgan Woodruff released his wife. "Probably an improvement," he said. "It will take some of the shine off this suit."

"Oh, Morgan, maybe we can squeeze enough out of your next commission to—"

"It's your turn. We spent your dress money for my shirts."

"Well—we'll see. Sit down, darling. You look pale. Are you all right?"

"I'm fine. It's those damn stairs."

"You take them too fast."

"Because I'm always in a hurry to get to you." He dropped into a chair and winced. "That no-good spring bit me again."

"We'll get it fixed soon. What did you do?"

"What would a rich guy like me do on his Monday off when his wife chucks him out of the house? I had lunch at the Gateau."

"No—seriously."

"Seriously. I set out for a walk, but I hadn't gone more than three blocks when I met Glen and he insisted that I join him for lunch."

"That was a nice break." But her face had clouded. "I'm baking a pie for dinner. I'd better get on with it."

"Joss—it's too hot to bake."

"But you like pie."

"Joss—"

She halted on her way to the kitchen. "Yes?"

"About that lunch with Glen—"

"You don't think I mind you swanking it once in a while without the old lady." She had a lovely smile, but now it seemed forced.

"You mind something."

She hesitated. "Not really—only it would be nice if you could go to places like the Gateau on your own, and not just when—when someone else chooses to take you."

He looked at her curiously. "You don't like Glen much, do you?"

"I did at first, but—"

"But what?"

"But I don't like him as much now as I did at first. That's all."

"No reason?"

"No reason."

"That would do for most women, but not for my straightforward, intelligent Joss."

"Your Joss has her moments. We're going to see him tonight. Aren't we?"

"No—I called it off. I had a suspicion you wouldn't mind."

"Swell. We'll get to bed early."

"Have you been out at all, Joss?"

"Only to the hardware store. The bulb in the bathroom burned out. See—" She glanced at the desk. "I left the note in the typewriter in case you got back before I did."

They were both trying to keep their voices light, but neither of them succeeded. She saw with concern that the stairs alone could not be held responsible for his pallor or for the fatigue lines on his thin, bitter face. She said, "That super-deluxe lunch didn't put any weight on you. Come into the kitchen and drink some milk while I get on with my baking."

In the tiny kitchen Morgan leaned against the refrigerator, sipped milk, and watched Joss wield the rolling pin. Love for her welled up and almost choked him. She had, he thought, a glow that rubbed off on everything she touched, so that even the drab, ugly apartment responded and became a wholesome, cheerful dwelling. The play of her strong body engaged in the simplest of household tasks was enough to make a man weep for joy, and whoever believed that beauty of face depended upon features should observe her when she smiled, or looked interested, or thoughtful, or tender. Brown-eyed Joss of the blunt nose, the generous mouth—

"What did you do after lunch?" she asked. "Did you go home with—"

"No." He answered before she could pronounce Glen's name. "I took my walk. I got as far as Central Park and sat down until the sun disappeared."

"I'm glad you had sense enough to sit down. You do enough walking in the normal course of things."

"The abnormal course of things," he said. "But I get too wound up to stop on my day off. I don't suppose I'll ever get used to having Monday off—instead of Sunday like everybody else. But my outfit only recognizes Sunday as the one sure day the prospect will be at home."

Morgan Woodruff had come out of the army an old young man, too old, he felt, to continue his interrupted formal education. Joss was waiting as she had promised she would wait, and his one full-fledged desire among a swarming of inchoate longings had been to embrace her and hold her forever. What was to follow after seemed unimportant at the time. So they had married. His mustering-out pay looked larger than it was, and on the deceptive strength of it he had insisted that Joss quit her own job.

He was talented. He could draw, write verse, play the piano, sing, and compose songs that compared favorably with many of those that came over the air waves to tickle the national ear. But he had soon become aware that without contacts it was impossible to buck the closed shop where such commodities were launched. Discouraged, he had walked the streets in search of a desk job. But he had little more to offer than charm and a quick wit, insufficient equipment in a world that demanded specialists for the most trivial work. When he had exhausted every lead, someone suggested that he was a born salesman and introduced him to an organization that sold encyclopedias.

Because the organization had nothing to lose, it employed almost everybody who applied. Beginners were subjected to a period of schooling in which they memorized yards of sales patter. During this period they received no remuneration. In the final week of preparation they accompanied an expert into the field in order that they might profit by his performance. For this and for all subsequent solo ventures they were required to pay their own carfare, an outlay which few could afford, else they would not be there. And if any of them fell by the wayside, the organization could take it philosophically.

Morgan did not fall by the wayside, but his physical and mental expenditures were large. He was not a born salesman. He was constitutionally unable to assume the "iron vest" which salesmen wore to protect their egos. He hated everything about the work: the ringing of strange doorbells in order to achieve entry into buildings that did not run to doormen, the dodging of doormen who barred his way, the endless stairs to be climbed, the furtive insertion of come-on cards into mailboxes. But most of all he hated the intrusion into apartments where innocents, lured by the tricky wording of the cards, had written for information and received, instead of the printed material they expected, a flesh-and-blood representative who would not leave until he either had been tossed out or had bludgeoned his prospect to weakness by means of the organization's prescribed tactics.

It was two months before Morgan made his first sale and received his first commission. Meanwhile he wore out two pairs of shoes and spent about a dollar a day for transportation. Therefore he felt committed to remain until he broke even. When presently he did break even, he could not bring himself to quit. He wanted to take care of Joss, and no other way presented itself.

His morale had been at its lowest ebb the day Glen Williams answered the door, listened courteously to his preliminary spiel, and asked him to come in. Glen had offered him a chair and a drink. Glen had suffered the spate of double-talk so timed that one sentence flowed into another, leaving no gap between for interruption. But before the spiel was completed, Morgan sensed an odd quality in Glen's attentiveness, a kind of tolerant amusement. Most of the people whose gates he stormed showed restlessness or irritation, frequently anger. He had learned how to deal with their ineffectual essays to shut him off or to interject questions. To be met with amusement was something new. It distracted him, made him stumble and repeat.

"Our encyclopedia is a 'must' in every home that aspires to culture," he said desperately. He had made the same nauseating statement in dreary cold-water flats, in stodgy remodeled tenements, and in upper-middle-class apartments throughout Manhattan, the Bronx, and Brooklyn. It had always sounded false and insulting, but never so false or insulting as it sounded here in Glen Williams' living room where culture had not only been aspired to but plainly won.

Glen Williams broadened his subtle smile. "How much—or is that a secret?"

It was a secret. The rules commanded that the price he broken gently and never until the "fish" was well hooked. Morgan reddened and went on quickly with the several hundred stock words that remained to be delivered. If the "fish" kept on about the price he was to be staved off with, "Can you afford to pay seventy-five cents a day? Fifty cents?" It went even lower than that if the nod was not forthcoming. The "Powers" considered it poor psychology to mention the fat sum total until the contract was signed.

Glen Williams did not permit Morgan to progress as far as the "Can you afford" routine. He said abruptly, "Very well—I'll buy it."

Cut off midsentence, Morgan had difficulty with his hanging jaw. "I—I beg your pardon?" He thought that the unaccustomed drink had affected his hearing.

"I said I'll buy it."

Morgan lost the next line of his interrupted spiel. He felt foolishly that he could recall it only by reciting the whole thing over again. But he had enough presence of mind to pull out a contract from his brief case. He saw the cursory glance it received, and held his breath as the bold signature took shape. Sales were not made this way, the rules said. He shook himself and rattled something about a down payment.

Glen raised an arched eyebrow. He said gently, "Down payment? If you'll trust me far enough to divulge the full amount, I'll give you a check for it."

Morgan divulged the full amount. He looked around the room while the check was being written. It won't bounce, he told himself, his eyes resting briefly upon the grand piano, the pictures, the radio-phonograph-television combination. The odds are all in favor of its being good. It can't bounce, not issuing from a place like this. I'm in. I've made a sale. My first!

"Now then," Glen said, handing him the check. "That's over with." Morgan, about to rise, was waved back into his chair. "Don't go. Do you mind my asking how you happen to be pursuing a—a career like this?"

Morgan felt the way he imagined a prostitute must feel when questioned as to how she happened to stray off the straight and narrow. Lightheaded, he simpered, "Oh, sir, you see I never meant to go wrong. I was raised strict but—" He was checked by Glen's laughter.

"Well done," Glen said. "And much more effective than 'mind your own business.'"

"Sorry." Morgan meant it. He was grateful to this polished, insulated article who could not be expected to know that any job was preferable to a roofless, foodless existence. He said, "I just fell into it, I guess."

Glen Williams nodded. "It's a manhole, all right. I'll bet they don't even give you a drawing account."

Again Morgan had to remind himself that his host, well made, well fed, whose cashmere jacket must have cost almost the price of the encyclopedia, was a paying customer. He said with considerable restraint, "Are you a writer?"

"You mean I should be to justify my prying into your affairs. No—I'm not in search of material. I've dallied with writing, though. As a matter of fact, I've dallied with almost everything but never made the grade." He noted Morgan's skeptical smile, his reappraisal of the surroundings. "Don't let this grandeur fool you. I didn't lift a finger to earn it."

"Don't be bitter about it," Morgan said. "I could accept an inheritance with no guilt at all."

Glen Williams made no comment. He refilled Morgan's glass.

"Thanks—but I've taken up enough of your time." He was in a hurry to tell Joss the unbelievable news.

"I've time to spare—especially when I'm interested. Stay awhile."

"Well—" He thought uncomfortably, Here's a switch—the angler hooked by the "fish." He said, "Why should you be interested in a run-of-the-mill salesman?"

"You won't be a salesman long." The cashmere shoulders, broad by grace of padding or nature, rose in self-deprecation. "You're welcome to think me a screwball, but I do have hunches about people."

Morgan humored him. "What's your hunch about me?"

"Success."

"Fine. When does it start and where do I go to meet it?"

"That depends on where your talents lie." Glen Williams got up, crossed the room, and returned with a thick, leather-bound book. He placed it on Morgan's knee. "I interrupted my dallying once—for long enough to complete this."

The binding of the book was a mellow delight. Impressed, Morgan wondered if the contents measured up to it. He opened it to the title page and read, "*Jester in Heaven*, by Glen Williams." He could think of nothing to say, so he turned to the first chapter. "Is it fiction?" he asked.

"Yes—it comes under the heading of fiction. I don't expect you to read it now. Some other time, perhaps." Glen relieved him of the book, returning it with tender care to its place on the desk. He laughed. "I've a confession to make. Actually I'm a vain man. I showed you that merely to undo the screwball impression."

"A lot of screwballs have written books," Morgan said. The second drink had been quite strong, or else skimping on lunches had given him a weak head. A short while later he found himself playing one of his songs on the grand piano.

"Bravo," Glen said. "My hunch paid off."

Morgan's hands crashed down on the keyboard. "Your hunch is all

that ever will pay off as far as this or any other of my songs is concerned."

"Don't be too sure. Are there words to it?"

"Yes, but—"

"Let's hear them."

Morgan sang, self-consciously at first, and then Glen picked up the
lyrics and joined him in the second chorus. Glen had a rather pleas-
ing baritone, and he seemed disproportionately delighted when Morgan praised it. Morgan became expansive and invited him to come and
meet Joss sometime. He thought that he was a modest, disarming sort
of man and that Joss would like him.

That was the start of their friendship. Glen visited the Woodruffs'
railroad apartment and was visited in return. He paid Joss extrava-
gant compliments and told Morgan that he was a lucky guy. He took
the Woodruffs under his wing. He had contacts. He had schemes for
launching Morgan. Once they got under way, he said, there would be
no more tramping from door to door. No more encyclopedias—

"Bravo," said Morgan. "Sure—bravo." The cold, disillusioned sound
of his own voice catapulted him back to the kitchen, to Joss. It served
him right, he thought, for pinning his hopes to anyone but himself,
and especially to the man Glen Williams had revealed himself to be.
He knew now that Glen Williams had never seriously intended to do
anything for him, and never would do anything.

"Did you say something?" Joss asked.

"No." He walked over to her. He put his arms around her and
pressed close, as though he were cold.

## CHAPTER 2

Betty Conway took the six-ten train out of Grand Central Station.
In a little more than an hour she was in Howardsville, Connecticut.
Howardsville was home.

She had left her car parked near the station. Mike Williams greeted
her as she was about to step into it. "Hi, Betty."

Glen's brother was no one she wanted to see just then, but she said,
"Hi," and waited for him to join her. He was a stocky, sunburned man,
just under average height. He had a strong, plain face. If an artist had
set out to draw Glen's physical opposite he would have drawn Mike.

Because his very white teeth flashed with the pleasure of seeing her,
she tried to smile too.

"You look so elegant," he said, "that I'd have known you'd been to New York even if I hadn't seen you get off the train."

Mike's sincerity was unquestionable, yet she knew that she never achieved elegance. She had no instinct for clothes. Jeans and tweeds suited her, but in more formal dress she lacked that which distinguished the city girl from her country cousin. She said, "I don't feel elegant. I feel as though half of New York's grime has settled on me."

"It doesn't show. You're a princess for my money—right out of a fairy tale."

"Coming from you, that's practically a sonnet."

His smile became sheepish. "Anyway, it's not a line."

She knew that. Glen's compliments had ranged from, "My awkward young colt" to "My blue-eyed, golden-haired Amazon," and it had always been a "line." She bit her mouth in her fight for self-control. She opened the door of her car and managed to say lightly enough, "See you around, Mike."

His eyes held her. "Were you in for some shopping? No—that's a foolish question, considering you're not weighed down with bundles."

"There is such a thing as a delivery service," she said. "But I didn't shop. I went in for a checkup."

He frowned. "Nothing wrong?"

"Not a thing. Just the annual visit. I'm so healthy I bore my doctor stiff."

His brow cleared. "You always were as strong as a horse, Betty."

"How alluring. I prefer the fairy-tale-princess description."

He said soberly, "I'm no Don Juan at that." He hesitated a moment. "You didn't run into that brother of mine in—"

"I didn't run into him or see him by appointment." Her voice had flattened.

"Excuse it. I suppose I'll never get it into my head that you and Glen— Well, when you were kids it seemed like a sure thing. I—if you'd quarreled seriously with him or anything, I'd know where—I mean I could understand—but your quarrels never seemed to amount to much—just—"

She said icily, "If you don't understand now, you'll never understand—and what difference does it make?" His expression made her repent the outburst. "Sorry, Mike. I'm tired and cross. I don't want to be rude, but I do want to get home and bathe."

"It makes a mighty big difference," he said, "because if you and Glen—" He stopped short.

"Well?"

"Never mind. I guess you're right. You're in a hurry and I'm not one of those glib fellows who can talk with a stop watch held on them." She gave him a brief, forlorn stare. Then she got into the car. "Goodby, Mike," She drove off, knowing without needing to verify it that he was standing where she had left him, gazing after her.

The fool, she thought. The stubborn, generous, bewildered fool. How could two men, so different in every way, be born of the same parents? Glen never deserved his loyalty—never. Glen's spoiled my life because Mike would sooner die than— Die. Be dead. Oh no. Impossible. She began to cry. When she reached the dirt road that led to her house she had to stop the car until she could see to drive again.

Hugging the brown paper bag to his chest, the big man stumbled past his own basement apartment and went into the furnace room. He closed the fire door behind him. His knees shook and he could feel the sweat trickling down the backs of his legs. He switched on the overhead light and prowled the cement floor. His thick lips moved silently in time to his slow-working brain. If I take too long I'll be in the soup. Dora could've heard me go by. I can't tell her I had to fix something down here. She knows I got nothing to fix. I got to think fast.

The brain's sudden click was all but audible. He wheeled and went to the room's far wall. He stepped into a large partitioned space that served the tenants as a storage place for the overflow from their apartments. In physical strength he lacked nothing. With no great effort he shifted a few trunks, came upon the one he sought, and tested its spring lock. Then he drew a hammer from the pocket of his overalls and struck a few expert blows. The lock sprung open. He lifted the lid and stooped. When he straightened his body the trunk was closed, the lock in place, and he was rid of the brown paper bag. He heaved the trunk to its former position, watching as it teetered and came to rest atop two of its fellows. He grunted with relief.

As he returned to the furnace room he heard loud guttural sounds coming from his apartment. He muttered, "Now! He has to pick now." But the sounds had tapered into silence before he reached the door of his apartment.

His wife was in the kitchen. She stood at the tub washing some of Billy's things. She turned at his entrance, wiping her hands on a dish towel. "Don't make no noise. I just got him to sleep. I had to run out for a minute and he fell down."

"Is he okay?"

"Yes—he didn't hurt himself."

She had scarcely enough flesh to cover her large bones. Fred Storch seldom remembered that once she had been handsome. He existed only in a present made horrible by Billy. It seemed to him that Billy had been with them always, Billy, who was responsible for nothing and who had so irresponsibly altered their lives.

Coffee bubbled on the stove. He got a cup and filled it, adding sugar and condensed milk. He stirred the mixture, blew upon it, and gulped it down.

She said irritably, "What are you drinking coffee for? It's supper-time. I'll fix something for you as soon as I hang up these clothes."

"I don't want no supper."

"You sick?"

He shook his head dumbly.

Her harsh voice softened a little, became the voice she used for their son. "What's the matter, Fred? You don't look good. You didn't have an-other run-in with that skunk on the second floor?"

"It ain't the second floor," he said, "it's the top floor. It's Mr. Williams."

"Mr. Williams? You never had no trouble with him, Fred. If you went and got fresh to Mr. Williams after all he done for us I—"

"Nobody's going to have trouble with Mr. Williams," he said heav-ily. "He's dead. Someone went and shot him."

She was wringing out a pair of shorts. She dropped them back into the rinse water. Her hand flew to her mouth.

"So that's why I don't want no supper," he said.

Her eyes were big in her pinched face. "Mr. Williams dead—shot—I can't believe it. Why, only this morning he—"

"You can believe it all right, Dora. It's the truth—I seen it for my-self."

"You seen somebody shoot him?"

"I didn't say I seen somebody shoot him. I wouldn't have let nobody shoot him if I seen them, would I? When I opened the door there was only him—dead—"

She was a woman accustomed to shocks. She came out of this one and took command. "Did you call the police?"

"I only just come from his apartment. I'm going to call them—right now. I didn't want to use his phone. They always tell you not to touch nothing."

"You call them, then—this minute—or they're going to think you had something to do with it. Go on—get to that phone. You should have done it as soon as you found him—before you told me."

He grumbled, "How are they going to know when I found him?"

"Fred—if you start off by lying to them, they'll get you so mixed up you'll wish you hadn't."

"Who's lying?" He went to the telephone in the hall.

When he came back she said, "What was you doing up there? What time did you get back from fixing that garbage violation? I come in at five-twenty from running to the store and I looked for you in the lobby because I thought you might be fixing the leg of that chair up there—you said you would when you got around to it—"

"I didn't get around to it."

"Fred—the police will be asking the same questions I'm asking, so you better tell me the whole business to get it clear in your mind."

He sat down at the round table in the center of the kitchen. He clutched his head. "I got it clear in my mind. You're the one who'll get me mixed up if you don't leave me alone."

"Fred."

When she used that tone she had to be answered. He fumbled for words. "There ain't much to it. Mr. Williams asked me to come up. This morning he asked me. He said he wanted the bookshelves in the bedroom pickled because he liked the job I done on that chest of his—and he'd pay me good on account of I wasn't supposed to do stuff like that on the landlord's time. So I said I'd be glad to oblige but I couldn't make it until about four-thirty—and he says not to make it no later than a quarter to five because he wanted to talk to me about something important and he might be busy after that—"

She interrupted him. "What did he want to talk about?"

"How do I know?"

"You was up there at a quarter to five? It's a couple of minutes to six now. The police could get pretty sore—you taking all that time before you—"

"Quit jumping on me. You're acting like I done it or something. I wasn't up there at a quarter to five. I tried, because I always liked to keep my promise to Mr. Williams and he—he'd got so he counted on me. But you know today was the day I had to go square that garbage violation—" He paused, reminded of a grievance that blotted out his more recent experience. "If I told that skinflint landlord once about needing new covers for the cans on account of the old ones wouldn't fit no more the way them sanitation workers bang them down, I told him a million times. But he sure hates to part. I just wish it was him who had to stand around waiting for some little squirt who didn't have nothing to do but collect fines—"

"Never mind that," she said. "They kept you waiting and you didn't get back till—"

"I got my tools and went straight up to Mr. Williams' apartment. It could have been maybe ten after five. I looked because I was worried about being late—but I can tell the police it was even later if they start squawking—"

"Did you unlock the door or was it open?"

"It was open. I called out who I was, but he didn't answer, so I thought he was in the bathroom and I walked in." He ran rough hands over his cropped head. "He was laying there—"

"You're sure he wasn't breathing? He could be just hurt—"

"Well, he ain't just hurt. I know a deader from a live one. The minute I got in the room I seen something was wrong. There was things knocked over and drawers opened—"

"A burglar? We never had burglars in this house. I wonder if they broke into anybody else's apartment."

"We'd've heard."

She nodded thoughtfully. "Them tenants don't keep nothing from us, so it ain't likely they'd keep burglars dark." Her voice became mournful. "Poor Mr. Williams—I guess some crook could've got wind of the expensive things he has up there. Fred—maybe you should've stayed with him. It don't seem right to think of him laying there—"

"He ain't worrying." He added stubbornly, "And like I said, I had to leave him to phone the police. Remember that movie we seen where the killer used the phone and the police found his fingerprints on it?"

"If it was a burglar and he didn't wear gloves and the drawers was pulled out and stuff knocked over, then they'll find plenty of fingerprints without any that was left on the phone. You sure you didn't see nobody on the floor?"

"Nobody—except a blond young lady coming out of the Delaney apartment."

She said, "Maybe you better make out to the police it was later than ten after five when you got up there. They don't know how slow you move sometimes when you're thinking about something."

He nodded. He scratched at his head.

Her hand descended upon his shoulder. It was a caress, rough and unaccustomed. "Fred—you ain't worried the landlord will blame it on you? He couldn't—"

"That don't bother me." For a moment he was tempted to tell her what did bother him, to unburden himself completely. The bell, sounding loudly through the small apartment, stopped him. It also woke the unfortunate child in the next room, and the child made its peculiar guttural demand for attention.

"Billy's hungry," she said. "I'll feed him. If that's the police, don't let them get you excited. Except for making out you came home a little later, all you got to do is tell them the truth."

"Yeah," he said.

Sarah Thrace pulled off her clothes, stretched, fitted a rubber cap over her hair, and got under the shower. She scrubbed herself meticulously, dried with large sweeping motions, and was putting on a shabby silk robe when the telephone rang. She went into the bedroom to answer it, moving with somewhat more speed than was usual to her.

She was a woman past middle age, but splendid still, her opulent body firm, her blue eyes unexpectedly clear and guileless. In a soft light the wrinkles that rayed out from them were almost imperceptible, and even the brassy quality of her dyed hair lent them no hardness.

The telephone stood on a table near her bed. Before she reached for it she settled herself upon a mass of pillows.

"Hello," she said. Alcohol and tobacco had added a not unpleasant huskiness to her voice. "Oh—it is you, Tom. That's a relief. I couldn't talk to a stranger the way I'm dressed." She laughed lustily at the outmoded joke.

The man at the other end of the wire said, "Turn it off, Sarah. I've been trying to get you for the last hour. Where were you?"

"Having a shower, old boy." She used her best stage diction. "I can't hear the phone when I'm in the bathroom."

He said petulantly, "It must have been the longest shower on record."

"You sound almost thrillingly possessive. And I was beginning to think that you didn't care even a little bit."

"Sarah—were you going to Glen's later?"

"I've been asked—but I wasn't sure of an escort."

"I'm coming over now."

"Masterful brute," she said. "It's not seven yet, is it? I'd been counting on a beauty nap, but who am I to—"

The telephone clicked in her ear. She looked at it reflectively before she set it back in its cradle. She got up and went to the dressing table. She eyed her face in the mirror and started with great industry to remodel it. She practiced a variety of expressions as she worked.

She had arranged her hair and progressed as far as girdle and stockings when her visitor arrived. She stepped into her mules, reassumed the silk robe, and went to the door.

Tom Gaudio barely greeted her. He stumbled into the living room. He was a slight young man with large dark eyes, all pupil. His nose was straight, his full lips well shaped, but he needed more chin. This evening he needed a shave, too, and a fresh shirt, and a crease to his trousers. And he needed something to steady his shaking hands.

"Give me a drink," he said without preliminary. "You'll want one too."

"I always do," she said. "Scotch?"

"Anything." He stood fidgeting with his buttons, his collar, his tie. "Straight."

"In that case, rye. It's a bit cheaper. Sit down. If I were a nervous woman I couldn't bear you."

He jammed his hands into his pockets. He sat down on the couch. She brought him a generous drink of rye. She could hear the hard, tight sound of his swallowing as she tilted the bottle over her own glass. When she turned she watched his face for a moment. It wore a look of eagerness, as though he might be waiting for the whisky to take effect. Then as she watched the look faded and his full lips drooped with frustration.

She sat next to him, took a few deep swigs, and said briskly, "Your impatience to see me is very touching, old boy, but I shouldn't have minded if you'd taken time out to shave and change."

"Drop the British act, Sarah."

"You are in a state." But she dropped it. "Nothing can be as bad as you look, Tom. What's happened—lost your best friend?"

He nodded wordlessly. He finished his drink and said, "Yes—I've lost my best friend—and so have you. Glen is dead."

She stifled a nervous giggle. His tone had reminded her of a childhood game where everyone stood in a circle and took chances at intoning, "King Dido is dead." She was afraid to say, "How did he die?" because that was part of the game too, and the answer was, "He died doing this way," whereupon the player who had answered would perform some ridiculous distracting gesture and keep repeating it while each of the players had a turn. And the game ended with each of them trying madly to concentrate upon the performance of his chosen idiocy.

After a moment she arose, slow motion, poured more whisky, and drank hers on the way back to him. She set the glasses down carefully. She said, "It always gives me the shivers to hear of anybody dying—

but I wouldn't say that Glen Williams was my best friend—or yours either."

"Women," he said bitterly, "a race apart. Glen is dead"—anger released his taut nerves—"and you don't even ask how—or when—or—"

"Calm down." She went on in the manner of one who is always ready to oblige, "How did he die?" and watched half fearfully for the expected gesture. "He wasn't sick that I know of. An accident?"

"Murder—shot through the chest—right in his own apartment—" Tom Gaudio's dark eyes filled, spilled over. He made a boy's gesture of shielding them with a crooked arm.

She got up and poured herself a third drink. She said in a kindly tone, "You're just feeling sorry for yourself, Tommy—not for Glen. Another drink? No—better not. You might wind up with a real crying jag. Take it from me, you haven't lost much. I shouldn't wonder if I hadn't made a mistake—introducing you to Glen in the first place. And that's an understatement, but we've been over the ground before. Aside from everything else, he made a lot of promises, but even with the best of intentions I doubt if he could have fulfilled them. You'll get along. You've got a lot of what's needed—and I'll try to help you to—"

He turned toward her. He flung himself upon her breast. Sobs shook him. She gave his straight black hair a few perfunctory strokes, her expression completely detached. She said, "That's right —get it out of your system." When he was a little calmer, she said, "How did you hear the news, Tom?"

He took out a soiled handkerchief and blew his nose. "I was supposed to drop in to see him at five—to talk to him about—about a project we had. But I was developing some pictures and I got interested and didn't arrive until—well—just before I called you."

"Couldn't you have saved what you had to say to him until tonight?"

"No—because he'd invited the Woodruffs too—and I knew there'd be no chance for a private talk."

"I see."

Something in her voice startled him. He stared at her.

"Well," she said, "you didn't get there until sixish. Go on."

"I told you I'd been working. When I came to and realized the time, I didn't stop to shave or change my clothes. I rushed over and saw the police just getting into the elevator. I didn't dream it had anything to do with Glen. I had to wait because they were taking the elevator to the basement. Some man had been nosing around the lobby and I asked him what it was all about. He said a Mr. Glen Williams on the top floor had been shot and killed—so I—I knew the police wouldn't let me in—"

"And there would have been no sense in your getting mixed up in it, since it was too late to do any good," she said. "Very sensible of you to come away. I wonder if there's anything on the radio about it." She reached out and turned the knobs of a battered console set. But the news broadcasts had come and gone. She tried the different stations. Scratchy fragments of song filled the room. When she gave up, the silence was not the relief it should have been.

Tom Gaudio had lit a cigarette. His face was almost obscured by smoke. He said, "Sarah—what did you do with yourself today?" He was trying to sound quite casual. But he was overdoing it.

She stared at him. She said, "Now really!"

"Don't say you didn't resent Glen for taking up so much of my time—because you did."

"Would you like to search the premises for my smoking gun?"

"Maybe you think it's funny now, but—"

She said, "Tommy, I'm very fond of you—but really you are a little fool."

## CHAPTER 3

Lieutenant Gridley Nelson, acting captain of Homicide in the absence of his chief, Waldo Furniss, studied without pleasure what had once been the living room of Glen Williams. Nelson's pointed, olive-skinned face wore the listening look of deep absorption.

The medical examiner had come and gone. The inelegant wicker basket was conveying Glen Williams morgueward. The laboratory squad had repacked its equipment and departed.

A small man, lost in a baggy suit, came out of the bedroom. Nelson's eyes questioned him.

The small man shrugged and turned up empty palms. "I combed every spot in the joint, likely and otherwise, Lieutenant. The marksman must've taken his gun with him. Should I have another go, just to make sure he didn't ditch it somewhere in here?"

Nelson shook his prematurely white head. "Never mind, Clevis. The boys took care of this room thoroughly, upholstery included." He stood at the desk, regarding the still damp traces left by the broken vase. The long, strong fingers of his right hand dabbled in the oblong depression cut into the wood's thick surface. A little pool of water had formed there.

Clevis, at his elbow, said, "The late Mr. Williams must've had the literature bug bad. He cuts a piece of his good expensive desk out just to make a bed for that number." He pointed to the book at the far corner of the desk. "What is it—a Bible or something?"

Nelson dried his fingers on a handkerchief before he picked up the book. "You have a good eye," he said. "Yes—it does look as though it would fit. But apparently the late Mr. Williams didn't always remember to put it to bed. Or else our marksman was thoughtful enough to move it out of the wet." Delicately, he ran his hands over the spotless leather binding. "Yes—it's suffered two small water blisters. So perhaps he's got the literature bug too."

Clevis's button eyes watched Nelson's way with the book. "You kinda like literature yourself—don't you, Lieutenant?"

"Hmmm." He had turned to the title page. "I wonder if this is literature. It was written by the deceased—and privately printed."

"Say—that was real foresighted of him. Could it help?"

Nelson consulted the date. "Published six months ago. A lot could have happened to him since the time he wrote it—new interests—new contacts. But we'll look into it."

"We?" Clevis sounded horrified. "I'm no reader." He changed the subject hurriedly. "Doc said if the murderer had been a patient man and waited awhile he could have saved himself the exertion. Doc liked that bullet wound a hell of a lot better than the others he found. By the way, I didn't spot no junk, but there was a hypo syringe stuck in back of a bureau drawer. Speaking of drawers—all right for me to go through the desk now? I'll be looking for out-of-keeping stuff—plus personal correspondence and an address book. He didn't have one on him. But his wallet was on him. One thing's for sure—this wasn't no small-time robbery. His wallet had better than forty bucks in it."

Nelson nodded. He was looking down at the book.

Clevis chuckled. "Funny thing about that towel in the bathroom. I could've sworn the brown smear on it was blood—and then one of the lab boys tells me it's nothing but chocolate."

"Yes—funny," Nelson said absently. He walked away from the desk. "Don't leave here until the policeman assigned to the apartment arrives. I'm going down to talk to the superintendent again."

"Right. If I get through in time I'll stop in for you." Methodically, Clevis tackled the desk.

Before he reached the door Nelson was arrested by his whistle.

Clevis said, "I'll bet it was a dame. I'll bet my bottom dollar it was a dame." His eyes were glued to a letter written on pink stationery.

"I thought you weren't a reader."

"They don't put stuff like this in books, Lieutenant. Things couldn't have changed that much since my teacher booted me into the public library."

"Pick up almost any best seller in your spare time and be prepared for a shock." Nelson went his way smiling. He liked the little detective who concealed unexpected muscular power beneath his ill-fitting clothes and unexpected brain power behind his illiterate speech. He liked a great many people and wanted to keep them alive. Life was so dear to him that he resented even the deaths of those he did not like and of those he did not know. That was the key to his vocation, to his patient pursuit of murderers at large.

He took the self-service elevator to the basement, walked down a dingy passage, and knocked upon the superintendent's door. He smelled food, but it was not a very appetizing smell. He thought of the dinner that awaited him at home. He thought of his wife and of his new little son. But when the superintendent opened the door to him, he thought only of questions and answers.

The superintendent was a solid block barring entrance to his castle. Immovable, he stared at Nelson. "You back?"

Nelson said, "Aside from a few details, Mr. Storch, we're through upstairs. A policeman will be stationed in the apartment for a while, in case there are visitors who don't read the news and who might be able to supply leading information."

The block became more vocal. "You don't need no policeman for that. I'm around most of the time."

"You weren't around today."

"So it's my fault I had to waste time squaring a garbage violation?"

"Of course not. I'm sure your account of your day will be confirmed." Nelson sounded surprised. He was not surprised. In the Williams apartment and here, the man showed a suspicious reluctance to cooperate. Yet experience had taught Nelson that most people carried a burden of guilt which swelled to oversized proportions in the presence of the law. And he knew that this guilt could more often than not be traced to an exaggerated sense of sin, accumulated over the years and rarely pertinent to a case of murder. He said, "I'd like to go over your story again. I may have missed a few facts."

"You didn't miss nothing. I told it all. I can't tell no more than I know, can I?"

A voice behind him said, "Fred, let the officer come in if he wants. Maybe he could use a cup of coffee."

Nelson said, "Thank you," and saw the superintendent's bulk shift to give him clearance. The white-shaded fixture that hung from the kitchen-living room's cracked ceiling gave him opportunity for at least superficial study of the superintendent and his wife. He judged by their size and bone structure, and by the earth-bound look of their stoic faces, that their ancestors had lived in a kitchen too. But probably it had been a rural kitchen, he thought, open to green fields and filled with the odor of baking bread. It had in no way resembled this basement trap where daylight was cut off by close high buildings and rancid air received no benefit of disinfectant sun to kill the stink of coal gas and laundry and human exudations, and coffee boiling endlessly upon the stove. The walls were broken on three sides by doors: the door through which he had entered, a door to what he supposed was a bedroom, and an open door through which he could see a toilet, a basin, and the front legs of a high, old-fashioned bathtub.

"Pull up a chair for the officer," Dora Storch said. And her husband obeyed sullenly, adding a third place to the round table where two chairs stood at ready. "Excuse us," she said, her hard thin arms reaching to set aside the last meal's litter. "I didn't clear away the dishes yet. We was late eating tonight." She rinsed out a cup at the sink, filled it, and brought it to Nelson. The room's predominant smell steamed out of it, hurting his nose. Nevertheless he sipped.

"Nothing like a good cup of coffee," he said.

"Yeah. Some people go for tea, but give me coffee every time. Take some milk and sugar."

"Thanks—I like it black."

"Well, you do get the full flavor that way."

He was getting the full flavor. He went on sipping bravely.

Her eyes moved anxiously from his face to the hostile face of her husband. She said, "How about you, Fred? You want some coffee?"

"I had coffee. What I want is sleep."

"Fred's tired," she said defensively. "He works hard—and he was up most of last night—"

"He don't want to hear our troubles," Fred said. "Look, mister, whatever you do want—get it over with."

Nelson's eyes were on the clothesline stretched across the kitchen. It told him nothing except that the pair of overalls and the several pairs of shorts hung up to dry were too small to fit his reluctant host. "Do you live here alone?" he asked.

"We don't take in no boarders," Fred Storch said. "The view ain't good enough."

His wife seemed bent on covering his rudeness. She said quickly, "There's just us—and our boy."

Nelson's attractive face showed genuine interest. "You have a son? So do I—but I'm a Johnny-come-lately to parenthood."

A wrinkle joined the set ones on her broad forehead. "A what, officer?"

He smiled. "I mean my son is two months old. From the size of those overalls on the line, yours must be a big fellow."

She said flatly, "Sure—a big fellow—he—"

Fred Storch groaned. Nelson was startled by the sudden blaze in his dull eyes. He said tentatively, "I suppose that when they get older they can cause quite a bit of trouble. Mine hasn't reached that stage yet."

"Poor Billy don't mean to make me no—"

"Shut up, will you." Fred's shorn head crouched low between his shoulders. His chair scraped as he shifted toward Nelson. "Mister—get this. No matter how long you sit here making company noises, we know you ain't no friend of this family. Someone give you a badge once which says you got a right to pester people—but not the way you're doing. You keep your kid to yourself and we'll keep ours."

Distress was a familiar to the woman's face. She said, "You got to excuse him, officer. He works hard and he ain't used to policemen butting—I mean—" She tried again. "The both of us liked Mr. Williams, and the whole business was kind of—kind of unexpected. Listen—if it's all right with you, Fred could go to bed and you and me could talk. He told me just how it was he went up there and—"

"I told the world." Fred looked at neither of them. He spoke to the peeling wall. "The whole world knows as much about it as I do. One of the cops upstairs even wrote it down in a book—about the way I'd pickled a chest of drawers for Mr. Williams and he liked it and asked me to come up and pickle—"

"All right." Nelson managed to catch and hold his eyes. "I won't ask you to repeat it again. But I want you to tell me anything you might have learned about Mr. Williams before his death."

"He was a swell gentleman," Dora Storch said. "A swell gentleman," she repeated with conviction.

"Yeah," said Fred. He had relaxed a little. He looked less hostile.

A hoarse cry came from the next room. Its quality was disturbing. Nelson's skin prickled in response to it. He saw Dora Storch rise and hesitate, as if torn between two powerful responsibilities.

"Sit down," Fred said roughly. "You sit down, Dora. I'll see to him."

He heaved himself out of his chair, lumbered to the closed bedroom door. The walls shook as he pulled it tight behind him.

Nelson had started to his feet, impelled by that disturbing cry. Dora Storch waved him back. "Billy ain't good with strangers," she said absently. He could almost hear her listening to whatever might be taking place in the next room. "See—he's good with Fred. He's stopped already. Fred wouldn't hurt a fly. I guess even Billy knows that."

Nelson drank the rest of the coffee without tasting it. "Is Billy sick?"

"He fell down on the stairs—it didn't hurt him none—but I guess maybe it scared him and he was dreaming about it." Then she said, "Otherwise he's like he's always been," and somehow her voice projected a picture of what Billy had always been.

"I'm sorry," Nelson said.

She looked at him. Her lips moved silently. She nodded as though she had weighed and accepted his sympathy.

His ears still cringed from that thick-tongued cry which now his mind associated with the broad, short skull and the slanting eyes of Mongolism. "What age is he?"

"Going on thirteen." Then she said proudly, "Big for his age, too. Real well-built," and in the next moment her face crumpled. "Mister," she said, "officer, excuse me—" She dropped her head to the table. She made no sound, but her large bony frame shook.

She wept as a strong man weeps when life has become too terrible to bear. After a while Nelson got up and brought her a cup of coffee. He had mislaid his reason for being in that room. He took her hand and brought it to the cup. "You'll feel better soon," he said, and heard a muffled, "Thanks, mister," before she raised her head.

He realized with something of a shock that her eyes, cleansed by tears, were dark and lustrous, that the mold of her features spoke of forgotten beauty. He pictured her with the color flooding her broad, high-boned cheeks and with the taut mouth loosened to a mobile curve. But the cellar had muddied her skin, and her mouth was set with cumulative anxieties, and she was scrubbing at her face as though she hated it, and she was saying in strident shame, "Good thing I don't do this in front of Fred. He's got enough."

Nelson, thinking of the healthy little scrap of humanity who was his own son, agreed with her and wished fervently that he could be God for a while. He said, "Being up all night is apt to strain anyone's nerves. Was it yesterday that Billy fell?"

"No—he was just restless—he don't seem to thrive in this hot weather. It was this afternoon he fell. When I ain't watching he gets into things. He'll start going up the stairs or hide someplace—"

"Oh. Then he can help himself to some extent. He can get out—"

She said hopelessly, "I don't let him out alone. I have to be with him. I tried sitting him in a chair in front of the house, but the other kids they don't know no better than to tease him—and with not having much time to spare, I can't be around to chase them. We got a yard—ain't no more than an areaway—really—but when he was smaller it was okay. Not now, though. He can get over the fence now—so most always I got to keep him indoors."

"There are institutions," Nelson said carefully. "Schools where he could be taught within his limits to cope—"

She said, "No."

"But it would be better for him—and for you and your husband."

"Maybe," she said. "I don't know. It ain't me that's against it. The doctor told us that if we ever had another child the chances were a hundred to one it would be—it would be like other children." Her eyes yearned. "He also said it wasn't no fault of ours about Billy—that it could happen to anybody. But Fred don't want to believe him. Fred acted from the start like he was disgraced—like the blame was all on him—and he won't hear of no institutions. It's his business, he says, and he'll take care of it. Me—I love Billy. He's mine and I want what's best for him. But I can't tell what's best. I ain't educated enough to figure such things out. Once I almost had Fred with me that an institution was the answer. But then Mr. Williams happened in and took Fred's side. Not that he meant any harm. He was real nice to us. He didn't seem to mind about Billy and he used to go out of his way to visit with him. But he said he'd heard some bad stories about what they did to the poor kids in institutions and that if Billy was his he'd find some other way. So that was that, and Fred wouldn't let me bring it up no more. Fred can be stubborn like a mule—"

Nelson said dryly, "Did Mr. Williams suggest any alternative to an institution?" He had been propelled back to the case by the mention of Williams' name. "I mean other than going on as you're doing?"

"No—he promised he'd think about it and let us know if he got some idea—like a small private place where Billy could get the right care."

"Small private places are apt to cost a great deal. Was it his intention to pay the bills?"

"He never came right out and said so, but I—well—I guess that's what he meant. We weren't asking no favors," she added defensively.

"Fred would've done everything he could—odd jobs and carpentry and
the like—for the rest of his life to pay him back. Tell you the truth,
neither of us cottoned to being beholden at first—except that Mr.
Williams kept on about what was money for but to help others."

"Did he have a lot of money?"

"He must have had plenty. Seems like a dollar to us was what a
penny would be to him. That's why it wouldn't have meant nothing
to him to help us with Billy. You seen his apartment, didn't you?" Her
voice grew hushed. "Ain't it beautiful? Them rich rugs and things—
and the way he always bought fresh flowers—and the television.
Sometimes when he wasn't busy he'd have me bring Billy up to look
at the television and I'd leave him there awhile so's I could get out.
But I don't think it was good for Billy. It got him kind of excited and
funny-acting, and anyways he can't never keep at anything for very
long."

"Did Williams have a regular job—or a business?"

"No—he was one of them authors. When he first moved in he was
always writing that book of his—and I almost felt sorry for him because he seemed kind of lonesome. But then when he finished the
book he began having people in. I don't know if he got his money from
writing books or not. They say authors make an awful lot—but I think
maybe his family was rich and left him a fortune. He said once his
mother and father died when he was small."

"Any brothers or sisters?"

"He never said. He had a lot of company in the last six months or
so, though, and I was real glad he wasn't lonesome no more. They was
nice people. I was finishing up once in the bedroom and when I come
out they all gave me the time of day."

"Could you describe any of them?"

"No—I didn't like to stand gawping—besides, on the days I cleaned
for him my cousin would sit with Billy and I was always in a hurry
because she didn't like to stay no longer than she had to."

"Didn't Williams employ a maid?"

"Not regular. Once a week some agency would send a girl to do a
thorough cleaning. He didn't like anyone around all the time fiddling
with his things and disturbing him. If he was having company, I'd go
up and give things a lick and a promise. He had the food and drinks
sent from Neuilly's." She struggled with the pronunciation.

Nelson had been employing a conversational tone throughout. He
used it now. "You'd probably know if he kept a gun in the apartment."

"A gun?" She shook her head slowly. Affronted dignity stiffened her voice. "I said I gave things a lick and a promise—like dusting and going over the rugs. I didn't pry or open no drawers—"

Nelson said pacifically, "People are often careless with guns. I thought that you or Billy might have seen one lying about."

"Billy? He don't know from guns—he—" Plainly she was disappointed in him. "I guess I didn't explain good about Billy, but you seemed to catch on without me drawing no pictures." She labored to put it into words. "Billy never grew up in his mind. He's like a baby inside—he—"

Nelson said, "I do understand," and tore his eyes from the overalls on the line. "Sometimes when I'm asking questions," he lied, "I get a bit absent-minded. Are the apartments in this house expensive, Mrs. Storch?"

Her face had cleared. "Well, it's an old house and it wasn't nothing fancy till they remodeled it. The rents depend on when the tenants moved in and if the ceilings could be lifted at the time. Mr. Williams paid a lot, on account of he wanted so many alterations. He said he hated them big snooty buildings on Park Avenue and give him a place like this any time." She sighed. "Poor man—"

There was a knocking at the door and she went to open it, returning to the kitchen with Clevis. "Somebody for you, officer," she said. "Will he want coffee? It ain't no trouble. It's always ready."

Nelson sent Clevis an almost imperceptible warning. Clevis caught it and said, "No, thanks. I got to go easy on the stimulants. I finished up there, Lieutenant. Sergeant Baldwin just arrived to take over until further notice. You set?"

"Yes." He turned back to Dora Storch. "You've been very patient."

"That's all right. I guess I didn't tell you much, though. From what Fred said, it must have been burglars. You got any notion—"

He shook his head. He had a notion which he hoped to keep from her forever. "There's a bit to be done before I can expect to get notions. One more thing, Mrs. Storch. You didn't happen to see any unlikely visitors entering the building this afternoon?"

"No—I was here most of the time—like always. I only went out for bread, and that was when Billy fell down. It was about twenty-past five when I got back. I went in the front way to see if Fred was in the lobby. I thought he'd be there fixing something if he'd got back from that garbage business. The only person I saw was a girl all dressed up in black. She was at the bells and she didn't look like the type we get here, so I asked her who she wanted. It wasn't Mr. Williams, though—it was Mr. Smith on third. I showed her what bell to ring and she didn't even say thanks. Kind of fresh she was—tough. It takes all kinds. Skinny as a toothpick and kind of Italian-looking. If I had a kid that age she wouldn't be wearing no fancy black dress. Fred didn't see nobody either when he went up later—only a blond lady coming out of the Delaneys', which is across from Mr. Williams. Mr. Delaney is an artist. He has models going in and out—but very respectable. Officer—will you have to talk to Fred again?"

"Not tonight anyway. I hope you both get a good sleep."

"Well—thanks." She saw them to the door.

Out on the sidewalk, Clevis filled his lungs. "A man has to work yet," he said, "to enjoy the luxury of a setup like that. Me, I'd rather be a bum on a park bench."

"You can't support responsibilities on a park bench."

"Oh. Kids, huh?"

"One." Nelson told him briefly about that one.

"Tough," Clevis said. "Maybe the toughest thing that could happen to people. Did you see him, Lieutenant?"

"No—not yet."

His tone made Clevis scrutinize him sharply. Clevis opened his deceptively slack lips to say something and then thought better of it. What he did say was obviously a substitution. "I got a line-up of real good suspects—and since it ain't an open-and-shut case of burglary, I'm still betting it was a dame. This Williams had the dames so groggy they generally walked away forgetting to gather up their possessions. I counted three feminine souvenirs in a desk drawer that weren't bought in no five-and-dime store. And letters—wow! By comparison, that first one I read was only a 'nice Nellie' introduction."

They had reached Nelson's car. Nelson said, "Where do you want me to drop you?"

"Ain't we going to headquarters?"

"No—you put in a full day—and I'll want you on the job early tomorrow."

Clevis grinned. "I'd argue, but my wife's got a funny idea she'd like to see me once in a while." He took a bulky package from under his arm. "Here are my findings—correspondence—addresses—souvenirs—and the famous book." He got into the car beside Nelson. "Any B.M.T. will do."

After Nelson had dropped him off he carried on a halfhearted debate with himself. His day had been fuller than Clevis's, and his wife too was possessed of a "funny idea" that she would like to see him once in a while. He never had any difficulty in conjuring up the image of

Kyrie, no matter how much physical distance lay between them. And now was no different from any other time. He could see her plainly against the setting of their pleasant living room. She was a slim ash blonde with a dark strength contradicted by her lovely fragile appearance. He glanced at the clock on the dashboard. It was a quarter to nine. She would probably be asking Sammy, the cook, to hold dinner for a little while longer. Or she might be in the domain of Grid Nelson, Jr., rechristened Junie by Sammy. And Junie, just beginning to acknowledge his parents with a bona fide smile not to be confused with the gastric spasm of ordinary babies, would be—

Nelson grinned and put an end to his inner debate. The laboratory reports on the Williams murder would not be in before noon of the following day. Clevis's findings could be studied at home as well as at headquarters. Kyrie had never been a hindrance to work. He turned the car east in the Fifties and headed toward Lexington Avenue.

Tall Sammy opened the door to him. Her dignified apricot-colored face broke into a slow smile. "Mr. Grid-dely—we about to give you up."

Kyrie, close behind her, said, "Grid," and took both his hands and pulled him into the fragrant atmosphere of home.

## CHAPTER 4

Morgan Woodruff had worked the bedclothes into lumpy pleats. When Joss got up she straightened them without waking him. She kissed his forehead lightly and it was moist to her lips. He had been restless most of the night and she wished that he could make up for the lost sleep. But he had an early appointment and she knew he would not thank her if she allowed him to miss it. She decided to give him another half hour, which was the time it took to get breakfast on the table. He could eat in his robe and dress later.

She went to the bathroom. She brushed her teeth, washed her face, combed her hair, and reddened her lips. She buttoned on a fresh cotton house dress and opened the door to take in the milk and the morning paper.

After she had put the coffee and the water for the boiled eggs on the stove, her own forehead was moist. It was going to be another hot day. The curtain on the open kitchen window was as immobile as a wood carving.

Joss was a country girl. She thought longingly of her origin, of a mountain stream known intimately in childhood, and of how much

Morgan would profit by a few weeks spent away from the city pavements. He was so white and thin, and one day off a week did little to
replenish his depleted physical reserve. But a vacation was out of the
question, even a stay-at-home vacation. As matters stood, they would
skimp on necessities to afford the occasional relief of an air-condi-
tioned moving-picture theater. And it was only June. And the two summer months that could be so beautiful or so ugly, depending upon personal circumstances, stretched menacingly and endlessly before her.
Her sigh contained no pity for herself.

She sat down at the kitchen table and quickly scanned the news.
This had become part of her routine, because at her insistence Morgan took the paper with him to read on his subway journeys.

She wasted no time on the headlines, which scarcely varied from
those of yesterday or from those of a month ago yesterday or for as
long as the world had teetered precariously between war and peace.
She was turning to the second page when the item she had missed
arrested her. The familiar name danced before her eyes, and she
brushed her little finger across the printed letters as though to erase
them. But they remained. And for proof that he was not just any Glen
Williams there was a cut of his face centering the item, and the cap-
tion beneath it said, "Shot to Death in West Side Apartment."

The egg water boiled unheeded as she read and reread. It was a
struggle to return to the simple chores of morning. She looked fearfully at the clock. Five minutes remained of the stipulated half hour.
She turned out the light under the coffee, put the eggs into the water, and went back to the bedroom.

She looked down at Morgan, his sprawled bones covered by a sheet,
his dark head pressed, as though for solace, upon the pillow where her
head had lain. She would not tell him until after breakfast, she
thought. She would see to it that he ate first. For Glen Williams had
been no more than a stranger met by chance. He had forcibly inserted
himself into their lives even though Morgan insisted that it was the
other way around. But Morgan was as innocent as a child in his relationships. He liked and accepted or he disliked and renounced. And
in his innocence he had liked and accepted Glen Williams.

Joss, warm, sympathetic, always quick to assume a share of suffering and pain that was not her own, wondered because she felt no
regret in that a young man's life had so summarily ended. Nor would
she put a name to what she did feel, nor would she dwell upon a recent day when Glen Williams had managed to burden her with a
weight of distaste which might now be shed for all time. She com-

pressed her full, generous lips. He was dead. According to the newspaper item, he had been shot through the chest by a burglar or burglars whose design he had apparently interrupted. Her sole concern was for the way in which his death would affect Morgan.

She knew well, although he tried to hide it from her, the depth and breadth of Morgan's discouragement. She had witnessed many times his angry focus upon some small, comparatively minor worry, utilizing it as a receptacle for all of his pent frustrations. How then would he react to tragedy visited upon a man he had called his friend?

"Morgan," she said softly. "Morgan—"

He turned over on his back. His eyes, screwed tight in sleep, opened with reluctant effort. "Wicked," he muttered. "Wicked—murder—"

"I know," she said soothingly, so concentrated upon him that the word "murder" had only one association for her, and that the murder of his sleep. "I hate waking you, but it's seven-fifteen and you told me—"

He shot upright. Groaning, he swung his legs over the bed. His feet explored the floor for his slippers.

"A little to the right," she said. "There—you've made it. Breakfast is ready. You can shower and dress after you've eaten."

"All right. I'll just stick my head under the cold-water tap."

She hurried to rescue the eggs and to make toast. She took his fruit juice from the refrigerator as soon as he appeared at the kitchen door.

He drank the chilled drink gratefully, but broke open an egg without enthusiasm. "None for you?" he said.

She sat opposite him and poured coffee. "I get hungry after you've gone. That's when I have my real breakfast."

He grumbled, "Well, you might have had the decency to give me only one egg. This isn't a day for food."

"You eat."

He smiled crookedly. "Yes, Mama." Then he said, "So it's getting to be that kind of relationship, is it? I'll bet it would be a nice change for you if I could be more of a man and less of a problem child."

"Morgan Woodruff, if I wasn't resigned to your pre-coffee moods I could get very angry with you."

"If you turned into the angriest shrew in the world I wouldn't blame you a bit."

"Yes you would. In your present state you'd blame me or anyone else for everything from a mosquito bite to an—an earthquake."

"Hey—you *are* angry." He looked at her in surprise. "Or—or something." He took a deep swallow of coffee, set the cup down, and smiled resolutely. "Now it's post-coffee and I'm feeling fine. So let's start again. Anything in the paper?"

"Quite a bit." She had folded it and laid it aside. He seldom read at breakfast, preferring, he said, to make the most of her companionship before his grind started.

"Good, bad, or indifferent?"

"Finish your second egg. They don't grow on trees."

"I know. I learned the facts of life when I was very young. What's the matter? I thought that was pretty funny. You haven't gone and caught my morning dumps at long last?"

"No, darling," she said, and started to refill his cup.

"Hold it. I'll have it when I'm dressed, if there's time."

"Morgan—"

He paused in the doorway.

She said, "I—I sewed the missing button on your blue shirt. It's in the drawer with the others."

"Thanks—I'll wear it. It's my lucky shirt." He headed for the bedroom.

She put a clean coffee cup at his place and cleared the rest of the table. She set the dishes in the sink and began to wash them. She wished that she had told him. She wished that she did not have to tell him. She wished absurdly that the news could have been broken to him yesterday, on his day off. Then at least he would not have had to try to sell encyclopedias. Yesterday. But it had happened yesterday. He had lunched with Glen Williams—and later— Later he had gone to the park to sun himself—and Glen—and it had happened.

She toyed with the idea of not telling him, and dropped it. He might miss the item. She herself had almost missed it. She, with Glen Williams as her mind's ubiquitous and unwelcome guest. She shook her head. She pictured Morgan wedged into a subway seat, hot, miserable, trying to lose himself in the news, combing the pages, recoiling, his face stark with horror in that surrounding sea of rigid masks habitually assumed by subway riders.

He came up behind her, encircling her waist with his arms. She jumped.

He said penitently, "That was a dumb trick. I didn't mean to startle you. Turn around, Joss, and take a look. Any difference between me and the Lord Calvert gents is purely a matter of shiny pants and a Van Buck cravat."

She turned, and her heart turned. Posing self-consciously, he appeared to her more like a sleeked-up schoolboy well washed behind the ears than a Man of Distinction. She wondered if his remark about their relationship had been true, if she was overcompensating because they could not afford a child. Then he pulled her to him and gave her a man's kiss.

She released herself. "You'll do," she said. "That tie's becoming—and the shine isn't noticeable—except on your shoes."

He spoke out of the side of his mouth. "Stick with me, baby, and you'll be wearing jools." He shed the parody. "Know what? I saw a dress in a Madison Avenue window—a real Joss dress. If this client I've got lined up bites, it will be on your back. The dress will, I mean."

She hated to disturb his determined cheerfulness. "Meanwhile will you have another cup of coffee?"

"Sure—if you join me. I'm still ten minutes ahead of schedule." He looked around for the paper and dropped it on the floor next to his brief case. He sat down. "No—don't bother to heat it. It couldn't have cooled off much in this temperature. Where's your cup?"

She got one and he filled it. She took a sip.

"Joss—I wish I could pack you off to the country."

"You can't pack me off anywhere. I'm sticking with you whether you like it or not."

"I banged around a lot last night, didn't I? I bet you didn't get any rest at all."

"I slept like a log."

"Liar—beautiful, gallant liar. You look like hell."

"Make up your mind."

His eyes clouded. "Sometimes I wish we could fool each other—but we can't, no matter how hard we try. Maybe it would be better if you let down your hair once in a while and staged a real honest-to-goodness tantrum. I wouldn't mind—"

"Why should I stage a tantrum? I've got you—and you're everything I want—and you know it."

"I know that you're feeling rotten. I knew it the moment I sat down to breakfast."

That was her cue and she grasped it hardly. "You don't know much if you think my feeling rotten has anything to do with our financial state. There are carloads of young couples who start off poorer than we are and with far less in the way of prospects. And they manage to make the grade. It's not that at all. It's something in the paper. It shocked me and it will shock you, and I've been trying to think of a way to tell you without—without—"

He left his chair and swooped to pick up the paper.

She said to his back, "It's about Glen. It's on the second page—the left-hand side under—"

"Oh," he said. She could not see his face. She heard the paper rustle. She waited for a few minutes, giving him time to read. Then she said, "Morgan, if you—if you don't want to keep your appointment, I could phone the—"

"Not keep my appointment?" His tone was that of a man who has just heard a most unreasonable suggestion. When he turned to her there was nothing on his face that she could read, but the paper was a tight roll in his hands and he seemed intent upon rolling it tighter.

He said aloofly, "My first thought was that you'd seen something about the encyclopedia firm going into bankruptcy." And in the same aloof voice he said, "I meant to bring my hat in with me, but I guess I left it in the bedroom."

"Morgan—I'm sorry—"

"Yes," he said, "that about expresses it. Anything else either of us could say would be redundant." He went into the bedroom.

She hesitated. Then she followed him. She found him staring at himself in the mirror over the bureau.

"Morgan—perhaps you'd better stay home—"

He backed away from the mirror. He said savagely, "For pity's sake, will you stop trying to treat me like an infant. Death is no news to me. I've met it over and over again—caused it, too. Me—the returned warrior—not Joss's little boy. Not so long ago I held a gun in my own little hand, and you'd be surprised at the number of times I made it go boom—all without benefit of a skirt to hide behind—" He stopped. He shook himself and the anger fell away. He saw her eyes go dark with pain. He took a step toward her. "Joss—I—"

"It's all right."

He held out his arms, dropped them as the doorbell rang. They stared at each other. He said, "Who—"

In almost her natural voice she said, "Probably Mrs. Jorgensen. I promised she could leave her little girl here this morning while she shopped."

"Well—I'll let her in on my way out." Then he said, "Are you close to me again?"

It was an old formula, used at the end of every small quarrel. There had never been any large ones. She achieved the right response. "Very close. I'll go to the door with you. Mrs. Jorgensen likes to talk to handsome men. She might make you late."

"Then I'd better duck into the kitchen to get my brief case. You steer her into the front room and I'll sneak out quietly. Good-by, my Joss."

"Good luck, darling."

The doorbell rang once more, but she waited to answer it until he had reached the kitchen. She was thankful that she had promised to look after Mrs. Jorgensen's little girl. It would be a distraction. Added now to what she wanted to forget was Morgan's closed, cold face as he contemplated himself in the mirror, the fury of his outburst. People, her mind told her, reacted in different ways to bad tidings. But she was not comforted. Morgan was not "people." He was a part of her, and for him to lash out at her was comparable to having her hand rise up to strike her cheek without a given signal from her brain. Or so she felt. Only feeling was not thinking, her mind told her. And even if countless themes had not been written upon the subject, surely she was intelligent enough to have discovered the dreadful separateness of every member of the human race, the loneliness born of a tragic inability to establish full communication. For no matter how great the effort to interpret another or to translate oneself by means of word and gesture, only at rare moments was unity achieved. A shared laugh might work the miracle, or the brief sharing of physical fulfillment, or a joint sorrow. But anyone, her mind told her, who assumed that such moments could be sustained, that loving was a kind of magic exposing all facets of the beloved, must be a stupid, arrogant fool. And she, Jocelyn Woodruff, her mind insisted, was neither stupid nor arrogant. And instead of seeking the impossible, she should be grateful for those rare moments of being at one with Morgan.

She opened the door, ready to gather in Mrs. Jorgensen's two-year-old daughter. She was not at all prepared to welcome Tom Gaudio. He said breathlessly, "Mrs. Woodruff, thank heaven you're home."

She caught the smell of sweat and alcohol as he stepped over the threshold, but was too preoccupied to express either surprise or resentment at his intrusion. She was thinking that Morgan's day had begun inauspiciously enough and that nothing must be added to his troubles. Determinedly, she led the way to the front room. She did not ask Gaudio to sit down. It was obviously at the insistence of his legs that he folded himself into a chair.

His hands behaved like the shaky hands of the aged. They made fumbling work of extracting a cigarette from a crumpled package, of conveying it to his mouth. He used three matches before he lit it. "Is Morgan in?" he asked.

She had been listening for the click of the latch. She heard it and expelled a breath of relief. "No. He had an early appointment."

"That's good. It was you I wanted to see."

"You're out pretty early too—aren't you?" Delayed annoyance overtook her now that Morgan had been granted safe exit. Then, for the first time, she noted Gaudio's appearance, his homeless, unwashed look. He seemed very far removed from the neat young man who had been a stock fixture at Glen Williams' parties. She said in kindness, "Have you had breakfast?"

"Breakfast?" He shook his head.

"I'll get you some."

"No—no, thanks. I guess—I guess you haven't heard—"

"You mean about Glen Williams?"

"You know? But you seem so calm. I thought—" The ashes from his cigarette dropped to the carpet. His inadequate chin trembled. "I'll never—as long as I live I'll never understand women."

She thought again that people reacted in different ways to bad news. And Tom Gaudio was definitely "people." She wished him well, but that did not prevent her from wishing that he had chosen elsewhere to react. It was odd, under the circumstances, for him to have sought her out. If he wanted a close link with his dead friend, a companion in sorrow, why not Sarah Thrace, with whom he seemed to be on terms of intimacy? Why Jocelyn Woodruff, whom he scarcely knew? She said formally, "I'll make some fresh coffee, and then you should go home and sleep. You—your eyes look as though you need it."

"Sleep," he said bitterly. "I've been walking the pavements all night—I—"

"The news has been a shock to you, but it won't do any good to—"

He was not listening. "I didn't know which way to turn until I thought of you."

He stared at her so expectantly that she was puzzled. She said falsely, "I'm glad you regard me as a friend, but I'm afraid—" She paused to find the words. "I hadn't known Glen Williams very long or—"

"As if that matters. You loved him. You'll want to—"

"I what?" Her own knees gave way. She sat down suddenly.

"It's all right. Glen told me. That's why I came. Together we can get to the bottom of this. Don't you see?"

She did not see. Her blank face showed it. "Glen Williams told you that I loved him!"

"Yes—but you mustn't mind. He wasn't being a cad. He trusted me. He knew I wouldn't—that I could keep a secret. We were like brothers—the way brothers should be. I never had one—and Glen didn't either—not in the true sense—because his own flesh-and-blood brother treated him like a dog—"

"Wait," she said, "I don't—"

But he went on, unheeding. "So you can be sure I'll respect Glen's wishes. He was fine—wasn't he—not wanting to hurt poor Morgan—protecting him even though it meant his own happiness. You're fine too. It must have been even harder for you, because Glen had so many interests to divert him, while you—"

"Be still," she said, "you don't know what you're talking about. You misunderstood something that Glen Williams said—or else you're drunk—that's it, of course—you're drunk—"

He was trembling. He said reproachfully, "I'm sober—I had a few drinks, but they—they didn't help. Please—you needn't pretend with me. This is no time to be conventional. Glen was your lover and my closest friend—and he was murdered—and I know who murdered him—"

"You—you know?"

"Yes—I know. And between us we must decide what steps to take." He fingered the edge of a newspaper protruding from his pocket. "Burglars!" He expelled the word as though it were a bone that had caught in his throat. "Yes—I know—and Glen knew. He saw it coming months ago. I begged him to go to the police, but he wouldn't. He had nothing to offer in proof, he said. But that wasn't his real reason. His real reason was his loyalty—he was loyal even to—to vipers."

Her lips were dry. "He told you that someone was going to murder him?"

"He didn't mention any names. He didn't have to—"

"You're confused," she said. "You're confused about everything—you've got everything wrong. You've imagined all this. You're sick. Your eyes look——"

The quality of his stare altered. Scorn made a hard frame for his words. "So you're going to play it that way? Now that he's gone, you're going to cling for dear life to what's left because you're frightened that Morgan will somehow discover what you probably consider a lapse from virtue—"

Her vital body inclined toward him and straightened again in victory over the urge to pick him up by his neck's scruff and throw him away. "Go home," she said softly. "I want to make allowances for you, but—"

"Allowances for me? That's a hot one. What Glen saw in you—" He

wavered under her steady gaze. "Well, I'm not here to question that.
Glen was a saint. He found only the reflection of his own good in oth-
ers—you—Sarah Thrace—" Then he repeated the name of Sarah
Thrace with such venomous force that it brought an echo from her.
"Sarah?"
"Of course."
"Of course what?"
"You're not even intelligent," he said wonderingly. "Just the usual
snare of a beautiful body. Who would believe that nothing more than
that could make a man of Glen's caliber fall—"
Her control broke its cage. "I don't want to hear any more. You'd better go." She was breathing fast.
He said, "That's more what I expected—you do care—you're not really cold." He jumped out of his chair and seized her arm. "You will
help me. Listen—Sarah Thrace murdered Glen—"
"You're insane." She shook free of him. She said desperately, "You listen. You and Sarah Thrace are practically strangers to me—but from
what I've seen and heard, she's been very kind to you. Why you should
be trying to involve her in a—in a murder doesn't even incite my curiosity. She probably got tired of you and you're using Glen Williams'
death as a means of taking revenge." She ended lamely, "All I can say
is that you ought to be ashamed of yourself," and closed her mouth,
finding that it was indeed all that she could say to this wretched
young man who was swimming so far out of his depth. She tried
again. "Don't—just don't spread anything like that around or you'll
find yourself in real trouble."
"Trouble? What do you think I'm in now? Glen was going to help
me—as he helped everybody—he was going to set me up in—Oh, skip
it." He collapsed into the chair again without taking his dilated eyes
from her face. He seemed to be deliberating something. After a moment he said in a peculiar tone, "You don't believe Sarah killed
Glen?"
"Of course not. Why should she kill him? You go home and get a
wash and some rest and you won't believe it either."
"She had motive enough—if that's all that's bothering you."
Among other swarming thoughts was the thought that Mrs. Jorgensen would ring the bell at any moment, and that at some time or
other she would make coy reference to Tom Gaudio's early visit,
quite possibly in Morgan's presence. Joss's clear skin flushed guiltily.
But if I mention it to Morgan I'll be unable to withhold any of it and
he'll—he'll— She did not want to contemplate Morgan's possible re-

action. She said truthfully, "That's not all that's bothering me," and added, "I've work to do—and I'm expecting visitors—"

He cut in, his eyes hostile. "No—perhaps that's not all that's bothering you. Perhaps you have reason to know that Sarah didn't kill Glen—perhaps the best of reasons. A husband can't be expected to stay blind forever. Do you mind telling me where Morgan was yesterday afternoon?" He was sticking out his weak chin. He was making a brave effort to narrow his dark eyes. He was trying to look astute and cynical. And he was looking like nothing so much as an outrageous travesty of "the boy detective."

Only that ludicrous seeming saved her from committing violence upon him. She bit her lip hard. She could not have said whether she suppressed laughter or tears.

## CHAPTER 5

Detective Sergeant Clevis shuffled across the small anteroom. He seemed to be giving himself up fully to the pleasure of picking his teeth, but his expert eye registered bilaterally the solitary male figure who sat waiting outside the acting captain's door.

Clevis opened that door just enough to insert his thin frame. He stood before the laden desk, only the toothpick moving in his mouth, until Nelson looked up. Then he said, "You been to lunch, Lieutenant?"

"No—but I observe that you have. When did you last see your dentist?"

"It ain't cavities. It's I can't resist getting something for nothing— and toothpicks is about all they're handing out free these days."

Absently, Nelson rumpled his curly white hair. "What time is it?"

"There's a watch on your wrist and a clock on your desk—but you're far too classy an operator to use common clues like that. It's five minutes to two."

Nelson had withdrawn his attention. He was turning the pages of a typewritten report.

Clevis coughed. His deceptively vacuous face was suffused.

"Well?" Nelson said, still reading.

"Excuse it."

"Excuse what?"

"The way I keep forgetting you're the chief—and acting flip same as if we were arms-around-the-neck pals."

Nelson said gravely, "You should give up cafeterias—free toothpicks notwithstanding. They seem to make you self-conscious."

Clevis discarded the toothpick. He grinned. "Did you know there's a fellow waiting to see you? Strong build from shoulders to waist—couldn't guess his exact height on account of he's sitting. Rugged face—plenty brown hair—brown eyes—"

"I know. Mike Williams—the brother of yesterday's victim. I'll see him and go to lunch."

"Why don't you go first? You look hungry and he looks like a citizen who's used to waiting."

"Did you have a session with him?"

"Nah—just took a squint in passing—but I could tell he ain't one of them nail-biters."

"He's a farmer," Nelson said.

"Which don't surprise me. I can see him with a hoe easier than I can see him connected with the deceased gent. Ain't a scrap of resemblance."

"You've done well for just a passing squint." Nelson was making an orderly arrangement of the material on his desk.

"But I didn't do so good on this morning's assignment. The Gaudio guy wasn't home—and hadn't been all night, according to the landlady. I went to a couple of places where he might've been—but he wasn't."

"Does the landlady know what time he went out yesterday?"

"She seen the tail end of him scoot through the front door. Between five and six is the closest she'll hit the time, though."

"Is it a rooming house?"

"Yeah—the kind of boxes that used to rent for maybe three or four bucks a week. Now most of the inmates are soaked from eight to ten, depending on how close they are to the bathroom. She gave me the usual landlady's earful, but it don't amount to much. He's a free-lance photographer and for two extra leaves per she's let him rig up a darkroom in the basement. Wouldn't let me see it at first, and I didn't want to put the pressure on yet—being you told me to keep it chummy until further notice. But after a couple of pretty pleases she took me down and I had a look. Nothing out of the way—all fixed up real neat—and the pictures mostly modern shots of flowers and miscellaneous stuff arranged to make designs." He added regretfully, "I guess he couldn't afford to hire live models. She says he's a nice quiet boy with some tony friends—namely, a dressy female old enough to have diapered him and a guy who could be the late Mr. W. from the way

Mrs. Landlady had him sized up."

"How did she have him sized up?"

Clevis started to spit, thought better of it, and wiped his mouth delicately with the back of his hand. "Well—you know—amateurs don't see nothing. But by poking hard I managed to pin her down to his hair was blond—his eyes blue—and his clothes expensive. Also she tags him as a polite, handsome, democratic gent who gave her a fat tip for showing him the way to Gaudio's room the first time he called."

"Was he a frequent visitor?"

"A couple or three times, to her knowledge—but of course she ain't always on the spot. Going to put out a call for Gaudio, Lieutenant?"

"I'll give him until evening to come home. According to these letters"—Nelson touched the pile on his desk—"he shares honors with a number of suspects. I don't want to deal out unfavorable publicity until I'm more or less sure it's been earned."

"But that note he wrote to the late Mr. W.—that don't sound too innocent to me. If I remember right, it hinted at secrets between them. Oh, it was double polite and affectionate and all that—but it could've been some kind of blackmail."

"I doubt it. Blackmailers don't usually kill the people they blackmail."

"That's so—it's generally the other way around. Still—" Clevis chewed on something. He said, "Lieutenant, maybe I'm off base, but last night I made it you was stuck with some notion about the janitor's son. Take it from me, it was Gaudio or a dame—not that the janitor's boy wouldn't be more convenient all around. They'd only stick him in an institution—"

"Did you have time to visit Miss Thrace?"

"I had time—only she wasn't home also."

"Then there you are," Nelson said.

"No comparison," Clevis protested. "Miss Thrace ain't just a dame. She's big-time. I seen her once when she played a bit part in some movie. Reminded me of a neighbor who gave me handouts when I was a kid—a nice soft—"

Nelson's mouth twitched. "Don't let your sentiments get the upper hand."

Clevis shifted his stance. "Besides, she only wrote to turn down an invite to one of Mr. W.'s shindigs." Then he said hardly, "Yeah—well—the neighbor—name of Mrs. Dowse—was a slob anyway—cockroaches in and out of everything. If I hadn't been the hungriest little bastard in Brooklyn, I couldn't have ate a thing she—" He came back to the present. "Get a load of me slapping my dirty past in your face like you was one of them psychiatrists. I ought to write a book myself. Which reminds me—did you get anything out of Williams' book?"

Nelson had gone through the book the night before. And it had been a task to keep his attention from wandering. Glen Williams had wielded a heavy pen. The pronoun "I" lay thick as pepper over every paragraph. But Nelson had needed no corroboration of his egotism. It was enough to know that he had paid money out of his own pocket to present his masterpiece to the world. The book was written about a character named Glen Williams. But it was fiction, Nelson judged, because no real-life character he had ever met possessed all of the charm and all of the dynamic qualities ascribed to Glen Williams, hero, by Glen Williams, author. The writing was circuitous and inept, wandering into vast purple areas at the drop of a hat. Yet, perhaps because of this, because of what the writer chose to write about, because of the emphasis he placed upon the most unimportant encounters, and the importance he attached to his own opinions on every theme from birth to any form of death, the true character of Glen Williams emerged. He had been a man who wanted desperately to stick his fingers in other people's pies, who interpreted a normal desire for privacy as base ingratitude, whose need was not for people but for puppets he could manipulate to his own greater glory. And because he had little use for people as people, he had little use for God. Not that he admitted this. Rather he placed God on a level with himself, a being of perverted humor who laughed at all the ridiculous situations through which mortals struggled. Hence, Nelson supposed, the title, *Jester in Heaven.*

Some of this Nelson tried to convey to Clevis. But he did not succeed in holding the little man's interest.

Clevis said, "Sounds like most books—nothing but a lot of malarky. Do I go back to squat on Thrace's doorstep?"

"No—you go back to the rooming house and wait for Gaudio. Get him to give an account of himself—and if he's reluctant bring him in."

"I'm on my way. Lab turn up anything?"

"Some fingerprints, including those of the corpse. The others we'll check with the suspects as we proceed. The corpse, by the way, had traces of chocolate on his fingers."

"So it was him who didn't wash his hands so good and smeared the bathroom towel. And me thinking it was blood."

"There were no traces of chocolate in the stomach."

"Well—he must've eaten it earlier. There was an empty candy dish on the desk. What about the bullet?"

"A thirty-two—deflected by the sternum, so they had a bit of difficulty in determining the angle from which it was fired. Powder burns
indicating that he was shot at very close range by someone he obviously didn't expect to shoot him. Numerous hypodermic wounds—one
administered shortly before death, which the M.E. sets somewhere between two and six."

"That's a big help. Was the junk heroin?"

"Yes."

"Maybe this Gaudio was the pusher."

"You find out," Nelson said, dismissing him. "And ask Mr. Michael
Williams to come in."

"One thing, Lieutenant—who else you got on this, if I need to swap
notes?"

"Baldwin on the Williams' house—Broder, who's checking to see if
any of the names have guns registered to them—and Judd, who took
the early train to Howardsville."

"Why waste Judd? Howardsville's come to you."

"Glen Williams' fiancée or ex-fiancée lives there too. She can't be neglected."

"That so?"

"One of the letters included in your sampling was signed by her—
Betty Conway."

"Oh, sure." Clevis added apologetically, "Truth is I was more hit by
the texts than by names and addresses—and from the texts, they all
should've been fiancées. Come to think of it, hers sounded less so than
the rest. You putting a man on Thrace?"

"We'll see what you turn up."

"Okay." Clevis shuffled out the door like a man going nowhere, but
Nelson knew from past performance that his goal was firmly fixed and
that he would reach it willy-nilly.

A few minutes later he said, "Good afternoon, Mr. Williams," and gestured the short, powerful man to a chair at the right of his desk. He
saw, as his visitor sat down, that he was greatly disturbed, and that
a yellow cast overlay what was obviously a healthy outdoor com-
plexion. He sharpened a pencil that needed no sharpening, in order
to give the roughly cut face time to relax. Nelson preferred people under questioning to be as relaxed as possible. Contrary to the theory
that anger or hysteria engendered truths that would not otherwise
see the light, he believed that it was easier to separate truth from fic-

tion when the answers were thought out. Then evasions were apt to
be more perceptible, lies easier to detect than they would have been
in a state of excitation. Unless, of course, he dealt with congenital liars.
But at first glance the man who had announced himself as Mike
Williams did not appear to be a congenital liar. Nelson waited, his
deep-set brown eyes seeming to hold no more than polite interest.

"Lieutenant Nelson?"

"Yes."

"You're the man in charge of investigating my brother's—"

"Yes."

"I went down to Centre Street first—but they sent me here. I—I'm
not a New Yorker—I don't know the ropes or much about police procedure—" He rubbed his face with a strong, square-tipped hand.
"This hits me hard—" He started again. "I'm ten years older than
Glen. I brought him up. My mother died when he was seven—my father a couple of years before."

"Would you like to smoke, Mr. Williams?"

"No—thanks. I didn't bring my pipe—and cigarettes don't seem
worth the trouble. I'm not much for the refinements, Lieutenant. I'm
a farmer."

"There are some very refined farmers these days," Nelson said.

"Yes—well—"

"When did you learn of your brother's death?"

"Last night. I listened to the midnight news. I—I couldn't believe it."

"I thought farmers retired at sundown."

"They do as a rule, but—" The silence that followed was like a muffled explosion of words.

Nelson said, "I suppose there isn't an occupation in the world that
doesn't call for an occasional departure from routine."

Mike Williams nodded. He spoke without hostility. "And you want
to know the occasion for my departure. It wasn't a guilty one. I had
certain things on my mind—things that had nothing to do with my
brother—or at least not directly."

Nelson waited until it became patent that Mike Williams could not
or would not continue. Then he said pleasantly, "Have you had lunch?"

The rugged face looked startled. "Lunch? No—I'm not hungry."

"I am—and it's long past my usual hour. Would you mind having coffee while I eat? There's a restaurant down the street where we can
continue this talk." He got up and did a little jig step to flex his long
legs. "Don't forget your hat—not that you need one in this weather.
June's behaving like mid-August. Has there been a shortage of rain

your way?"

"Yes—but we manage by irrigation." Williams' voice sounded less strained. He followed Nelson out of the office, standing apart while he paused to speak to a group of uniformed policemen in the corridor and to have a few words with the desk sergeant.

The restaurant, a small, rather shabby place modeled on an old English chophouse, featured cooking of the hearty variety. The luncheon crowd had deserted it more than an hour ago, but there was a party of stragglers talking loudly over wedges of apple pie. Nelson ordered lamb chops, his mind apparently elsewhere, so that the waiter misunderstood and brought lamb chops for Williams as well. Williams did not comment, but he looked surprised when his empty plate was removed. And in the same detached manner with which he had eaten, he downed two cups of strong black coffee. Rid of that drawn yellow look, he might have been any man enjoying a leisurely meal with a friend. He even made the required responses to Nelson's general observations.

Then Nelson, without changing his tone by so much as a shade, said, "Do you visit the city often, Mr. Williams?"

"No—once a month or so for supplies." A moment ago Nelson had seen his white teeth flash at something said at the other occupied table. Now he was grave again. "I came in yesterday. I took the six-ten train back to Howardsville. I didn't see Glen. I wish I had. I might have prevented—he might have been alive today."

"Do you usually see him when you come in?"

"If he's at home."

"But doesn't he expect you? Don't you have a regular schedule for your trips?" Nelson decided that the face was oddly sensitive for all its rough cut.

"Glen knows my schedule all right. But I couldn't expect him to juggle his plans to fit in with it. His life is—was—given over to new friends and new interests after he came to New York—and I guess he found me pretty dull company. He never considered our being brothers any reason for pulling his punches about what he thought of farms and farmers. And I don't blame him. Why should he?"

"Did you meet any of the new friends he had made?"

Mike Williams stared at him. He said simply, "You'll have to look somewhere else for the man who murdered Glen, Lieutenant."

"I'll have to look everywhere."

"Yes—I see that, of course. But these friends of his—they're famous—artists—actors—song writers and the like. They're not criminals. They'd have no reason to kill Glen. They thought the world of him."

Nelson repeated, "Did you ever meet any of them?"

"No—but I feel as though I did. Glen talked about them so much—their names and what they do and what they eat and what they talk like and look like. When Glen got started he could make people as real as if they were right in the room. He really liked people in a big way—and they him. Even when he was a sprout he'd wander off from his chores as soon as my back was turned and start up with strangers and have them eating right out of his hand. He'd come back and tell me about it so pleased and excited that even if I'd made up my mind to wallop him I didn't have the heart. I guess I was a fool to think he'd ever be satisfied to stay on the farm in Howardsville."

Nelson, remembering the minute, self-destructive wounds in the dead body, thought, Perhaps you were a fool not to wallop him. But he did not express the thought. "How big a town is Howardsville?" he said.

"About eight thousand."

"Big enough for Glen to have made quite a few friends there—and probably enemies, too, since the more popular a man is the more people seem to hate him."

"Glen had no enemies that I ever heard of."

"Then we'll stick to friends. Did he keep in touch with the ones he'd made in Howardsville?"

"I don't believe so. You see, people change—and although Glen was born and bred in Howardsville, he was smarter than most of the boys and girls he went around with—and I guess he kind of outgrew them except for—" He shook his head. He said too firmly, "No—he didn't keep in touch."

Nelson said, "He outgrew them except for—"

"Nothing—no one. My mind was on something else."

He lied badly, Nelson was pleased to note. He said, "You came here of your own accord to further the investigation of your brother's murder. So I think if you can possibly help it you should try to keep your mind from wandering to other matters." He saw the tanned face redden. He persisted without enjoyment. "Is this person you're so reluctant to mention in need of your protection?"

"Protection—good God, no—she's always been quite self-sufficient." It sounded bitter.

"I mean do you suspect her of having a hand in the murder?"

"Betty—me suspect— Of course not. It's just—there's no reason for involving—"

"Betty Conway?"

"How did you know I meant—"

"The police looked through your brother's desk as a matter of routine. Her name appeared on a letter or two."

"Oh." Then he said with distaste, "It don't seem right to root through a man's private business."

"We have to use whatever tools are at hand for our work."

The doglike eyes were tormented. "No matter—Glen wouldn't have anything to hide. As for Betty—Betty isn't the kind to put anything on paper she'd be ashamed of—or to do anything she'd be ashamed of either." Nelson could almost see himself fading out of the man's retina. Mike Williams was alone, locked up inside himself, as he went on broodingly, "She was Glen's girl—at least that's what I'd always thought. I was as sure as anything Glen would settle down and they'd marry and raise fine kids." The cords of his strong throat stood out. "I wanted it that way. I—"

Nelson thought, So that's it.

Mike Williams was saying, "But they drifted apart. They couldn't seem to agree about anything—and from what Betty said yesterday, it's been over and done with for a long time."

"What did Betty say yesterday?"

"Nothing. At least not in words." He seemed to be mulling it over to himself rather than answering a question. "I asked her if she'd happened to run into Glen in New York—and she said something about she hadn't happened to—and that she didn't see him by appointment either. It was as though she had no interest in ever seeing him. But I don't know. I just don't know. I can't believe— They always had spats. Maybe this is only another spat and they'll make it up again. You see, I can't be sure—and unless I'm sure I can't tell her how I—"

Nelson said gently, "They won't make this quarrel up again. Your brother is dead."

It caused Mike Williams to emerge from himself, the pupils of his eyes shrinking as though against a sudden light.

Nelson said, "At what time and where did you talk with Betty Conway yesterday?"

"At the Howardsville station. We must have taken the same train home—it arrived late—close to seven-thirty. I didn't see her until we got off, though. She was stepping into her car. She'd left it parked in the station lot—"

"She'd been in New York too?"

"Yes—for a medical checkup—not that she needed it. Betty's the picture of health. I told her so and she made a joke. She said she bores her doctor—"

"Do you know the name of her doctor?"

"No, I don't. After Howardsville's old Dr. Henshaw retired, a new man came in. But most people don't like him very much. Of course we've got a fine hospital, but still they—" Mike Williams was not a subtle man. He had been slow to realize where the conversation was leading. Now he sat up stiffly and said, "Don't waste your time on nonsense, Lieutenant Nelson. I want to help all I can. That's why I'm here. But Betty and what she did yesterday have nothing to do with the case—and I won't have her plagued—" He looked ready to do battle.

Nelson appeared quite willing to drop Betty Conway. "Are you a rich man, Mr. Williams?"

The broad, low brow wrinkled. "Not what you'd call rich. I make out. I can support a—" Again he had to stop because for him all roads veered toward Betty Conway.

"Your brother was rich, wasn't he?"

"Glen? No. He only had— He wasn't rich."

"But judging by the way he lived, he spent a great deal of money. He must have had a good income."

Mike Williams' firm, square jaw came into prominence. He said shortly, "He had no income at all."

"Then how did he manage?"

"That can't be any business of—"

"Look here, I'm not the village gossip. I want only that information which I consider important to the investigation. How did your brother maintain himself if he had no income and no money?"

"I didn't say he had no money. He had some. Dad left the farm to me as oldest son—with the understanding, of course, that I'd look after my mother and Glen. And when Mother died she left Glen what money she had—about six thousand dollars. He came into it on his eighteenth birthday, and it was to be used for his education and whatever else he'd want at the time. It was only fair. My mother knew I'd be able to take care of myself and that the only education I wanted had to do with farming. But from the minute Glen learned to recognize his letters he was never without a piece of printed matter in his hand—even if it was no more than a drugstore pamphlet. So it stood to reason he'd be the scholar in the family."

"Was he?"

"Well, he didn't stick college very long—but he went on reading—

and writing too." His voice was proud. "He wrote a book."

"Did you read it?"

"Well—no. It was—it was kind of over my head. Glen said I shouldn't worry, because it was over the public's head too. I guess he was fooling—but maybe not, because he didn't make any money on it."

"When did he take the New York apartment?"

"He— About eighteen months ago."

"And his sole capital was six thousand dollars?"

"No—I guess there couldn't have been much of that six thousand dollars left, although I—"

Nelson waited a few moments. Then he said, "Go on, please."

Williams obeyed reluctantly. "Well, the farm prospered—and so long as he stayed there he had no living expenses. Under the circumstances, Dad would have expected me to furnish his board and lodging and clothes. As for that six thousand—Glen paid for his own car out of it—and he was always one to keep his end up, treating his friends and such—"

"Did he work on the place in return for his board and keep?"

Williams said defensively, "Farm work just wasn't his line—and I could afford experienced hired help." He seemed to sense Nelson's unspoken comment. "That's neither here nor there. I always felt the farm was half his anyway. He was entitled to a share of the profits."

"So when he wanted to live in New York you advanced him his share of the profits?"

Mike Williams nodded.

"How much?"

"Eighteen thousand dollars." Nelson's expression forced him to elaborate. "You see, I'd just had an offer of thirty-six thousand for the whole place—but it's worth a lot more than that, what with the improvements I've— Well, I figured I was buying Glen out. That's the way he wanted it—and it was fine with me, knowing as I did that he could never take any real pleasure in farming."

Nelson did some mental calculation. He calculated the price of the apartment's furnishings, and the clothes in Glen Williams' closets, and the entertainment catered by Neuilly, and when he had subtracted it from eighteen thousand dollars he found that there was very little left. It came to him, too, that the drug habit must have been recently acquired, since drugs devoured fortunes at a speed that seemed faster than light. He said, "Did he invest the money?"

"No—no, he didn't. Glen never had any notion of the value of money. Eighteen thousand seemed as much to him as maybe two hundred thousand—and both sums looked big enough to last forever, from the way he acted. He wasn't a businessman at all. I offered him a reasonable quarterly allowance for as long as he needed it—which would be until he settled down to something that suited him. It would have been better for me, because in farming you have to keep putting money back into— Well, aside from that, I'd have been much easier in my mind about him—but he wouldn't have it. He was anxious to cut loose completely, and I didn't feel I had the right to stand in his way."

Nelson managed to keep his sympathy from showing. He talked impersonally about farming in general, and discovered that by harnessing love and labor Mike Williams had converted a modest little home place into a prosperous modern enterprise. Then he reached for the luncheon check.

Mike Williams said, "I'll take that. There's no reason for you—"

Nelson ignored it. Deliberately and without zest he hit below the belt. He had no idea of what Betty Conway looked like, but he said, "A girl answering Betty Conway's description was seen on Glen's floor last night. The superintendent saw her just before he discovered the body."

Mike Williams, who had been more or less relaxed, made and shook a durable fist at Nelson. "That's a lie. Nobody answers Betty's description except Betty herself. And she wasn't there." Nelson could see the collar tightening on his strong neck. "Do you think she could have talked to me as calm as you please and even made a joke if—"

"I didn't say she killed him."

Mike Williams took a deep breath. "Then what are you saying—and what are you making me say? I tell you she wasn't there. If she'd been there I'd have run into her, because the papers say the superintendent found my brother at half-past five—and I was just entering the house at half-past five, and if she'd been there I'd have run into her coming out." In the face of that statement he sounded astonishingly triumphant.

Nelson's "Oh?" did not sound triumphant. It sounded defeated.

## CHAPTER 6

In this one instance Mike Williams produced without prompting. "I had some time to spare before the train left and I thought I'd take a chance and call on Glen. Generally I phone first. He liked it better that way—but it would have been foolish to waste the little while I had in a phone booth. So I went along to his place, thinking if he was in all right and if he wasn't—all right too. I rang the downstairs bell and there was no answer. Maybe if the girl who came rushing out right then hadn't let the downstairs door slam shut, I'd have gone up anyway to see if Glen was home and hadn't answered the bell because he wasn't expecting anyone. But she was in an almighty hurry. She saw me and could have held the door for a minute. I guess she was one of those city kids—raised wrong—"

"A kid?" Nelson said. It was an automatic question touched off by the fact that someone had rushed out of the house during the suspect period.

"Well—not much more. Spindly. I remember thinking she'd borrowed her mother's black clothes." He went on, impatient with his own digression. "Anyway, I began to think it was just as well. If Glen was home he might have had company or private business he didn't want me to horn in on. So I decided I shouldn't have come in the first place without phoning, and I took myself off to the station and read the paper until the train came in. But you do see, don't you, that Betty couldn't have been there when the superintendent said—because I must have been downstairs at least five minutes and I'd have seen her come out."

Nelson made no comment, but he was not impressed. The superintendent's hesitancy about the time he had found the body could have meant that he had found it earlier and dawdled, for one reason or another, before he called the police. And if that were so, he would have seen his blond young lady earlier too. But Judd, the operative sent to Connecticut, would take care of all that. Judd would not return without the name of Betty Conway's doctor or the time of her visit to his office, if she had been there at all, or any other facts that seemed pertinent. He said, "Why didn't you tell me at once that you'd called on your brother yesterday?"

"I didn't think I'd have to mention it. I didn't see him, and I thought it would only give you wrong ideas. You don't know me from a rotten potato—how I feel about Glen or—or anything else." He stared at Nelson, and the effort he was making to read Nelson's mind was all but palpable. He said doggedly, "Whatever you think—it had nothing to do with the case. Poor Glen must have been dead when I rang—"

Nelson said, "Did you know that he was a drug addict?"

"A drug addict—Glen!" There was a pause. He might have been waiting for Nelson to smile, to say it was a joke, to apologize for the tastelessness of it. Waiting, he suffered. He had taken a lot and he would probably take a lot more. But all of it would leave a carved record upon his open face. "Glen had no vices. He didn't even drink much. You must be mistaken."

"I'm not mistaken. Your brother's arms and thighs were plainly marked with needle punctures. I hoped you could tell us something about it—something that might connect with his murder."

"Maybe Glen was sick and didn't want to worry me. Maybe a doctor prescribed some of the injections they give people nowadays."

Nelson shook his head.

Mike Williams offered no other theory. He seemed robbed of further speech until he was led back to headquarters. There he managed to dictate and sign a statement, and when he was made to understand that for the time being nothing further would be required of him, he went mutely on his way.

Nelson reread the statement several times, wondering bleakly if here was another case where love and loyalty had turned to hatred and destruction. He did not think that he had been wrong in his appraisal of Mike Williams' character, but he did not know. He called the apartment of Glen Williams, and to the man assigned to cover it he said, "Any visitors, Baldwin?"

"No, sir—well—that is—"

Nelson could have sworn he heard the man struggling with his conscience. "Well?"

"Well—a half hour ago I hear somebody fumbling with the lock and I sneak up and pull the door in as quiet and sudden as I can—which isn't quiet or sudden enough. I'm all set to grab, but when he sees me he squeaks and jumps back out of reach and turns and makes a beeline for the back stairs. I chase, but the door slams in my face and I can't open it. So I come back in here and try to raise the super, whose number I have handy by the phone—only he isn't there and his wife answers—taking her time about it—and then it's too late and the guy is long gone. I don't see how I could have done different, Lieutenant."

"You couldn't. Did you get any kind of a look?"

"A dark, thin guy—seemed about average height. I couldn't see his features clear, the way he jumped and scooted. I know that ain't any kind of a make. I wish I could have done better, but—" Baldwin was a newcomer to Homicide who had already earned the reputation for being the most apologetic cop extant. "I hope this won't be no black mark against me?"

"No black mark. I'm sending a relief over. When he arrives you're to go across the hall to an artist named Delaney. Get a description from him of the models who posed for him yesterday—the times of their arrivals and departures—and ditto for any other visitors he may have had."

"Yes, sir." Baldwin repeated the instructions.

"Good. After that go down to the third floor and see the tenants named Smith. Get a list of their visitors too—with special attention to a thin young girl dressed in black. Report as soon as you have the information."

His phone rang as soon as he had replaced the receiver. The desk sergeant said, "A woman here—name of Thrace, Sarah. Wanted to see the commissioner but settled for you. Something to do with the Williams murder."

"Send her up—and hold any other calls until she's left."

Sarah Thrace made a musical-comedy entrance. Nelson, who had seen many startling sights, managed to keep his face impassive as he greeted her. He looked down, almost expecting to find the worn linoleum on his office floor obscured by the greensward.

Slowly she removed her white summer gloves. She touched a plump, manicured hand to a lock that peeped from under the wide brim of her picture hat. Then she rested upon her tall parasol. And when Nelson invited her to sit down she nodded graciously, lowered her opulence, and billowed her organdy ruffles over the uncompromising wooden chair that faced his desk.

The illusion of an English garden party was so strong that he wanted to say, Tea will be along in a moment. He said, "If you can cast any light upon the death of Glen Williams, Miss Thrace, I shall be very glad you came to see me."

The coquettish toss of her head was the pattern of her life, of her dealings with men. He thought he might be in for something until she raised her eyes. They were very blue and very friendly eyes. And there was nothing of coquetry in their frank appraisal of him. And when she spoke, her whisky-flavored voice was earthy and matter-of-fact.

"Lieutenant Nelson, I was going to say that most men would be glad to see me anywhere, anytime, with or without information. But I'll try to skip the badinage." She sighed and aged a little. "All I hope is that I'll be glad I obeyed the impulse to come here."

"Impulse?"

"No—I'll skip that too. This is no spur-of-the-moment business. I've been weighing the pros and cons of it since last evening."

"Since the murder of Glen Williams?"

She corrected him. "Since I *heard* of the murder of Glen Williams." She took her eyes from his face. She looked around the office. She sighed again.

"Will you have a cigarette, Miss Thrace?" He pushed the box toward her.

She brightened, but when he got to the word "cigarette" she shook her head in disappointment. She aged a little more and sank back heavily in the wooden chair with no thought to the arrangement of the organdy ruffles. He understood what she wanted even before he heard the small sound of her tongue patting the roof of her mouth. He opened the bottom drawer of his desk and took out a bottle of scotch and two clean glasses.

"Well," she said, "that's real kind of you." The diction she employed for the cliché might have issued from Clevis's neighbor in Brooklyn. "I don't want you to think I make a habit of drinking in the afternoon." Then she laughed lustily. "Hell, I drink whenever I get the chance. You're a good fellow, so why should I lie to you, Lieutenant?" She tasted the drink he had poured, and eyed the token drops his own glass contained. "Your scotch is good too. You should try a bigger sample to get the full flavor. No—no more for me—at least not for the moment. This isn't the first I've had today, and I don't want to fall on my face until I've unloaded."

"I'm listening," Nelson said.

"Have you ever heard of me—or are you just naturally nice to everybody?"

"Of course I've heard of you. I've seen you on the stage too."

"I wouldn't like to call a gallant gentleman a liar, but if you did see me it must have been when you were too young to appreciate my performance. That curly white hair doesn't fool me for a moment. Nothing does, if you'll excuse me for boasting."

He said patiently, "I'm sure you're not easily fooled. That's why I'm sure you've brought me some information—"

"I'm leading up to it, Lieutenant. Don't rush me. Let me tell it in my own inimitable fashion. First it's required that I make a confession. No, not the sort of confession your sweet pointed ears are accustomed to hearing—I just want to confess that I'm a 'has-been.' But believe it or not, I was and am a damn good actress—a character actress— not a star. At no time in the career of Sarah Thrace did she thirst for stardom. Juicy character parts were her meat and drink. That does- n't seem overambitious, does it? And yet wherever she seeks for roles the light brush is carefully applied. The field is overcrowded and no- body wants to make the teensiest entering wedge for dear old Sarah Thrace." She smiled suddenly and shed a few years. "You look worried, Lieutenant. I expect you've had more than a baker's dozen of women blubbering on your wide shoulders. You're the type to draw them. Well, ease your mind about me. I'm not building to the crying scene. I'm merely establishing myself as a 'has-been.'" She was the English lady again. "And to have been a 'has-been' in the court of Glen Williams is, I assure you, a rare distinction—because the people he associated with are 'never-wases,' and, with perhaps one exception, 'never-will-bes.'"

"Is a man called Gaudio the one exception?"

She showed no surprise. She said, "If you know Tom Gaudio, perhaps I'm bringing coals to Newcastle."

"I know his name."

"Good for you. Now I made the mistake of knowing more than his name, and I regret to inform you that the experience hasn't been en- tirely rewarding. Expansive, outgoing Sarah Thrace has made many mistakes in her dealings with the human race—" With complete de- tachment she lifted the bottle and poured scotch into her glass. It might indeed have been tea she was pouring, for quantity and for her grand manner. "Shall I tell you about my dealings with the human race?" She glanced at the scarred desk, the linoleum floor, the dingy walls. "This is a charming spot for it—eminently suitable to my tale, as a matter of fact." She took several deep swallows of whisky. "Your face wasn't designed for patience, Lieutenant, or for this setting. It's rather a beautiful face. It has a fawnlike quality. You'd be more at home in a woodland grove—"

Nelson said firmly, "We were speaking of Tom Gaudio. Did he bring you the news of the murder?" He returned the bottle to the bottom drawer.

"You hated to do that, didn't you, Lieutenant? Your mouth is a dead giveaway—much too generous to let you get any satisfaction out of be- ing inhospitable or stingy. But I understand. I realize that the big wheel of the Homicide Squad can't really afford to hold drunken parties in his sanctum. Shall we adjourn to my house?" Her words were coming out slurred. She seemed to be listening to them, because a look of wonder crossed her broad, good-tempered face. "Sorry—perhaps that last drink was one too many," she said, giving precise attention to each syllable. "I *am* sorry. I didn't come here to make a nuisance of myself. I don't often overestimate my capacity, but I suppose that highballs for breakfast instead of coffee are unwise in the last analysis."

Nelson liked her. He found himself hoping that she would be all right, get a job, regain to that Sarah Thrace she spoke of with affection and respect. His absent chief, Inspector Waldo Furniss, had often accused him of having mush for a heart. He said, "Would some coffee help now?"

"No. I'll be all right. If you give me another moment I'll tell Sarah Thrace to sober up and deliver." Whatever it was she told herself worked. She readjusted the organdy ruffles, sat straight in the hard wooden chair, and began to talk sense. She appeared to take no notice when Nelson pressed a buzzer on his desk.

"Tom Gaudio came to my house at a bit after six last evening. He rang up first and made a point of saying that he'd been trying to get me for an hour. That was exaggeration—but whether deliberate or not I can't say, because people do exaggerate about such matters. What I can say is that I came home before six and took a quick shower. These days theatrical agencies always down me—and showers are morale-lifting." She paused. "I'm telling you this so that you'll get the whole picture. I'm not trying to suggest that Tom killed Glen Williams. But he's more than trying to suggest that I did. And I've a feeling he can make himself believe anything he chooses—especially since— Never mind—he's a very intense young man—or maybe fanatic is the word. He rarely bothers to let his conscience know what his mind is up to."

"And you came here because you thought he might come here first to put us on your trail?"

She nodded. "An ignoble errand, isn't it? But I don't set myself up as a public-spirited citizen who co-operates with the police in order that justice be served. I never went in for abstract causes. I don't even like people en masse. Individuals—yes or no, as the case may be. And permit me to boast that I've brought quite a lot of sunshine to individuals from time to time." She added, "And one at a time—if you should be harboring the wrong impression. No—relax—I'm not going off at a tangent again. What I'm trying to indicate subtly is that I've brought quite a lot of sunshine to Tom Gaudio. I'm not ashamed of it, either. He's young enough to be my son—but then who isn't?"

Her back was to the door. She could not see the silent policeman who had answered Nelson's summons. He was writing busily, his notebook backed by the wall, his sharp features a study in discipline.

"I met Tom about a year ago," said Sarah Thrace, "and I felt sorry for the poor devil. At first my intentions toward him were strictly honorable. He looked all kinds of starved, and I thought I could attend to one phase of it by asking him to my apartment for a home-cooked meal. I'm rather an artist in that field too. Well, he accepted my invitation with alacrity, as they say, and pretty soon it became a habit with him. He does—did love his food—and one habit led to another. Luckily I was working when he entered my life. I'd landed the part of dear old nauseous Aunt Flo in a soap opera—so I could afford to nourish Tom and even buy him an occasional pair of socks or whatnots. He wasn't a costly item—not in the beginning—although I did feel the pinch a little when the sponsor's wife had the author of the soap opera kill off Aunt Flo because the characterization made her self-conscious. Tommy boy was a bit irritated. Perhaps he liked me better employed—or perhaps the novelty was wearing off. At any rate, his circle had widened some through his association with me and he had other places to go—so he wasn't quite the poor friendless stray he'd been at first." She paused for a moment. "All in all," she said, "I didn't do so badly by Tom until I brought him to one of Glen's parties."

Nelson opened his mouth to speak, thought better of it.

She went on, "He fell for Glen—fell hard. Nothing queer. Call it the birth of ambition. Glen's drawing-room manner, his assurance, his clothes, his furniture, his car. Duplicates of these could be Tom's—and Tom meant to get them. He would get them. Glen told him so. He had great talent, Glen said. If he went about it in the right way, there was no reason why he couldn't become the country's leading photographer—the *world's* leading photographer. Of course it would take some doing—but that's why Glen was there. Glen meant to see that it was done, to provide the necessary advice and the very necessary capital. What was money for but to help others? Tom need have no false pride. And Tom didn't have any. He lapped up every morsel of it and drooled for more. And I listened too—secondhand. But I wasn't so enthusiastic. When you have the same diet for breakfast, dinner, and supper, it gets to be something less than a treat. And I may have been influenced by the fact that in the early stages of my acquaintance with Glen he'd dished the same stuff out to me—and even then I couldn't swallow it for very long. So one morning I told Tom to put a little salt on it, and he walked out in a flap and went back to his furnished room. Our situation changed considerably after that, although he continued to honor me with his presence whenever he wanted a meal or had an idle moment. He'd even consent to squire me places if it suited his schedule. And that's the story of Glen and Tom—or as much of it as I know up to last evening when he came riding hard to inform me that Glen was dead." Her broad nose crinkled. She gave a sudden throaty chuckle and clapped a hand over her highly painted mouth. She removed it and said, "Lieutenant, you look shocked—or probably as nearly shocked as you can look. But believe me, I'm not hardhearted—just old enough to be glad that everything has its funny side. I wasn't laughing because a murder had been done. I was laughing at Tom's announcement of it." She told him about the children's game, about King Dido who had died doing this way. Then she said, "And I wouldn't be surprised if that's how Glen Williams died. He died doing this way."

Over her shoulder Nelson saw the expectant face of the writing policeman clouded by disgust. He had obviously believed that Sarah Thrace intended to reveal motive, method, and murderer then and there.

Nelson offered her a cigarette, and lit one for himself when she declined. She did not, however, repeat the motions of expressing thirst. She pressed her ample body as far back as the straight chair permitted, her eyes fixed upon his face.

He said, "Did Gaudio accuse you at once of being responsible for the death of his friend?"

"He didn't accuse me at all—not in so many words. He asked for a drink and I gave it to him—a stiff one. It didn't seem to steady his nerves—in fact, he stared at the glass as though it were a Judas. He— Well, that's extraneous. Finally he sniffled a bit and blew his little nose and gave an account of the business. It seemed he'd been working in his darkroom and came out of his absorption to remember that he had an appointment with Glen. We were all due at Glen's last night—but Tom's appointment was private." She grimaced. "Dealing, I imagine— and it doesn't take much imagination—with Glen's plans for his career. Anyway, he was late—he didn't even stop to change his shirt or wash—just rushed out the way he was, for fear he'd incur the royal displeasure—and when he arrived he saw policemen in the lobby— and some man talked to him and explained what had happened."

"According to Gaudio, exactly what did the man say?"

"That Glen Williams had been shot and killed. At least that's all Tom repeated of it. He might have been going to say more—but I got a bit feline at that point and said something about how sensible he'd been to run away instead of staying to get involved with the police."

"Do you know of any reason why he'd be afraid of such an involvement?"

She lowered her blue eyes. "No—I told you I was just being feline."

"What made you feline, Miss Thrace?"

Her poise had returned. "That question's a compliment, Lieutenant. You wouldn't have asked it if you thought I was a chronic cat. You're right. I'm not. I expect I was fed up in general—and fed up specifically because Tom always took it for granted I'd be on tap when he telephoned and got ratty because he'd rung for a few minutes without an answer."

"Is that all?"

"Yes," she said, registering surprise. "That's all."

"Do you think Gaudio's accusal or hinted accusal was a reaction to your cattiness?"

"I guess so. It followed on the heels of it, anyway. He started to dig around in the most extraordinary way for an account of my activities yesterday afternoon. He acted just like Guido, the Gimlet of Ghent, if you know your Stephen Leacock, Lieutenant."

Nelson smiled. "If Gaudio is as unsubtle as Guido, it won't take us long to discover what really is on his mind. What time did he leave your apartment last night?"

"About an hour after he arrived. I wanted him to eat something, but he wasn't interested in food. As a matter of fact, he hasn't been for quite a while—" She bit her heavy lower lip.

"Miss Thrace—would you mind elaborating upon something you said—something about not having done badly by Gaudio until you took him to one of Glen Williams' parties."

"Did I say that? Yes, I could have said it." Her friendly eyes evaded Nelson. "But I have elaborated, haven't I, about Glen filling him up with hopes—promising him the earth—and as sure as I'm sitting here, never meaning to follow through."

"Does Gaudio have as much talent as Williams led him to believe?"

She shrugged. "He's not a bad photographer—some of his studies in design are rather interesting. He might do very well if he stopped trying for short cuts."

"Then encouragement and flattery wouldn't necessarily hurt him—even if it wasn't implemented. Glen Williams was guilty of a more tangible sin, wasn't he?"

"I don't know what you mean."

"Yes, you know. You know that Tom Gaudio became a drug addict. Several things you've said and half said, coupled with odds and ends I've picked up from other sources, point to the fact that you know. You've indicated that he changed from a hearty eater to a man not interested in food. You mentioned that the stiff drink you gave him had no effect—that he can make himself believe whatever he—"

"I'm no match for you, am I, Lieutenant? Yes—Tom started taking dope after I introduced him to Glen. I've been around enough to detect the signs—and on him the signs were easy to read. You had only to look at his eyes—the pupils splashed all over the irises. At first he seemed to get a real charge out of whatever it was he took. He'd never been what you'd call the life of the party—more the other way— moody—shy. Hypochondriacal too—always mewing about his little aches and pains. But after he'd been initiated his personality changed. He was riding the crest—whooping it up like a real outgoing, back-slapping boaster from Butte—"

"You're describing the effects of heroin," Nelson said, "but that riding-the-crest phase doesn't last. Tolerance for the drug is acquired so fast that its pleasures are short-lived."

"You can say that again. Heroin or whatever—his pleasures deserted him at the rate of knots. He developed a foul temper. And jumpy! He'd break into a cold sweat if you so much as touched his sleeve. Seemed scared to death half the time and kept complaining of a queasiness in his stomach. Once when I was out with him he disappeared into the bathroom and stayed there for years—very embarrassing."

"But he felt better when he emerged."

"Better? Remade—mentally and physically. You'd think he'd discovered a fortune in the plumbing fixtures."

"Did you ever discuss it with him?"

"I tried." She sounded weary.

"Addiction to drugs is one of the most expensive hobbies in the world. Do you think he was financed by Glen Williams?"

"He might have been. I know I didn't finance him—just a few dollars here and there when I could spare it and it seemed urgent. Of late it's seemed urgent in the extreme." She thought for a moment. "In fact, one day last week I confessed to being short of cash and I thought he was going to try to knock me down. I said *try* advisedly."

Nelson's pleasant voice was dry. "Addicts have been known to kill their own mothers to get the price of a 'fix.'"

She said as dryly, "Mother Thrace sees what you mean." But she looked sick. After a pause she said, "I'm beginning to be sorry I came—sorry I told you all this. It *was* an ignoble impulse. I have nothing against Tom, although I've taken an odd way of proving it. The truth is"—there was a slight break in her voice—"I'm still fond of him. I don't think he murdered Glen."

"If Glen had started him on the habit and was withholding his supply—"

She shook her head. The incongruous garden hat wobbled on its perch. She said miserably, "I'm not even sure he did start him. Perhaps I've cut it out of whole cloth. If I may descend to personalities again, you strike me as being rather wise, Lieutenant—not the type to go off half-cocked. If I'd known there were men like you in the department I wouldn't have been so afraid of my own skin. I'd have sat it out at home."

"What about Williams himself? Did he evidence the same symptoms as Gaudio?"

"I've seen progressively less of Glen in the last few months. And you could never tell about him. He was something like what the analysts describe as manic—way up or way down." She paused again. "I don't want you to get the wrong impression from anything I may have said. Could be I *am* becoming just a spiteful, catty old woman. Glen wasn't a bad sort. Quite charming actually. I got sore at him because he seemed to make a business of flattery—of leading people up alleys that any fool could tell were dead ends. But maybe his motives were innocent—maybe that was his way of making people happy."

"Did you, by any chance, read Glen's book?"

"Who—me?" Her reaction reminded him of Clevis. "He gave me a copy, and I honestly tried to read it, so that I could make the right responses when he sounded me out, but—" She raised her eye-brows. "Paper-backed, too, so that it didn't even gladden the eye. I believe that leather-bound copy he prays to is the only one in existence."

"Prays to?"

"Well, he's had a niche carved out for it, and there always seems to be a floral offering there."

Nelson did not comment. He said, "You still insist that no more than a veiled accusation made by a man you knew to be unstable brought you here?"

"Isn't that good enough? I—my reputation—I can't have stories like that spread." She drew herself up in the wooden chair. She seemed to be engrossed in some game with her ruffles. "In the theater the slightest hint of anything fishy would ruin what chances I—"

"Have you seen Gaudio since he left your apartment last night?"

"No—I haven't."

"Whom did you see?"

"Why—no one."

"But you talked to someone."

She raised her eyes to his face again. "Lieutenant, I brought all this on myself. I should be kicked around the block. I am being kicked around the block." For a large woman she looked astonishingly helpless.

He smiled. "You paid me a compliment before. You said I wasn't the type to go off half-cocked. Are you taking it back?"

"No—it's just that if through sheer stupidity I involve myself that's one thing. But I don't want to involve some rather pleasant people who innocently and through no fault of their own wandered into the wrong pew." Then she said almost crossly, "Take that patient, waiting gaze away, will you? Oh—all right—it was Joss Woodruff. She phoned me. She said Tom had been to see her early this morning. She thought that I should be warned about the stories he was spreading about me—and she—she wanted my advice—about how to deal with him, I mean. He'd said a lot of irresponsible things that—"

"Irresponsible things—about you?"

"Yes—of course."

"No—not of course. Why would Miss Woodruff want your advice if he hadn't included her in the irresponsible things he said?"

"*Mrs.* Woodruff." The correction was mechanical, but she seized upon it as an excuse to change the subject. She said rapidly, almost gaily, "Joss is a wonderful girl. Morgan, her husband, is a darling too. It wasn't Tom I meant when I said Glen's circle included an exception to the 'never-wases.' It was Morgan Woodruff. That lad really has talent. Given the right break, he—"

Nelson said, "If necessary, we'll come back to Morgan Woodruff. First I'd like you to answer my question."

"What question?"

"Why did Mrs. Woodruff want your advice?"

"Hell—oh hell." Then her voice became defiant. "Why wouldn't she? She was worried about the way he acted, and she's seen me with him so often that she thought I was the logical person to call. After all, he was practically a stranger to her, and it was obvious, I suppose, that he needed help. She didn't know he took dope—his calling so early and shooting off his mouth must have seemed like sheer insanity—"

"She thought he was insane because he accused you of murder?" She tried to be flippant. "Now that you've met me, wouldn't you draw the same conclusion?"

"And he went to her with his suspicions even though she was a stranger to him? Why her? Are you and she close friends?"

"No, but— Dammit, I've told you why. He was unbalanced—doped—"

"I'm afraid you'll have to do better than that, Miss Thrace."

Reluctantly, she did better than that. She told him that Joss Woodruff had called her, not knowing where else to turn, because Tom had accused Joss of being Glen's mistress. And Joss was afraid he would take the story to Morgan, and Morgan wasn't too well and had enough to disturb him without that. "And if ever," Sarah Thrace concluded, "there was anything more absurd, I'll lose what little faith I have in human nature. Because Joss and Morgan—well, I wish you could see them together. It's beautiful. It's a modernized version of any pair of historically renowned lovers you care to mention."

## CHAPTER 7

Nelson could not accept the absurdity of Joss Woodruff's guilty relationship to Glen Williams. He did not say this to Sarah Thrace. He caught the writing policeman's eye and gave a slight nod. The policeman interpreted the signal correctly and went off to transcribe his notes. Then Nelson, his mind half occupied with other matters, put Sarah Thrace through a few more paces from which he drew no important conclusions. By the time the policeman returned to lay the typescript on his desk, she had openly asked for and been granted another drink. She was gratefully devoting herself to it.

Nelson pushed the typescript toward her. "Would you mind signing this?"

She looked at him in bewilderment. "Signing what?"

"Your statement."

She almost dropped her glass. Incredulously she scanned the thin sheaf of papers. "You took down everything I said? How—with mirrors?"

"You couldn't see the stenographer from where you're sitting."

"An accident, no doubt—carefully arranged to make me feel more at home."

"Do you find the statement in order?"

"I find it very much out of order. I find it a dirty trick. All that stuff about Joss—it makes me positively sick—and what it will make her—"

"We'd have got to her sooner or later," Nelson said, thinking of the cross section of letters pre-empted by Clevis.

"How, may I ask?" Her voice was laden with sarcasm.

"We're making it our business to interview as many of Glen Williams' acquaintances as possible."

"Oh. Glommed on to his address book, I suppose. Well, if I ever get bumped off—and I feel like a candidate for it this minute—you can take it from me that I'll destroy every bit of paper in the house, so that my friends won't be annoyed by people like you."

"I wish I could make you understand that you haven't betrayed a confidence," Nelson said gently. "You may even have helped Mrs. Woodruff by the stand you've taken that she's not the type to indulge in extramarital affairs."

"Do I have a choice about signing this?"

"I shouldn't think so."

She signed with no further protest. But her hand shook a little. "Anything else I can do for you?" she said bitterly.

He said there was nothing else, thanked her for coming, and escorted her to the door. Before she billowed through it she drew herself up and cried in a ringing voice, "Keep your jails clean, Buster."

He returned to his desk grinning. But the grin faded as he found what he was searching for in the folder containing Clevis's haul.

The letter signed "Joss" seemed out of key among the feminine bits of stationery. But it was a love letter in spite of the fact that its format was unromantic. It had been typed single-spaced upon a battered machine with a worn ribbon, and the manuscript paper employed was of the kind used for second sheets. The text started high on the page and left a generous margin of white space beneath. Reading without pleasure, Nelson thought that either Joss Woodruff was an inferior typist or that the stress of her emotions was responsible for the number of Xed-out errors.

Glen Williams had been "My darling Glen" to Joss Woodruff. But notwithstanding her deep and indestructible love for him, she did not mean to sit back and let him have things all his own way. She was, in many more words than seemed necessary to make her point, not going to permit him to renounce her out of his pity and loyalty for Morgan. She could not help but admire his nobility—his integrity. She herself had made countless sacrifices for Morgan, but what that poor soul did not know could not hurt him, and how could she force her love to go where it would not go. Clichés were almost as thick as the errors. "We only live once—and then too short a time—and the hours spent in the arms of my Glen are the only hours that hold purity or rightness in an evil, guilty world ... so I'll be there tomorrow—and you'll be there—because something stronger than both of us—something that makes us as helpless as leaves in the wind ..." That was the gist of the letter. Considering the purple tinge of its text, it ended rather suddenly in stark black and white. "I'm running down to the corner mailbox. Then I'll come back and cook dinner for my lawfully wedded husband. All my love, Joss."

Nelson placed the letter in a separate folder, marked it "Lab," and rang for a messenger. His mind etched a picture of one Joss Woodruff. In spite of Sarah Thrace's warm praise, he saw her as a hard-faced beauty with a second-rate intellect and third-rate-morals, discontented with her lot and clutching at her sordid version of romance with both greedy hands. He saw, as well, the meek, struggling, lawfully wedded husband who had nothing and probably went about believing he had everything.

The desk sergeant had followed instructions, withholding telephone calls while Sarah Thrace was in the office, putting them through the moment she departed. Nelson gave the ringing instrument a cold stare that would have silenced a human being. Joss Woodruff's letter did not suggest that she was ready to divorce the poor husband and marry the lover. But perhaps, Nelson thought, she had acquainted the lover with such an intention and found no need to restate it. And perhaps it was not so much integrity as fear of a marriage trap that had caused Glen Williams to make his renouncement. And perhaps when she had gone "there" she had been faced with the true nature of his "nobility" and killed him. Or perhaps her husband was not so unsuspecting after all, and had followed her "there," and harked to the voice of his outraged manhood which clamored for revenge. Nelson smiled crookedly. The purple prose must be catching, he thought. It seemed to be affecting his brain, lending it a new vocabulary. The letter bore no date. The envelope was missing. But the "tomorrow" might easily have referred to the day of the murder.

It seemed to Lieutenant Gridley Nelson, Acting Captain of Homicide, that a visit to the Woodruffs was strongly indicated. The present time was twenty minutes after four, and there was no time like the present, or, failing that, a quarter of an hour later.

So for the next fifteen minutes he took the most urgent of the telephone calls, advising and instructing on matters departmental and listening to the report of the detective stationed in the Williams apartment.

Operation Delaney and Smith, Baldwin, the detective, assured Nelson, was completed. Delaney, the artist, residing opposite to Williams, had used only one model for the past three days and had received no visitors. The model was named Vita Suarez, and she was a Spanish-looking type, dark and "kind of pushed out above and below, if you get me, Lieutenant." Nelson could visualize the involuntary pantomime that accompanied the description. "And I asked to see his wife, Mrs. Delaney, and he called her and I put the question to her before they could cook up anything together, and she said the same, positively no other visitors. So I think they're on the level. They're both nice-spoken and wish they could move because they don't like murder except at a distance, only it's hard to get a suitable place for Mr. Delaney's work— Sure, Lieutenant, excuse me, I'll cut it short. I went down to the third floor and that was a different story. Mrs. Smith was home. Her husband's away on a business trip since last week. If I was him I'd stay away— Yes, sir, I'm sorry but— Yes, sir. She got real sore and said she had no visitors at all yesterday—especially no girl who was skinny and wore a black dress. It was like she thought I was crazy to come and bother her with such foolishness. I guess none of this is what you wanted, Lieutenant, but—"

Nelson said it would do for a starter and broke the connection. He picked up a telephone directory. He recorded the address of the only Morgan Woodruff listed. He strode out of the office, out of the building, trying to concentrate on those members of the force who interrupted his swift passage, and exchanging surface pleasantries with a reporter who had a hang-over. He got into his car and drove to the Woodruff apartment house, wondering why Clevis had not checked back and whether the skinny young girl in black encountered by the superintendent's wife and by Mike Williams had said "Smith" for the obvious reason that it was the first name she could think of to account for her presence, which she dared not account for by uttering the name of the person she had really come to see. Williams, for example. For obviously, according to the adjectives "skinny" and "spindly," used by the superintendent's wife and by Mike Williams, she was not the Spanish-looking-type model "pushed out above and below."

The Woodruff street was mean, yet not too mean to display the American phenomena of the car-lined curbstone. Nelson had to park his Buick in a lot several blocks away.

The Woodruff house was mean, too, a dingy, soot-seasoned walkup.

The door clicked open in response to his ring and he made the steep climb. By the time he reached the hot, musty landing near the roof he was willing to concede that Joss Woodruff might have reason to be discontented with her lot. His own walk-up apartment near Lexington Avenue was a paradise by comparison, well-kept and clean. He had rented it at the onset of the housing shortage and had been fortunate enough when he married Kyrie in the thick of the shortage to take over the adjoining apartment too. So he and Kyrie, and now Junie, had plenty of space. And they had Sammy to add to their peace and comfort. And he was a lucky man, and let him not condemn others less lucky, sight unseen. He tried to strip himself of bias as he pressed the bell on the Woodruffs' door.

It opened at once. The woman standing there was no one he expected to see. He said, "Is Mrs. Woodruff at home?"

"I'm Mrs. Woodruff," Joss said. She added a polite "Good afternoon," because it occurred to her that this caller might be a salesman like Morgan and that she had nothing to give him but courtesy. "Perhaps I ought to tell you," she said, "that I'm—we're not in the market for anything. I'm sorry, but—" She lost the rest of the sentence. It was not that she found his scrutiny offensive, but that its steadiness was unnerving. It went on even while he took a leather folder from his pocket and opened it in a manner that must have been perfected by practice.

"My name is Nelson," he said. "Lieutenant Nelson, Homicide." He extended the folder. "Perhaps you'd like verification."

She did no more than glance at the credentials. She said, "Come in," and when they reached the living room she said, "Sit down."

He sat down. She resented the relaxed attitude he managed to achieve even though he had chosen the chair with the treacherous springs. She resented his well-tailored summer worsted and the youth implicit in his olive-skinned face under its contradictory shock of curly white hair. She herself sat tense and waiting in the opposite chair.

He said with no more than passing interest, "Is your husband at home?"

"No—he's not." She hated herself for being unable to let it go at that. "You see, my husband sells encyclopedias—I thought you might be a salesman too and—" She bit her lip. She was Joss Woodruff, among whose attributes Morgan had listed serenity and unshakable poise. But things had happened to her that—

Nelson said, "It doesn't matter. It's you I want to talk with at the moment."

"About what?" The words were quiet, but her face showed that she wanted to scream them, wanted to know why she was being harassed by a man from Homicide.

He made a show of surprise. "Glen Williams' death. Sorry—I didn't mean to be so abrupt about it. I thought you'd have heard by this time."

She said, "I have heard—or read. It was in the morning paper. Burglars broke into his apartment—didn't they?"

"It looks that way."

She repeated, "Looks that way?"

Nelson's voice was rueful. "It's not unusual for newspapers to cavil at the slow methods of the police and to try to jump the gun. Actually we have no means of knowing why or by whom Glen Williams was killed. We haven't had time to check thoroughly—but we have observed that a number of small valuables which should have tempted a burglar were left untouched in the apartment. Of course that could mean that the burglar was intercepted before he had time to complete the job."

She said nothing.

"However, there are a few other factors which war with the burglary theory—"

She said, "Other factors?" and then imposed a stricture upon herself to speak only when a direct question was put to her. In that way no inadvertent light could disclose her secret thoughts about Glen Williams. She lowered her eyelids. She looked through her fair stubby lashes at the man from Homicide and hoped that he was unaware of her constraint, or that he accepted it as born of the natural distress of one unaccustomed to even slight contact with murder.

His voice, at least, was sympathetic. "You and Mr. Williams were close friends."

It was a statement, not a question. It took her off guard. "No—we were not close friends. My husband—it was through my husband's job that we met." Again she was unable to check herself. "Mr. Williams had been kind to my husband and naturally we wanted to make some return—so we invited him here and he seemed to enjoy coming—"

"I don't wonder," Nelson said. His eyes traveled the simple little room. "You've made this extremely attractive."

Joss was momentarily diverted. "I hadn't much to work with," she said without bitterness. "If you look closely you'll realize that everything's a bit seedy—but having a home is very important to my husband and to me—" Her brown eyes met Nelson's and she tensed again at the expression she surprised in them. She could not know that it was induced by the remarkable fact that each time she said, "My husband," she seemed to wave a bright banner symbolizing her reason for being, and that the man from Homicide was trying to reconcile this with the typewritten letter he had marked "Lab."

He said abruptly, "You corresponded with Williams."

"Corresponded?"

His pleasant voice sharpened. "Mrs. Woodruff, you look as though you're trying to determine just what foreign language I'm speaking."

"I am. Why should I correspond with a man who lives in the same city? I have a telephone and so has—had he."

She saw that he was angry. She did not know what had provoked his anger.

He had expected and rather enjoyed the histrionics of Sarah Thrace. But somehow histrionics coming from this girl were an insult. Everything about her looked honest, her strong free body, her face. And yet she had written a letter proving dishonesty. He said, "We'll use no more words than are necessary. You and Glen Williams were lovers."

Her heart was thudding, interfering with the honest volume of her voice. "You've been listening to Tom Gaudio. He sent you here."

"A letter sent me here—a statement of your relationship to Glen Williams—signed with your name."

Her face was pale. She stood up, gripping the arms of the chair. Beneath her the room rocked like a ship. That letter—the only letter she had sent to Glen was—

"Can I get you some water?" he said.

She did not hear. She was thinking, If it could be a very bad dream—if I could wake up some morning last week with Morgan there sleeping beside me—

Nelson said, "Are you all right?" and to her his voice had become ice and he loomed before her clouded eyes as a machine which could produce nothing but ice. She said, "Yes—excuse me—I felt strange for a moment. I'm all right now. That letter—the letter I wrote to Glen Williams—was a statement of the way I felt about him. You seem to be reproaching me for it—I can't imagine why. And knowing him—having known him—I can't imagine why he didn't destroy the letter—but of course he didn't if you found it—and you wouldn't—there'd be no sense in your lying." She was sitting down again, glad of the supporting chair since there was no other support. "But I don't see why the letter should interest you unless—"

"Unless?"

Her color was returning, and with it some of her poise. "Unless you think that in a fit of outraged virtue I killed him."

"Did you?"

"No." This time she felt no inclination to elaborate. She looked down at her left wrist, at the little disk that had been Morgan's mustering-out gift to her, that on several grim occasions she had needed to pawn, and had not, because Morgan saw the transaction as a knuckling to defeat. The little disk said a quarter to six. For once she hoped that Morgan would be late, late enough to miss the Homicide man.

"Your husband might have killed him," Nelson said. "Other men have been made desperate by the same goad."

The sickness was returning. She fought it. "My husband isn't other men," she said. And then, "He didn't know—I didn't tell him."

Nelson said tonelessly, "I'm sure you didn't. But sooner or later rumors have a way of reaching the concerned party."

"No—I'd have realized if he knew. He can't hide his feelings from me."

"But you can hide yours from him."

"If necessary."

"That must be quite a comfort to you." His hostility surprised himself. He had met quite a few women who for one reason or another ignored convention, and he had not thought of judging them for their sins. But they had not been like this woman, this girl who was anybody's clean, wide-eyed sister to be protected against—

She stared at him. She said evenly, "Why are you talking to me this way? I'm aware that the police have to question the innocent and guilty alike in a murder case—I'm not objecting to that—but I see no reason for your antagonism—and you're being extremely antagonistic."

He said, "Then I apologize. It's bad practice for a detective to show antagonism—or anything else, for that matter."

She did not analyze the apology. She saw with relief that he had risen from Morgan's chair. He will be gone before Morgan gets home, she thought.

He said, "I wonder if you have a typewriter? It would save us both a bit of trouble if I could write something before I return to headquarters."

She bit her lip at the prospect of further delay. "I have one, but it isn't much good."

"No matter—as long as it works at all."

"Well—over there—under the desk. We bought it secondhand, and I'm about the only one who can manage it—"

"Thank you." He strode over to the desk, stooped and lifted the heavy old Remington as though it were a light toy. He set it upon the desk.

"You'll find paper in the top drawer," she said. She watched him take a sheet from the stack of cheap paper, insert it, and start to type.

He said over his shoulder, "Two-finger system. You're probably an expert."

"I'm quite good." He had finished. She sighed as he took the paper out. Then she saw that he was offering it to her along with a fountain pen.

"Will you read this and sign it, please. It's the gist of our conversation, and I've left space for you to fill in a brief account of the way you spent yesterday."

"I spent yesterday at home—except for the few moments I was out shopping."

"Well, please write it in—it may save you from having to make a formal statement later."

She did what he asked. He folded the paper neatly and put it in his pocket. "What time does your husband get home?" he said casually.

"His hours are irregular—depending on his appointments."

"Then will you ask him to come to headquarters—at his convenience. I'll leave the address."

"Do you have to see him?"

"Yes."

There seemed no more to be said. She felt his measuring stare and met it helplessly. She imagined that the expression in his deep-set eyes was kinder, and suddenly she wanted to pour out all that troubled her, all that she had been unable to say on the phone to Sarah Thrace, all that she could not say to Morgan. She held her arms stiffly at her sides, her fine capable hands clenched. She shook her head to dislodge the idiocy that had crept in to possess it. To want to weep on the shoulder of a cold, strange man because she had surprised kindness in his eyes—

He had turned from her. He was looking at the bookshelves. He said, "I see you have a copy of Glen Williams' memoirs. It has a different binding—a bit less elaborate than the one in his apartment."

She nodded.

"Have you read it?"

"Yes." She wished he would stop making conversation. Or was it just conversation?

"What did you think of it?"

She said tiredly, "This seems an odd time to give literary criticism. However, the book didn't interest me very much. It was pure Glen Williams all the way through—" She shrugged.

"And you'd had enough of Glen Williams?"

She did not answer at once. She took time to dam her first spontaneous rush of words. "I'd had enough of the details of Glen Williams' life. I'd heard them repeated and repeated—and what a man eats for breakfast on certain mornings or how many miles he drives and what he says to some chance acquaintance and how popular he is with women are neither matters of universal importance nor exciting reading unless they're handled by a professional with a special touch."

"Was that your husband's opinion too?"

"My husband didn't read it. He hasn't any patience with that sort of thing. He wouldn't even pretend he'd read it when Glen asked him. He's too honest. He—he even joked about it to Glen—said he didn't believe Glen had read it himself, because that beautiful leather binding was much too new-looking and that something ought to be spilled on it to give it a used look."

"I see," Nelson said.

It seemed to her that he really did see something. But she was too preoccupied to speculate. Her next words were involuntary. "You didn't have a hat, did you?"

"No hat—but I do have one more question before I leave. What made you type a letter of that nature?"

Her face was blank. "That nature?"

He said, "The letter we were discussing—the one I found—"

"Oh." Now she had the look of one who is forced to discuss private affairs with a tradesman. But she showed no evidence of guilt, only the normal distaste of a reticent person. "I don't type personal letters—I—"

"Surely your point of view is unique—I'd be interested to know what you call personal—"

She interrupted hotly, "Glen's point of view was unique. I can't help what he thought—or wanted to think—and I can't help or even understand what you're— Oh—please go. I'm expecting someone. I—"

"Whoever you're expecting is here," Nelson said as a key turned unmistakably in the lock. "Your husband?"

Her clear skin flushed. She said passionately, "Of course not. It's my custom to make wholesale distribution of keys to my apartment."

Then she turned and walked swiftly to the door.

Nelson stood listening. A man's voice said, "Joss!" and it was the voice of a man who had everything. And the silence that followed was the silence of a man who holds everything he has in the tight circle of his arms.

## CHAPTER 8

Tom Gaudio walked lightly down the dark creaking stairs. Compared to this house, the one that the Woodruffs lived in was a mansion. But Gaudio, for the time being, was giving the Woodruffs no thought. Nothing troubled Gaudio. Even the aggressive hall toilets he passed, one to every five families, did not affect his sudden rise of spirits. He reached the street and breathed its used and tepid air as though it had been compounded on a high mountain for his special intake.

Aloof, yet kind, he moved aside to allow an old gnarled female to enter the house, ignoring her sharp hostile glance, waiting until she was out of sight to flick his coat free of imaginary contact with her greasy brown paper bundles. With magnificent tolerance he eyed the little people who filled the sidewalks, wheeling or lugging or chastising their progeny, chattering about their petty concerns. Unhurried, he lingered on the Acevedo stoop, head up, hands nonchalantly in the pockets of his shabby trousers. There was no hurry about anything now. Everything that had been important several hours ago could wait upon the god who was Tom Gaudio.

Godlike, he smiled as he thought of the inspiration that had led him to the Acevedos, of the treasure he had uncovered in their sordid quarters, of what he had left behind him on the rumpled bed. The humor of it struck him so forcibly that he opened his mouth to let the smile mature into a strapping laugh. Then he choked the laugh to stare reprovingly at a rubbernecking monkey who had stopped to stare. "Who are you looking at?" he said, and was answered with a barrage of Spanish, and would have returned it in the good Bleecker Street Italian of his childhood except that good Bleecker Street Italian would be wasted on this monkey, and anyway, a commotion had broken loose behind him.

He did not like noise of any kind. It made him jump. It penetrated his supreme well-being. It made him feel that after all there might be a need to hurry. He was not afraid of what the little people could do to him, but he did not want his dignity impaired by contact with them. So he muttered, "When in Rome do as the Romans," and floated off the Acevedo stoop in the general direction of the subway. Subways were not for gods. Low cream-colored cars such as the one poor old Glen had driven were for gods. Taxis might substitute, but even he, the great Gaudio, could not conjure a taxi from the welter of this slum.

He did not float for long. A hard hand reached up to stay him. Hard fingers made a clamp around his arm. And from his height he looked down upon a specimen in baggy clothes. He jerked his head around to see what lay behind him, as had become his habit in time of stress. Swarthy foreshortened figures were racing out of the Acevedo house. By twos and threes they came, by threes and fours, by— The old woman led them, her knotted arms empty of bundles, her face full of sorrow and hate. She pointed at him. She shrieked. She closed in and spattered him with boiling words. Other hands reached out to clutch, to hurt, to violate his person. Then the thin, piercing blade of a whistle severed his nerve ends and he toppled.

Morgan Woodruff walked into his own tidy living room. He had no eyes for the personable figure of Gridley Nelson. He saw only the invader of his privacy, and to that invader his words were addressed. "It's my turn now. You've finished with my wife."

"Not quite," Nelson said.

"Yes you have—and managed to upset her thoroughly."

"Mrs. Woodruff does not appear to be a woman easily upset," Nelson said. What Mr. Woodruff appeared to be, he thought, was a man making a valiant attempt to swim to shore through a heavy sea of fatigue, and he thought further that in spite of this and in spite of the sensitive quality of his mouth and eyes, Woodruff managed to convey an impression of gristly toughness.

"Mrs. Woodruff is not easily upset," Morgan said. "So you must have really put your shoulder to it. I suppose policemen are the same the world over. I noticed that during the war, with few exceptions, men who put in for M.P. jobs were too cowardly to become honest criminals. They had to satisfy their sadistic urges under a blanket stamped 'legal.'"

Nelson's tone expressed polite interest. "Did you have many encounters with M.P.s during the war?"

"If your curiosity outlasts this session, I doubt you'll have difficulty in checking my war record."

Joss said proudly, "His war record was wonderful." She had re-entered the room quietly. She had taken time to comb her hair and wash her face. Moisture still clung to her eyelashes.

Morgan said, "You needn't have come back, darling. He's through with you. And don't bother to defend us, because he's not out to believe anything we say."

Unexpectedly, she supported Nelson. "I don't think that's true. I think he's only trying to do his work."

"I wouldn't call it a very good try," Morgan said.

They might have been discussing an absentee. It was a new experience for Nelson, accustomed in similar circumstances to painful awareness of his presence. Morgan ended the brief exchange with a yawn. "That's not to express nonchalance," he said. "Annoyance, probably—or maybe hunger. It's dinnertime, isn't it, Joss? Hadn't you better start preparations?"

"Dinner's ready to serve. We'll have it as soon as the lieutenant leaves." She had obviously caught the pleading note in his voice, but was as obviously determined to remain in the room.

Nelson said, "I don't want to prolong this. Mr. Woodruff, where—"

Morgan cut him off. "If you really don't want to prolong it," he said, "I know a short cut." As though he were engaging in a one-man vaudeville act, he assumed the dual role of detective and suspect. "Woodruff, where were you at the time of the murder? Who—me? Yes—you. Well—it was my day of rest, so I went for a walk. Who did I bump into but Glen Williams. He invited me to lunch and I accepted." He thrust his hand out to grip the lapel of the unseen suspect who was himself. "You had lunch with the victim? Now we're getting somewhere. Sure—don't hit me, officer. We're getting to the Gateau and the hour is one-ten. How did you know the exact hour, Woodruff? I'm glad you asked that. It's like this—I don't wear a watch—put it down to eccentricity, which it isn't—but my host took a squint at his and announced the time as we were tying our napkins around our little necks. Well, sir—"

Joss said, "Morgan!"

He looked at her, at Nelson. He seemed more nonplused by Nelson's grave, attentive air than by her exclamation of his name. He frowned and said in his normal voice, "Maybe I haven't laid you in the aisles, but I can't help it if the script was dull to start with." He sat down wearily.

Nelson said, "Did you go home with Williams after lunch?"

"No. We parted outside the restaurant."

"Was he going home?"

"I didn't ask him."

"And he didn't mention any appointment he might have had?"

"No—and thank you kindly. But if that's an out for me, I can't take it."

"How long did you spend at lunch?"

"An hour or so."

"Did you go straight home after that?"

"I went to Central Park." He made a return to his attempt at flippancy. "I'm in arrears on sun—see? Me not getting my usual trip to the Riviera last winter."

"Did you meet any acquaintance in or on the way to the park?"

"You can walk for days in New York without meeting a familiar soul. I know because I'm always walking for days. Wait a minute. Come to think of it, there was another bum sharing the bench with me—a sociable gent with whiskers and plain and fancy patches. He's my alibi from about two-thirty onwards—and a smart operator like you should dig him up easy—even if all the best bums are wearing whiskers and patches this year." Joss sat down on the arm of his chair. His hand went out to hers. There was no change in his facial expression to show that the gesture was a conscious one.

"What time did you reach home?"

Joss said quickly, "Four-fifteen. I looked at the kitchen clock when he came in."

Morgan turned his head toward her. Consciously or unconsciously, he withdrew his hand. She said, "Sorry. I didn't mean to answer for you, Morgan."

"You can answer for me any old time you like—except that right now it might seem too eager-beaver to the lieutenant here. It might give him the idea we've something to hide or that you're afraid I'll pull a boner."

"Afraid you'll— Why should I be?" But her eyes were afraid.

"Never mind. You only read the morning paper. But one of the later editions I picked up gratis in the subway said the medical examiner's best guess was somewhere between two and six. It was after two when I left him, but you still haven't managed to clear me—"

"Clear you? Morgan—please don't joke about—"

"Joke? If I'm joking, our constant visitor here has no sense of humor. Look at him. He hasn't even tittered."

Nelson said, "Mrs. Woodruff, I think you can start getting that dinner ready to put on the table while I ask your husband a few more questions that might save him a trip to headquarters."

Morgan got up. He raised her from the arm of the chair and faced her toward the door. "Go on, darling. When a policeman sounds almost human you've got to do what he says."

She had a protest ready but she closed her lips upon it. She went from the room and Morgan Woodruff returned to his chair. "Alone at last," he said. "Not very cosy—but alone." Then he said challengingly, "You'll never have the good fortune to meet another woman as forthright as my wife. Must be she's had a stinker of a day—with you to put the topping on it. Otherwise she wouldn't be taking this so big."

Wouldn't she? Nelson thought. And he thought that Morgan, too, must have had a stinker of a day—or a series of stinkers. He waited, saying nothing.

"And while we're on the subject of being forthright," Morgan said, "I might as well tell you that there was a point during lunch when I wanted not just to murder Glen Williams but to cut him up into bite-sized chunks. I didn't because the joint was too classy and Emile kept too close to give me elbowroom."

"Emile?"

"The waiter. Glen kept Emiling him all over the place. I didn't kill Glen later, either, for the simple reason that my little tempers never warm me for more than a couple of minutes."

"Why did you want to murder Williams?"

"A personal matter—very boring to the outsider."

Nelson said what, considering the facts, he had been oddly reluctant to say before Joss. He was reluctant to say it now. "Was it because Williams and your— Did you quarrel with Williams because he and your wife were in love with each other?"

Morgan Woodruff came out of his chair.

"It's a logical assumption based on your wife's—" Nelson sidestepped the thrown fist and caught Morgan, who had flung himself off balance. It was like grappling with an armful of live coals.

Morgan panted, "Let go—the take-off was wrong—if I'd been on my feet you'd be off yours—"

"Stop it—you'll only add to your wife's distress." Nelson managed to pinion his arms. "All you'll gain if you insist on a battle is temporary release from what's eating you."

"Shove it. You're what's eating me—and what I want is permanent release from you. Get a warrant—get anything—but get the hell out—"

Nelson released him. "If you were in better condition," he said sincerely, "we'd be fairly matched—"

"Sure—sure—a psychologist too." He was breathing heavily, but he made no move to swing again.

"You gave me some voluntary information, Woodruff, either because you thought I'd check with your Emile at the Gateau or because you're an honest man—"

"Don't flatter me. I gave it to you because I thought the waiter might come forward with a statement as soon as he saw Glen's picture in the paper. He did, didn't he? That's what brought you here."

"I'd have come anyway," Nelson said. "And now I want your version."

"You won't get it. I'll co-sign anything the waiter said. That should be good enough."

"It isn't good enough." Nelson sat down. His eyes glanced off the typewriter on the desk. He shrugged his wide shoulders and turned back to Morgan. "And I want my dinner too."

"You mean they actually feed you?" Morgan met Nelson's gaze squarely. A latent awareness of something he had failed to note before flashed across his features.

Nelson said, "You've just decided that in a dim light I might pass as any honest citizen."

Morgan caught himself returning the smile and tightened his lips. After a minute he said, "Was it shock tactics or what—that business about Glen Williams and my wife?"

"It could have been Emile, the waiter."

"Oh." There was another pause. "I take it back. I won't co-sign his statement. He's got it garbled."

"But the quarrel was about your wife?"

"No—not directly. Joss didn't even like Glen. She tolerated him because she thought I liked him. Bringing Joss into it was something he thought up on the spur of the moment to make matters worse."

"What matters?"

"You win," Morgan said. "A little background music, please." He took off his coat and flung it over the chair arm. He wriggled in his damp shirt and began. "After I came out of the Army and after a few hundred false starts I landed on my feet—and I do mean feet—in the fine upstanding job of selling encyclopedias. Glen Williams was my first customer—that was how I met him—and oh what a high-type guy he was. Oh what an interest he took in his fellow men—in me—in my career—" The lines deepened on his scowling, thoughtful face.

"In your career as a salesman?"

"No—as a song writer." Then he said defensively, "I really liked him—it wasn't opportunism—at least not entirely. Aside from being

a little precious, he seemed okay. The run-around he gave me was unnecessary. I didn't ask for it."

Nelson recognized the familiar pattern. "He promised to launch your
songs?"

"Yes. He said he knew everybody. A word in the right ear at the right
moment and I was in. With my talent and his connections I couldn't
fail. He made it sound so real that I could see Joss in sables—enjoying the sort of life she deserves—"

"That's what you meant when you said the quarrel only concerned
her indirectly?"

"Of course. Joss was the one big reason why I forced myself to believe everything Glen said against what I foolishly choose to call my
common sense. The big reason. There were little reasons too. You see—
I'm what they mean when they speak of a maladjusted man." He gave
an involuntary turn toward the kitchen. "Not in my home life. If you're
any kind of a detective you can tell that at a glance. But in my job. I
don't like my job. I keep being rubbed raw by the idea that I'm fitted
for something more stimulating. You wouldn't know what I'm talking
about, would you?" He minced it out. "I'm sure you simply adore your
job."

Nelson said, "For the most part, yes." He might have added that he
did know what Morgan Woodruff was talking about, but he was not
sure that it would be true. Princeton had provided Nelson with an education but with no clue to his place in the world. And he had arrived
at that place through a series of jobs including work in a research laboratory, in a garage, in a little-theater group, and as a rookie on the
police force. He had many influential friends, but he had elected to go
his way alone without specific aid, and now he was indebted only to
the sum total of every experience that had befallen him. Yet there had
been no economic pressure behind his essay to become what he was,
the round peg in the round hole. His mother had left him an adequate
income which robbed the process of urgency. And looking at Morgan
Woodruff, he thought that, common belief to the contrary, poverty was
not always the best nourishment for ambition. He said, "Quite probably you *are* equipped to do something more stimulating."

Morgan seemed to be searching his tone for sarcasm. "Yeah—well,
there was no 'probably' in Glen's line of chatter. It was all 'for sure,'
and he ladled it out with a king-size spoon."

"And when he stopped ladling, you were naturally—"

"He didn't stop. I stopped believing. It suddenly looked like too
much—and I could only smell it but I could never get near enough to

taste it. Maybe if he'd allowed me the smallest taste—say a glimpse of New York's leading publicity agent, who was his close friend and who was itching to take me on—or an introduction to New York's leading producer, boon companion, whose tongue was hanging out for fresh new songs for a fresh new show—or a shakedown to his buddy, New York's leading crooner, whose silver throat could make the public like any song—or even a black look from Petrillo, ditto close friend, buddy, and boon companion—" His mouth twisted. "But curiously enough, these close close friends were always apologizing profusely because they had to rush to the Coast or something and plans would have to be deferred until further notice. Yeah—that was Glen's story—and I was stuck with it."

"So you decided to have a showdown."

"I didn't decide. The showdown happened. The only decision I'd made was to drop Glen by degrees. As a matter of fact, he'd invited us to a party last night and I'd intended to start dropping him by being indisposed. But I ran into him and found myself accepting an invitation to lunch because he was so insistent—and face to face, it was always easier to accept his invitations than to argue. And I didn't feel like arguing. That sounds funny, doesn't it, not feeling like arguing—and later— Well, Glen was in fine form—his usual form. We'd no sooner got seated when he asked me if I had any new songs. I said no and he reproached me. He said he'd dined with a Mr. So-and-So—I'd stopped bothering to remember the names quite a while ago—who was president of the biggest music-publishing firm in America—and he wanted to see me as soon as he could find a blank spot on his calendar. And he said it might be a good idea if I dropped in at the apartment around five so that he could brief me on the coming interview. He said that he knew Joss and I were coming that evening but that he might not have a chance for a private talk then." Morgan breathed deeply. "The waiter had just set a dish of shrimps in front of me. I looked down at them and they looked at me and I was embarrassed. For some reason or other the shrimps brought everything to a head. I felt that what intelligence I had left was being clubbed to death by Glen Williams. And then I got angry and let loose. Glen gave the waiter an apologetic look and asked me to lower my voice. I did—but I lowered my vocabulary at the same time. I said all I wanted to say, and when I'd said it I wasn't angry anymore—just tired and wanting out."

"You left right after that?"

"No. I told you we parted outside the restaurant. I started to leave, but Glen put up his hand to stop me. He had a funny expression on his face and—so help me—because there were people staring our way and I felt like a dope for making a scene, I sat down again. Glen shed the funny look. He smiled and said he couldn't let me go off angry and that he was making allowances because he knew my nerves were on edge and that in turn I must make allowances for him too. I said I'd make anything provided I didn't have to listen to any more talk about my genius. Then he played tremolo and accused me of losing faith in him—of not giving him an opportunity to explain why there'd been such a delay in the flowering of his plans. He said he'd hesitated to burden me with his own troubles, but the truth of the matter was that he'd had a financial setback and that there'd be no point in trying to proceed until he could get the publicity man on the job—because without publicity I'd be just another song writer and I couldn't get half the money I'd get if my name became a household word. And unfortunately, even though the publicity man was a close friend, business was business and he'd need a good lump sum waved under his nose before he'd start pulling—and Glen just didn't have that lump sum at the moment—merely a temporary nuisance—a carload of dividends would be coming along any minute and all I had to do was sit tight."

Morgan tugged his coat off the chair arm and rooted through the pockets. Something fell to the floor. He did not look to see what it was or make an effort to retrieve it.

"Cigarette?" Nelson said.

"Thanks—I've got a pack somewhere." He found what he was seeking, struck a match, and drew smoke with difficulty through a squashed cigarette. Nelson's following of the procedure seemed to amuse him. He grinned naturally and said, "Well, anyway, the matches are high class—straight from the Gateau."

"Where you left Glen talking about his financial setback."

"Yes." The grin faded. "He sure talked volumes. Then at last he must have noticed a kind of skepticism on my part, because he paid the check and got up and we left. Outside, after I'd been the polite guest and thanked him for the lunch I couldn't eat, he made one more try. He asked me please to drop around for a cocktail at five, if only to show there were no hard feelings. I told him there were no hard feelings except the ones I cherished toward myself—and I guess he realized that I didn't mean to drop around that afternoon, or ever, because it was then he tried to plant the seed about Joss. It didn't take root—it was strictly for the birds. And at that moment the waiter came rushing out with a cigarette case Glen had left on the table. He took it and went

right on talking. And the waiter, maybe thinking he was talking to him
or maybe expecting a tip or a thank-you, got an earful before he decided to return to his station."

"What exactly did Glen say about Joss?"

"It doesn't bear repeating," Morgan said calmly, "but it did provide
me with the exit cue I'd been waiting for. I stalked off."

"You reacted by stalking off. Yet when I dug up the same seed you
swung at me. So perhaps it did take root. Perhaps you changed your
mind and dropped in to see Glen—"

Morgan said, "Congratulations. It's a real high-grade theory." He got
up stiffly and stretched. "I'll bet you'd be more comfortable with it if
you hadn't met my wife."

That at least was true up to a point, Nelson thought. Meeting Joss,
he could have dismissed the theory entirely if it had not been for the
letter. He left his chair and bent his knees to retrieve the article that
had fallen from Morgan's pocket.

"Where the hell did that come from?" Morgan said.

"It fell out of your pocket." He extended the flat cardboard packet,
holding it delicately by its edge. Its cellophaned window showed two
glistening hypodermic needles.

"What is it—victrola—? No—well, I'll be—"

"Don't you want it?"

"In the pig's eye." Morgan put his hands behind him. "Nix." He gave
Nelson a level stare. "This is the clumsiest frame since Adam's day—
and I was almost beginning to like you. Look—I've only got about two
dimes on me—so if you're so anxious to put me behind bars you could
make a vagrancy charge stick easier. Nix, I said. You don't get me to
put my fingerprints on that—"

"My guess would be that they're on it now. Smudged beyond recognition, perhaps, but—"

"Guess again." He kept his eyes on Nelson. They looked bewildered.
"I don't get it. Why hypodermic needles? What could they have to do
with the case? Glen was shot—"

"They might have a great deal to do with the case. Glen was an addict."

"Glen? He was?"

"You didn't know?"

"I—sometimes I thought he took Benzedrine or something, but—"

"It was heroin."

"Heroin? Well, that could account for his pipe dreams—the poor—
" He came back to his own immediate predicament. "Do you, by any

chance, think I peddled the stuff to him? Is this more shock tactics—
flashing those in the hope I'll break down and tell all? Listen—is selling encyclopedias supposed to be a cover for my real activities? Some
hard cover!" He wilted on his feet. "And is this luxury I'm surrounded
with the fruit of my ill-gotten gains? Get your head examined, will
you?"

Nelson could not make him admit that the needles had dropped out
of his coat pocket. He did not think he could make him admit it at
headquarters, even if he employed aids to which he had never sub-
scribed. His efforts produced nothing more than a white ridge around
Morgan's lips, and suddenly Morgan was struggling into his coat and
shouting, "Come on! If there's only one way to get you out of here, I'll
buy it. Let's go to headquarters. Maybe I can find an honest cop there
who'll recognize the truth when he hears it—"

"Calm down," Nelson said. "I haven't charged you with anything. For
the time being I'm letting it rest with the usual caution not to leave
town—"

"Save it," Morgan shouted, "unless you can tell me how to leave town
on a shoestring." Then his drawn face smoothed out a little. His voice
dwindled. "You're not arresting me?"

"The unattached needles aren't good enough," Nelson said. But all
things considered, he had no full belief in the words.

Remembering the detective's account of the "thin, dark guy" he had
frightened from the door of Glen Williams' apartment, Nelson extracted the names and addresses of the clients Morgan had visited
that day, along with the approximate times of the visits. According to
Morgan, they had all taken place a good distance away from the
Williams house, and Morgan was above average height. But then Morgan had ample reasons for lying, and the detective had received no
more than a brief impression of the unsuccessful intruder.

Morgan, coatless again, accompanied him to the door, not out of po-
liteness, Nelson thought, but out of a need for corroboration of his exit.
Radio music was seeping under the closed kitchen door at the end of
the hall. It created an atmosphere of normalcy. Nelson wondered if
that was Joss Woodruff's intention.

## CHAPTER 9

Gridley Nelson felt depressed when he left the Woodruff apartment. He phoned Kyrie from a drugstore on the corner. He told her among other things that he would not be home for dinner. She said, "Are you sounding sorrowful to ease my feelings or have things gone wrong?"

"They're not going too well," he said. "How's Junie?"

"Almost too well." He heard her tap the wood of the telephone table. "But I'm sure the first words he lisps will be, 'Where is my wandering daddy tonight?'"

As always, her low, throaty voice conjured up a life-sized picture of her. He took time out to contemplate it.

She said, "Grid—are you still with me?"

"Always. Junie will never call me 'Daddy.' He's too tough. Pop or the old man, more likely."

"How soon will you be home, Grid?"

"As soon as I can."

"That's a sane answer to a foolish question. I'll have Sammy put some choice bits aside for you. Meanwhile get a sandwich and coffee to stave off the pangs."

He promised. He said, "Good-by." He hung up feeling better. Talking with Kyrie had performed the miracle of re-establishing him as a warm-blooded human being with a private life, and for a moment he experienced quite human resentment as he thought that the Woodruffs, murder suspects, would have the pleasure of dining together that night. Then he thought that Kyrie would like the Woodruffs, and that their likeable qualities accounted for much of the conflict that was raging in his head.

He strode the three blocks to his car and drove to headquarters. It was late enough for the night shift to be on duty. The sergeant on the desk was an old-timer who had known Nelson since rookiehood and who called him by his first name on all save official occasions.

"Grid—Clevis wants you on urgent business—"

"Where is he?"

"In the ready room. There's also a little dark fellow name of Acevedo and—"

"Let Clevis know I'm back, Rufe."

"Okay. It seems there's been a follow-up to— Excuse it, Grid." He picked up a ringing telephone.

Nelson did not wait to learn what had been followed up. He hurried to his office.

While he waited for Clevis he called the Gateau. The waiter named Emile had gone off duty, but Nelson asked for and received his home telephone number. A woman with a French accent answered, and Nelson identified himself. She summoned Emile, whose accent was even heavier than hers.

He admitted that Mr. Glen Williams had been a regular patron and that he had served him on the afternoon of his death.

"Then you overheard the quarrel?" Nelson asked.

Emile admitted that too.

"And when you read about his death didn't you realize that it was your duty to come forward?"

Emile stuttered something about not wanting to make trouble for anybody or for the restaurant or for himself, and Nelson, by persisting, received the same account of the incident that Morgan Woodruff had given, including the fact that M'sieu Williams had left his cigarette case behind and that he, Emile, had rushed to the pavement to present it to him. But M'sieu Williams had been in such a disturbed state that he had not even thanked him.

Nelson asked him what he meant by a "disturbed state," but Emile's own state was disturbed and he seemed unable to explain. So Nelson told him to come in on the following morning to make a detailed statement, and hung up.

Clevis shambled into the office. His beady eyes, bright with excitement, were the only signs of urgency he showed. "Well, Lieutenant, I think we got it nipped. Too bad it had to sprout an extra branch—but the way it looks now, two will be the total score."

"Two?"

"Didn't old Rufe brief you when you came in?"

Nelson shook his head.

"Then I better lay some groundwork before you see Gaudio. I brought him in—him and the girl's uncle who couldn't bear to be parted from him. Grandma wanted to come too, but she was stretched two ways—wanting to stay with her dead and—"

"Start at the beginning."

"Will do. Guess I'm rattled—the whole thing was so unexpected." He did not seem rattled. "When I leave you I go express to Gaudio's rooming house. I make a deal with the landlady, smearing it on how important it is for me to have a talk with Gaudio—and she plays along about giving me the signal as soon as he shows. I stake out opposite the joint and I stand for a good hour with nothing to reward me but a few stragglers going in and out. Then I see a beat-up young guy climb the steps and something tells me. I don't wait for the landlady's signal, which comes when I'm halfway across the street. But before I can raise my foot to the curb Gaudio's out again, heading west. I tail him. He's so wrapped up he wouldn't notice a tribe of Ubangis at his heels. We go underground at Lexington and take the train to One Hundred and Tenth Street. Then we walk some more. He knows where he's headed and gets there fast even though I can see he's short on energy. Goal is a tenement job on One Hundred and Seventh to which nobody's donated a nickel's worth of spit and polish since it was built. The lock on the street door has been blitzed long ago, so Gaudio don't have to ring a bell to get in. I hang behind on the street, which is crowded. Reason I don't follow him, I figure I'm not risking a thing, there being only one exit—and I want to see if the names in the bells tie in with the Williams killing. They don't. I pick myself a vestibule on the other side, and just when I'm beginning to wonder why a guy with free choice and a real tony social list should be slumming forty minutes of his life away, he comes out. I'm primed to go where he goes, but he ain't in a hurry no more. And from clear across the street—which ain't so wide at that—I can see a change in him. It's something in the way his shoulders are straighter and his head higher, and in the way he's acting as leisurely as a tycoon taking the air from the terrace of his million-buck estate. Right away it hits me. I get a kind of movie flash of the hypo scars on Williams, deceased—and I connect. You get it?"

Nelson nodded briefly.

"Yep—it stands out that Gaudio's just had a fix—and it stands out likewise that a peddler lives at the selfsame address where he's now standing. A pretty dumb peddler—or he wouldn't let his customers come to the house, let alone linger on the doorstep. So it ought to be a cinch for me to tag his contacts because, while I ain't working for the Narcotics Detail, it never hurts to help a good cause along. Well— I'm keeping my eye on Gaudio and chewing over what's my best move. I could go see if he's got the junk on him as well as in him—but I'm solo—and the sidewalks are packed—and it don't seem to me they're packed with people a cop could look to for sympathy. Luckily I don't have to decide. He leaves the stoop and starts walking, and I walk over and clap the mitt on his shoulder because the way he's moving I wouldn't be surprised if he spreads wings and flies away. And almost simultaneous an old woman hops out of the house. I make her as the same old woman who passed Gaudio on the steps a few minutes back. She's yelling blue murder—and that's what it turns out to be." He slowed up. "The murder of her granddaughter—age eighteen—name of Bernice Acevedo."

Nelson said angrily, "Go on, Clevis." His anger had several ingredients, among them the time he had wasted while another murder was being committed and, in lesser proportion, his apparently unnecessary invasion of the Woodruffs' privacy.

"You think I handled it wrong? You think I should have followed him in? How could I know—"

"Of course you couldn't know. Go on."

Clevis seemed satisfied that the anger was not directed at him.

"Well—Grandma makes like a homing pigeon straight for Gaudio— a homing pigeon gone haywire because it looks like she's trying to peck him to death—and she's assisted by a troop of tenants who've followed her into the street and by some fun-loving folks who are already on the street. I'm taking steps to protect my interests. I've got a grip on Gaudio and I'm flashing my badge at all and sundry and trying to find out what's what. And because Gaudio's an outsider too, I'm getting co-operation—only it don't amount to much because it's mostly in Spanish—so I blow my whistle and raise two harness bulls who come running from opposite directions. One of them stands by while the other calls the wagon. The one who stands by is an up-and-coming rookie of Puerto Rican descent, and he interprets for me and keeps some kind of guard over Gaudio, who's meanwhile passed out and is laying on the pavement—which don't stop Grandma from taking kicks at him when she can get near enough. Some kinder soul thinks to run for a doctor for Gaudio, but I figure that will keep—and I thumb the doctor upstairs with me—and we're chaperoned by Grandma's son, who turns out to be the dead girl's uncle Luis—bachelor. She's dead all right. The doctor can't do her no good. He ain't even willing to say how she died—nor how recent—which is sensible enough from his angle, because while rigor hasn't set in, the room being like an oven might have staved it off. But she's got bruises on her skinny upper arms and on her skinny throat, and her tongue's swollen and her face is cyanosed—so it seems open- and-shut to me how and when she died." He closed his beady eyes for a moment as though the act made him see better. "There ain't much to her. A sharp-faced dark little number. She don't look a full-fledged eighteen so far as her shape goes—and yet she looks older—which may be due to the way her face is twisted up. She sure didn't die happy." He opened his eyes. "Plus being hot, the room's sour because she's been vomiting. It's messed up in other ways too. Stuff all over—tossed out of the bureau and out of one of them ready-made beaverboard cupboards you buy when you ain't got enough closet space. I make it Gaudio is responsible for most of the mess on account of I judge by her habits she's been trying hard to rise above her surroundings. Her nightgown and the bed linen is clean except for where she was sick. Her underwear is folded neat on the one chair in the room, and there's a fancy new-looking black dress on a hanger which dangles from a hook near the bed." The voice of Clevis rose thinly. "That black dress gets me, Lieutenant. It's hanging there like it might be a new toy the kid wants to see first thing when she wakes up. It makes me itch to run down and take a few kicks at Gaudio myself. The way I see it, he came there for the junk and she wouldn't part, so he killed her and tore the room up and got what he came for—and was in such a state by that time he couldn't wait. He took a fix on the spot—after which he sailed so high he got the notion he was above the law. He must've snuffed it that time instead of main-lining, because there wasn't a needle or a spirit lamp in the room and he had none on him."

"How do you account for the vomiting?"

"I thought you'd ask. Before I climb into the wagon with Gaudio and the uncle who don't want to be left behind, I naturally leave a harness in charge and I advise the medical examiner and the lab boys to move in—and I suggest they take a sample of the vomit—which they inform me they'd do anyway. They came back fifteen minutes ago and are going to work on it. But we don't have to worry, because Grandma explained it through the uncle. Seems something this Bernice ate didn't set right and she had cramps last night and chucked. Grandma don't believe in doctors, but when she went out to do her shopping she bought something in the drugstore guaranteed to cure anything from corns to a spoiled stomach. She said she washed Bernice before she went out, and left her sleeping."

"How long was she gone?"

"About two hours. She'd stopped in to see a daughter-in-law who lives in the neighborhood."

"And you say Gaudio stayed forty minutes."

"On the nose—so that would have given Bernice time enough to wake up and be sick again before he arrived."

"Have you booked him?"

"I thought you'd want me to wait till you saw him—or maybe till you got the lab story."

Nelson nodded.

"You going to inspect the scene of the crime? I gave orders for the morgue to refrain until you said the word."

"You can tell them to stop refraining. I might have a look at the room later, but I'm sure there was very little you missed."

Clevis said without conceit, "I did do a thorough job, at that—and the lab boys took up where I left off."

"Did anyone else in the Acevedo family complain of cramps and nausea?"

"No—but Grandma says Bernice ate out a lot."

"What does the family consist of?"

"Grandma—the uncle—and two male boarders. Seems everybody in the house takes boarders. They were away at work, though."

"Are the girl's parents living?"

"Legally she never had more than one—and not much of that one— a mother who got into trouble and skipped, leaving the trouble with Grandma."

"Did you find any drugs in the room?"

"No—not in the other rooms either. I had Mack Hanley of the Narcotics Detail send one of his men to give the whole place a going over. But Gaudio had enough in his pocket to keep him going for a week. Heroin. According to Hanley, it's high-grade stuff—better than forty per cent. Hanley's real sore because the girl died before he could talk to her about her contacts. He didn't get to first base with the uncle. Uncle, by the way, ain't what you'd call a sweet personality. I found two hundred and thirty-one bucks in the girl's handbag. I didn't get a chance to examine the rest of the stuff in the bag, so I took it all along in case it might be evidence—and also I didn't like the way Uncle was looking at it."

"Where was he during Gaudio's visit?"

"In a cigar store around the corner. Somebody ran and got him. He works nights in a joint called Ramondo's. That's how come Grandma can take boarders. They're getting up when he goes to sleep. Maybe it's a good arrangement in winter, with the bed not getting a chance to cool off."

Nelson smiled, not because he thought it was funny, but because he felt that Clevis had done a good job and was entitled to what humor he could squeeze from it. He said, "What's Gaudio's story?"

"At first he not only swore he didn't kill her, but he wouldn't even admit she was dead. He put on we was slipping him a frame that didn't fit no picture. Later he wouldn't talk at all—and now all he does

is sweat and beg. Believe it or not, he's on the nod already, and it was-
n't more than a couple of hours ago that he snuffed the stuff—but I
guess only main-lining can give him any kind of a lasting charge at
this stage. He's hooked—but good. It takes four or five fixes a day to
keep him happy—and Hanley says that runs into heavy dough."

"Did the girl show evidence of being 'hooked'?"

"No—not a mark of that kind on her. Course she might have got
bored with peddling it and tried one of her own samples—them cap-
sules they sometimes pass out free to make new customers. Hanley
says the first try often brings on a vomiting spell."

"One more thing. The grandmother must have met Gaudio before,
if she could single him out on that crowded street."

"She hadn't met him—but she'd seen him a couple of times on the
corner talking to Bernice. She thought from the way Bernice looked
at him that it could lead to monkey business, and she didn't think any
good would come of it because he wasn't their kind. Also—once before
she'd seen him coming out of the house when she was going in—and
it worried her. She didn't want Bernice to get into trouble like her
mother. She'd tried to raise her nice—beating the hell out of her so
she'd know right from wrong—but she was too old and too weak to
keep beating the hell out of her after she grew up—so what could she
do?" Clevis added, "Don't glare at me. I'm just quoting."

"I'll see Gaudio now."

"And you'll be seeing something!"

"Bring a stenographer," Nelson called as Clevis shambled out of the
room. Left alone, he picked up the telephone and asked if Judd, the
man he had sent to Connecticut to cover Betty Conway, had checked
back. The answer was no. Not that it mattered. The probabilities, he
thought, were that Judd, too, had spent a wasted day. More to be doing something than with the conviction that what he did was important, he pressed the buzzer, and when a messenger appeared he
handed him the hypodermic needles that had fallen from Morgan
Woodruff's pocket and asked him to take them to the lab. As an af-
terthought he included the typewritten statement signed by Joss
Woodruff and said it was to be compared with the letter he had sent
down earlier over the same signature. Then he glanced at some assorted papers and memoranda that had been placed on his desk during his absence. One of the sheets dealt with the financial status of
Glen Williams, deceased. It declared that Williams had overdrawn his
checking account, that no savings account had come to light, and that
in so far as the operative had been able to ascertain, he had died poor.

The operative promised that a complete bank statement of deposits and withdrawals would be available the next day.

So from one point of view, anyway, Nelson thought tiredly, Williams could not have come to a more timely end. He was still thinking about it when Clevis and the stenographer appeared with Gaudio between them. They dumped Gaudio, who seemed unable to manage without support, onto the chair that had been occupied by Sarah Thrace.

"Quit sliding," Clevis said, "What do you want—a seat belt or something?"

Gaudio made an obvious effort to hold to the chair.

Nelson said, "Has he had medical treatment?"

"Sure. Them brown stains on his face ain't dirt. They're iodine—and except for a few bruises on his body, he's as good as he ever was—which ain't—"

"Well, Gaudio?" Nelson said. He had meant his voice to be harsh. It was evident that Gaudio had expected it to be harsh. What stamina remained to him fled at the kindly inflection. His large eyes swam in his white face.

He wailed, "Please—I'm sick—"

"The doctor will give you something to make you sleep as soon as this is over. You can hurry it along if you'll help."

Clevis, as though he were divorcing himself from the proceedings, walked to the wall and leaned against it. Disgust showed on his face.

Gaudio spoke just above a whisper. Nelson had to crane to hear. Clevis craned too, in spite of himself. And noiselessly the stenographer who had sat down near the door pulled his chair closer. "How can I help?" Gaudio said. "It's all mixed up. I don't understand why they say I— She isn't dead—she was sleeping and I tried to wake her so she'd—so she—please—"

"We know why you went there," Nelson said, "so you're not incriminating yourself on that score. You were found with an illegal drug in your possession, and you'll be charged with it in any case. But we are giving you a chance to prevent a murder charge." Again he leaned forward to hear the reply.

"I didn't kill her. When I went in I called her name. She wouldn't answer. I thought she was sleeping—but she wasn't lying in a comfortable position—her head was in the pillow, and nobody could sleep that way—it was too hot—and so I thought she was pretending because she was mad at me, and I went over and I turned her around and shook her. I took her by the arms—then I put my hands on her throat just to scare her so she'd stop fooling and give me—sell me—then I noticed that she'd been sick and I thought she'd been drinking and passed out—so I thought it would serve her right if I looked for it and helped myself. I thought it would teach her a lesson when she woke up—not to drink so much—"

Clevis's mouth dropped open. He tried to catch Nelson's eye.

"So I found it," Gaudio droned, "and after—after that I went downstairs. I was fine—I was fine until that man—" His head wobbled in the direction of Clevis. "He stopped me and—" He was sweating. The sweat crawled down his weak, handsome face. He could hardly get his shaking hands up to wipe it away. He said, "I'm sick—I hurt all over—please—give it back to me—make him give it back—"

Nelson said, "Why was the girl angry with you?"

"I need—she was in love with me—"

Clevis snorted.

Nelson gave him a warning glance.

"She was just a crazy kid," Gaudio said. "I didn't encourage her. I had to see her because—but I never—well—once. But I had to—and after that I stood her up whenever she wanted a date—except when—" He floundered. The sweat kept crawling down his face.

"Did she supply Glen Williams with heroin too?"

The question jolted Gaudio. He stopped shaking for a moment. For a moment he was rigid. "You leave Glen Williams out of this." Even his voice was braced.

"That's the second biggest laugh of the year," Clevis said.

"Glen was my friend," Gaudio said. "Why don't you find out who killed him? He knew it was going to happen. He told me—"

"He told you that he expected to be murdered?"

"Yes—he told me—"

"Why didn't he tell the police?"

"He wouldn't—he was too good—"

"Did he tell you who was going to murder him?"

"No—but it was—it was Sarah—or the Woodruff girl—or her husband—" The stiffening had left him. "My friend," he repeated on a dwindling note, "everybody's—but not Bernice's. When she came there it wasn't for social—social—" His eyes skittered in his head. "I'm sick—I need it—make him give it back. Glen paid for it—he would have wanted me to have—he wouldn't have liked this—"

"You killed Glen because he stopped supplying you," Nelson said.

"Glen was my best friend—Sarah killed him—jealousy—she wanted me all to herself or—Woodruff—Woodruff killed him because Glen and Joss—women—"

"Did Woodruff get his supply from Bernice?"

"Woodruff didn't—it was just Glen and me—it was private—nobody else knew—private—" He brought his hands to his head. He winced as his fingers probed.

"Did he get a head injury?" Nelson asked Clevis.

"Nah—didn't even hit it on the sidewalk when he fell."

Gaudio moaned, "It hurts—tingles—my feet too—all over—"

"Why did you go to Glen's apartment this afternoon?"

The skittering eyes came to a brief rest on Nelson's face. "I didn't go in—there was someone there—I went because Glen never let himself run short—and the last I had was early this morning from a fellow I met in a bar—only he wouldn't give me any extra—he said he didn't have it—so later I went to Bernice—I'm not the kind—I was never rough with a girl. I just wanted—I want—please—" He slid into his refrain. It was the only thing that held importance for him. Nothing else mattered.

Nelson said slowly and distinctly, "You didn't mean to be rough. You only meant to scare her—but you killed her."

"No." Gaudio turned his wobbling head from side to side to implement the weak denial. The effect was grotesque.

Nelson stood up. He said abruptly, "Take him away, Clevis. I've finished with him for the time being. Get the doctor to prescribe—"

Clevis came away from the wall. "Lieutenant—you can't." His voice was incredulous. "It will never be easier than now to get a confession—"

Nelson did not look at him. He said to the stenographer, "Lend a hand, will you, Hodge."

After they had gone, Nelson did what he never did when he was alone. He took the scotch from the bottom drawer of the desk and poured and downed a stiff drink. As he returned the bottle to its place he could almost hear Kyrie saying reproachfully, "Grid—you haven't eaten!" And for some reason that created more warmth in him than the whisky.

He sent out for a sandwich and coffee. What he received was neither a good sandwich nor good coffee, yet the joint effect made him feel less hollow. The misery of Gaudio did not torment him quite so much, and he was able to view with more balance the sordid picture of the Acevedo tenement as evoked by Clevis. He lifted the telephone receiver and asked if the dead girl's uncle was still on the premises. He held the line while the hands of the clock on his desk dragged from eight-fifty to eight fifty-four. He said, "All right, send him in," and at three minutes past nine Luis Acevedo entered his office. Nelson dismissed the accompanying policeman and gave Acevedo his undivided attention.

He saw a small, dark-skinned man with a smooth, taut face upon which all the hair seemed concentrated in long sideburns. The man looked familiar, but only, Nelson realized, because there were many copies of his physical type in the city's Puerto Rican districts. He could have been nineteen or fifty, depending on whether the judgment was based on his unlined face or on his wary old eyes. There was a wariness, too, in the way he handled his light body.

"Sit down, Mr. Acevedo," Nelson said.

He sat down. The half-smoked cigarette seemed very white against his dark red mouth. He removed the cigarette with a quick gesture, dropped it to the floor, and crushed it out with his pointed black shoe.

"I'm sorry about your niece," Nelson said.

"That's all right."

It could have been interpreted as awkward acceptance of sympathy or as indifference. Nelson did not yet know how to interpret it. He said, "Were you waiting to speak to me?"

Luis Acevedo crossed his legs. His knees pushed hard against his tight trousers. His voice was thin and brittle. "I'm waiting to see this bastard don't get off easy. What you done with him?"

"He's getting the proper treatment."

Luis Acevedo grinned. "The works? That's good. I wish I'm in on it. Maybe then I can make the old woman believe it when I tell her. She thinks you cops don't give the works to nobody except people like us." He stared at Nelson, measuring him. "This bastard gets the chair, huh?"

"If he committed murder he'll be punished."

"Who says he didn't—him? You keep giving it to him right he'll change his tune. I got him sized up."

"Do you know him well?"

"I never seen him before today. I don't have to see him more than once to size him up." He was still measuring Nelson. He said, "Listen— I—" He hesitated.

Nelson, maintaining a casual front under the stare, knew with certainty that he was not meeting the Acevedo standards for a "cop." He said, "Well?"

Luis Acevedo stood up. "Nothing. Glad to know you. I got to go to work now." He started for the door.

"Wait a minute."

He halted. "What for? I'm on duty at Ramondo's—a Hundred and Sixteenth. We get a big crowd. Ramondo don't like it if the waiters come late—"

"Yet you were willing to stay here all night, if necessary, to see justice done."

"Justice!" He made it sound profane.

"Sit down."

He perched, his tightly covered rear contacting no more than the chair's edge.

"You know, of course, that your niece was peddling drugs."

"Who—me? I don't stick my nose in her business."

Nelson said, thinking how sententious yet how true it sounded, "Things like that are everybody's business."

Luis Acevedo misunderstood, or pretended to misunderstand. "Not mine—I don't do no peddling. I work steady as a waiter."

"How old are you?"

"Twenty-nine." Then he said, "Why you start asking me questions?"

"Are you married?"

"Me? What for? You think I need a chiseling wife and no-good kids? The only dame sees my dough is the old woman."

"Your mother?"

"Sure my mother." The look in his eyes might have been a proclamation of the fact that he had just discovered Nelson's intense stupidity. The discovery seemed to give him courage. "Talking about dough—I seen that cop lift a roll from Bernice's pocketbook. Maybe he don't mention it to you, but I seen it and so did the quack."

"Is that what you waited to tell me?"

"Sure—I got my rights. That dough belongs to nobody but me and the old woman—and you're the cop's boss, ain't you?" His eyes said that he could not imagine why Nelson should be anybody's boss. "How about it?"

"Bernice was probably holding the greater part of that money for her boss," Nelson said expressionlessly. "We need a clear claim of ownership in cases like this—so perhaps you'd better take it up with him."

For a brief moment the old eyes of Luis Acevedo looked thoughtful. Then he sucked in his cheeks, darted from his chair, and leaned over the desk, his face close to Nelson's.

"Don't do it," Nelson said. He used the voice that almost always worked, but to make sure that it worked this time he raised a hand and shoved.

Luis Acevedo did not do it. He braked a few feet from the desk, swallowed the gathered saliva, and spat venom instead. He seemed to have only one adjective at his command and he attached it to almost every noun. What he said in substance was that every so-and-so cop was a so-and-so robber, that the old woman was right, and that his people were always given a so-and-so crooked shake, that so-and-so Nelson and Clevis intended to split Bernice's money, but not if he could help it, because maybe Nelson had a so-and-so boss too who would want to know what was going on—

The ringing telephone stopped him. He looked at it, at Nelson regarding him sadly from behind the desk. He shouted, "You got nothing on me," and turned and ran out of the office.

Nelson picked up the receiver. He said rapidly, "Rufe? ... I'll take the call in a moment. Is Fernandez in the ready room? ... Good. Get him on the double. Luis Acevedo just left my office. Hold him on some pretext and tag him for Fernandez. It will take him a good five minutes to find his way down, because I doubt if he'll ask anyone for directions. Fernandez is to stick with him until further notice and check back at convenient intervals."

He hung up. The phone rang again. He regarded it absently. Before he answered he wrote a memo to "Narcotics" suggesting that when Fernandez checked back he be relieved by one of Hanley's operatives. It was possible, of course, that Luis Acevedo was more of a concern for Homicide than for Narcotics, but he did not believe it.

He silenced the ringing telephone. "Who? ... Clevis? ... Put him on."

The voice of Clevis had altered since their last encounter. It was now a compound of apology and awe. "My hat's off to you, Lieutenant."

"Put it back on before you catch cold."

"Okay—I rate a ribbing. I wish I knew how you did it. You must have had more than a hunch that Gaudio had an out. You still there?"

Nelson said he was still there and asked where Clevis was.

Clevis took the question literally. "In the lab. Maybe it ain't news to you, but they found traces of poison in that vomit. Still, you got to admit I had a leg to stand on—the swollen tongue and the color of her face and all. But they tell me oxalic acid will do that—so it don't look like Gaudio killed her after all—anyway, not with his hands—"

Nelson said, "How long does oxalic acid take to act?"

"Berman here says it varies—sometimes three minutes—sometimes an hour—and it's been known to take as long as fourteen days. He says the bruises on the throat were surface. Also he says he didn't like the look of that vomit to start with. I wouldn't know—not being a connisure. But if she starts throwing up during the night, Gaudio's clean as far as today's visit goes. Berman's rarin' for Doc to get busy with the autopsy. He's betting her insides are pickled—"

Nelson said, "I'd like to have a look at the girl's handbag."

"Coming right up. The way you're cooking, you're set to find all the answers right there."

Nelson's wry smile was turned upon himself. He decided that it would only lower the morale of a realist like Clevis to learn that his chief's failure to follow through with Gaudio had been prompted by compassion rather than astuteness.

The phone rang again almost as soon as he replaced the receiver. A woman's impersonal voice asked if he were the acting captain of Homicide. She said that Detective Sergeant Gilbert Judd had asked her to say that he would be detained overnight and to please notify his wife that he was on a job. She hung up before Nelson could ask her to elaborate. He had the call traced immediately. It was from the Sellars Memorial Hospital in Howardsville, Connecticut.

## CHAPTER 10

That night a scattering of people who had been on more or less intimate terms with Glen Williams slept poorly or not at all.

In Howardsville, Connecticut, long before dawn, Betty Conway struggled out of a nightmare's ugly grasp to find reality no marked improvement. She reached for the light over her bed, switched it on, and tried to take reassurance from her surroundings. But the bedroom's gaily papered walls, the furnishings adapted to her changing tastes since childhood, had suddenly assumed an aspect of smug self-righteousness, and every object her eyes touched seemed to say, "You're not the girl we know. You don't belong here."

She was alone in the house. Her mother and father had left a week ago for a visit to California. She told herself that at least she was spared the effort of dissimulation their presence would demand. But it was very cold comfort, because she would have given much to run to either of them.

She got out of bed and, barefoot, walked to the open window. The still air had no healing in it, and no friendly whisper came from the leaves of the tall elm outside. She retreated into the room. She went to the dressing-table mirror and stared. Her nightgown clung damply, her short yellow curls were any old way, and her eyes stared back, dark blue and smudged beneath. Fairy-tale princess, she thought.

Witch! She picked up a brush and dropped it, smiling an ironic little smile. She lit a cigarette. She thought of a man named Judd, and of what Mike had done to him. And she thought that it was all her fault, and it would be her fault if Mike was arrested. Because if she had used her head there would have been no need for Judd to come to Howardsville. And when he did come she had not used her head either. If she had answered the bell earlier, Judd would have been and gone before Mike got there. But she had not answered the bell because she did not want to see anyone, and when at last its persistent ringing had forced her to answer in spite of herself, she had behaved like an idiot. And then Mike rang. And that was the time not to answer. But Judd, with a great play of innocence, had offered to go to the door, so she had no choice. And she had continued to behave like an idiot. That drive back from the hospital. A hussy as well as an idiot! Poor Mike. I made him say it at last. I made him.

She giggled. It must be nerves, she told herself. Certainly I have nothing to giggle about. She covered her face against the room's smug gaze. She longed for daylight, so that she could go to New York and do what she had to do.

Mike Williams did not go to bed that night. He made much of a sick cow's need for his attention. Only when he took periodic trips to the barn to minister to her could he forget his own misery. Between trips he sat in the living room of the farmhouse and thought about Glen, and about Betty Conway, and about Mike Williams, fool. The living room was stuffy and drab. The alterations and improvements he had made on the farm proper had not extended to the house, because in the back of his mind had lurked the thought that when he married, his wife would apply her magic womanly touch and transform what had been shabbiness and general disrepair to new and shining beauty. Now, sitting in the worn chair, a stocky, deep-chested man with a bruised face, hot-eyed and wide awake, overalled and booted, vaguely conscious of his own aroma of sweat and barn, he extracted the thought, examined it, and deliberately tore it to shreds. There had never been and there never would be any woman he wanted to marry but Betty Conway. And seeing himself as surely she must see him, he could no longer even weigh his chances. He had been a lout seeking the moon, with nothing for barter but callused hands and a stumbling tongue. And if there was any doubt in Betty Conway's mind, he had extinguished it by offering indisputable proof that his physical seeming matched what it contained.

When he left the office of Homicide's acting captain he had been terribly disturbed at the turn the interview had taken. Not that he held anything against the acting captain for doing his duty as he saw it. His disturbance was due to his own shortcomings, his blundering stupidity in being unable to keep Betty's name from cropping up. Glen would have handled it easily. Glen, by brilliant sleight of hand which he, Mike had always found so difficult to follow, would have hog-tied that acting captain. Or would he? Unbidden, the doubt crept in, the doubt that had seldom been granted admittance while Glen lived. That Nelson fellow was clever. Not in a showy way, but quiet-clever. And Glen? Had Glen ever been pitted against anybody like that? Certainly not among the constantly changing group of Glen's companions that he had been permitted to meet before Glen left the farm. They were— Drop it. Glen was dead. And it was bad enough that Glen's death, let alone the nature of it, left room for anything but grief and guilt. Face it. Guilt. He was responsible. He should have whipped sense into Glen long ago instead of waiting, watching him drift until—until it was too late. And while he was alone and facing the truths he might as well admit that neither grief nor guilt had been the first emotion aroused by his brother's death. Love had been first. Love for Glen's girl. Instantly, like a clear cool spring, it had come welling up from its buried source. And he had been ashamed. But not too ashamed to want to drink. Yes, he might as well admit it. Here in this shabby room that would never be transformed, that would never be anything but the shabby reflection of a shabby soul, he might as well admit it.

He had gone from the acting captain's office to the station and waited for the next train to Howardsville. He had boarded the train and sat until the end of the trip painstakingly trying to recall every word he had said to Nelson and every word that Nelson had said to him. It had ceased to matter to him whether or not the investigation unearthed the murderer. What mattered was that Betty be left untouched by it, and he kept wondering if there was anything he could have said or left unsaid to spare her. Oh, he had made a mess of it. But one thing he could do, he had thought. He could warn her of a possible visit from the police, so that at least she'd be prepared. And too, before she read the sordid details in the newspapers, before the cold printed word could inform her that her sweetheart, her beau, had died with the stamp of vice upon him, he, Mike, could tell her himself. Break it gently. Say that Glen had been ill and had needed the drug to ease his suffering. Something like that.

At Howardsville he had stepped into his rickety old car and driven straight to the Conway house. But when he turned in at the front gate his own inadequacy caught up with him again. How should he account for his presence? He could not burst in upon her and with no preliminary blurt out what he had come to say. As never before he longed for polish and tact. He knew that just the fact of his visit would surprise her. He knew that she was alone, and even when her parents were there he came by invitation only. His impulse was to turn back, to wait until he could think of a suitable opening. But there was no time for that. The police might invade her privacy at any moment. And aside from that, the longing to see her was stronger than shyness or fear of intruding. So he went up the cobbled walk and climbed the porch steps and rang the bell.

Betty answered the bell. She looked much as usual to him except that her cheeks were pale. She said, "Mike!" And his ears were at first deceived into hearing a note of gladness in her voice. But her next words were bleached and dry. She said, "I'm sorry about Glen," as though she might be saying, "I'm sorry your hens aren't laying," or, "Too bad we don't have rain."

He had forgotten that this must pass between them. He stood there making a clumsy to-do of wiping his feet on the mat, forgetting that his city shoes had been exposed to nothing more than dry pavements. He muttered foolishly, "So you've heard." And he thought that Glen's death would account for her pallor, and knew a treacherous stab of pain for which Glen's death was not accountable.

She said, "I'd ask you to come in, Mike, only I—I have a caller here on business. Could you come back later?"

Closed in with his pain, he had not understood. He had crossed the threshold to stand beside her in the entrance hall. He had seen and aped the involuntary turn of her head toward one of the rooms that gave on to the hall. It was her father's study and it was occupied. A strange man stood facing the open door.

Betty had made an odd, uncertain gesture. Then she had stepped into the study, he following automatically. She had performed no introduction. She had said flatly, "This man is just leaving."

Mike had looked from her to the man, a nondescript man of average height and indefinite coloring, impossible to classify. Mike had stepped aside to give him room to pass. But the man had stood firm, eying them both with impersonal curiosity, and he had said politely enough, "I can't go, Miss Conway, until you've answered a few questions. If I'd got to see you earlier, this would have been over and done with."

"I won't answer your questions," she cried. "I can't—not now. Please go."

The man had looked at her almost pityingly before he turned to Mike. "What's your name, mister?"

"Don't answer him—it's none of his business." She had seemed on the verge of panic.

And it had caused Mike to forget the reason behind his errand. Conscious only that his lady was in distress, he had come to the rescue. "Don't you understand English? Go on—scat—out." He had not even heard the argument that the man started to advance. He had grabbed him by his arm and started to drag him toward the door. But the man was agile beyond ordinary for all his ordinary appearance, and he had twisted free. He had thrust a hand into his pocket, and Mike, bemused by some memory of a Western he had seen, believed that he was reaching for a gun. And that, so far as he could recollect, was how the fight began.

He huddled deeper into the chair. So help him, he had assaulted a police detective. Not only assaulted him but knocked him flat. He touched his own face, as though seeking solace by counting the bruises he had received in return. But the detective had received more than bruises. There had been a bad bump on the back of his head where he hit the hearth, and because they could not raise a doctor they had driven him to the hospital. He came to on the way and seemed to have some foolish notion that he was being taken for a ride. But perhaps he was raving. In the hospital a staff doctor insisted that he spend the night and pumped a sedative into him before he could say much more than, "For Pete's sake phone headquarters and get Acting Captain Grid Nelson to tell my wife I'm working." Mike had asked him if he wanted to press charges, and he had answered, "Just don't try to skip. I'll attend to you later."

After that, Mike had insisted that Betty drop him at the Howardsville police station. They had driven to the hospital in her car. He was not in the police station very long, and when he came out again he was surprised to find her waiting. He had told his story to Chief Brundage, and Brundage, an old friend, had listened incredulously and refused to put him under arrest. "The man hasn't preferred charges, Mike. You go home and get a good night's rest and we'll see what happens in the morning. Don't know as I blame you much. You didn't know who he was, and if I caught anybody bothering Betty, I'd haul off myself. Besides, I can't see that he had business in her house. Not if she didn't want him there. Not without the proper papers—"

So he told Betty that Chief Brundage was reserving judgment, and she drove him back to her house to reclaim his car. Mike found little to talk about on the way. He had fixed things up for fair. His fists had been as quick as his wits were slow. He had caused trouble for the girl he would have given his life to shield. Right in her house, before her eyes, he had engaged in what was no better than a barroom brawl. Several times he had tried to make fumbling apology. But she scarcely seemed to listen. Quite naturally she had more important things to occupy her. But when they reached her house she invited him in for a drink or a cup of coffee or whatever he wanted. Of course he had refused. He was not going to add insult to injury by taking advantage of her good manners.

He groaned. And then what had he done? He had added insult to injury, all right. Of all the times to choose—with Glen not even buried—

He was getting into his car when she said, "Mike—why did you do it?"

"Hit him? I told you—I lost my temper. I didn't know he was a policeman. I should have known it but I didn't—"

"I know—but why did you lose your temper?"

And with no warning at all the words had jumped to his lips. "I love you. I'll love you as long as I live—and as long as I live nobody's going to hurt you—" Then his foot had come down hard on the starter and he had driven off. Too bad, he thought, that he could not have driven off the earth.

Joss and Morgan Woodruff lay side by side in the double bed. Neither dared to stir for fear of disturbing the other. But finally Morgan was unable to control his right leg. It twitched, and Joss jumped.

"Sorry," he muttered. "I tried not to wake you."

"I was awake."

"Hot—isn't it?"

"Yes—but the window's open as far as it will go."

"I know." He knew, too, that the heat was not responsible for their unrest. "What time is it?"

Joss sat up and looked at the radium dial of the alarm clock. "Five after three."

"Oh lord—I thought it was later."

"Be glad it isn't. You can still get in a good few hours' sleep."

"An oversimplification if ever I heard one."

"Try."

"You don't sound like you."

"Voices always sound strange in the dark."

"A nice kind of strange—not—"

"Morgan, don't talk any more. You'll be dead tomorrow."

"That's a pretty thought. It ties in so well with—with everything."
She did not answer.

"Joss?"

"Yes?"

"What did the detective say that upset you so much?"

"We've been over all that. I'm not used to entertaining detectives.
Just the fact of his coming to question me was upsetting."

"It wasn't any specific question that he asked?"

"Morgan—please stop thinking about it."

"He didn't, for example, ask if you and Glen had been—had been interested in each other?"

She lay quite still. He turned toward her. He flung an arm over her,
the flat of his palm resting against her heart. He said, "Whoa—
Joss—darling—what's that African tom-tom doing in there?"

"Did the detective tell you he'd asked me that about Glen?"

"Only after I gave him the lead."

"You gave him the lead?"

"I couldn't avoid it. He wanted to know about my lunch with Glen—
and it was that among other things that made it such a gala occasion."

"You mean Glen told you we—and you never said anything?"

"I didn't take it seriously. I wasn't ever going to mention it. But you—
you've been acting so unlike yourself that I thought if we brought
everything out into the open you'd—we'd feel better."

Her voice was choked. "Glen must have been crazy to invent a story
like that."

"He was taking an awful risk—because if I'd believed him I'd have—"

"Don't!"

"Don't what? Where are you going?"

"To get a drink of water."

"I'll go."

"No—I'm up."

At the end of five minutes he called out, "Are you all right?"

"Yes—I'm coming. Shall I bring you some water?"

"Please." He switched on the light. He saw her shrink from it. He
said, taking the glass from her, "I wanted to see you." He drank
thirstily. He leaned over and set the glass upon the night table. "No

dark, devious thoughts stand a chance with you in sight."

She sat down in a chair away from the bed. "And when I'm not in sight you think it was true about Glen and me?"

He said, "What is this? Are you suspecting me of—of suspecting you? You couldn't stand him. I know that."

"Do you?"

"Joss!"

"I'd better tell you the whole business. Perhaps it's too late—but I'd better tell you."

"You don't have to tell me a thing." Then he said, "What do you mean about it being too late?"

"I don't know what I mean. Glen told me he loved me. He begged me to leave you."

"When was this?"

"A week ago."

"And you kept it to yourself? If I'd known, I'd have—"

Again she cried, "Don't!"

He stared at her. He said slowly, "You think I'm going to say I'd have killed him? Maybe you think I did kill him."

Wordless, she shook her head.

He said, "A guy goes along certain he has no secrets from his wife— or she from him. He doesn't have to be a stupid guy, either—just a guy like me." Frost touched his voice, hardened it. "Did Glen make you this sweet little offering in person?"

She nodded.

"Joss—why did you keep it dark? You couldn't have thought it would bore me."

"I didn't want to spoil things between you. I thought I could handle it myself. I said he was never to mention it again, and I wrote to him making it absolutely plain, in case he had any room for doubt."

"He said you'd written. Only he seemed to have been more encouraged than otherwise by your letter."

She breathed sharply. Then she said, "The detective has the letter. He'll probably let you see it if you feel the need."

Their eyes seemed entirely detached from the conversation. Joss studied the wall above his head. Morgan gazed intently at the bureau behind her. He said to the bureau, "I'd be more interested in seeing Glen's reply."

"There was no reply. There was nothing to reply to."

"That's not his version."

She stopped staring at the wall. "Morgan—look at me. You put the light on because you wanted to look at me, didn't you? You've got to make a choice. You've either got to believe everything Glen said—or you've got to discount it entirely."

It seemed to both of them that the choice involved their love, their marriage, everything they had been or ever would be to each other. But neither of them was ready to admit it.

Morgan got out of bed. He went to her. He knelt beside her chair and put his arms around her waist. He said, "I don't care—I wouldn't blame you—I—after dinner I was looking through the desk for some paper clips and I found a scrap of a letter in his handwriting—"

"A letter in his handwriting? You must be mistaken. I wouldn't even know his handwriting if I saw it."

"I would. I've seen it often enough on notes he's written on my song sheets." His voice was pleading. "Joss—think—please think. It said, 'Thank you, my sweet. We'll—' and then the rest of the sheet was torn off. If you say so, of course it wasn't what he said it was—he always flung endearments around, and I'd be the first to grant he couldn't help lying about anything and everything—but maybe he sent some invitation you forgot to mention." Still holding her, he watched her face, dismayed because she seemed to be concentrating so hard on what should have been a simple, straightforward answer.

"No—he didn't write to me—not ever. He telephoned or dropped in, but he never wrote. That scrap of paper must have fallen from his pocket when he was here. I don't know how it got in the desk—"

Morgan broke his hold upon her waist. He stood up. There was comedy to be extracted from his tousled black hair, from the cotton pajamas, shrunken by many washings, that fell inches short of his thin wrists and ankles. There was no comedy in his face. He wore the look of a man crucified.

"Morgan," she said, "something's happening that I don't understand."

"That makes two of us. At least we have that in common—or have we?"

"I won't let you do this, Morgan." The words were ripped from her.

"Won't let me do it?"

"Yes—you. You're destroying yourself—us."

Don't let me, he begged silently. Say something—anything that will restore my balance—my faith. He took a cigarette from the open pack on the bureau. He lit it.

Long habit made her ache to tell him not to smoke, because what with lack of sleep and the poor pretense he had made of eating dinner, smoking would— She put aside the humdrum concern, realizing its relative unimportance. Deliberately, she whipped herself to anger as the only means of reaching him. "Apparently you aren't Glen's sole confidant in regard to his love life. You aren't the only one who believed him, either. You share honors with Tom Gaudio. Tom Gaudio came to see me this morning, his object being that I, as Glen's bereft lover, join forces with him in tracking down the murderer."

"What?"

"So you see—the letter you said you found just adds to my guilty confusion. This is the truth, Morgan, whether you want to accept it or not. The only inkling I had about the peculiar ideas Glen was fostering came on June fourth out of a perfectly clear sky. He never mentioned them before or after—either in writing or in person. I'd remember the date quite well even if he hadn't made it a—a what you'd call a gala occasion. Because it was little Brigid Jorgensen's birthday, and I'd been downstairs helping her mother to entertain some of the neighborhood babies. I'd been home only about ten minutes and I was just going out again to shop for a few things when Glen rang the bell. I asked him to come in. I didn't expect—" The false anger evaporated. "Oh, Morgan, it was so ugly. I ran out and left him—and when I came back he was gone. Can't you see why I didn't want to tell you?"

Blindly, she reached out her arms. And like a sleepwalker he came into them, hiding his tormented face in her neck.

In the basement apartment only Fred Storch slept. Dora, his wife, prodded him. "Fred—Fred—you having a bad dream?"

He made incoherent protest. He thrashed about. Then, under her insistent repetition of his name, he heaved himself to sitting posture. He said, "Huh?" and, not fully awake, thrust off the light cotton blanket.

"Fred—you don't have to get up yet—it ain't morning—but you was yelling fit to raise the house—"

His head turned automatically toward the other bed in the room.

She sensed or felt the movement. "It's all right. Billy ain't there. I took him to the bathroom a few minutes ago. He'll call out when he's ready to get back to bed. He can go by himself now, but I'm always scared he'll hit against something in the dark. What was you dreaming, Fred?"

"How do I know?"

"You ain't been sleeping good at all lately—turning and twisting until I—"

He said sourly, "Maybe your ladyship would like me to buy a pair of them twin beds."

"What are you getting sore for? It ain't my own rest worries me."

"You don't have to worry about mine." He was scratching his head, his fingernails scraping the cropped hair. He said laboriously, "What was I yelling?"

"You know—them crazy noises you make in bad dreams when you think you're really saying something only it don't come out."

"Oh." For the first time he became aware of the sound under their voices. He looked toward the streak of light that came from the bathroom door. "Want me to get him? He's got the water running like—"

"Leave him be. It won't hurt nothing. I turned it on for him and he's probably dabbling in it. He can do that by the hour and he won't catch cold in this heat. It makes him awfully restless—the heat does."

He muttered, "Maybe things ain't always going to be this way."

He was given neither to optimism nor to idle remarks. She said, "What do you mean? Fred, you ain't changed your mind about putting Billy in—"

"No charity home is ever going to see me or mine—that's for sure."

"Then—"

"Forget it."

She said fearfully, "You—you ain't been up to something?"

He stretched his length along the bed again. He yawned decisively.

"Fred—you answer me. You been carrying on in a funny way lately—not eating enough to keep a bird alive—not hardly sleeping—"

"I notice you ain't in such a hurry to let me sleep now."

"No—nor to let you start dreaming and yelling again, either. I want to know what's the reason for it. If you're sick you'll go to a clinic—and if it ain't that, it's something you got on your mind."

"Ain't I always got something on my mind? Ain't you?"

"That's got nothing to do with it. You been different since Mr. Williams got himself shot. You can't hide nothing from me, Fred. I'm your wife."

"Who's trying to hide—"

"You are. Whatever it is, you tell me and we'll—"

"Shut up and lay down or I swear I'll shut you up."

"There—in all the years we're married you never talked to me like that. Now I'm sure you ain't yourself. You been a good husband—a good man—"

"And where did it get me?" He heaved himself over on his side. Deliberately he began to snore.

She stopped talking, and presently the snore became the rhythmic breathing of a sleeper. Sighing heavily, she pulled the light blanket over him. She longed to obey the demands of her own tired body, to lie back and rest for a few moments before she went to fetch Billy, but she dragged herself out of bed. She hoped as she neared the lighted bathroom that he would not be mulish and refuse to come. He had evidently heard her approaching steps. He was not at the sink. She turned the water off before she attempted to rout him from his crouch behind the door. He had taken to doing that a lot lately, she thought wearily, to hiding from her in any place where he could squeeze his poor overgrown body. With infinite patience she started to coax him out.

By grant of a police doctor's injection, Tom Gaudio was temporarily released from his misery. And in another part of the city a sturdy nightcap performed the same service for Sarah Thrace. But during the period before it took effect she thought unhappily of the Judas role she had played that day. She thought about the trouble that Glen Williams had stirred up alive and dead. She wished that she could have kept Joss Woodruff out of her session with the acting captain of Homicide. She wished that she had met the acting captain under other circumstances, socially for choice, and in her younger days. Yet she conceded glumly that even in her younger days, when men swarmed, her special brand of honey had succeeded in attracting none on a par with Gridley Nelson. More on a par with Tom Gaudio, and it was strange how some women never learned but just kept repeating and repeating their mistakes. She wondered where Tom Gaudio was, and what would become of him. She wondered what would become of herself if she kept on drinking and if she did not get work. Her last conscious thought was a comforting cliché. Tomorrow was another day. She would go on the wagon tomorrow. Tomorrow she had that audition for the new television program. It just might pan out.

Acting Captain Gridley Nelson tried to sleep on his problems. They made a lumpy mattress, and each lump had a name like Glen and Bernice and Betty and Mike and Joss and Morgan and Sarah and Tom. There was even a composite lump named Storch. At about four o'clock in the morning it caught him at the base of his spine. He sat up and said, "Oxalic acid."

Kyrie murmured, "What, Grid?"

"Oxalic acid—for pickling."

"As in Heinz?"

"No—furniture."

"Oh—you mean what Stella did to that desk she bought at auction for six dollars?" Then Kyrie laughed. She was one of those who made almost instant transition from sleeping to waking. Her laughter was a lovely normal sound. It seemed to flood the dark room with sun. "Grid—I've had weird conversations in the night, but this one wins. Does it lead to anything?"

"It might." He drew her softness closer. And for a while the problem lumps receded.

## CHAPTER 11

Nelson awoke to the hot June morning and reached headquarters before 9 A.M. He started his official day by telephoning the lab. While he waited for an answer to his inquiry, he stared at the handbag of Bernice Acevedo which lay open upon his desk. He had gone through its contents with care the night before, finding of special interest a stiff, self-conscious picture of a thin girl in a black dress, obviously spot-developed by a street-corner photographer, a brown stain on the otherwise clean lining of the bag, and a damp squashed chocolate which had burst through its wrapping of silver foil to make the stain. Almost before his eyes had recorded the chocolate and the stain his mind had leaped swiftly to connect the tiny raised letters on the foil with the voice of Dora Storch saying, "He had the food and drinks sent from Neuilly's."

"Yes, I'm here," he said into the telephone. "Yes, Ralph, go ahead."

"The candy was loaded with it, Grid. Doc hasn't started the autopsy yet—the body arrived too late last night—but there doesn't seem to be much doubt as to the cause of death. Looks to me as though one piece of that confection would have been sufficient—"

"Doesn't it have a taste?" Nelson asked.

"I don't know," the laboratory technician said without humor, "I never tasted it. And the crystals as such have no odor except when they're mixed in a solution of hot water. But our malefactor didn't bother with a solution. What he started with is a date—dipped in chocolate and stuffed with a mixture of chopped nuts and some kind of liqueur like a strong brandy. He cut the date in half lengthwise—removed the stuffing, and put it back after he'd mashed the crystals in with it. On the piece you sent down you can see the signs of doctoring plainly even though the chocolate's been smoothed back over the jointure, but I guess the poor girl wasn't looking for it. If she noticed any irregularity she might have put it down to the hot weather." "What's oxalic acid used for?" Nelson said not very hopefully. "Dyeing—also some kind of printing on fabrics—and on giving old furniture a new finish. That's about all I can tell you offhand." "Thanks." "Don't hang up. Fields has just handed me this report on the hypo needles and the letter. Just smudges on the needle package. The typing on the letter and on the woman's statement match. So do the signatures—of course there's a difference in touch, but the machine's the same." "All right. Return the material and the reports when you get time." Nelson could not put much feeling into the request. Both the needles and the defection of Joss Woodruff seemed vastly unimportant as compared to the latest evidence. He sat trying to weigh it.

Neuilly was the trademark of one of the most expensive caterers and purveyors of sweets in the city. Glen Williams had been a Neuilly client. And someone had poisoned his last purchase. But drugs might have dulled Glen Williams' appetite for sweets, and therefore the impatient someone had used the thirty-two as a surer, quicker means of accomplishing his purpose. And it followed that Bernice Acevedo, visiting Glen Williams on the afternoon of the murder, witness the description given by Mike Williams and by the superintendent's wife, had helped herself to the chocolates. Nelson winced, sidetracked by the thought of the superintendent's wife, whose miserable privacy was shortly due for another invasion because the oxalic acid so directly pointed to her husband. He thrust the thought aside and went on with the interrupted saga of Bernice.

She had helped herself to the chocolates, carried some of them away in her handbag, probably made a clean sweep, witness the empty candy dish. She, who had so patently put away childish pleasures, had been brought to her end by childish greed.

Yes, thought Nelson, it was easy enough to establish her presence on the day of the murder. And if it needed verification, he could get it by means of showing the street-corner photograph to the two who had encountered her. But then what? What else could be established? Neither the murderer nor the motive for the murders.

Assuming—and it seemed a safe assumption—that the same person had poisoned the chocolates and used the thirty-two, it was also safe to assume that the criminal had not been the victim of said chocolates. Which exonerated Bernice as a murderer. And little such earthly exoneration meant to her now. And little did it serve the ends of earthly justice.

But wait a moment. It did introduce a variation on his theorizing. It cast no light upon Glen Williams, corpse number one, but it did suggest a secondary motive for a secondary corpse. Say that the poison had not been intended for Glen Williams at all. Say it had been a deathtrap for Bernice because she knew and could have named the criminal—

All right, say it, he thought angrily. Say it until your own doomsday. She can no longer name anyone. Get back on the track!

He got back on the track. Deliberate poisoning by oxalic acid was rare. Impossible, then, to dismiss as coincidence the fact that it was an indispensable item in the process of pickling furniture, and that Fred Storch, superintendent, had pickled furniture in Glen Williams' apartment. And the thought of what this might mean to the superintendent's wife, Dora Storch, could no longer be set aside. It swelled to such proportions that it seemed the woman herself stood before him. "Fred wouldn't hurt a fly," she said, and her ravaged, bony face was sick with fear.

In fancy he could hear the thick-tongued utterance from the other room of the basement quarters. And he could hear himself saying, "I'm not accusing Fred of anything. But I must question him." And suddenly Junie was in the picture too. Junie, whose sturdy little body he had hefted a short while ago, whose face was already stamped with bright new intelligence.

The phone rang. Nelson answered it and was informed that a man named Emile Renaud wished to make a statement concerning the Williams case. Nelson asked that a stenographer take the statement, type it, and put it on his desk. Confused, he wished that Emile Renaud, waiter at the Gateau, was sufficient reason to delay what must be done.

He pushed his chair back. He arose, experiencing an unaccustomed resistance to action throughout his length and breadth. Ever since his latest promotion, Kyrie had accused him of doing a great deal of unnecessary leg work instead of delegating it as was fitting to a man of his exalted status. Quite naturally she hated the often dangerous paths he traveled in his quest for firsthand information. But her protesting was only half in earnest, because she understood that he was not the stuff of which desk-sitters are fashioned. Yet now, for once, he would have preferred to delegate the leg work that was indicated.

And why am I making such heavy weather of it? he thought. It doesn't mean that the man is implicated. He might have forgotten to take the leftover crystals with him when he finished his work in the apartment. He has no criminal record—not so far as we've been able to check. And certainly he has enough on his mind to explain his surly attitude toward life in general. Nevertheless, Nelson went on to wonder unhappily if the personal affairs of Fred Storch fully explained his unwillingness to co-operate with the police in Glen Williams' apartment on the eve of the shooting. There had been long and painful pauses between questions and answers. And he had deliberated with more than ordinary caution before he undertook to approximate the length of time that had elapsed between his discovery of the body and his call to the police. He was a slow-witted man. That much was apparent. But was he all that slow? And if not, what had he been attempting to conceal from the Homicide Squad, whose specialized interests lay solely in tracking down a murderer?

Nelson slid the photograph of Bernice Acevedo into an envelope and put it in his pocket. As he walked toward the door he heard voices in the anteroom and placed one of them as issuing from a reporter who had covered several of his cases. The morning papers had given no headlines to the passing of Bernice Acevedo. In most instances it was tucked away on the back pages. The presence of oxalic acid was undiscovered at the time the press arrived on the scene. Therefore the public had been told briefly that the condition of the body pointed to foul play, and that a man named Thomas Gaudio had been taken into custody. Drugs were not mentioned, nor was Bernice Acevedo linked with Glen Williams. Nelson had given Clevis full counts for his handling of the matter. He could well imagine the little detective assuming his village-idiot stance as he spouted the special brand of double talk he reserved for such occasions.

Nelson hesitated before the door, shrugged, opened it, and walked into the anteroom. There were three reporters waiting. The man whose voice he had recognized represented a respectable evening paper. The other two represented tabloids with wider circulation.

One of the tabloid men spoke first. "At least we can't say you keep banker's hours, Lieutenant."

"What's the least you *can* say?" Nelson asked mildly.

"Oh—it's like that, is it?"

"For the moment. I may have something for you later in the day."

"Not so fast." The short, fat spokesman blocked his exit. "We're early birds too. We got a right to get a worm."

"Just what worm are you after?"

"The one that ate the Puerto Rican tomato. I understand you got him under lock and key—which is pretty quick work—or would be if you'd booked him—which you haven't—and why?"

The other tabloid man gave tongue. "That's not my pigeon. My paper wants the love angle on—"

The representative of the evening paper grinned. "Why bother the lieutenant? Why not ask an expert like me? How's this? Crime of Passion. Young photographer kills luscious Latin-type sweetheart in jealous rage."

The second tabloid man looked interested. "You got an inside line?" Then he said sulkily, "I'm not on that case. Mine is the Williams murder." He narrowed his eyes at Nelson. "I have it that yesterday you sent a plain-clothes man named Judd out to Connecticut to work over Williams' ex-girl friend, who turns out to be some kind of prize fighter because Judd's just checked in with plaster on his head and a mouse on his right eye. I horn in while the desk sergeant is kidding him—but he's not in the mood to talk—"

The fat man said, "Maybe the mouse got his tongue," and laughed fatly.

Nelson looked at the reporter who worked on the evening paper. "What's yours, Garvey?"

"Williams case. Any angle you can give me, including the man and his mouse."

Nelson glanced at his watch. "Come back later in the day—bring your friends and I'll make a statement."

"Good enough." He addressed his vocally dissident colleagues. "Do what the acting captain says, boys. He's a leveler from way back."

Nelson eased out quietly while they were arguing about it. A sheepish, battered Judd waylaid him in the corridor.

"I caught the milk train in. I was just heading for your office."

"Change your mind. My office is full of reporters."

"Yeah—I ran into one downstairs."

"Rumor has it that you ran into something else."

"A closed fist. I—"

"Should you be up and around, Judd?"

"I'm not hurt—just my feelings. That damn hospital doctor had me pounding my ear before I could—"

"Later, Judd. Go home and take it easy for a while. I'll talk to you this afternoon."

"You mean the trip wasn't necessary? Something else broke?"

He left Judd looking insulted as well as injured. He managed to quit
the building without further interference.

The bell marked "superintendent" did not respond to Nelson's first
pressure. He had to ring several times at reasonable intervals before
the catch on the door was released. In the lobby he was received by
Dora Storch.

Her scraped-back hair was damp with sweat, and there were damp
patches on her cotton dress. She did not recognize him at first. She
said, "We got no vacancies, if that's what you want. And if it's something else, you should have come down them stairs on the street. They
lead to the basement. I can't be letting anybody and everybody into
the house." As he came closer she studied him for a moment and said,
"Excuse me—you're the officer who—"

"I'd like to talk to your husband, Mrs. Storch." He tried to steel himself against the strain that tautened her face. "Is he downstairs?"

"No—no, he ain't. But I got to go down right away. I left my boy
alone." She tugged at the door of the elevator.

Nelson opened it for her, followed her into it, and pressed the basement button. She looked at him helplessly. "I don't know how long
Fred will be—"

"I'll wait for him, if you don't mind."

She did mind. But when the elevator came to a stop she led the way
submissively to her apartment. The electric light was on in the hot
kitchen-living room, and what seemed to be the same clothes Nelson
had observed on his first visit hung limply from the line.

He glanced at the dry kitchen sink. He said, "You've left the water
running somewhere." He located the sound and turned toward the
closed bathroom door.

"My boy's in there. He don't want to do nothing lately but splash
himself. I guess it keeps him cool. Ain't it fierce the way this heat don't
let up? Early for it, too, and we still got July and August to go." Her
nerves had surfaced to egg her on. "Reason I kept you waiting upstairs, he ain't satisfied unless I turn the water on full for him—and
it kind of drowns out the bell."

"Is your husband in the building?"

"I guess so. He overslept this morning—and the owner was due to
talk over some repairs. I guess they're stopping in at the different
apartments to find out what's wanted—not that the owner's going to
order it done—he—" They were both standing. She said, "You can sit
down if you want to—but like I say—"

"I don't want to keep you from your work. If you can give me the names of the tenants who need repairs, I'll try to locate your husband."

"From the way they been complaining, they all need them. Do you have to see Fred, officer? He ain't been feeling good, and it will only— Can't you ask me what you have to know?"

"I'm sure you told me what you could when I talked to you before, Mrs. Storch." He tried to make his smile reassuring. He took the envelope from his pocket. He removed the photograph and showed it to her. "But there is one way you can help."

She took the cardboard-framed oblong from his hand. She stared at it, wrinkling her bony forehead. She nodded. "I seen her someplace— where I don't— Oh, sure—that dress—it's the same dress, all right. She was the one come looking for the Smiths' bell."

"You're sure," he said, more to divert her from the real purpose of his visit than because he doubted the identification. "You saw her only for a moment or so."

"I couldn't forget that dress—and the way she was too skinny to fill it out. Her face don't seem as sassy as it did—but people always put on their best face for a picture." Her own face had relaxed. "Is that why you're here, officer? Did this girl—did she have something to do with Mr. Williams being shot? If that's all it is, you don't have to ask Fred, because he didn't see her. He wasn't back yet from settling the garbage violation." She looked almost happy with relief.

"You say he hasn't been well. I hope it's nothing serious."

"No—he ain't exactly ailing. It's just that ever since—" She turned away as though the words she had almost said might be written upon her face. Then she gave a suppressed exclamation.

He followed the turn of her head. Water was seeping from under the bathroom door, forming a steadily growing pool upon the linoleum. He strode toward it, but she was there before him, fumbling with the knob.

"He must've somehow went and put the stopper in." Pride entered her voice in spite of her annoyance. "You'd be surprised how smart he is sometimes. I never put the stopper in for him—I just let it run so's he can dabble. Will you look at the way this door sticks. If I told Fred once I told him a hundred— Billy—Billy—be a good boy—see can you open the door for Mama—" She managed it herself. She looked behind it. She said coaxingly, "I know you're hiding—come out now. Billy! Say—he ain't—"

Nelson removed his coat and bared an arm. He reached past her, closed the taps, plunged and pulled the stopper from the high tub. The water began to drain off with a sickening gurgle. She stood transfixed, the overflow soaking her flat-heeled shoes.

Nelson backed out. He tossed his coat on a chair and, rolling down his sleeve, went to the kitchen's one window. He leaned into the bare sooty yard that was set off from other yards by a shoulder-high fence. Dora Storch crowded him. "He ain't there," she said unnecessarily. "And he couldn't climb over—not without a chair to stand on—and he didn't have a chair. He ain't in the bedroom neither—he must have got out when I went up to let you in."

"He couldn't have taken the elevator. Can he climb stairs?"

"He can climb stairs—he falls, but he can climb."

"Is there anywhere down here he might be hiding?"

"The furnace room—he could be there. He likes to hide—he's full of mischief." Again, in spite of her fears, the pride was in her voice. "Sometimes I think he knows as much as other folks. Sure—that's where he's got to—the furnace room." She hurried to confirm it. She called over her shoulder, "I don't care, so long as he ain't loose upstairs. The owner would kick up and Fred would get awful sore—"

Nelson, close behind her, saw the large wet footprints she left on the cement flooring outside the apartment. Evidently Billy had ventured forth before the tub overflowed. There were no signs to show that he had passed that way.

The heavy fire door of the furnace room opened easily. It opened upon nothing but the furnace and the intricate sweating pipes that branched over wall and ceiling. "Billy," she called. "Billy!" And her voice was hoarse with renewed fright.

Then Nelson heard that thick-tongued utterance once more. It tortured his spine. He and the frantic woman collided at the door of the storage room a moment before the crash came. His hand reached the knob first. His eyes were the first to see the queerly angled leg jutting from under the piled trunks.

Instinctively he moved to block her vision. "Go for help," he said.

But she was beside him, her back bent, no sound coming from her but the sound of her labored breathing. She teamed with him, and as a team they worked to free the boy of the crushing pressure.

And when the boy was free she knelt, and with her skirt dabbed at the blood that trickled from his nose and mouth. She gathered him to her breast. "It's all right, Billy. You didn't mean to do no harm. It's all right. Mama ain't going to scold. Mama's here, Billy. You ain't hurt bad—nothing but a little nosebleed. Mama will—"

She did not hear the footsteps angrily pounding the cement. She crouched and crooned to the weight in her bony arms.

It was Nelson who turned at the outraged roar, Nelson who stepped back into the furnace room to confront Fred Storch.

"Who the hell is in there?" Fred roared. "What goes on? Why are you—"

Nelson told him. And showed him. And watched a great hulk of a man disintegrate.

## CHAPTER 12

The metal corner of a trunk had cracked the boy's skull. He was dead before a doctor arrived to make official pronouncement.

After the body had been carried to the basement apartment, Nelson lingered alone in the furnace room. He could not remember when the demands of his calling had waged such bitter warfare with his emotions. Several times he had started purposefully toward the cement passageway, and several times he had been halted by an intangible barrier. He could not bring himself to scale it. He could not intrude, even though the words of Fred Storch were a mocking echo in his ears.

"I killed him," Fred had howled. "I killed him same as if I went for him with my own two hands—and I never meant it. I didn't want it this way, Dora. You got to believe me. I guess I must've known no luck would come of it—but I swear I done it for Billy's good—"

Head bent, Nelson stood in the cubicle that had been the boy's next-to-last hiding place. Absently he stirred the littered floor with the toe of his shoe. The lock on the trunk responsible for the boy's death had been sprung by the force of the lethal blow. The tray had fallen out, scattering such articles as people habitually store in old trunks. There were schoolbooks, a faded sweater, a box of dominoes, a few photographs, a large crumbled silk handkerchief, a split brown paper bag, a box camera, an assortment of rolled woolen socks, a fishing reel—

Could there be any verdict but accidental death? thought Nelson. Could Fred Storch have meant anything but that he had been careless in stacking the trunks, and by that carelessness guilt-stricken, his plodding mind shocked to conscious realization that he had been harboring a death wish? But would that explain his anguished "I did it for Billy's good"? Had Billy hidden in the furnace room before, and had his father actually planned his end? His grief was real enough. But grief was often real enough after the fact.

Then go, thought Nelson, intrude upon that grief. Demand the answers. And he repeated to himself the words that Clevis had said the night before: "It will never be easier than now to get a confession." But Clevis had been referring to Tom Gaudio. And Clevis had been wrong. And Nelson's foot, about to take the initial step, kicked at the split brown paper bag.

The split widened. A funny sort of container, he thought inconsequentially, to lock away in a trunk. He stooped to retrieve its contents. He stooped and stared at the roll of bills, at the revolver with the ebony handle.

The revolver had bounced from the bag to land on the faded sweater. He judged it to be a thirty-two. And when he had examined it, using the sweater sleeve to preserve it from his own prints and to preserve the doubtful existence of other prints, his judgment was substantiated. It was of English make, and one shot had been fired from it. Later, Ballistics would fire another, a test bullet to be compared striation by striation with the bullet probed from Glen Williams' chest. But Nelson was convinced without benefit of Ballistics that here was the missing weapon.

He wrapped the revolver in the silk handkerchief, secured it with twine from the fishing reel, and returned it to the torn paper bag. Then he counted the money. There was a fifty-dollar bill on the outside of the roll. The rest were fives and tens and ones. The total was one hundred and fifty dollars, and he thought that under the circumstances it was a paltry sum. The circumstances, as he saw them at first glance, were that Fred had known there was money in the Williams apartment and killed to get it. But then why had he left the money in the dead man's wallet? If he had killed for one hundred and fifty dollars, would he have scruples that prevented him from adding forty or more to his little hoard? Unless some interruption had prevented him from completing his project. Bernice?

No, it did not make sense. The untouched bills in the wallet indicated that Glen Williams had not carried the one hundred and fifty dollars on his person. So if the motive was robbery, Fred, who possessed keys to the apartment, could have entered it at any time during Williams' absence and helped himself without resorting to murder.

An alternate and sounder theory was that someone had paid Fred Storch to kill Glen Williams, and that Fred had wanted the money to ease life for his son. Not that one hundred and fifty dollars could provide more than transient ease in these days of inflation. But perhaps it was merely a down payment. Accepting that, Nelson went on to absolve Fred Storch of deliberately planning his son's death. There Fred's guilt was by indirection. In his haste to conceal the weapon and the blood money, he had neglected to set the trunk firmly in place. Could he be absolved in much the same manner from the poisoning of the girl, Bernice? Nelson thought so. He thought that whoever had paid Fred for his one overt criminal undertaking had made use of the forgotten oxalic-acid crystals. And his earlier guess as to motive still held: namely, that Bernice alive would constitute a menace, a potential betrayer. Then he thought of certain other aspects of the case and both theories collapsed and he was back where he started.

He dropped the roll of bills into the bag. He stood up, flexed his long legs, and leaned over to inspect the trunk's sprung lock. He nodded as he saw the impress of the hammer. It was an old trunk, and it might have been tampered with before Fred used it as a receptacle, but the chances were that he had done the tampering, since it seemed unlikely that he would be entrusted with keys to the tenants' luggage.

The trunk was not initialed. It bore the traces of several labels that had been scraped off. But there was one label intact, pasted to the side. Nelson moved the trunk a little in order to read it. It said "Glen Williams" over the apartment-house address.

He was not a superstitious man. Yet for a moment he felt the cold breath of superstition and heard it whisper something about a dead man rising from the grave to take revenge. He shook himself impatiently. He tried to shake off the clinging sympathy he had been entertaining for the Storch family. He picked up the brown paper bag and pulled the split ends together so that it would be a secure package. And he tried resolutely to act as a policeman should act. The effort brought him to the door of the Storch apartment. He knocked.

Dora Storch came quickly. In the dim light she was a gaunt, red-eyed figure of tragedy.

She said, "Please don't make no noise. He was carrying on something terrible. The doctor made him take pills for his nerves, and now I just got him to lay down. Maybe he'll fall asleep if—"

"I must see him, Mrs. Storch."

"Shhh—I don't want him to know you're here. He keeps raving he wants to talk to you. He wants to go to the police station and give himself up—"

"He wants to—"

"Yes—he thinks it's his fault about Billy. It ain't. He wouldn't hurt a fly if he could help it." She scrubbed at her dry red eyes. "It don't do no good for him to take the blame." Then she said in a low, fierce voice,

"Go away. It's your fault as much as anybody's. If you hadn't come horning in, I wouldn't have left my boy alone and he wouldn't—" Her voice broke. "Excuse it—I'm talking as crazy as Fred."

Nelson, the man, said, "I'm sorry, Mrs. Storch." And the policeman added, "May I use your phone?"

She showed him where it was in the little dark hall outside the kitchen. She left him to it. He heard the bedroom door close softly as he dialed headquarters. After that his muted voice was the only sound in the apartment.

He gave the street and number of the building and said that he wanted two plain-clothes men immediately. One was to stand guard in the furnace room to see that nothing was disturbed should developments require the services of the lab. The other, armed with a warrant for the superintendent's arrest, was to stand outside his basement quarters. He was not to make his presence known until he heard activity in the apartment. Then he was to bring Fred Storch in for questioning. He was not to use the warrant unless Storch refused to come.

Quietly, Nelson let himself out into the passage. He waited for the arrival of the operatives, repeated his instructions, and drove back to headquarters. Because it was past lunch time he stopped at a restaurant along the way. But he had seldom felt less like eating.

At headquarters he entrusted the thirty-two to a policeman, along with a precisely worded order. Clevis was waiting in the anteroom of his office.

Clevis looked at him, looked away, and said offhandedly, "You going to take a vacation this summer? Must be a long time since you had one."

"And it's showing," Nelson said. He had not taken a vacation since his chief, Waldo Furniss, had departed for Florida to convalesce from wounds received in the line of duty. And he was beginning to think that Furniss intended to convalesce permanently. The thought brought him no cheer. As always, when downed by the ramifications of his job, he missed the flamboyant old extrovert who was his friend as well as his superior officer. Furniss drew a sharp line between right and wrong and was seldom troubled by the psychological factors behind a crime. He leaned toward oversimplification in his appraisal of human beings, whereas Nelson, with whom he had worked closely, tended, in his striving for the secret of human complexities, to inhabit empathically almost everyone with whom he had dealings. Between them, he and Furniss had achieved a good balance, and now he longed for the old man's ear, his unsparing criticism, his advice. He went further. He wished he were Furniss. He wished he were in Florida— And then, thinking of the comment such self-pity would have drawn from Furniss, he smiled.

Clevis said hopefully, "Ain't it as bad as it looks?" He followed Nelson into the office.

Nelson sat down behind his desk and tried not to wish he had been sitting there all morning. He put the brown paper bag containing the money in a drawer. "This is how bad it is," he said, and gave Clevis a summary of his recent activities.

Clevis said, "You got nerves of iron," in a tone that was flooded with censure. "Me—I wouldn't have let that Storch out of my sight until he opened up with who paid him to shoot Williams. Well, it looks like it's all sewed up—or will be when they bring Storch in." He looked at Nelson doubtfully. "Provided you ain't pulling the kind of switch on me you pulled last night."

Nelson wished he could pull a switch that would permit Dora and Fred Storch to go their way unmolested by the law. He happened to glance at the folder containing the Woodruff reports, and he sighed inwardly because that was not the switch he wanted. Clevis was waiting for him to speak, so he said, "Have you seen Gaudio this morning?"

"Him?" Clevis said without interest. "Maybe he ain't no murderer, but he's sure a mess. The doc wants an order for him to be removed to that hospital in Lexington, Kentucky." He went on more enthusiastically, "He didn't get us any further, but he tossed a nice plum to Narcotics. Hanley wants to thank you personal for having the Acevedo jerk tailed. Seems he made tracks for the restaurant where he works, but he wasn't in no hurry to go on duty. Instead he beards the boss of the joint, a fat slob named Ramondo, and they disappear into Ramondo's office. Fernandez, a strictly A-1 operative, manages to ease within earshot and he hears Acevedo relate the sad story of how we glommed on to Bernice's lawful earnings and how he wants a reasonable facsimile of same to keep his mouth shut about who she's been pushing for. He thinks it's only fair, seeing as how he introduced her to Ramondo in the first place and how she did real good business for him. Fernandez don't linger to hear more. He leaves quietly and phones. And Narcotics takes over, the press co-operating to keep it out of the papers because even if Ramondo ain't exactly small fry he's no whale—and Hanley ain't satisfied with less—his ambitions being encouraged by finding on the premises five ounces of high-grade Mex-

ican heroin—market value about a grand and a half. Hanley's been
working on Ramondo on and off since he was booked last night. He
hasn't cracked yet—but he will on account of Hanley's boys ain't got
no maternal instinct when it comes to dealing with riffraff." He gave
Nelson a sidelong glance.

"Good," Nelson said absently.

"Sure—and could be you been casting some bread by helping Narcotics. Could be this Storch clunk will finger Ramondo for the Williams
job. For both jobs."

"I doubt it."

"Yeah—me too. Unless Williams was more mixed up in the racket
than being just a customer, it ain't likely Ramondo would have personal interest in him. I'm beginning to get some kind of an idea that
the dope angle don't tie in with the Williams murder at all. So with
Gaudio being more or less scratched, and with Storch being no more
than a tool, how does the brother strike you for a candidate? I hear
by grapevine that Judd came back from Connecticut with a shiner—
and sober citizens don't generally take a poke at cops unless they got
a special reason for hating them." He waited for Nelson's reaction. He
shuffled his feet. He said, "I keep forgetting you don't need my
guesses—or won't when Storch is brought in. If."

"Do you mean if he doesn't beat up the man watching him and skip
town—or if I get maternal with him?"

"Neither is preferable," Clevis said genteely. Then he grinned and
said, "You were acting so far away I thought you missed that maternal crack. Seriously, though—like they say on the radio—even if
Storch does finger X, we by no means got an airtight case. Because
X's mouthpiece could spout all kinds of arguments to discredit a guy
found with dough and a gat on his home territory. Any smart mouthpiece could make it stick that said guy did the job solo, motive being
robbery."

"Not if the jury thinks it through." Nelson advanced his reasons for
dismissing robbery as a motive.

"I'm with you," Clevis said pessimistically, "but who thinks on a jury?
I still say that unless we get real seeable, touchable evidence it would
be only Storch's word against X's—and Storch ain't exactly the type
to win twelve new friends with his personality. So leave us hope and
pray the gat is registered to X."

"Leave us," Nelson said. If the gun was registered to X, he thought,
then X was not one of the present suspects.

Clevis seemed to follow the thought. "That would put the Williams social list in the clear, wouldn't it? Because nobody on it has got firearms registered in his name—which of course don't mean he couldn't have come by that thirty-two illegal." He hesitated. Then he said almost diffidently, "When we do flush X—and if the gun ain't registered to him—I've a feeling I could get to know him real good if you left him alone with me and a few of the boys for a while."

Nelson shook his head. "I'm in full sympathy with all your doubts of me, Clevis, but—"

"It ain't that, Lieutenant—"

Nelson quoted one of his cook's favorite expressions. "There are more ways of killing a cow than slitting its throat."

Clevis said stubbornly, "There's only one way of milking it dry. Hey—company!"

Nelson had been aware of voices in the anteroom for several minutes. "Have a look," he said.

"Sure—maybe—" He re-entered the office in a few minutes, making no attempt to hide his disappointment. "You got everybody but Storch waiting to see you."

"Who's everybody?"

"The pals of the late Glen Williams—minus Gaudio and minus—"

"Never mind the minuses."

"Well, there's Mr. and Mrs. Woodruff—also an outdoor-type blonde who won't state her name and business, but I can guess—also Mr. M. Williams, dark horse. And Sergeant Judd's there too, with his one good eye wide open and his mouth shut."

"Did the Woodruffs say what they wanted?"

"No—they're saving it for you. It's their second try. Seems they were here this morning while you were out."

"Is the blond girl with Mr. Williams?"

"They ain't conversing, but it figures. Betty Conway, huh?" He added suspiciously, "You didn't call for this gathering, did you?"

"No."

"Shucks." He gave a fair imitation of Mortimer Snerd. "I was just going to volunteer to get Sarah Thrace, so we could start the meeting."

Nelson said gravely, "If Sarah Thrace is X, I might take you up on your offer to supervise operation rubber hose. Meanwhile, I'll see the Woodruffs."

"Tease!" Clevis muttered. He made short work of ushering in Joss and Morgan Woodruff. "Want me to stay, Lieutenant?" he asked.

Nelson shook his head. "You might remind Ballistics that I'd like a rush job on that package I sent them."

Even the baggy rear view of the little man looked reproachful as he closed the door behind him. Joss and Morgan Woodruff seemed relieved by his exit, but they did not seem happy. Nelson had arisen at their entrance. He greeted them and they made mechanical response. He held the chair at the desk's side for Joss. She sat down. Morgan, after a glance at her, took the chair that was near the door. He dragged it across the linoleum until he was sitting opposite to Nelson, who had returned to his place behind the desk.

Morgan said, "I hate to give you any false hopes, Lieutenant, but we haven't come to make a confession. Our presence is purely irrelevant to murder."

Nelson's silence was inquiring. Joss sat quietly, her hands in her lap. Both she and Morgan bore the signs of a sleepless night. Morgan fumbled in his pockets. Nelson slid a box of cigarettes toward him. He hesitated, shrugged, and took one. He lit it and drew hard. Nelson offered the box to Joss, but she said, "No, thank you," in a remote voice. Then she said, "He didn't want to come."

Nelson's silence was still inquiring.

Morgan said, "Yes—let that be understood. I have full faith in my wife—but she seems to think it needs bolstering. Psychologists might have the answer—the theory being that when people believe others are suspicious of them it's because they're harboring suspicions of others."

Joss stared at her hands.

Nelson spoke. "You didn't come here to discuss psychology."

Joss said distantly, "He came because I insisted. I want him to see the letter I wrote to Glen Williams."

Nelson's eyes went to the top folder on his desk. He heard himself saying hurriedly, "Events have happened since yesterday to make its bearing upon the case doubtful. So I don't think it's necessary for—"

Morgan did not let him finish. He said defiantly, "You're right it isn't necessary—and furthermore, I couldn't be less interested."

"Please show it to him," Joss said.

Nelson stared at her. He drew the folder toward him.

Morgan said loudly, "I'm much more interested in discovering how those hypodermic needles got in my pocket—if they ever were in my pocket."

"They were," Nelson said, quite willing to change the subject, But Joss said, "Please," again, and the tone of it impelled him to open the folder.

Puzzled, he extended the cheap sheet of typewritten script, not to

Morgan but to her. He watched her gesture as she held it out to Morgan, watched the arrested motion of her arm, the abrupt way she recalled it and began to read, brow's shirred, eyes unbelieving. Could she have forgotten how freely she had written? he wondered. Could she have been nursing the hope that the outpouring would appear innocent to a trusting husband?

She laid the letter on the desk. Her eyes were level with his. She said, "I didn't write this. I told you that I never typed personal letters. This isn't the one I sent to Glen."

Again the contradiction of her clean, straightforward appearance stirred Nelson to anger. He said coldly, "It has your signature. Experts have established that fact."

Morgan leaned forward in his chair. "Here—I don't like your tone." He reached for the letter. He glanced at it but did not read. "We're not hillbillies. That paper's for my own artistic jottings. My wife wouldn't use it for a letter—not even to a man she despised. You might not believe it to look at us, but we do own a box of decent stationery." He waved the sheet at Nelson. "Let's have done with these broken-down traps you seem in the habit of springing. I've changed my mind. I'll see the real letter—"

Nelson said, "This one will have to do. It's written on your typewriter and it's signed by your wife."

"If my wife says she didn't write it, then you can be sure it's a forgery—experts notwithstanding." He bent over the paper. After a moment he said without raising his head, "Joss, you've got grounds for a libel suit. Imagine anybody having the nerve to accuse a skilled typist like you of turning out copy like this. The lieutenant—who knows everything—doesn't know you were private secretary to a V.I.P. before you married me." His eyes traveled down the page. "As for the prose—brother, what talent! If you had it, you could write for the pulps and I could sit back and take life easy." He squinted at something. He said, "Well, what do you know. For Pete's sake!" Then he laughed.

Joss turned toward him as toward the light. She left her chair and looked over his shoulder.

He jabbed with his index finger at the letter's ending. He said, "Don't you get it, Joss?"

She nodded slowly. She said, "But you didn't need that. You believed me anyway."

"Of course. I must have had rocks in my head last night."

"Morgan—he was alone in the apartment only once—that day when he—when I ran out and left him. He must have written it then—"

"And left that other little sweet nothing caught prominently in the back of the drawer where I'd be sure to find it. The guy was nuts—plain, unfancy nuts—"

They had managed to exclude Nelson in the same way that they had excluded him in their apartment. He leaned forward in his chair, not sure if he was witnessing a remarkable piece of gallantry on Morgan's part or a remarkable piece of acting. He said loudly, "What other sweet nothing?"

Morgan condescended to explain.

Nelson made no comment. He said, "May I have the letter, please? Evidently I've missed something."

Morgan said kindly, "Don't blame yourself too much. Here—I'll read the punch line. Up to now it's been a family joke, but I don't mind sharing it. In fact, I don't have to read it. I know it by heart." Without consulting the paper, he recited, "'I'm running down to the grocery store. Then I'll come back and cook dinner for my lawfully wedded husband,' et cetera."

Nelson corrected him automatically. "You don't know it quite by heart. It says, 'I'm going down to the corner mailbox.'"

"Sure. Grocery store's been erased. I guess with all the other Xings out and erasures you couldn't be expected to notice that one particularly. But I noticed it because it comes in the only line in the whole works that Joss wrote. It's her standard note for me whenever I'm due home and she has to run out for something. In fact, one of her lesser economies or timesavers is to use the same note over and over until it wears out—even if her last-minute errand doesn't happen to be at the grocer's. You know—the way you use one of those printed 'Out to Lunch' signs." His amused eyes darkened. "Glen found it lying around and used it for his own ends—whatever those ends were."

Nelson had stretched across the desk for the letter. He studied it, seeing in the light of foreknowledge the way it crowded the top edge of the page, leaving a wide area of white space at the bottom, noting that "corner mailbox" was written over an erasure, a fact which had seemed unimportant because of all the other erasures.

He said, "You believe that Glen Williams wrote this?"

"I believe it," Morgan said. "He had the opportunity when Joss left the apartment. Fantastic as it sounds, it's not half so fantastic as your belief that Joss would or could be responsible for such drivel. All things considered, it seems to me that Glen Williams was more fantastic than met the eye—my eye, anyway—and after that lunch at the Gateau nothing I learn about him is going to give me even a slight shock. I suppose he composed this effusion so that he could confront me with it if I didn't believe his invention about Joss. Of course the letter she actually did send him wouldn't have done at all. He probably burned it behind drawn blinds so that no one would ever suspect he didn't have everything that every woman wanted. Why he itched to break up Joss and me is anybody's guess. Fractured ego, maybe—or the revenge of a man spurned—or just plain jealousy because we had something he didn't have. Thinking back, he wasn't too pleased with the Thrace-Gaudio relationship either—not that there's any comparison—but he probably wanted everybody's undivided attention." He clenched his fists. "Dammit—I wish he were alive so I could punch him in the nose."

Joss sighed. And then she smiled at him.

Nelson looked up. "Somebody took more drastic measures."

"Somebody sure did," Morgan said. His eyes widened. "You're still not satisfied that the somebody isn't me? Well—you're up the wrong tree, and the sooner you climb down the sooner you'll get places. It wouldn't surprise me a bit if Glen Williams planted that hypodermic-needle package on me—the same as he planted that scrap of paper in the drawer."

It would not have surprised Nelson either. He was beginning to rearrange his whole concept of the Williams case. But it was a slow operation because the bulky figure of Fred Storch kept getting in the way.

He stood up. He looked at Joss Woodruff. It was a look, although he did not realize it, of complete vindication. He knew only that she smiled at him with an extraordinary sweetness which transformed her plain face. He said, "I'm glad you came."

Morgan was on his feet too. A thought seemed to strike him suddenly. "I've a hunch that says you haven't seen the last of us—and not for the reasons you're toying with. Come on, Joss. We're going to see another man about the same dog."

## CHAPTER 13

As soon as the door closed behind the Woodruffs, Nelson lifted the receiver and asked for the signed statement of Emile Renaud. When it was brought to him he read it carefully. If Glen Williams' last luncheon had dwindled in importance as a murder factor, the unexpected visit of the Woodruffs had brought it into the foreground again. And Nelson sought to work it into the new pattern his mind was weaving.

Two thirds of the waiter's statement repeated with a great deal of unnecessary wordage what he had said on the telephone. He kept asserting that he wanted to do his duty, and had not come forward of his own volition only because people of his calling were expected to hear and see nothing that did not directly concern them, and he hoped the police would understand that an affair of this nature would scarcely reflect credit upon an establishment such as the Gateau whose clientele was above reproach. Then, toward the end of the statement, he vouchsafed additional information, insisting that he had not mentioned it before because telephones confused him, but that he had recollected it under the stress of formally committing his thoughts to paper.

When he had rushed to the pavement to present Monsieur Williams with his cigarette case, Monsieur had been distrait. He had gone on talking to his companion as he put the case into his pocket. His hand had remained in his pocket, and with his other hand and from another pocket he had produced a large white handkerchief. But he had not employed it. There had been a strange expression upon his face, not quite a smile. The other man's face had been full of anger and perhaps scorn. Monsieur Williams had withdrawn his hand from his pocket and let it fall at his side. He had continued to talk, once bringing his two hands together as in the earnestness of his emotions. Then Emile, realizing that he was not to be thanked for his trouble, had walked back to the door of the restaurant, turning, he knew not why, for one last look. And he had seen Monsieur Williams, under cover of the handkerchief, drop something into the other man's pocket. The other man had appeared to notice nothing. He and Monsieur Williams had then parted, each taking an opposite direction.

Nelson put the statement down. He entertained briefly and dismissed the idea that Morgan had been in contact with Emile and had bribed him to amend the statement. He had a stronger idea that Mor-

gan was now on the way to see the waiter in the hope of eliciting just
such an amendment.

He looked up. The door of the office had opened several minutes ago,
and Clevis stood before it in an attitude of impatient waiting. Clevis
drew a deep breath and said, "Didn't like to interrupt genius at
work," and went on without pause between sentences. "Those
Woodruffs don't look like respectable married folks to me. They went
out with their arms around each other as if this trap was a country
lane. Regarding the thirty-two, Ballistics and lab co-operated as per
instructions. First it was dusted for prints, which resulted against the
odds in bringing up a couple of clear ones, which same are being
checked with prints of the various suspects. Storch's, which the boys
got on the night of the murder—Conway's, which were lifted off her
letter—Williams', Mike, from statement—Sarah Thrace's, ditto—
Mrs. Woodruff's from something you sent to the lab—and a couple of
miscellaneous ones picked up in the Williams apartment, including
those of the corpse. Also, test bullet has been fired and is in process
of comparison." His expression made it clear that he had saved the
best for the last. He drew another breath. "Storch is here. I moved the
others down the hall to spare their nerves if things got rough in here.
They didn't appreciate it. Acted like I was doing them out of their next
at the barber's. I got a stenographer ready and waiting. Are you?"

Nelson nodded without eagerness, and Clevis stuck his head into the
anteroom and signaled.

Storch came over the threshold, prodded by the operative who had
been detailed to bring him in. Storch's eyes were filmed and sunk deep
in his puffed flesh. He moved like a man asleep. The stenographer
brought up the rear. He moved the chair that Morgan had displaced
back to its original position near the door.

The operative cleared his throat. "I didn't have any trouble, Lieutenant Nelson. He came like a lamb."

"And now for the slaughter," Clevis said. "Will you take him standing or sitting, Lieutenant?"

Nelson gave him a look that held no amusement. He thanked the
operative and dismissed him. He said, "Sit down, Mr. Storch."

Storch had been gazing about him stupidly. Slowly he seemed to
awaken to his surroundings, to Nelson. He shook his cropped head in
the manner of a fighter after a punishing blow. He sat down.

"Your wife said you wanted to see me," Nelson said.

Storch said dully, "I didn't need nobody to come and get me. I was
coming in myself."

"Good. Your willingness to co-operate will make it easier for you."

Storch hunched his shoulders. He muttered, "Nothing's going to make it easier for me, mister. I knew it was wrong when I done it. I'll take what's coming."

Clevis nodded approvingly. His nod meant, This won't be any trouble at all.

Nelson said, "Who paid you to kill Glen Williams?"

"Huh?"

Nelson repeated the question.

Storch clutched the desk's edge. Rage seemed to burn the film from his eyes. "I told Dora I was coming here—I told her why—and she said you were okay. She said you had a boy of your own and you'd play fair and square. She said I had to come and I had to take my medicine but you'd play fair and square. Mister, if I felt like laughing, I'd laugh in your face. Taking my medicine don't mean taking no frame—"

Clevis said, "Uh-uh."

"Who paid me to kill Mr. Williams?" Storch said, clinging desperately to the stimulus of his rage. "Nobody paid me to kill him—I didn't kill him—"

Nelson opened the top drawer of his desk. He took out the brown paper bag and shook the roll of bills onto the desk.

Fred Storch looked at the bag and at the bills. He sagged in his chair. His mouth fell open.

Nelson said, "I have the revolver too."

Storch raised his hands to his head. He groaned, "I was going to bring it—the policeman wouldn't let me go into the furnace room to get it—"

Clevis looked expectant. His ears seemed to stretch and grow. Then his own mouth fell open.

Storch said despairingly, "But the money—I thought Dora could have the money when I was locked up—"

Nelson said, "It wouldn't take her very far."

"It wouldn't?" He dropped his hands. Again the anger helped. "Mister—maybe it wouldn't take you very far, but we ain't fancy. Two thousand dollars ain't chicken feed to us—not the way we sweat for it."

"Then this is a down payment. Did he promise you the rest of it after you did the job?"

"He didn't promise me— Down payment? What do you mean?"

Clevis shrugged.

Nelson said, "Have you counted the money?"

"No—I stuck it away. He told me it would look funny—me using it until—until after they"—he seized almost triumphantly upon a cinema phrase—"until the heat was off. Anyways, I didn't have to count it, and there wasn't no time to do nothing but stick it away fast."

"Count it now," Nelson said.

Storch looked at him doubtfully. He took the roll of bills. His large fingers fumbled with the elastic band. He moistened his thumb. His lips moved as he counted. When he reached the last few bills his face was an ugly purple. He bent them back to see their denominations. Then he wadded the lot in his hand and flung it on the desk. His words were choked. "Framers—robbers—where's the rest of it?" He swooped over and grabbed a handful of Nelson's shirt. "I don't take no more pushing around from nobody. You better—"

Clevis rushed forward like a small charging bull. Nelson said, "Hold it." His hand closed on Storch's wrist. His shirt ripped as he stood up. It looked like a simple maneuver, but the big man might have been a leaf for the way he spun around and landed back in his chair.

Nelson rearranged his ripped shirt. He thought fleetingly that a low opinion of police tactics seemed to be universal. He sat down and said, "There was the same amount of money in that roll of bills when I found it as there is now. You were cheated, Storch."

Storch looked at him. He was sweating and bewildered. He said, "A hundred and fifty dollars—a lousy hundred and fifty." It was a stumbling block beyond which his mind seemed unable to progress.

"Why did you want to come here of your own free will, Storch?" Nelson asked quietly.

"Because I done wrong. I done wrong for two grand—not for no hundred and fifty bucks. It ain't even enough to bury my boy."

"What wrong did you do?"

"Mr. Bones," Clevis muttered.

Nelson went on patiently, "I want to help you."

Storch shook his head. "You want to frame me. Dora said you'd play fair and square, but—"

"Dora was right. I am playing fair and square."

"Then why did you say I killed Mr. Williams? If you say I killed him, I ain't going to talk—it don't matter what you do to me. It don't matter anyway."

"Very well. Who did kill Mr. Williams?"

"I dunno. I dunno even if it was a man or a woman. He didn't tell me."

"Who didn't tell you?"

"Mr. Williams."

Clevis said, "A clown yet. A real circus clown. Lieutenant, he ain't going to make sense unless you convince him you mean business."

Nelson said, "Do you mean that Mr. Williams was still alive when you entered his apartment and that he talked to you before he died?"

"No—he was dead when I found him."

"Let's get back to the money," Nelson said. "Who gave it to you?" "Mr. Williams did—"

Clevis flung his arms ceilingward. Then he made a clamp of thumb and forefinger and pressed his lips together.

"Only it wasn't supposed to be no lousy hundred and fifty—it was supposed to be two grand."

"And what did you do to earn it?"

"What I came here to tell you. He told me he'd always leave the money ready on the bedroom closet shelf—and he said it would be enough to send Billy to a home where they'd treat him good and teach him to take care of himself. It ain't no charity place—you put down a lump—as much as you can—but it's got to be at least two grand—and they take care of him for the rest of his—" He raised a clenched fist to his mouth. He bit down on it.

Nelson gave him a few moments. "What did you do for Mr. Williams?"

Storch gazed at the flecks of blood on his knuckles. "I took the gun like he wanted me to and I went to the shelf in the closet and got the money. I found a bag in the kitchen and then I went down to the furnace room and stuck the bag with the money and the gun in it in the trunk. I done everything the way he wanted me to. He shouldn't have cheated me."

Nelson waited.

Storch looked at him. "Mister—do you swear on your boy's life that you ain't got the rest of that money?"

"Lieutenant—" It was an outraged protest from Clevis.

"I haven't the money, Storch," Nelson said.

Storch seemed satisfied. His voice was pacific. "I'm sorry I tore your shirt, mister, but—" He continued to struggle with the problem. "Do you think maybe the killer found out about it and stole it? Yeah—it has to be that way. Mr. Williams wouldn't do nothing dirty like that. And the worst of it is, the killer has to get away with it, because that was the whole thing. Mr. Williams didn't want him caught."

It was much too much for Clevis. He could not contain himself. "I could die right now and I wouldn't have missed a thing on account of nothing will ever top this."

The stenographer coughed. His face expressed absolute sympathy for Clevis.

Nelson said, "We'll start with the day of the murder. Then we'll work back from there. Try to think, Storch. Try to remember everything you did from the moment you entered the Williams apartment."

"I couldn't forget it if I tried. I come back from fixing the garbage violation and I go up to do the work he wants. I don't have my stuff to get—it's there from the last time because he said he'd want more work done soon. I walk in. I ain't expecting nothing. The time he put the deal to me he only said if and when it happened—and I guess I couldn't get it into my head that anybody would really want to kill a nice fellow like him. But sure enough—there he was—laying dead on the floor—and the room all messed up—drawers open and everything. So as soon as I took it in I done like I promised. He was laying near the couch and I put him on it and straightened him out. And I took the money and the gun and beat it to the furnace room to think—and I thought his trunk would be safe enough until I could find a better place. I was in such a sweat I guess I didn't make sure it was sitting steady on top of the other trunks when I heaved it back. I never meant nothing but good for my boy—"

Clevis's face was a blank. It went blanker, if possible, when Nelson said, "You saw that the vase of flowers had fallen over. Did you move the book Mr. Williams wrote out of the wet?"

"No, mister, I didn't do nothing like that. I didn't touch nothing but him and the money and the gun."

"Was the safety catch on or off the gun when you picked it up?"

"It was off. I put it on. I don't know much about guns. They didn't take me in the war even—on account of Billy. But Dora's cousin is a bank guard and he showed me about safety catches once on his big revolver. It was the same as on the little gun. I picked it up by the barrel—I was scared to touch the right end in case I touched the trigger by mistake—and I fixed the safety catch before I put it in the bag."

"Then your fingerprints will be on the barrel."

"My fingerprints." A new burden of distress settled upon his face "Jeez—Mr. Williams told me to be sure and wipe off the gun and I forgot. I didn't even remember it when Dora was asking me why I didn't use his phone to call the police and I made like I couldn't because they always tell you not to touch anything that could have prints on it. Real reason I didn't call the police in no hurry after I hid the stuff was because he'd asked me to be sure to give his friend plenty of time to get away in case I found him right after he'd been shot." He shook his head hopelessly. "I'm dumb—right or wrong, I shouldn't never have tried a job like that. We was bad off, but we made out. And now—"

Clevis, too, was shaking his head hopelessly. His shoulders almost met his ears.

Nelson picked something from the chaos of the man's thoughts. "Mr. Williams asked you to remove the prints from the gun?"

"That's the whole thing. He didn't want the killer to be arrested or get the chair or nothing. He was like a saint when he put the deal to me. There was this friend of his—see—who was going to kill him. He said he seen it coming for a long time and even knew that the friend had bought a gun to do it with. He said he loved this friend and this friend loved him—only the friend had got sick in the head and turned against him. Mr. Williams used some big words in telling about it, but I knew what he meant. He just didn't want this friend who couldn't help going crazy to take no murder rap. So my job was to make sure that the friend got off and I was to see there was nothing laying around to put the police on the track or else Mr. Williams said he wouldn't rest happy. That's how it was, mister." He added earnestly, "You see, it didn't mean nothing to Mr. Williams, because he was going to die anyway. Maybe he wouldn't want me to mention it, but he told me he had some kind of disease that the doctors couldn't do nothing about and he couldn't last no more than a few months and it didn't matter to him if he went sooner. He said this poor friend didn't know how it would be doing him a favor to shoot him—saving him a lot of suffering and all. So maybe you can see, mister, how it didn't sound so terrible bad to me—and why I done it."

Clevis shambled over to the desk.

Nelson said, "Yes?"

Clevis produced two syllables. He said them loudly. "Eyewash."

Nelson said, "Does Storch appear to be a man of imagination—a man who could invent a story like that?"

"Lieutenant—you're not going to sit there and tell me it's true. Listen—did the autopsy show that Williams had an incurable disease? He had the habit—sure—but—"

"I didn't say it was true."

"So?"

"When we questioned Gaudio don't you remember that he said Mr. Williams expected to be murdered?"

"I also remember he tried to pin it on the Woodruffs or on Sarah Thrace." He gestured toward Storch. "Gaudio was in the same class as this joker—only he got there by a different route is all."

Someone was knocking on the door. At Nelson's nod the stenographer moved his chair aside.

Nelson said, "Who's there?"

"Package from Ballistics, Lieutenant." A policeman stepped into the office. He handed the package to Nelson, saluted, and left.

Nelson opened the package. He laid the thirty-two on the desk and rapidly scanned the typewritten report. Storch was staring at the revolver as at a mortal enemy.

Clevis said, "It checks, don't it, Lieutenant?"

"Yes—it checks."

"Then what are we waiting for?" He scowled at Storch. "I move we get down to it."

"Bring a few more chairs, Clevis, and ask Betty Conway and Mike Williams to come in."

"Chief—you want a party—now!"

"Don't waste time. We've wasted enough as it is." Nelson's voice was incisive. "Tell the desk there are to be no phone calls or visitors until we give the clear signal."

Clevis seemed to take a hitch in his loose bones. Stiffly he walked to the door, a lowly sergeant obeying the command of a superior officer against his own superior judgment. "Give me a hand with the furniture," he said to the stenographer. Together they moved three chairs from the anteroom and set them before the desk. Clevis addressed Storch. "Don't let your nose get out of joint. You're still the guest of honor for my dough."

## CHAPTER 14

Betty Conway reached the office first. Her eyes glossed over Fred Storch. She subjected Nelson to a brief examination and said clearly, "If you're the man in charge of investigating Glen Williams' death, I want to speak to you alone. My name is Betty Conway. I came in from Howardsville, Connecticut, and I've been waiting for over an hour—"

Nelson said, "I've been waiting for longer than that, Miss Conway. Sit down."

A pink tide rose from her neck to her brow. She moved awkwardly to the chair he indicated. The rayon suit she wore was a small-town model, divorced from the lines of her well-formed body. Her flippant hat had been designed for a lesser head. Nelson thought in passing that she would look splendid in country tweeds or riding clothes.

Storch was staring at her in a puzzled way. Nelson said, "Have you seen Miss Conway before?"

Storch shifted his eyes. "She's kind of familiar. Maybe I seen her in the house—"

Betty Conway looked at him. "You're the superintendent. You were going into Glen's apartment that night."

Nelson said, "And you were standing at the door of the Delaney apartment across the hall—as though you'd just come out."

"I guess that's right," Storch said uncomfortably. "I didn't look good, but she was a big girl—a big blonde—"

"It's right," Betty Conway said. "I'm not trying to deny it. I want to explain it—but Mike Williams, Glen's brother, is outside—and he'll be here in a moment. I can't explain it in front of him. I rushed in ahead to ask you to make him wait until—" She turned in her chair.

Mike Williams had crossed the threshold, uneasy in his city clothes, and as wary of his reception as a lost dog. Behind him, Clevis said resignedly, "Judd came too." He gestured over his shoulder.

Judd said, "I thought you'd want me, Lieutenant."

"All right. Close the door."

Hesitantly, Mike Williams took the chair next to Betty Conway. She did not look at him. She seemed to be searching about her for an exit. Clevis and Judd stood, leaving the third chair empty.

Nelson said, "Sit down, Judd, if you're still feeling rocky."

"I'm okay, Lieutenant."

Mike Williams spoke. "I'm sorry about hitting him. I lost my fool head. The chief of police in Howardsville didn't want to arrest me, but—"

Betty Conway raised her clear voice. "He didn't know the man was an officer. He was only trying to protect me."

Mike's eyes were grateful. "That don't excuse it. I should have known—"

Nelson said, "Judd will decide whether or not he wants to prefer charges. I'm not minimizing the offense of striking an officer—but we have something even more important on hand. Yes, Miss Conway?"

The pink tide had ebbed. She seemed to be fascinated by the thirty-two on the desk. She had to tear her eyes away.

The chair creaked under Fred Storch. He coughed. He said, "Mister—my missus will be worrying—could I—"

Clevis said threateningly, "In the pig's eye."

Nelson ignored the exchange. "Miss Conway—you've seen that revolver before?"

"Yes—I think so—I—"

Nelson picked it up. He offered it to her. "Do you want to examine it closely to make sure?"

She reached out her hand. Mike Williams said, "Wait—I don't know what this is all about, but I've heard of cases where—"

Nelson said tonelessly, "Where the police tried to frame suspects by tricking them into putting their prints on the murder weapon? Don't worry, Mr. Williams. This particular weapon has been through Ballistics and the lab. I have the report on it right here."

Betty Conway drew a quick, sharp breath. She said, "Oh?" She took the revolver. She turned it around in her hands.

"Do you recognize it?"

She nodded. "Yes—of course—I've seen it many— Look—I want to talk to you alone."

"I'm sorry, Miss Conway. I believe you had your opportunity to talk to me alone and chose to let it slip by."

"I didn't choose," she said hotly. "I did what seemed best at the moment. I'd probably do it again—"

"Betty," Mike Williams said, "I wish you'd tell me what this is all about. It don't seem right—you being here at all—"

"*You* being here isn't right," she said.

Nelson said, "Miss Conway is in this office to give information she's been withholding from the police. If you want to help her, stop interrupting."

"You're talking nonsense. Betty has nothing to do with it, and I'm not going to sit quiet and let you—"

"Mike—you can't keep beating up everybody who looks cross-eyed at me." She lowered her voice a little. "But it's nice of you to want to try, and I can understand the impulse because—because— Oh well!"

"Because your own actions were probably dictated by an impulse to spare Mr. Williams," Nelson said. "But he's a grown man—and if there's any sparing to be done between you, he wants to be the one to do it. You haven't been realistic. You'll be doing him much more of a service to let him hear a firsthand account than to wait until the newspapers—"

"The newspapers," she said. "Must— Yes—all right." She sounded defeated, but her chin was firm. She opened the clasp of her handbag and drew out a square white envelope. She said, "It's from Glen. I brought it along in case you doubted my word—and I wouldn't blame you. Read it."

Nelson took the envelope. He looked at the postmark before he read the enclosure. He refolded the sheet of paper and summarized its contents. "Glen Williams wrote to you. He asked you to come to his apartment at five o'clock on the day which turned out to be the day of his death. He said he knew that the request would surprise you because he'd been out of touch with you for quite a while—but he begged you to come for old times' sake since it was a matter of grave importance. Go on from there, Miss Conway."

She swallowed. "Glen had seemed very dashing to me once. I suppose it was no more than a very severe childhood crush, because as soon as I got any sense at all he cured me by simply being himself. But, being himself, he never really believed I was cured—and every so often he'd take it up again—not because he cared—just to keep in practice—or else because he knew the way Mike felt and it amused him to keep Mike guessing. I'm sure it didn't occur to him that I could possibly prefer Mike to—to a man like him—"

Mike said, "Betty—" putting his soul into it, making it cover all that was incomprehensible to him.

"Wait," she said. "Let me finish." She stared straight ahead. "I went to Glen's because I thought he might have run out of money and would ask me to use my influence with Mike. He'd done that before—about six months ago—and I'd refused. This time—once and for all I wanted to convince him that he was nothing to me except as a threat to Mike's peace of mind. I was going to tell him to stop bleeding Mike and get a job and stand on his own feet. I didn't think it would do any good, but I meant to try. Everybody in Howardsville knew that Mike couldn't go on making sacrifices—jeopardizing everything he'd worked so hard to—"

Mike said, as though talking to himself, "Glen couldn't have run out of money—he couldn't have spent all I— That couldn't have been the reason he wrote—"

Nelson said, "You're forgetting his expensive hobby, Mr. Williams. It used up every cent you gave him. We have proof of that. Go on, Miss Conway."

She struggled with her thoughts. "I got into town early. I didn't want the trip to be a complete waste, so I'd made an appointment with my doctor for a checkup. It was a few minutes to five when I reached Glen's. I rang the bell and I didn't wait for the thing on it to click because some man came in at the same time and used his key. He went to the ground floor and I went up to Glen's. I'd telephoned from the doctor's to let him know I was coming, so I expected him to be waiting at the door of the apartment. He'd received me that way the time before. But the door was closed. First I rang—then I knocked a few times. I was getting annoyed—thinking it would be just like him to keep me waiting on purpose—"

Nelson cut in. "How did he sound when you telephoned?"

"A little out of breath—the way you sound when you've just come in to find the phone ringing—otherwise about the same as usual—even more pleased with himself than usual—as though he might have had one drink too many—not that I'd ever known him to drink a lot. He said he was delighted I still had a soft spot for him—that kind of thing."

"What time did you telephone?"

"At half-past three. My appointment with the doctor was for then, but the nurse said I'd have to wait a few minutes." She went on without being prompted. "I gave one last knock at the door and he didn't answer, so I took hold of the doorknob and rattled it. I was really annoyed. I must have turned the knob, because the door opened and I walked in shouting something like, 'Where are you—why don't you answer your bell?' Except for the noise I was making, the apartment seemed awfully quiet. Then I remembered that he'd always gone in for practical jokes, and I walked to the living room, bracing myself in case he was set to jump out at me. Just as I got to the living room I smelled something—a smoky, powdery smell—it made me think of the hunting season in Howardsville. And then I saw him. I suppose I called his name, because it seemed to echo back from the walls. And the next thing I knew, I was on my knees beside him—still trying to believe it was a practical joke and that he'd get up in a minute and laugh. But it wasn't. His wrist was warm when I touched it—warmer than mine—but there was wet blood on his shirt—and I couldn't find any pulse. I got up somehow. I didn't faint." She tried to smile. "I couldn't faint because my doctor had told me I was the best physical specimen he'd ever"—her voice ascended nervously—"he'd ever seen—"

Clevis looked at Fred Storch. Then he looked at Betty Conway as at a usurper. He opened his indignant mouth.

Her voice was controlled again. She said, "I looked down at the revolver and I kicked it away. I was going to pick it up and take it with me, but I couldn't make myself do it. I went out, and I wasn't panicked or anything—just numb. I started to look for the stairs, because I didn't want to wait for the elevator. And then this man—the superintendent got out of the service elevator—so I turned quickly and pretended to be coming out from the door across the hall. As soon as he went into Glen's apartment I went down the stairs."

"What time was that?"

"I don't know—about ten after five. I couldn't have been in there more than ten minutes—if I was there that long."

Her recital had seemed to hold no meaning for Fred Storch. Through it he had sat, head bowed, like a man unable to peer out from the cage of his own dark thoughts. The mention of the word "superintendent" made him stir uneasily. "That's right," he mumbled. "About ten after five. Mr. Williams told me not to make it no later than a quarter to five on account of he had something important to say to me and he'd be too busy after that. And I promised—and he knew he could count on me, but how was I to know I'd be kept so long over that garbage violation?"

Nelson glanced at Clevis. "Do you want to say something?"

"Lieutenant, I want to say plenty. Firstly, in my opinion this don't clear Storch by a long shot. It could have been a return visit to see if he'd forgotten anything or"—he paused a moment—"the lady could be our X—"

Storch stirred again. He tried to free his voice. "Listen—"

"I've been listening until it's coming out of my ears. Secondly, I don't know what game the lady is up to now—but whatever it is, she ain't playing it very smart." He turned to her. "What's with this kicking-the-gun routine?"

"Don't you see?" Helplessly she appealed to Nelson.

Nelson said, "Sergeant Clevis is usually very quick to see the point. I know you've tried—but perhaps you haven't made it clear—"

The door was pushed open with considerable force. A resplendent Sarah Thrace entered the office. She did not get very far, because the chairs blocked her. Nonetheless it was quite an entrance, accompanied by the sighing sound of released tension as the heads of the audience turned her way.

She said in her husky, theatrical voice, "Oh—you *are* busy, Lieutenant. I was told to stay put downstairs, but I thought that the man at the desk was merely being bureaucratic, and since I knew the way up I decided to dispense with red tape. I'm afraid I was rather devious about waiting until his attention was diverted. Naturally I wouldn't think of bothering you unless it was important. I wanted to come as soon as I read about poor Tom Gaudio, but I had this television interview and it meant a possible source of income for me, which in turn meant that I'd be in a better position to give Tom aid and comfort. By the way, I'm sure you'll be glad to know that it panned out. Tell me— Tom didn't—I mean aside from being in possession of heroin, there's no other charge against him? Because you see—I'll have money enough now to finance a cure—and there's another matter concerning that delightful Morgan Woodruff—"

Nelson partially recovered his powers of speech. "Miss Thrace, I'll have to ask you to—" He saw that Clevis was looking pleased for the first time in hours. Every inch a gentleman, he stood behind the empty chair, holding it in readiness. "I'll have to ask you to sit in the other room," Nelson said sternly. It was a matter for stern measures or for loud, unseemly laughter, and he reminded himself sharply that there was really nothing to laugh about.

"But of course." She was quite gracious. She might have been easing him out of an awkward social situation. "And you will arrange for me to see poor Tom, won't you? I'm frightfully sorry I interrupted." Her apology included each separate member of the audience. She said, "I'll be waiting, Lieutenant. Whenever you're ready, of course," and made her exit.

Clevis said, "She's got as much right to sit in as—" He shrugged and returned his attention to Betty Conway. "About this kicking—"

"Wait a minute," Nelson said. "You mentioned something before about having seen the revolver many times. Explain that."

"I *had* seen it many times—but not for years. I gave it to Glen."

"Now we're hearing something," Clevis said.

She ignored him. She ignored Mike, who had jumped convulsively. "When I was about twelve years old," she said, "my mother's brother died. He'd been fond of me and he left me a little money and a small cottage he owned on the outskirts of Howardsville. Mother decided to rent the cottage until I was old enough to know what I wanted to do with it, and I went there with her to straighten things out for the tenants. She said I could look in Uncle's study and see if there was anything I'd like to take home. I chose a few souvenirs, and then I found the revolver in a drawer and I took it for Glen. I didn't tell my mother, because I knew she wouldn't approve, and I did want to give Glen something special. It was a secret between us. We never told anyone else about it. Glen managed to get some blanks for it and we'd go to the woods and shoot at things." She added forlornly, "If it hadn't been that gun, it would have been another—wouldn't it?"

Nelson nodded. "Tell Sergeant Clevis where the gun was before you kicked it away."

She said obediently, "Next to his hand—and the fingers of his hand were spread out as though he'd just loosed his hold on it with—with his last strength. All I thought about when I kicked it away was that

Mike mustn't find out that his brother had committed suicide."
Nobody spoke, not even Clevis.
She went on, "I didn't think of a murder investigation or of anyone
being accused. I just thought that Mike mustn't know—because, be-
ing Mike, he'd be sure to blame himself for having failed Glen in some
way."
Mike was staring at her.
Nelson said, "Miss Conway, did you touch anything else in the
room?"
"No. Later I wondered why everything seemed so upset—but at the
time nothing really registered except finding Glen that way."
"You didn't move the book he wrote out of the path of the water from
that overturned vase?"
She shook her head.
Clevis said flatly, "Lieutenant, are you buying this?"
"Yes. I think I am."
"You're writing it off as a suicide, after the way we've been knock-
ing ourselves out—just because she gives you some rigamarole about
the gun. Listen—I'll stick with her as far as the body being warm
when she touched it—no farther. It was warm because Storch shot
him either while she was there or while she was on the way up. If they
ain't in cahoots—"
Storch said, "No—"
Nelson silenced him. "Judd, take Miss Conway and Mr. Williams into
the anteroom and wait there with them." He nodded to the stenographer. "You take a breather too."
Storch said, "Mister—"
"All right, Storch. Judd will get someone to show you out. You'll be
hearing from me tomorrow."
"Show me out? Home?"
"Until further notice."
"Mister—what'll I tell her?"
"Tell her she's not to worry. Tell her I said so."
His large face was working. "Mister—" He gave it up. He lumbered
out after the others.
Clevis closed the door. He said truculently, "That clunk has nothing
on me when it comes to being mixed up. How come you swallow her
story hook, line, and sinker—no witnesses—no nothing—Lieutenant,
I don't like to say it, but you—"
"Don't say it," Nelson said. "It's not just her story. It's the sum total
of everything. We'll start with the book Glen Williams wrote. He de-

voted some space to unveiling his views about people and about his relation to people—but his subject matter wasn't all that interested me. Clearly, no one in the group respected that book enough to have moved it from the path of the spilled water—no one but Glen Williams himself. Perhaps overturning the vase was an accident, but—"

"Books yet."

"All right. We'll go on to Bernice Acevedo. He murdered her and set the stage so that his suicide would look like murder—and he planned it so that everyone he had dealings with would be suspected of the crime. But his timing went off because he'd counted on Storch to remove the gun before the others showed up—Betty Conway and Tom Gaudio and possibly Morgan Woodruff. Remember he asked Storch to come no later than a quarter to five—"

"It seems a long way for a guy to go to prove something."

"You were given certain assignments, Clevis, which prevented you from getting an all-over picture of the case." Nelson reviewed succinctly the matter of Joss Woodruff and the letter, the luncheon at the Gateau, the hypodermic needles planted on Morgan Woodruff. He mentioned the appointment that had been made with Bernice Acevedo, who must have arrived when Storch was hiding the evidence in the furnace room, which would have been immediately after his wife returned from the grocer's.

Clevis said, "But why?"

"A distorted sense of humor. He'd had it to start with, and it became even more distorted under the influence of heroin. He wanted to control everybody, and when he couldn't swing it in the higher echelons he tried it on a lower level. Even then he found it hard going, so he decided to make his subjects pay for their small rebellions."

"He puts the joint at sixes and sevens—pays Storch to stash the gun so we won't guess suicide—and deliberately gives all his dear pals the high sign to rally around so they'll be on tap when the police arrive—and underpays Storch, at that? I'm surprised he didn't give him stage money."

Nelson said dryly, "Probably because the hundred and fifty dollars was about all he had left and he could afford to be generous with it. Besides, Storch was doing him a great service. He realized that with the revolver gone from the room, the powder burns and the angle of the shot would receive exactly the interpretation we gave them—that someone he knew well had taken him off guard and fired at close range."

Clevis was a die-hard. "Always providing that the Conway-Storch yarn holds water."

"You don't want to believe it does hold water—and I sympathize with you. I don't enjoy being made a fool of either—and that's what it amounts to." On the other hand, he thought but did not say, if it was a choice of being made a fool of or holding for murder any of the people concerned, he would cheerfully go down as a fool.

Clevis was still trying. "Bernice Acevedo," he said. "He poisoned her just for the hell of it?"

"I suppose he poisoned her for the further confusion of the police should they entertain any doubts that he was murdered. And he may have planted the hypodermic needles on Woodruff on the off-chance of establishing a connection—or just to give Joss Woodruff food for thought—because more likely he counted on Gaudio to provide the link to Bernice. People meant very little to him aside from his desire to manipulate them—and a girl like Bernice would have meant even less than most. Don't you remember the chocolate on the bathroom towel—and the traces of it on his fingers? He must have known she liked sweets and laid his trap accordingly. He made it his business to know everybody's vulnerable spot."

For the first time, Clevis's skepticism wavered. "You're building it up good," he said grudgingly.

"Perhaps this will convince you," Nelson said, touching the report from Ballistics. "Storch's prints were on the barrel of the gun. As usual, there was nothing identifiable on the trigger—but there was a smear of chocolate on the ebony handle, along with Glen Williams' prints. After he prepared the chocolates he probably fingered the gun in preparation. He could afford to be careless, because he banked on Storch to remove any telltale signs. Bernice must have been asked to come earlier than she did, and arrived late for some reason."

"Yeah," said Clevis. "Yeah—it figures." He looked very glum.

"Have a cigarette," Nelson said.

They smoked in silence for a few minutes. "I could murder that guy myself," Clevis said. "What was that title again—the title of his lousy book?"

"*Jester in Heaven.*"

"He should've called it *Jester in Hell.*"

Nelson agreed. He realized now that Glen Williams had been referring to himself and not to God in the title.

"What are you going to give the press?" Clevis asked.

"The truth—that Bernice Acevedo was murdered by a hopped-up suicide."

"Brother!" He brightened. "Well, at least the taxpayers can't say we didn't solve her murder. What about Storch and Conway for monkeying with the evidence?"

"As little as possible—and I hope we can manage to let them off with an admonition."

"I don't know. Storch will be meat for the sob sisters, Lieutenant, and everybody who reads about him will send him carloads of cash and groceries until the next tear-jerker takes the spotlight."

Nelson stubbed out his cigarette and arose. He did a little jig step to flex his long legs. "We must go to our guests in the anteroom."

Mike Williams sat close to Betty Conway. Judd stood behind them. Joss and Morgan Woodruff had returned to add themselves to the group. Sarah Thrace was backing them into a corner.

She said, "Lieutenant, you must help me. I can't convince this stubborn boy that I'm not being altruistic. He's simply got to appear on my program. He can't let me down. You see, I'm to be mistress of ceremonies on a television program called The Old and the New." She grimaced. "Me to be the 'Old,' and to introduce new talent to the waiting world. We'll be recruiting that talent from the ranks once we get started—but for the first few shows it's up to me to round up all my promising friends. And Morgan's a natural. He has a good voice and I've heard at least two songs of his that are topflight. He'll be paid for his appearances and undoubtedly win the thousand-dollar prize to boot—and he's being so stiff-necked I—"

Morgan stepped around her. He said excitedly, "That waiter—Emile—he saw Glen Williams drop that package of needles in my pocket—he said he put it in his statement, and I'm here to make sure you—"

"I went over his statement after you left," Nelson said. "You have a clean bill of health. Everyone here has except—"

"Me," Betty Conway said in a small voice.

"Tampering with evidence is a serious matter, Miss Conway. I'll get in touch with you when the penalty's been decided upon." He looked at her troubled face and added weakly, "I hope it won't be a harsh one." He knew that he would be severely criticized for not holding her and Fred Storch. Both had obstructed what should have been a simple investigation of suicide. And yet, he thought, there were extenuating circumstances. Without that obstruction, the connection between the suicide and the murder of Bernice Acevedo might never have been discovered. So, in the end, Glen Williams had outfoxed himself.

Mike Williams was standing, holding out his hand. Nelson shook it.

Mike Williams said, "The sergeant's not going to charge me, Lieu-tenant." He smiled at Judd, who looked sheepish. Mike Williams had more to say. He said it with dignity. "Glen will be cremated. That was always his wish. And I thank you for—for everything." He nodded to the Woodruffs and to Sarah Thrace. "I'm glad to have met you." His voice held new authority. "Come along, Betty." They left, arm in arm.

Sarah Thrace said, "Isn't he sweet? It's hard to believe Glen was his brother. What's this about a clean bill of health?"

Nelson told them.

Sarah Thrace shed her social graces. She said intensely, "The louse—the real Lane Bryant-sized louse. When can I see Tom?"

"Tomorrow morning. Arrangements are being made for him to go to the hospital in Lexington, Kentucky. You can speak to the doctor about that. I don't know whether or not they accept fees, but I'm sure you can find some way to make a contribution."

"Thank you, Lieutenant. May I say that you're a love—an absolute love."

Morgan said, "I'm not prepared to go that far." Unexpectedly, he too held out his hand. "So long, Lieutenant."

"*Isn't* he stiff-necked," Sarah Thrace said. "Please—won't you con-vince him that I have nothing up my sleeve? Just because that louse gave everybody the run-around—"

"Just because," Morgan said.

Nelson looked at him. He said, "It sounds like a good idea. I would-n't be too stiff-necked if I were you."

He liked Joss and Morgan Woodruff, and he liked Sarah Thrace. He wished them well, but he wished they would leave. He was in a hurry to phone Kyrie. He wanted to tell her that he would be home for din-ner.

## THE END

Made in the USA
Monee, IL
05 February 2020

7